"I'm Grant Hardesty, volunteer doctor of the month."

The woman's chocolate-colored eyes seemed made for smiling, but they held a cool reserve when she looked at him. "I'm Maggie Davis. Permanent nurse."

"Nice to meet you, Maggie." It hadn't been so far, but things might improve.

Maggie lifted the envelope she held. "Your paperwork arrived the same day you did, Doctor. That's the way the mail usually functions up here in the mountains. I didn't think they'd send us a new doctor until after the holidays."

"You got lucky," he said lightly.

"Yes." She looked him over. "Now that you've seen what Button Gap is like, do you still intend to stay?"

There was a challenge in the words that he didn't miss. For whatever reason, Maggie Davis either didn't want him to stay or didn't think he would. Or maybe both.

He lifted an eyebrow, smiling slightly. "Sorry to disappoint you, Ms. Davis. I fully intend to stay."

A COUNTRY

Christmas

MARTA PERRY

& USA TODAY Bestselling Author
# Lee Tobin McClain

Previously published as *The Doctor's Christmas*
and *The Twins' Family Christmas*

LOVE INSPIRED
INSPIRATIONAL ROMANCE

LOVE INSPIRED®
INSPIRATIONAL ROMANCE

ISBN-13: 978-1-335-94070-4

A Country Christmas

Copyright © 2020 by Harlequin Books S.A.

The Doctor's Christmas
First published in 2003. This edition published in 2020.
Copyright © 2003 by Martha Johnson

The Twins' Family Christmas
First published in 2018. This edition published in 2020.
Copyright © 2018 by Lee Tobin McClain

CONTENTS

THE DOCTOR'S CHRISTMAS
Marta Perry

7

THE TWINS' FAMILY CHRISTMAS
Lee Tobin McClain

225

THE DOCTOR'S CHRISTMAS

Marta Perry

This story is dedicated to Bjoern Jacob,
Greta Nicole and Ameline Grace,
with love from Grammy.

And, as always, to Brian.

Worship and serve God with your whole heart and a willing mind. For the Lord sees every heart and understands and knows every plan and thought.

—1 Chronicles 28:9

Chapter One

Grant Hardesty strode into the clinic's waiting room. Empty and quiet, until a child's wail issued from an exam room beyond the counter. He tossed his jacket onto a chair. Whether he wanted it to or not, his stint as a volunteer doctor at the isolated mountain clinic was apparently starting right now.

The exam room door stood open. A kid of about nine or ten sat crying on the table, while his mother stood next to him, wringing her hands. A woman who must be the clinic's nurse struggled to pull the boy's hands away from the cut on his face without knocking over the suture tray.

He gave a cursory knock on the door frame, barely breaking his stride. "I'm Grant Hardesty. It looks as if you have a patient for me already." He headed for the sink, folding back his sleeves with a nod to the nurse. "I'll do the suturing. You settle him down."

The woman swung toward him, moving in front of the child protectively. "What are you talking about? Who are you?"

Grant did a quick assessment. Jeans, boots, a flannel shirt over a white tee. What had happened to lab coats and name badges? The woman had thick glossy dark hair, short and straight, a pair of startled dark eyes and a stubborn chin. She did not look welcoming.

"I'm Dr. Hardesty," he repeated. He started to take her place next to the patient, but she didn't move. "From Volunteer Doctors. They must have informed you I was coming."

The surprise in her face told him the answer to that one. She hadn't expected him. Some bureaucrat must have fouled up.

The woman's surprise was accompanied by something else. Before he could analyze what, the kid wailed again, the mother echoing his cry.

"Look, we'll have a welcoming ceremony later. Let's get the patient taken care of first."

He didn't have to analyze her reaction to that suggestion. Anger and indignation battled for supremacy.

"If you think I'll turn my patient over to you without knowing more than that, you must be crazy." Western Maryland accents were softer, lazier than Baltimorese, but hers had sharpened with anger.

The mother stifled a sob. "Maggie, if he's a doctor—"

"We don't know that." She darted an annoyed glance at the woman. "Somebody walks in off the street and you want him to treat Tommy without knowing a thing about him just because he claims to be a doctor? I don't think so."

Maybe he should appreciate her caution, but he just wanted to cross off one day from his sentence here. Grant yanked his hospital ID from his pocket and tossed it to her. "Grant Hardesty, M.D. Okay?"

She let go of the kid to catch it, and the boy made a determined lunge to escape. Grant caught him, plopping him back on the table and getting a kick in the stomach for his trouble.

He clenched his teeth to keep back a groan. "Satisfied? Let's get this done. I repeat. You hold, I suture."

She frowned at his ID for another moment, then gave in with a reluctant nod.

"Gloves are on the tray." She took the kid's hands. "Come on, Tommy. The new doctor will take good care of you."

She probably didn't actually mean that reassurance, but at least she seemed done arguing.

He snapped on the gloves and checked the tray. He'd dealt with antagonistic medical personnel before. He could handle this one, even if she did dress more like a female lumberjack than a nurse.

He sensed her gaze assessing his every move even as she talked to the kid, distracting him while Grant cleaned up the boy's forehead. The cut was nothing too drastic—no doubt she could have handled it herself, but that was why he was here. Wasn't it?

He half listened to her chiding the kid about crossing some creek on a log. He'd committed himself to tending the medical needs of this western Maryland mountain county for the next month. It wasn't what he'd intended to do after completing his residency, but the eventual reward would be worthwhile.

So here he was, lost in the wilderness until Christmas. He suppressed the edge that always entered his mind at the thought of the holiday.

At least, this job would get him away from his mother's round of society parties. That was something to appreciate, anyway.

The boy had stopped wiggling, listening intently as—what had the mother called her? Maggie, that was it—as Maggie told him a story about encountering a bear in the woods. Fanciful, but it kept him quiet.

"There you are." He stood back, pleased with the neat stitches. He hadn't lost his touch. "The nurse will give you a sheet of follow-up instructions."

He went to the sink to wash up. Before he treated any more patients, he'd get a lab coat out of his bag. It didn't look as if he could count on the free clinic to provide them.

He heard the soft murmur of the nurse's voice as she took mother and son to the outer office, explaining the instructions to the mother. Nurse Maggie seemed to have all the kindness in the world for her patients. And none for him.

Well, that was too bad. Presumably she was used to working with different doctors, since they rotated in and out of this place. She'd just have to adjust to his way of doing things.

If he stayed. The thought that had recurred since he left Baltimore came again. He didn't have to stay.

The outer door had closed. He went back to the reception area, noticing pale green walls that needed a new paint job, posters urging flu shots and well-baby checkups, a row of metal folding chairs. Maggie whatever-her-name-was stood at the desk in the little cubbyhole behind the counter, frowning down at an envelope in her hand.

"Let's start over again." He leaned against the doorjamb, giving her what he hoped was a friendly smile. "I'm Grant Hardesty, volunteer doctor of the month."

The woman's chocolate-colored eyes seemed made for smiling, but they held a cool reserve when she looked at him. "I'm Maggie Davis. *Permanent* nurse." She laid a faint stress on the word.

"Nice to meet you, Maggie." It hadn't been so far, but things might improve. He slid his jacket back on.

She lifted the envelope she held. "Your paperwork arrived

the same day you did, Doctor. That's the way the mail usually functions up here in the mountains. I didn't think they'd send us a new doctor until after the holidays."

"You got lucky," he said lightly.

"Yes." She looked him over, seeming to estimate the cost of his leather jacket and Italian loafers. "Now that you've seen what Button Gap is like, do you still intend to stay?"

There was a challenge in the words that he didn't miss. For whatever reason, Maggie Davis either didn't want him to stay or didn't think he would. Or maybe both.

Well, she was wrong. With faint surprise, he realized that at some point in the past half hour, he'd made a decision.

He lifted an eyebrow, smiling slightly. "Sorry to disappoint you, Ms. Davis. I fully intend to stay."

In her need to get rid of him, she'd given herself away. Maggie gritted her teeth. She should at least pretend to be welcoming.

"I'm not disappointed. It's just that the last volunteer doctor they sent us from the city couldn't make it twenty-four hours without his mocha lattes."

His eyes, as changeably blue and green as Elk Lake, narrowed a little at the implied criticism. His eyebrow quirked in a question. "Does that mean people will be taking chances on how long I'll stay?"

The county board that ran the clinic would undoubtedly not appreciate her antagonizing the new doctor the first hour he was here. She tried to smile.

"It won't be that bad. But outsiders do sometimes find staying in Button Gap a bit of a culture shock."

"I'm here to provide medical services, not run for citizen of the year." He abandoned the casual posture, straightening to an imposing six feet or so. The height went well with his classic, even features, his expensively cut brown hair and the tilt of his head that seemed to say he was better than everyone else.

She stiffened her spine. Aunt Elly would call him a "fine figure of a man," no doubt. Well, Aunt Elly didn't have to work with him.

"No, they won't elect you citizen of the year," she said. "But they'll probably arrive bearing welcoming casseroles."

"I'll have to count on you to tell me how to respond, won't I?" He gestured toward the doorway. "For now, you can give me the grand tour."

She nodded, moving reluctantly past him, getting a whiff of some expensive, musky aftershave. She knew his type. She'd certainly seen it enough times. Dr. Grant Hardesty was your typical doctor-on-the-way-up, filled with the arrogance that came from an expensive education, a doting family and a hospital staff who'd probably catered to his every whim.

She was stuck with him for the next month, and he couldn't have come at a worse time. A fleeting surge of panic touched her, and she beat it back down. She didn't panic.

In spite of the determined set to the man's firm mouth, she doubted he'd last a week, let alone a month. He probably had an elegant girlfriend back in Baltimore and a list of holiday parties a mile long. She'd just make sure he didn't tumble onto her secret in the meantime.

"You've already seen our exam room." She started down the hall.

He stopped her with a light touch on the arm. "Room, singular?"

The criticism in his voice annoyed her all over again. "One exam room." The words were crisp. "One waiting room. One nurse/secretary/receptionist. This is a free clinic, not

Johns Hopkins. We're lucky the county provides the building and my salary."

He lifted his hands. "Okay, truce. I was just surprised. I know you serve most of the county."

She nodded. At least he realized how big this job was. "Lots of miles, but not so many people. Not enough, anyway, to convince a doctor to stay full-time since old Doc Harriman died, and that was fifteen years ago."

She gestured toward the door they passed. "That's locked storage. We have to keep meds on hand, because the nearest pharmacy is twenty miles away."

He frowned, absorbing that information. "Where do you take patients if it's something we can't handle here?"

"Hagerstown has the closest hospital, and that's a good forty miles. They have a Life Flight chopper they can bring in, unless the weather's bad."

"You make Button Gap sound like the last frontier."

"Maybe it is, when it comes to medical care, anyway."

He wouldn't appreciate the significance of that. How could he? Someone like Grant Hardesty couldn't understand either the terrifying challenge or the immense satisfaction of providing the only medical care some of Button Gap's residents would ever have.

They reached the end of the hall. "The office." She swung the door open. "You can use it, but some of the patient files and insurance forms are stored in here, so I'm in and out all the time."

She'd found it best to make that clear right away with the visiting doctors. Otherwise, they'd assume it was their private sanctuary.

He glanced dismissively at the tiny room with its battered oak desk, flea-market chairs and office-supply-overstock file cabinets. "It'll do."

"The clinic's hours are over for the day, so if you want to get settled—"

She left it open-ended, wondering how he'd respond. He so clearly didn't want to be here that she couldn't imagine why he'd volunteered to come in the first place. Maybe he'd thought it would be a nice addition to his résumé.

He just nodded. "My bags are outside."

Apparently he intended to give the clinic a try. At any other time, she'd be grateful. But now—

She spared a fleeting thought for Aunt Elly, who'd taken over for her at home when she'd had to rush into the clinic.

The elderly woman hadn't lost any of the loving spunk that had once made her the perfect foster mother for a scared, defiant eleven-year-old. She'd be all right until Maggie could get back to take over.

"I'll help you bring your things in and show you the apartment."

She led the way outside, wondering what he saw when he looked at Button Gap. The village was only a few hours' drive from his busy hospital in Baltimore, but to him it probably looked as if it had not changed for the past century.

White frame houses and a couple of log cabins clustered around a village center composed of a general store and café, the post office with a flag flying in the wind and the medical clinic. White picket fences enclosed neat front gardens, their late chrysanthemums killed by the last frost. The heavily forested mountain ridges surrounded the town on all sides, rearing upward to cut off the gray November sky.

Maggie looked at it and saw home. He probably saw a hamlet with no coffee bar or decent restaurant in sight.

She might have predicted the new SUV he drove. It had probably been shiny clean when he left the city, but miles of mountain road had splashed it with mud.

He opened the back, and she grabbed the nearest duffel while he picked up two other bags. They matched, of course.

She nodded toward the long frame building that had been first a private home and then a grocery store before the county bought it for the clinic.

"The apartment for visiting doctors is on that side of the office. Mine is on the other side."

He sent a cursory glance from one to the other. "Okay." He took a computer bag from the front seat and slammed the vehicle's door, locking it with an electronic key. "Let's have a look."

She unlocked the apartment's front door and ushered him in, trying not to smile as he glanced around the living room. The county had been cheap with the furnishings, figuring none of the volunteers stayed long enough to make it worth fixing up the place. The beige carpet, brown couch, faux leather recliner and small television on a fake wood stand gave it the air of a motel room.

"The kitchen's through here, bedroom and bath there."

He took it in with a comprehensive glance. "I trust your place is a little better than this, since you're the *permanent* staff." His stress on the word said he hadn't missed her earlier dig.

"Mine was the living room and kitchen in the original house, so it has a bit more charm." She dropped the bag she'd carried in. "This part was once a grocery store. They knocked down the shelving and put in the kitchen to make it livable."

His expression suggested he didn't find it particularly livable. "Is it always this cold?"

"The county can't afford to heat the place when no one's here." She indicated the cellar door. "I'll start the furnace, but you'd better come with me to see how it works, just in case it shuts off on you in the middle of the night."

She'd prefer he not think she was at his beck and call for household emergencies.

Taking the flashlight from its hook, she opened the door, letting out a damp smell. She vividly recalled the female doctor who'd flatly refused to go into the cellar at all. Grant looked as if he were made of sterner stuff than that, but you never could tell.

She took a steadying breath and led the way down the rickety wooden stairs. Truth to tell, she hated dark, damp places herself. But she wouldn't give in to that fear, not anymore.

Grant's footsteps thudded behind her. He had to duck his head to avoid a low beam, and he seemed too close in the small space.

"There's the monster." She flicked the light on the furnace—a squat, ugly, temperamental beast. "It's oil fired, but the motor's electric."

She checked the oil gauge, knelt next to the motor and flipped the switch. Nothing.

Grant squatted next to her, putting one hand on her shoulder to steady himself as he repeated her action. His touch was warm and strong, giving her the ridiculous desire to lean against him.

"Doesn't sound too promising."

His voice was amused, rather than annoyed, as if he'd decided laughter was the best way of handling the situation. Maybe he was imagining the stories he'd have to tell, back in the city, about his sojourn in the wilderness.

"It's just stubborn." She stood, putting a little distance between them. She closed the door that covered the switch, then gave it a hearty kick. The furnace coughed, grumbled and started to run.

"Nice technique," he said. "I'll remember that." His voice

was low and rich with amusement, seeming to touch a chord within her that hadn't been touched in a long time.

She swung around, the beam of the flashlight glancing off rickety wooden shelves lined with dusty canning jars. A wave of discomfort hit her, and she went quickly to the stairs.

"The furnace will keep running until the thermostat clicks off, but it's always a little drafty upstairs. I hope you brought a few sweaters." *I hope you decide this isn't for you.*

If he left, they'd be without a doctor until after the holidays. If he stayed—

She didn't have any illusions about his reaction if he discovered the secret she hid. No one else in Button Gap would give her away, but he might.

"I'll make do," he said. He closed the cellar door behind them.

Grant wouldn't have a chance to give her away, because he'd never know. She'd make sure of that.

"Do you have a family, Maggie?"

Her heart stopped. "No. Why do you ask?"

His gaze fixed on her face, frowning, as if he considered a diagnosis. "I thought I saw a kid at your window when I arrived."

"That must have been Callie." She tried for a light laugh. "My cat. She loves to sit in the window and watch the birds. You probably saw her."

He gave her a cool, superior look that said he wasn't convinced. "Must have been, I guess."

Oh, Lord, I'm sorry. Really I am. But isn't protecting some of Your little ones worth a white lie?

Somehow she didn't think God weighed sins the way she'd like Him to.

And she also had a sinking feeling that told her she might not get rid of Grant Hardesty anytime soon.

★ ★ ★

"So you lied to the man, child?" Aunt Elly looked up from the piecrust she was rolling out on Maggie's kitchen table, her faded blue eyes shrewd behind her steel-rimmed glasses.

"I didn't want to." The defensive note in her voice made her sound eleven again, trying every trick in the foster-kid book on Aunt Elly before realizing the woman knew them all and loved her anyway. "But I didn't want him to find out about the Bascoms."

She shot a glance toward the living room, where Tacey, five, and Robby, four, were playing some kind of a game. Joey, at eight considering himself the man of the family, wasn't in her line of sight. He'd probably curled up with a book on the couch, keeping an eye on his siblings. She lowered her voice.

"You don't know what he's like. Stiff-necked, by-the-book and arrogant to boot. I can't take the risk of letting him know about the kids. He's the type to call social services the minute he knew."

Aunt Elly fitted the top crust over apple slices from her own McIntosh tree. "So you been saying, child. But you don't know that for sure. Might be good to have a doctor handy with three rambunctious kids in the house."

"I can take care of them. Besides, Nella will be back soon." She wouldn't give in to the fear that Nella Bascom, having lived with an abusive husband for too many years, just didn't have it in her to raise her kids alone.

"You heard anything more from her?" Aunt Elly slid the pie into the oven and closed the door.

"Three cards and one phone call." She nodded at the Christmas card she'd taped on the refrigerator where the children could see it every day. "She says she'll be back for

Christmas. That's what she said in the note she left with the kids in the office."

Shock had hit her when she'd opened the office that morning and found the Bascom kids in the waiting room. Tacey and Robby had been curled up like a pair of kittens, sleeping since Nella had left them at dawn. Joey had been watching over them.

"Nella will come back," she said again firmly, as if Aunt Elly had argued with her. "Once she gets used to the idea that her husband isn't around to hurt her anymore, she'll adjust."

"You could go looking for her."

She could. The postmarks told her Nella had run to the small West Virginia town where she'd once lived. "I've thought about it. Prayed about it. But—"

Aunt Elly nodded. "You figure if Nella's going to have strength enough to raise those youngsters on her own, she'd best come back on her own."

"She will. And I'm not going to let those kids get sucked into the system in the meantime. Nella would probably never get them back if that happened."

They both knew what Maggie had experienced in the foster care system. It lay unspoken between them.

"I reckon Button Gap can take care of its own," Aunt Elly said. She glanced out the kitchen window. "But it looks like you'll have to tell the new doc something."

"Why?" She slid off her stool, dusting her hands on her jeans.

"'Cause here he comes, and he's got ahold of Joey by the collar."

Before Maggie could move, a knock thundered at the door. Shooting Aunt Elly an appalled look, she moved to open it.

Grant stood on her step, holding Joey by his frayed jacket collar. "This kid belong to you?"

"Not exactly." She grabbed the boy, pulling him inside the kitchen. "He's a friend. What are you doing with him?"

"I found him in the cellar." He stepped inside without waiting for an invitation. "He was trying to dismantle my furnace."

"He can't have been." Her rejection was automatic, but her heart sank. Actually, he could. Joey was fascinated by all things mechanical. Worse, he might have heard her earlier and decided to help the new doctor go away.

"Yes, he was." Grant planted his hands on his hips, glowering at her. Then he seemed to become aware of Aunt Elly, watching him with what might have been an appreciative twinkle in her eyes. And of Tacey and Robby, standing in the doorway, looking scared. "Sorry, I didn't realize you had company."

"Not company." Aunt Elly wiped her hand on the sprigged apron she wore over a faded housedress, then extended it to him. "I'm Aunt Elly. I guess you're the new doctor."

"Grant Hardesty." He sent Maggie an annoyed glance. "I thought you said you didn't have any family. Your aunt—"

"Nope, not her aunt." Aunt Elly was obviously enjoying herself. "Ellenora Glenning, if you want to be formal."

"Mrs. Glenning—" he began.

"Call me Aunt Elly," she said. "Everyone does." She grabbed her bulky gray sweater from the coat hook inside the door. "I'd better get, Maggie. Watch that pie. And you children behave yourselves, you hear?" She twinkled at Grant. "You two can probably fight better without me here."

She scooted out the door, leaving Maggie to face the music.

Maggie gave Joey a gentle push toward the living room. "You go in and play a game with your brother and sister now. We'll talk about this later."

Joey sent a sidelong look at Grant. "I won't be far off, if you need me."

She tousled his fine blond hair. "I know. Go on, now."

When he and the other children were out of sight, she turned back to Grant.

"Why did you lie to me?" he asked before she had time to think.

"I didn't, not exactly." Well, that sounded feeble. "You asked if I had any family. I don't." She pointed to the windowsill where the elderly calico cat slept, oblivious to the hubbub. "And you might have seen Callie."

"I might have, but I didn't." His frown deepened. "It's obvious these kids are staying with you. Why didn't you want me to know?"

Part of the truth was better than none. "Their mother is a friend of mine. She had to go out of town for a few days, so I'm watching them while she's gone."

"That doesn't explain why you didn't tell me the truth when I asked."

"Look, I just didn't want you to think the children would interfere with my work." She hated saying it, hated sounding as if he had the right to disapprove of anything she did. "They won't. I have plenty of people to take care of them when I'm working."

"Your system didn't seem to work too well when the boy decided to take my furnace apart."

"Joey. His name is Joey." She took a breath. He had a point, unfortunately. "I'm sorry about that. He's interested in how things work. Do you need me to come over and fix it?"

"I can manage." There was a note to his voice that she didn't like. "But I don't want to work with someone I can't trust."

She wanted to lash out at him, tell him she didn't want

to work with him, either. Tell him to take his changeable eyes and his chiseled profile and go right back to Baltimore where he belonged.

But she couldn't. Like it or not, she was stuck with him.

Chapter Two

Maybe he shouldn't have been that rough on her. Maggie's face looked pale and stiff, her promise delivered through set lips. They'd definitely gotten off on the wrong foot, mostly her fault, but he didn't need to contribute to it.

Not being told the truth was a flash point with him, maybe because his parents had spent so much of their time either avoiding the truth or prettying it up until it became palatable to them.

Still, he had to work with the woman for the next month, and he was the temporary, not she. He needed to establish normal business relations with her, or his time here would be even more difficult.

He forced a smile. "Look, we've had a rocky beginning. What do you say we start over?"

Emotions flitted rapidly across her face. Maggie wasn't as impassive as she probably liked to believe. He could see her questioning his motives and wondering whether he meant what he said. He could see her distaste at the thought of cooperating with him. And then he saw her reluctant acceptance.

Why reluctant? What made her tick? His own curiosity surprised him.

She tilted her head, considering. "Maybe that would be best." She took a deep breath, as if preparing to plunge into cold water. "Welcome to Button Gap, Dr. Hardesty." She extended her hand.

He took it. Her hand was small, but firm and capable in his.

"Call me Grant. After all, we're going to be working closely for the next month."

"Fine." The reservation was still there in her dark brown eyes. "Grant."

He'd held her hand a little longer than necessary. He released it and glanced around, looking for some topic that would ease the tension between them.

"This is a lot nicer than the temporary doc's quarters."

The big square kitchen had exposed beams in the corners and crossing the ceiling, with rough white plaster between them. Old-fashioned dish cabinets with multipaned glass fronts lined one of the walls, and a wood-burning stove took up floor space on the worn linoleum. In the corner nearest the door, she had a square oak table, its surface worn with the scars of countless meals.

Maggie managed a more genuine smile. "You should have seen it when I moved in."

"I can imagine." He saw the work she must have put in, now that he looked for it. The faded linoleum was spotless and brightened by rag rugs in bright colors. Someone, presumably Maggie, had polished the wood-burner to a black gloss. Red-and-white-checked curtains dressed the three small windows, and each windowsill sported a red geranium.

"No one had lived here for a lot of years. I had to fight the mice for control of the kitchen." Satisfaction laced her words, and she glanced around possessively.

"I suppose the cat helped."

"Callie?" Her face softened as she glanced at the white-orange-and-black ball of fur. "Callie's way too old for much mouse-catching, but we get along okay."

"How long have you been here?" He leaned his hip against the counter, wondering if she'd ask him to sit. Or if she was just waiting for him to leave.

"Five years."

Something shadowed her face when she said that—some emotion he couldn't quite decipher.

"You've made a nice nest here." He sniffed the aroma filling the kitchen—apples and cinnamon, he thought. "Is that the pie I smell?"

She nodded. "Aunt Elly always claims I'm her one failure in teaching the fine art of crust-making."

"If that means she bakes for you, failure might be worthwhile."

"Don't you dare tell her that."

Her smile was the first genuine one he'd seen directed at him. It lit the face he'd been thinking plain, brightening her cheeks and making her eyes sparkle. He realized he was leaning toward her without meaning to.

"I promise," he said solemnly.

"Well." She glanced toward the pot on the stove, her color still heightened. "Supper's almost ready. Aunt Elly left us stew and biscuits. Why don't you stay and eat with us? I know you can't have gotten any food in yet."

He hadn't even thought that far. "Thanks, but I can just go out and grab a bite."

"Not unless you want to make do with a sandwich from

the general store. The café doesn't serve supper except on weekends."

He really was in the boonies. "In that case, I'll set the table."

"You don't have to do that." She lifted a stack of plates and bowls from the cabinet.

He took them from her hands. "My pleasure."

It only took minutes to set the scarred table. Maggie poured milk from a mottled enamel pitcher and scooped stew into bowls, then called the children.

Joey gave him a sidelong look as Grant slid onto a chair. "He staying for supper?"

"Yes." Maggie's return gaze was cautionary. "You be polite, you hear?"

"We'll get along fine, as long as Joey doesn't try to repair my furnace again." Grant studied what he could see of the kid's averted face. "What made you decide to work on the furnace, anyway?"

Thin shoulders shrugged. "I dunno."

He wanted to pursue it, but Maggie held out her hand to him. Startled, he took it, then realized they were all holding hands around the table. Joey frowned at him, ducking his chin. Apparently they were going to pray.

"Father, we ask You to bless this food." Maggie's warm, intimate tone suggested she spoke to a friend. "Please bless and protect Nella and bring her back to us soon." There was an almost imperceptible pause. "And we ask Your blessings on the guest at our table, Lord. Make his time here fruitful. Amen."

He didn't remember the last time anyone had prayed for him. It made him uncomfortable and touched him simultaneously. He and God hadn't been on speaking terms in years, but he didn't suppose he'd ever tell Maggie that.

"Good stew." Joey was well into his bowl already.

Maggie caught Grant's eyes and smiled. "He's a growing boy. He eats like a bear."

Joey growled, making his little sister and brother laugh. The kid's answering grin was pleased.

The girl, Tacey, was a mouse of a child, thin and shy, with light brown hair tumbling into her eyes in spite of the pink plastic barrette that was pinned in it. The smaller boy laughed at Joey's antics, then glanced around as if maybe he shouldn't have.

An interesting combination. Maggie seemed to lose that perennial chip on her shoulder when she talked with the kids. Her brown eyes warmed with caring.

When he'd first seen her that afternoon, he'd thought he was looking at an overworked nurse with an antipathy toward outsiders, doctors or both. Now he saw another side to Maggie, one that was ruled by protectiveness toward the three kids, the old cat and probably also the elderly woman.

She glanced up and caught him watching her. Her eyes widened, and for an instant he didn't hear the children's chatter. Their gazes caught and held. Awareness stretched between them like a taut cord.

Maggie broke the contact first, looking down at her bowl, her cheeks pinker than they'd been before. He yanked his attention to his stew, stirring the brown gravy as if that was the only thing on his mind.

What had just happened?

No sense asking the question. He already knew the answer. He'd looked at Maggie and felt a shockingly strong wave of attraction. Maggie had felt it, too.

That wouldn't do. He rejected the temptation. This month would be difficult enough without that kind of entanglement.

A pleasant, professional relationship—that was what was

called for here. Maybe he shouldn't have tried to move beyond that instant antagonism. Maybe he should have settled
for being sparring partners with Maggie, because anything
else was out of the question.

Maggie stood at the reception desk checking charts. At
least, she should have been checking charts. She definitely
should not be thinking about those moments at supper last
night when attraction had sparked between her and Grant.

She couldn't dismiss the memory. Like the proverbial el-
ephant in the living room, it took up too much space. She
couldn't ignore the warm wave that had washed over her,
waking every cell in her body and reminding her she was
alive.

All right, be rational. She couldn't pretend that moment
hadn't happened, but she could understand her reactions.
After all, she hadn't had anyone special in her life for a long
time—since she'd come back to Button Gap, in fact. She
could hardly be surprised if working in close quarters with an
attractive man roused feelings that were better left sleeping.

Grant *was* attractive. With his classically handsome face
and his assured manner, he looked like what she suspected he
was—a sophisticated, upper-class urbanite who'd been born
with a silver spoon in his mouth. A greater contrast to herself couldn't be imagined.

Well, she wasn't trying to measure his suitability for her,
was she? She'd simply recognized the feeling for what it was
and shut it down. She'd shut down worse emotions than this
in her life. She could handle it.

She shuffled the charts into a stack and plopped them
firmly on the desktop. No problem.

The exam room door opened. Grant came out with a patient—old Isaiah Martin, come to see if the new doctor could do anything about his "rheumatiz."

"Just see if those new pills help you." Grant carried a parcel wrapped in brown paper gingerly in one hand. "Check in with us next week."

"Thanks, Doc." Isaiah tucked a handful of pill samples into the pocket of his dusty corduroy jacket, waved to Maggie and limped out, banging the door behind him.

Grant turned to her with a grin and held out the package. "What am I supposed to do with this?"

A parade of butterflies fluttered through her stomach at the grin. Okay, maybe she hadn't eliminated the feelings. She could still settle for controlling her reactions so Grant never suspected.

She took the parcel and peeked inside. "Well, I'd suggest refrigerating it until you're ready to eat it." At his blank look, she smiled. "It's venison sausage. Haven't you ever had any?"

"Not that I can recall. I take it the barter system is alive and well in Button Gap." He leaned against the desk, way too close for her state of mind. "Don't they realize that the county pays the bills?"

She carried the package to the small refrigerator. "People here don't like to accept charity. I've tried explaining that their tax dollars support the clinic, but most folks still want to pay their way."

He shook his head. "They're out of step with society, then."

"That's not a bad thing."

"No." His smile warmed those cool blue eyes. "Anyway, you can have the sausage if you want it."

"What's the matter? Too rough for your sophisticated palate?"

Instead of responding with a smile or a jibe, he studied her face for a moment, as if wondering what lay beneath the skin. "That sounds like a criticism," he said. "And I'm not sure why. What do you have against me, Maggie?"

She shouldn't have let the remark pop out of her mouth. She knew better.

Grant waited, expecting an answer. At least he didn't look angry.

"Sorry." She forced herself to be honest with him. "I guess the problem is that I see the volunteers come and go. Don't get me wrong. I'm grateful. We couldn't run the clinic without them."

"I sense a 'but' coming." He folded his arms across the front of the white lab coat he wore over a pale blue dress shirt.

She shrugged. "But sometimes they're more trouble than they're worth. And sometimes I get the feeling that the only reason they're here is to fill in the line for public service on their résumés."

"That's a pretty harsh judgment, isn't it?"

That was what Aunt Elly had said, in different words. She'd reminded Maggie that being judgmental was a sin.

"That's how I feel. If I'm wrong, I'm sorry."

He shoved himself away from the desk and came toward her, frowning. She had to force herself not to back up. He stopped, inches from her, his gaze intent on her face.

"Okay, fair enough. Why are you here, Maggie?"

Not for any reason I'd like to confide in you. "That's a long story."

"Give me the condensed version." He didn't look as if he intended to move until she did.

She looked up at him, then was sorry. He was too close for her state of mind. The tiny refrigerator was at her back, and he filled the narrow confines between the desk and the wall. She couldn't walk away without brushing against him, and she wouldn't do that. She had to say something.

"I worked in Pittsburgh for a time after I finished school, but I never got rid of my longing for the mountains. Button Gap felt like home to me, and I heard the county needed someone to run the clinic. So I came. End of story."

"It's a nice story." His voice had lowered to a baritone rumble that did funny things to her. His fingers brushed hers. "You're a dedicated person, Maggie."

Her breath caught in her throat. Warmth seemed to emanate from his touch, flowing through her. She wanted to lean into him and feel that warmth encircle her.

She couldn't.

What she'd told him wasn't the whole story, and a large part of her particular story wasn't nice at all.

That was just one more reason why she shouldn't be letting herself feel anything at all when Grant was around. Unfortunately, that seemed easier said than done, especially when he looked at her with what might be admiration in his eyes.

"Grant, I—"

The door sounded, flooding her with relief. He moved, and she slipped around him. Aunt Elly came toward them. The heavy wool jacket she wore had probably belonged to her late husband, and she carried a basket over her arm, with a napkin tucked over something that smelled of cinnamon.

"Those aren't cinnamon buns, are they?" Maggie leaned against the counter, smiling in welcome.

Movement beyond the plate-glass window caught her eye, and the smile faded. A county sheriff's car pulled into the parking space in front of the clinic.

She felt instantly guilty, and it didn't do any good to tell herself that the presence of the sheriff's car meant nothing. It might well mean trouble if Grant was here when the occupant of that car came inside.

She rounded the counter quickly, taking Aunt Elly's arm.

"You're just in time to see the doctor." She glanced meaningfully at the car, then back at Aunt Elly's face. "Keep him busy," she mouthed.

Aunt Elly followed her gaze, startled, then nodded. Her eyes sparkled with mischief. "That's good. I want to talk to the doc about my knee."

"You go on back." She yanked open the file drawer to pull out Aunt Elly's chart and hand it to Grant. "Dr. Hardesty's coming right now."

Only Grant's slightly lifted eyebrows indicated he thought she was rushing them. He took Aunt Elly's arm, and together they disappeared into the exam room.

Just in time. As the exam room door closed, the front door opened. Deputy Sheriff Gus Foster ambled toward the desk.

At least the sheriff's department had sent someone she knew. *Thank You, Lord.*

"Hey, there, Maggie, how's life treating you?" Gus lifted the dark felt hat from his white hair. With his snowy hair and beard and his comfortably round stomach, Gus visited the Button Gap schoolchildren as Santa every year.

"Fine, Gus. And yourself?" The formalities had to be gotten through before Gus would get to the reason for his visit, but her stomach tightened with the fear that Grant would come back out for some reason.

"Can't complain." He leaned against the desk. "Hear you've got a new doc."

She nodded. "From Baltimore. Just until Christmas." Had they'd chatted enough? It felt like her nerves were rubbed raw. "What brings you in to see us?"

"Well, now." A shade of reluctance, maybe even embarrassment, touched Gus's ruddy face. "It's this way. We had a call from Mrs. Hadley."

Maggie's stomach lurched. Mrs. Hadley, head of the county's social services department, wouldn't have called the sheriff's office for fun. Her thoughts flickered to the Bascom kids, safely tucked away with retired teacher Emily Davison for the afternoon, except for Joey, who was in school.

"What does she want now?" She tried to keep both face and voice expressionless.

"Now, Maggie, I know the two of you don't get along. Reckon I know why, too. But I can't ignore her when she calls." He gave a wry grin. "Leastways, not unless I want her trampling over my head again."

"If you know how she is—"

"I've got a job to do," he said with heavy finality. "Mrs. Hadley's had her eye on Nella Bascom and her kids. She stopped by to see them a couple of times and didn't find anybody home. She wants to know what's going on."

Her heart sank. She'd been hoping against hope that the woman had enough to do without running all the way up to Button Gap. She'd prayed that no official notice would be taken of Nella's absence before she was back home with her kids.

"Why did you come to me?" She tried to sound unconcerned.

Gus didn't look convinced. "Everybody knows you've been helping Nella get by since that no-count husband of hers sent himself to perdition by crashing the logging truck. I figured you might know something."

She could tell him Nella had gone away for a few days, leaving the kids with her, but that would only lead to more questions. "I don't." Another lie.

I'm sorry, Lord. I don't want to lie, but what choice do I have? Mrs. Hadley would snatch those kids away in a minute. Nobody knows that better than I do.

"What business is it of Mrs. Hadley's what the Bascoms do, anyway?"

"Now, Maggie. The way I see it, if something comes to my notice, official-like, I'd have to do something about it. If not, well, I don't."

Her tension eased. "Thanks, Gus."

"I'm not saying I know anything. But you want to be careful."

The exam room door opened, and a wave of panic raced through her. "I'll be careful." She rounded the desk, wanting to hurry Gus out.

He straightened, immovable. "You know as well as I do that those paper-pushers at the county seat would just as soon close down the free clinic if somebody gave them a reason."

"Close down?" Grant stalked into the outer office, frowning. "What's going on? Can I help you, Officer?"

Maggie looked at Aunt Elly, who gave a helpless gesture seeming to indicate that she'd done everything she could to hold him back.

"Nothing's going on," she said. "Dr. Hardesty, this is Deputy Sheriff Foster. Gus is an old Button Gap boy, just stopping in to say hi."

Gus extended his hand. "Welcome to Button Gap, Doc. Hope you enjoy your stay here."

"I'll enjoy it more if I don't hear talk about closing down the clinic," Grant said, shaking hands. "What did you mean?"

Maggie held her breath.

"Oh, that's nothing." Gus smacked his hat against the side of his leg. "Maggie's an old friend. I was just teasing her."

Thank you. She should have known Gus wouldn't give her away to an outsider.

Aunt Elly bustled between them. "Gus, I'll give you a cinnamon bun for a ride in that sheriff's car." She swung the basket in front of him.

Gus patted his stomach. "Always room for one of your cinnamon buns, but I don't want to deprive the doc."

"Plenty for everyone." Aunt Elly handed Gus a napkin-wrapped bun from the basket. She took his arm. "Now let's see about that ride."

"You've got it." Smiling, he escorted her to the door. "Nice to meet you, Doc. Be good, Maggie."

The door closed behind them. Maggie drew in a relieved breath.

Grant grasped her arm to turn her toward him. One look at his frown told her that her relief had been premature.

"What was that all about?"

She tried for a casualness she didn't feel. "Nothing. You heard Gus. He just likes to tease me."

"About closing down the clinic?"

She shrugged. "He has an odd sense of humor."

"It didn't sound like teasing to me." His mouth was set in an uncompromising line. His determined gaze pinned her to the spot, demanding answers she wouldn't give.

"Look." She pulled her arm free, letting annoyance show in her face. "I can't help what you thought it sounded like. Gus and I both know that some of the penny-pinchers in county government would be happy to close down the clinic, so they could do something else with our tax dollars. But that's not going to happen." *Please, God.*

"I'm glad you feel so confident about it." His eyes were the blue-gray of a stormy sky.

"I do."

He wasn't satisfied—she could see that. But there wasn't anything he could do. As long as he didn't learn the truth about the Bascom children, they were safe.

"I hope you're right, Maggie. Because I have no intention of letting the clinic be shut down while I'm in charge here."

He tossed Aunt Elly's chart onto the desk and stalked back toward the office. The door banged behind him.

Lord, what else could I do? I have to protect those kids.

She had to. But there was one thing she *didn't* have to do any longer.

She didn't have to worry about any more moments when attraction sparked between her and Grant. He'd obviously decided she wasn't to be trusted.

Chapter Three

Grant prodded the limp green beans in the frozen dinner he'd just taken from the elderly oven. Saturday night, and he was dining on what looked like leftovers from the hospital cafeteria. If he were back in Baltimore, he'd probably be eating seafood at Thompson's with friends or a date.

He glanced at the clock. Well, no. He wouldn't have dinner anywhere near this early on a Saturday night in his normal life. Here in Button Gap, without city lights to dispel it, the November darkness seemed darker, the hour later.

Picking up his plate, he wandered into the living room and settled into the faux leather recliner in front of the television. This wasn't exactly the right ambience for dining, but it beat sitting at the Formica table in the kitchen.

He'd been in the village for nearly a week, and he had to confess the time had gone quickly. After a couple of quiet days, things had picked up at the clinic. Routine cases, for the most part, but they had kept him busy enough to forget he was stuck in the middle of nowhere for the rest of the month.

Okay, Hardesty, stop acting like a baby. Anyone would think this was a lifetime commitment.

Three more weeks, and he'd be free to leave. So life in Button Gap wasn't exciting. So what? The benefits to his future career certainly outweighed a little discomfort and a hefty dose of boredom.

The clinic seemed to run effectively, in spite of the jolt he'd had at hearing some county bureaucrats wanted to shut it down. Maggie had been scrupulous in following clinic procedures. She'd even exchanged her jeans and flannel shirt for a lab coat worn over a sweater to ward off the drafts that slipped through the chinks in the frame building.

At least, he'd prefer to believe the chill in the air came from the drafts. Possibly, however, the frost might be emanating from Maggie.

Had he overreacted to that overheard conversation with the deputy sheriff? Judging from the coolness she'd shown him the past few days, Maggie certainly thought so.

He didn't have anything for which to apologize. He was the doctor, and any problems with the clinic would reflect badly on him. He could just imagine the reaction of Dr. Rawlins, the man he hoped would soon be his senior partner, to hearing that his pet project had closed down while Grant was in charge.

Still, Grant wouldn't mind seeing Maggie's smile again.

A knock was a welcome interruption. He swung the door open to reveal Aunt Elly, swathed in a plaid wool jacket several sizes too large, topped by a discordant plaid muffler.

"What brings you out on this cold night?" He ushered her inside and snapped off the television news.

"Cold? Wait 'til you've been through a winter here and then talk to me about cold." She loosened the muffler. "I came to bring you along to pageant tryouts."

The only thing that came to mind was Miss America. "Pageant tryouts?"

"The Christmas pageant," she said, as if it ought to be self-explanatory. "Everybody in Button Gap comes to church the night they pick the cast, just to cheer them on."

Apparently he couldn't escape the holiday, no matter where he went. "I'm afraid I don't have any dramatic talent."

"Shoot, you don't have to try out, boy. It's mostly kids anyway. But you ought to jump into Button Gap life whilst you're here. 'Sides, Maggie's directing it." She glanced at his discarded plate. "We have dessert after they pick all the parts, y'know. More kinds of homemade pies than you can count."

He didn't need any reminders of the Christmas season. On the other hand, he didn't want to hurt the old lady's feelings, and just about anything was better than sitting here staring at the television.

"Your company and homemade pies sounds like a winning combination." He reached for the jacket he'd hung on the bentwood coatrack next to the door. "You're on."

He pulled the door shut behind them and started to take Aunt Elly's arm to help her down the two steps to the street. She'd already trotted down herself.

"It looks like your knee is feeling better."

She glanced up as if startled, then nodded. "It comes and goes." She snuggled the muffler around her chin. "Smells like snow in the air."

They crossed the quiet street. No one else seemed to have ventured outside tonight, unless the hamlet's whole population was already at the church. He slipped his hand under Aunt Elly's elbow.

"You and Maggie are pretty close, aren't you?" The question came out almost before he realized he'd been thinking about Maggie.

"Everybody knows everybody in Button Gap, if they live here long enough."

"You wouldn't be evading the question, now, would you?"

He could almost feel her considering. She wouldn't answer anything she didn't want to—he felt sure of that.

She looked at him as if measuring his interest, and then seemed to make up her mind.

"Maggie lived with me for a bit, when she was eleven," she said. "Guess that made us close, no matter how many miles or years there might be between us."

He digested that. "But you're not really related."

"No." She shrugged. "Folks round here take care of each other when there's trouble, blood kin or not."

The white frame church was just ahead, its primitive stained-glass windows glowing with the light from within. A chord of music floated out on the chilly air, followed by a burst of laughter.

An urgency he didn't understand impelled him. "What kind of trouble?"

Aunt Elly stopped just short of the five steps that led up to the church's red double doors. He felt her gaze searching his face.

Then she shook her head. "I 'spect that's for Maggie to tell you, if she wants to."

She marched up the steps, and he had no choice but to follow.

The small church had a center aisle with pews on either side. At a guess, the sanctuary probably seated a hundred or so. Plain white walls, simple stained glass, a pulpit that had darkened with age but had probably never been beautiful— he couldn't imagine a greater contrast to the Gothic cathedral–style church of his boyhood.

The atmosphere was different, too. There, he recalled the

hushed rustle of women's dresses, the soft whisper of voices beneath the swelling notes of the organ. Here, laughter and chatting seemed acceptable. More than half the people in the church were children, and they trotted around as comfortably as if they were on the playground.

"Okay, come on." Maggie, standing by the piano at the front, had to clap her hands to make herself heard over the babble of voices. The deep red sweater she wore with her jeans brought out the pink in her cheeks.

"Let's have a look at everyone who wants to be a wise man," she announced. "Come up front, right…"

The end of that sentence trailed off when she saw him. Fortunately, the thunder of small feet would have drowned it out anyway.

Maggie's eyes narrowed as she looked from him to Aunt Elly. Irritation pricked him. She had no reason to look as if he didn't belong here. He'd been invited.

He'd have slid into the back pew, but Aunt Elly grasped his arm and marched him down the aisle to near the front. Their progress was marked by murmurs.

"There's the new doctor."

"Young, ain't he?"

"Hi, Doc."

He nodded to those who greeted him and tried to ignore the other comments. He slid into the pew after Aunt Elly with a sense of relief. Then he glanced toward the front and found Maggie still watching him.

She blinked as their gazes met and turned quickly toward the children, but not before he saw her color heighten.

"Well, that's great." She seemed to count the small figures who bounced in front of her. "I think we need to narrow this down a bit."

"Can't we have more than three kings?" one of the kids asked.

It was Joey, he realized. The boy's face shone with scrubbing and his blond hair had been plastered flat to his head.

So the little monster wanted to be one of the magi. Grant would have expected a shepherd or a donkey was more his speed.

"I don't think—" Maggie began.

Some mischievous part of his mind prompted him. "The Bible doesn't actually say there were three wise men," he pointed out. "Only that there were three gifts."

"That's right." The man in the pew in front of him turned, smiling, and extended his hand. "Welcome. You'd be Dr. Hardesty, of course. I'm Jim Michaels."

Pastor Michaels, to judge by the Princeton Theological Seminary sweatshirt he wore. Grant tensed as he shook hands, and had to remind himself to relax.

"Sorry, Reverend. I didn't mean to start a theological quarrel."

"Jim, please." The young minister had a wide smile, sandy hair and a faded pair of jeans to go with the sweatshirt, which looked new enough to suggest he hadn't been out of school long. "Discussion, not quarrel."

"I think we'll stick with the traditional three kings," Maggie said firmly.

She frowned at him, and he smiled back, unrepentant. This was different enough from the church he remembered that it didn't bring up unhappy memories. And he enjoyed watching take-charge Maggie being ruffled by a crew of rug rats.

"Three kings," she repeated, in response to a certain amount of sniveling. "But the rest of you get to be angels or shepherds. Won't that be fun?"

As she went on with the casting, he had to admit she

seemed to have a talent for making people happy. Even the most reluctant angel was brought around by the promise of having a gold halo.

Pastor Jim kept up a quiet commentary about the pageant, which Maggie seemed to tolerate with an amused smile. Unlike the look she'd darted at him when he'd intervened, he noted.

Well, presumably Pastor Jim was her friend, along with everyone else in the sanctuary. He thought again about the bombshell Aunt Elly had dropped on their walk to the church. The trouble in Maggie's family must have been fairly serious for her to be farmed out to a neighbor at that age.

He studied Maggie's face as she announced the parts for the pageant. Did that uncertainty in her childhood account for her fierce protectiveness toward these people? Maybe so. He knew as well as anyone the influence a childhood trauma could have on the rest of a person's life.

"Let's finish up with a carol before we go downstairs for dessert." Maggie glanced toward Pastor Jim, who obediently seated himself behind the piano.

"What will it be?" he asked, playing a chord or two.

"'Away in a Manger,'" several children said at once.

"You've got it." He began to play.

Grant tried to open his mouth, to sing like everyone else. *Away in a manger, no crib for his bed.*

But something had a stranglehold on his throat, and he seemed to see his brother's face, his eyes shining in the light of a thousand candles.

He'd thought he could cope with this, but the old anger and bitterness welled up in him so strongly that it was a wonder it wasn't written all over him.

Maggie had her arms around a couple of the children as

they sang. She glanced at him, and apparently his expression caused her to stumble over a phrase.

Maybe his feelings *were* written on his face. All he could think was that the moment the song was over, he was out of there.

The expression on Grant's face when the children began to sing the old carol grabbed at Maggie's heart and wouldn't let go. Dr. Grant Hardesty, the man she'd thought had everything, looked suddenly bereft.

She couldn't have seen what she thought she'd seen. That glimpse into his soul shook her, rattling all her neat preconceptions about who and what he was.

The last notes of the carol still lingered on the air as people started to make their way to the church basement and the homemade pies. Grant looked as if he intended to head straight back the aisle and out the door.

Aunt Elly didn't give him the opportunity. She grabbed his arm as soon as they stood, steering him toward the stairs at the rear of the sanctuary.

Maggie followed, shepherding the flock of children along the aisle. She was close enough to hear Aunt Elly as they reached the back of the church.

"Come along now." She hustled him toward the stairs. "You don't want to get last choice of the pie, do you?"

Grant was out of Maggie's sight for a few minutes as they started down. By the time she and her charges had reached the church basement, he had resumed his cool, well-bred expression. That brief moment when she'd glimpsed an inner pain might have been her imagination, but she couldn't quite make herself believe that.

The children scattered, some racing for the table, others searching for their parents. She hesitated. Should she go up to Grant and introduce him around? She hadn't brought him. That was clearly Aunt Elly's idea.

"Come on, Doc." Isaiah Martin, looking better dressed than he had been for his clinic visit, waved toward Grant. "Get up here and pick out a slab of pie."

Friendly hands shoved him toward the table on a wave of agreement. Feeding him was their way of welcoming him. Would he recognize that?

"Here you go, Doc." Evie Moore slid a piece of cherry pie onto a flowered plate. "That's my cherry pie, and you won't find better anywhere, if I do say so myself. Those cherries come right off my tree. Now, what else will you have?"

"That's plenty," he began. Then he stopped, apparently realizing from the offended expressions on the other women that he'd made a strategic mistake.

He wasn't her responsibility. Still, maybe she'd better rescue him. Maggie slipped closer.

"You'd better try all of them," she murmured. "You wouldn't want to insult anyone."

"I can't eat fourteen pieces of pie unless you want to let out my lab coats." He slanted a smile at her, apparently not surprised to find her at his elbow. "How about getting me out of this?"

Suppressing that little flutter his smile provoked, she took a knife and split the piece of pie, sliding part onto a different plate. "Let's give Dr. Hardesty a little sliver of each kind," she suggested.

The pie bakers greeted that with enthusiasm. Evie might be acknowledged as the best cherry pie baker, but no one else intended to be left in the dust. Before Grant escaped from the serving line, they'd managed to add slivers of dried apple, rhubarb, lemon meringue and mincemeat pie.

Maggie helped herself to coffee, then realized that Grant

had headed straight for the table where Joey sat. Her nerves stood at attention.

By now, all five hundred and three residents of Button Gap knew about the warning Gus had delivered. They were all on the lookout for Mrs. Hadley. Everyone, in other words, but Grant.

She reached the table quickly. She thought Joey understood how important it was to keep quiet about their mother's absence, but kids were unpredictable, and it was her job to keep them safe.

Joey wore a rim of cherry around his mouth. "Sure is good pie," he said thickly.

"You better take it easy, or you won't be able to sleep tonight." Relieved, Maggie slid into the seat next to Joey. Unfortunately, that put her directly across from Grant.

His level brows lifted. "Are you talking to Joey or to me?"

"Both of you."

"You're the one who made me accept all of this," he protested.

"You didn't want to insult anyone, did you?"

He glanced at the crowded plate. "If it's that or my arteries, I think I'll take the arteries." He took a bite of Evie's cherry pie, and then gave a sigh of pure pleasure. "Although this might be worth the risk."

Their smiles entangled, and her heart rate soared.

You're mad at him, remember? she reminded herself, but it didn't seem to be doing any good. Maybe she'd better concentrate on finishing her dessert and getting the kids home.

Unfortunately Grant seemed to be eating at the same rate she was. He put his plate on the dish cart right behind her, grabbed his coat while she was getting the kids into theirs and walked out the door when they did.

"It's chilly out here." He buttoned the top button of his jacket.

She nodded. "Winter comes early in the mountains. We usually have a white Christmas."

By Christmas, Nella would be safely home with her children, and one source of Maggie's concern would be taken care of. By Christmas, Grant would be back in his world, probably forgetting about Button Gap the moment he crossed the county line.

The kids romped ahead of them. Joey stopped in the middle of the deserted street. He spun in a circle, his arms spread wide. "Snow!" he shouted.

Maggie looked up. Sure enough, a few lazy flakes drifted down from the dark sky.

"It is snow." She felt the featherlight touch of a snowflake on her cheek. "Look!"

Her foot hit a pothole in the road, and she stumbled. Grant's arm went around her in an instant, keeping her from falling.

"You're as bad as the kids." His voice was low and teasing in her ear. "Next thing you know you'll be dancing in the street."

"Is that so bad?"

She looked up at him and knew immediately she'd made a mistake. Grant's face was very close, his eyes warm with laughter instead of cool and judging. His arm felt strong and sure, supporting her.

The laughter in his eyes stilled, replaced by something questioning, even longing. Nothing moved—no one spoke. The children's voices were a long way off, and the world seemed to move in a lazy circle.

He was going to kiss her. She couldn't let that happen. She had to stop it.

But she couldn't. Whatever her reasonable, responsible brain said, her body had an entirely different agenda.

It didn't happen. Grant seemed to wake himself, as if from a dream.

"Well, maybe we'd better say good-night." There was something almost questioning in the words.

"Yes." She could only hope she didn't sound as stupid as she felt. "Good night."

She turned and ran after the children, knowing she was trying to run from herself.

Grant let out a sigh of relief as Maggie closed the outer door of the clinic behind the final patient on Monday afternoon and snapped the lock. She flipped the sign to Closed, not that it would actually stop anyone.

"Are we really done for the day?"

He'd been busier than this in the hospital emergency room, of course. Certainly he'd worked longer hours, especially as an intern. But somehow the clinic seemed a heavier responsibility, maybe because there was no one here to back him up except Maggie.

"That's the last of them." Maggie gathered files from the desk. "Congratulations."

He lifted an eyebrow, trying not to think about how soft her lips looked, or how he'd almost made the mistake of kissing them on Saturday night. "For what?"

"That was a good catch on Elsie Warner's pregnancy. Some docs wouldn't have seen it."

He shrugged. "Hopefully it will be nothing, but the ultrasound will tell us for sure. Better to be forewarned than caught unprepared."

It had been routine, of course. There was no reason to feel elated at the glow of approval in Maggie's eyes.

"Well, you did a good job. And you've been accepted. That steady stream of patients means that the word has gotten around that you're okay."

He considered that, ridiculously pleased. "Sure it wasn't just the lure of a free checkup?"

"I told you, they don't take charity." She nodded toward the desk's surface. "You now have three jars of preserves, two of honey, a pound of bacon from the hog the Travis family just slaughtered and a couple of loaves of homemade bread."

He took a step nearer to Maggie, reminding himself not to get too close. He didn't want to feel that irrational pull of attraction again, did he?

"So deluging me with food is the sign of acceptance in Button Gap?"

"It is." Her full lips curved in a smile. "Don't tell me the big-city doc actually appreciates that."

"Hey, nobody ever brought me honey before." He picked up a jar, holding it to the light to admire the amber color. "You sure this is safe?"

"Of course it's safe." Her exasperated tone seemed to set a safety zone between them. "Toby Watkins's bees produce the best honey in the county."

"Well, I can't eat all this stuff on my own, and you have kids to feed. We'll share."

"You could take some back home to Baltimore with you when you go. Give it to your family."

He shook his head. "My mother doesn't eat anything but salads and grilled fish, as far as I can tell." He grimaced. "She might gain an ounce."

He tried to picture his cool, elegant mother in Button Gap. Impossible.

"You live with your family, do you?"

"No." He clipped off the word. The Hardesty mansion,

as cool and elegant as his mother, hadn't been a place anyone could call home in years. But he wouldn't tell Maggie that.

"I have an apartment close to the hospital. It only made sense to be nearby when I was doing my internship and residency."

"Will you stay there when your month here is up?"

"Well, that depends." He put the jar down, and his hand brushed hers. At once that awareness he'd been avoiding came flooding back.

And they were alone in the quiet room with dusk beginning to darken the windows.

Maggie cleared her throat, as if she'd been visited by the same thought. "Depends on what?"

"In a way, on what happens here." He folded his arms across his chest, propped his hip against the table and kept talking to block feeling anything. "I'm being considered for a place in one of the best general practices in the city. The chief partner is a big supporter of the Volunteer Doctors program."

Maggie stared at him. "Is that why you came here? To impress him?"

"He suggested it. He said volunteering would be good experience—that I'd learn to relate to patients in a whole new way."

Actually, Dr. Rawlins had been rather more direct than that.

Technically, you're a good doctor, Hardesty, but you keep too thick a wall between yourself and your patients. I don't want a physician who gets too emotional, but I have to see some passion. Maybe you'll find that if you get into a new situation.

Rawlins was the best, and Grant wanted that partnership. So he'd taken the advice, even though he wasn't sure passion was his forte. Being a good physician ought to be enough.

"And is it working?" Maggie's question was tart, and he

remembered what she'd said about volunteers coming here to pad up their résumés.

Anger welled up, surprisingly strong. She didn't have the right to judge him.

"What's wrong, Maggie? Isn't that an altruistic enough motive for you?"

She stiffened, hands pressed against the desk. "It's none of my business why you came."

"No? Then why are you looking at me as if you're judging me?"

"I'm not." She turned away, the stiffness of her shoulders denying the words. "I suppose we're just lucky that our needs happen to coincide with yours."

They were lucky. The people of Button Gap got his services for a month at no cost to the community, and he got the experience he needed to land the position he wanted. It was a fair exchange.

So it didn't matter to him in the least that knowing his motives had disillusioned Maggie.

Not in the least.

Chapter Four

"You sure keeping the boy out of school is the only way of handling this?" Aunt Elly still looked worried on Tuesday morning as Maggie headed for the office.

Maggie paused, wishing she didn't have to hide Joey away from his friends. Was she overreacting? Letting her own fear of the county social worker govern what she did with the children? The memory of the deputy's visit was too fresh in her mind to allow her to judge.

"I know he doesn't want to stay home."

She glanced toward the living room, where Joey was trying to convince his siblings to play school. They didn't seem impressed with the idea of sitting still.

"I just don't know what else to do. If he's in school, it's too easy for Mrs. Hadley to find him."

Aunt Elly gave her a searching glance, as if plumbing the depths of Maggie's soul. "What did his teacher have to say about it?"

"She agreed it was just as well." Nobody at the small Button Gap elementary school would want to give them away, but they also couldn't risk running afoul of the county. "That way they're not to blame. It's not long until Christmas vacation anyway, and Emily Davison will tutor him. He won't fall behind."

"Guess maybe it's for the best." Aunt Elly's agreement sounded reluctant, but really, what else could they do? "How are you going to explain it to Grant?"

Her fingers clenched. "I'm not." She shook her head. "Honest, we can't take the chance. He can't know about Joey being out of school."

"I don't want to lie to the man." Aunt Elly's blue eyes darkened. "I'm not saying I won't, in a good cause, but I surely don't want to."

"We can't risk telling him the truth." Aunt Elly might think Grant could be trusted, but Maggie wasn't so sure. She kissed the older woman's cheek, its wrinkles a road map of the life of service Aunt Elly had lived. "Trust me. We can't depend on him."

Aunt Elly nodded, clearly still troubled. "I'll go along with you, child. But keep your mind open. The doc might be a better man than you take him for."

Maggie slipped out the door, shrugging her jacket closer for the short walk to the clinic's door. Aunt Elly always gave everyone the benefit of the doubt.

We can't depend on him. She didn't even *want* to depend on the man. He was an outsider, and he didn't mean a thing to her except as an obstacle to keeping those children safe. Not a thing.

She opened the clinic door. Grant, in the hallway pulling on a lab coat, turned to her with a smile lighting his normally serious face. Her heart gave a rebellious jump.

"Morning."

She concentrated on hanging up her jacket. What did Grant have to smile at, anyway? Certainly the last words that had passed between them the day before had been anything but friendly. She reached for her lab coat, only to find that Grant was already holding it for her.

"Thank you."

"Sure." His hands brushed her shoulders as she slipped the coat on.

With an effort, she steadied her breath and took a step away from him. It was just the effect of his closeness in the dim, narrow hallway—that was all. She certainly didn't have any longing to lean against him or to rely on him. Absolutely not.

"You came in early." She slipped past him, rounding the corner into the reception area and snapping on the overhead light.

He followed, leaning against the door frame. The harsh light picked out the fine lines around his eyes, the slant of his cheekbone. His usual neat pants, pale blue dress shirt and lab coat seemed to advertise the fact that he was out of his sphere.

"There's not much else to do. What's on our plate for today?"

Grant sounded determined to be friendly if it killed him. He'd probably decided that it didn't pay for the two of them to be at odds.

She might feel that way, too, if she weren't weighed down with the secret she had to keep, to say nothing of that ridiculous little flutter she felt every time he got too close.

She sat down at the desk and glanced over the list of appointments. "This looks pretty routine, but I imagine we'll have some walk-ins. Cold and flu season is on us already."

"Nothing like having a waiting room full of people sharing their germs." He leaned over her shoulder to look at the schedule, running his finger down along the list.

His nearness made her voice tart in self-defense. "People come because they're sick, remember?"

His hand paused on the schedule, then pressed flat. "Come on, Maggie, give me a break. You know I was kidding."

"Sorry."

That abrupt word certainly didn't sound very gracious. Aunt Elly would be ashamed of her, if she heard. She took a breath, trying to find something better to say. The trouble was, she just couldn't forget why he was here.

Grant leaned against the desk and folded his arms across his chest, looking down at her. He did that disdainful expression really well. People like him were probably born with the ability.

"What is it, Maggie? Are you still bothered by my motives for volunteering?"

She pushed her chair back, its wheels squeaking, to put another few inches between them. "I'm sorry," she said again, knowing she still didn't sound convincing. "It's really none of my business why you're here."

"That's right—it's not." His lips tightened. "Most people have a little self-interest in what they do. Probably even you, truth be told."

"I don't know what you mean. I'm here because they need me here."

"And because you like to be needed." He whipped the words back at her.

For a moment, all she could do was stare at him. "That's not true." Was it? She tried to search her conscience, but that wasn't easy when she was feeling thoroughly annoyed with him.

He shrugged, as if it didn't really matter to him at all. "Have it your way. The point is that your motives don't affect the care you give people. Nor do mine."

They'd drifted into dangerous territory. She had no desire to let Grant Hardesty know anything about the forces that drove her. That was between her and God.

She took a steadying breath. *I need to get out of this conversation, Lord. I can't afford to say one more thing that annoys him.*

"You're right." She stood, because she couldn't sit there any longer with him looking down at her. "I don't have any complaint about the care you're giving our patients. We're lucky to have you, no matter why you came."

She started to brush past him, but he didn't move. She cleared her throat.

"I'd better get the door unlocked. It's almost time to open."

He looked at her for another moment, then stepped back to let her go by. As she did, she glanced at his face and then was sorry.

She'd created a barrier between them with her attitude. She shouldn't have done that. The last thing she needed was to make Grant any more annoyed and suspicious than he already was.

"Take a deep breath for me."

Grant listened to the patient's breathing sounds, realizing he'd been functioning on automatic pilot for the past half hour. That was Maggie's fault, actually. He was still conducting a silent argument with her in his head.

Why couldn't he just dismiss her opinions for what they were?—the typical self-righteous proclamations of a woman who thought people had to have the highest of motives for every single thing they did.

Probably because he didn't really believe that. Maggie might be prickly, but she did have the best interests of Button Gap at heart.

She belonged here. He didn't. It was as simple as that. For

a moment he seemed to see her the way she'd been Saturday night at the church, her eyes lit with laughter as she joked with the children, her face glowing.

Not a helpful image. He was not attracted to Nurse Maggie, not in the least.

He took the stethoscope from his ears and made eye contact with the elderly woman who'd fulfilled Maggie's prediction about cold and flu season starting.

"That doesn't sound too bad. You go ahead and get dressed, and I'll leave a prescription at the desk with Maggie. Take the pills and get some rest, and you'll be feeling better in no time."

Her thanks followed him as he strode out of the exam room door.

He was trying to take this morning at his hospital pace, he realized. He may as well slow down. There was no point in rushing through the Button Gap clinic as if it were a city hospital—he couldn't even see the next patient until the current one was out of the exam room.

Inefficient. He frowned. Maybe he ought to give Dr. Rawlins some suggestions about running the clinic more efficiently.

He rounded the corner, to see Maggie leaning across the counter in animated conversation with someone in the waiting room. Any suggestions he made wouldn't reflect adversely on Maggie. He was thinking about the physical setup, not the staff.

He tossed the file on the scarred oak desk as she turned toward him. He pulled the prescription pad from his pocket. "I'm giving Mrs.—what was her name?"

"Robbins. Addie Robbins."

He scribbled quickly. No use trying to slow down. Ingrained habits died hard. "I'm giving her an antibiotic for that bronchitis."

He ripped off the script and handed it to her. She looked at it, frowning. He could almost hear her thinking.

"What?" he snapped. She had some criticism loitering in her mind, he could sense it.

"Maybe it would be better if you considered prescribing—"

He slapped his palm down on the desk. Then, mindful of the room full of waiting patients, he jerked his head toward the rear of the clinic.

"Come back to the office for a moment, Maggie. Please."

She pushed her chair back, and he heard her footsteps behind him as he stalked back down the hallway. As soon as they were inside the crammed office, he swung to face her.

"I'm the doctor, remember? I don't need you second-guessing me on the meds I prescribe. I don't need you second-guessing me on anything."

If his harsh words intimidated her, it didn't show. She just looked at him for a long moment, her dark eyes giving nothing away. Then she went to the glass-fronted cabinet against the wall and pulled out a box. She thrust it into his hands.

He looked at the contents of the box, frowning. "Drug samples. So what? If I say the patient should have a particular medicine—"

"A particular medicine that she'd have to drive twenty miles to get." Maggie's voice didn't betray any emotion, but her dark eyes narrowed dangerously. "If she had a car, which she doesn't. And even if she could get to the pharmacy, she couldn't afford the medication."

All of a sudden he was on shaky ground. He tried to regroup. "If she has to have it—"

Those soft lips of hers looked as if they were carved from ice. "If she has to have that particular antibiotic, I'll drive down and get it and pay for it myself. But if she doesn't have to have that particular one—" She jerked a sharp nod at the box in his hands.

"You want to give her the medicine."

"If we give her the antibiotic samples, saying the medicine is part of her office visit, she just might take the pills instead of going home and treating bronchitis with herbal tea and coneflower."

His irritation drained away. He looked again at the box's contents, packed tight with everything from beta blockers to Zithromax. "You've probably got enough to supply Button Gap for most of the winter. Where did you come by these?"

She shrugged. "Some of the drug reps know how hard up we are. They've been freehanded when it comes to samples." She glanced down briefly, then looked at him with a certain amount of caution. "I wasn't trying to second-guess you. I just wanted to be sure Addie got what she needed."

He lifted an eyebrow. "Don't you ever get tired of being right, Maggie?"

She looked startled, but then her face relaxed in a smile. "Careful, Doctor. I might remind you of that when you don't want to hear it."

That smile did nice things to her face. And he shouldn't be noticing that.

"Okay." He flipped quickly through the contents of the box and pulled out what he needed. "Give her these, and make sure she understands she has to take all of them. I don't want to see her back again because she decided to save some for a rainy day."

"Will do." She turned, then paused at the door. "Grant... thanks. I appreciate your listening to me."

"When you're right, you're right." It was easier to admit than he'd have expected. "Just don't make a habit of it."

Her eyes danced. "I'll try not to."

She was gone before he could say anything else. That was probably just as well.

He frowned absently at the dusty file cabinets. He and Maggie had moved from antagonism to an easy banter in a matter of moments. In most hospital circumstances that would be fine, but he and Maggie were alone here. They'd both be better off if they kept things strictly business.

But he had an uneasy suspicion that if he made Maggie laugh too often, "strictly business" would be a tough policy to follow.

She might actually begin to enjoy Grant's presence if she had a clear conscience. Maggie stacked patient files and glanced at the clock. Morning office hours were over—Grant would be out soon with the final patient. She'd lock the door, and then they'd be alone again.

And again, she'd be tempted to relax, to laugh with him, to talk. To tell him more than she should.

She touched the faint scar that crossed her collarbone. Faded now, it barely showed, but her fingers could trace the line. It was a vivid reminder of how easily a child could be hurt.

Of what her responsibilities were. She had to protect Joey and Tacey and Robby. There wasn't anyone else.

So she wouldn't let her guard down with Grant. She couldn't.

The exam room door opened, and Grant ushered the patient out. Maggie followed Evie Moore, who was still talking, to the doorway. She nodded, she smiled and once Evie was finally outside, she snapped the lock and flipped the sign to Closed.

"Will you look at this?" Grant put a cardboard box on the counter.

"I don't need to look—I can smell." The aroma drew her closer. "Evie brought you a whole cherry pie."

Grant flipped the lid back. Dark sweet cherries peeked through the flower-petal slits in the top crust.

"If this is anything like the one I had at the church the other night, I just might eat the whole thing myself."

"It's even better." Maggie inhaled, enjoying the rich scent, enjoying even more the relaxed look on Grant's face. "She got up early to bake this before she came. It's still warm from the oven."

He sniffed and sighed, the corners of his eyes crinkling. "Okay, Maggie, you and the kids have to help me with this. Otherwise I'll have an added fifteen pounds to show for my month in Button Gap."

"That's what you keep saying, but I don't see you turning anything down."

"Hey, nobody told me about the fringe benefits to volunteer doctoring. I might have come sooner if I'd known what awaited me."

His gaze was warm on her face, and for an instant it was almost as if he included her in the benefits he'd found in Button Gap. She pushed that thought away. It was silly. If he could have, Grant would probably have brought his own nurse with him on this assignment. Then he wouldn't have to argue all the time.

In an instant her imagination had created a picture of that perfect nurse—skilled, supportive, eager to serve.

She flicked the image away with the tip of an imaginary finger.

"So you think a few cherry pies and homemade preserves make up for the lack of coffee bars and fine restaurants?"

"Never been crazy about coffee bars." Grant took a plate and knife from the shelf next to the refrigerator and cut into the pie. Cherry juice shot out, making her mouth water. "Seafood restaurants—now them I miss. Baltimore has some of the best crab in the world."

"I know. I was there once. We ate down at the Inner Harbor."

"I hope you had steamed crabs." Grant handed her the pie and cut another slice for himself.

"I did, as a matter of fact." She smiled, remembering. "It was the first time I'd ever seen a whole crab. I didn't know how to get into it."

He closed his eyes, as if remembering the tastes she'd conjured up, then shook his head. "It'll taste even better when I get back."

"Counting the days already?" she asked lightly.

"Not exactly." He shrugged, looking a bit surprised at himself. "Oddly enough, I'm not as impatient to be finished as I thought I would be. Maybe I'm actually learning something from this experience."

"Can I have that in writing? Maybe we can use your endorsement to recruit future volunteers."

Future volunteers. For an instant her smile faltered. Grant would leave, and someone else would come. That was the way things were.

He didn't seem to notice her momentary lapse. "Sure, I'll give the program an endorsement. How about—"

He stopped when the door at the back of the office opened. For an instant her heart seemed to stop, too, when Joey poked his head in.

"Maggie, can I have—" He sniffed. "Hey, you got pie in here?"

Grant waved his fork. "Come on in. You can help us eat this."

Maggie fought to control the tension that galloped along her nerves. What was Joey doing out of the house when she'd told him to stay put? And how long would it take Grant to realize the boy should be in school?

"He needs to have lunch first." She caught the boy's shoulders and turned him toward the door. "You go on back to the kitchen. I'll bet Aunt Elly has lunch ready."

"But, Maggie—"

"Go on, now."

Grant slid a piece of pie onto a paper plate. "The woman's a slave driver, Joey. Here, have this after lunch."

Joey turned back to take the pie.

Get him out of here, her mind shouted. *Get him out fast, before Grant realizes he shouldn't be here.*

"Okay, off you go." She shepherded Joey and the pie to the door, then closed it behind him.

She could breathe again. Grant hadn't caught on.

She turned back to him, planting a smile on her lips. And found him looking at her with raised brows.

"Nice job, Maggie. You want to tell me why Joey isn't in school today?"

She'd relaxed too soon. And she didn't have a plausible story ready to offer him.

Grant folded his arms, waiting. "You're not going to tell me he's sick. The kid's the picture of health."

"No." She tried to force her limp brain to work. "I'm not going to tell you that."

"Well?" He shoved himself away from the desk, taking the two strides that covered the space between them. "What's the story, Maggie?"

This might have been easier if he'd stayed where he was. But he didn't want to make it easy, did he?

When she didn't speak, his gaze probed her face. "Something's wrong. What? You can tell me."

Could she? She wanted to. It would be such a relief to trust him.

But then Joey's face formed in her mind. For a moment it seemed her own face flashed before her, back when she'd been lost and alone.

No. She didn't know Grant well enough to trust him with a secret like this one. She never would.

She took a deep breath. "It's nothing that serious. Joey's just been...a little upset, that's all."

Upset. That was putting it mildly. His world was turned upside down, but he was still managing to smile.

"Upset about what?"

"About his mother being away." That part was true enough. The rest of the story held the difficulty.

"Natural enough. That doesn't explain why he isn't in school."

Grant certainly wouldn't make this easy.

"I talked with his teacher." Also true. "With his father's death only last month and his mother away, it's been hard on him."

She might as well stop rationalizing. The words were true enough, but all of the things she left out turned them into one big falsehood.

"We decided it might be better to keep him out of school for a few days. His mother will be back soon, and he'll settle down then. It's almost time for Christmas break anyway, and there's a retired teacher who's offered to give him some individual help."

She managed to look at Grant, gauging his reaction. He shook his head slowly.

"Poor little guy. I didn't realize he'd lost his dad so recently."

Joey was a poor little guy, but not for the reasons Grant supposed. "It's been a difficult time."

Grant touched her hand. "You're a good friend to help out this way." His eyes were as warm as his fingers against her skin. "If there's anything I can do, let me know."

"Thanks." She managed a smile. "I can't think of anything, but thanks."

Somehow it had been better when he'd doubted her and criticized her. His sympathy just made her feel worse. And if he ever learned the truth...

Well, she wouldn't need to worry about dealing with his sympathy then. He'd have none at all if he ever found out how she'd deceived him.

Chapter Five

If guilt were a disease, she'd be flat on her back by now. Maggie beat the cookie batter with a wooden spoon, taking some pleasure in the vigorous activity, as if the batter were to blame for her predicament.

Unfortunately, she was the only one at fault, and she knew that perfectly well. For the past two days she'd been playing and replaying in her mind that conversation with Grant about the children, trying to find some better way of handling it.

She hadn't. She couldn't tell him the truth, and she couldn't stomach lying. So somehow, she'd have to learn to live with this uncomfortable feeling.

"Isn't it ready yet, Maggie?" Tacey propped her chin on the wooden table, her blue eyes huge in her small face.

"Almost ready." Maggie sprinkled flour on the table and then began rolling the cookie dough with the heavy wooden rolling pin Aunt Elly had given her. Maybe her piecrust always crumbled to pieces, but she had a good hand with Christmas cookies.

"I want to cut out a wreath." Tacey clutched a metal cookie cutter in one hand, tapping it against the table. "Can I?"

Maggie smiled at her, her heart filling. "You sure can, sweetheart."

At least she still knew one thing for sure, no matter how many sleepless nights it cost her. These children had to be protected until Nella came back.

"I don't want to do any old wreath." Joey scrambled onto a chair. "I'm gonna make a reindeer."

Robby reached up to snatch a piece of dough and pop it in his mouth, then looked around as if to be sure no one was watching.

"You can all make whatever you want," Maggie said. "They're your cookies. But remember, it's only right to share them."

Three little heads nodded solemnly. The Bascoms had never had much, but what they did have, they shared.

That was a sign of how good a mother Nella could be, now that Ted wasn't around to make her life a misery. As soon as Nella herself realized that—

Soon, Lord. It will be soon, won't it? I know Nella needs to come back on her own, so she knows she's strong enough to do the right thing. But please, let it be soon.

"Okay." Maggie made a final pass at the dough. "You guys can start cutting out, while I take the last batch out of the oven."

She moved to the stove, a blast of heat warming her face as she slid the cookie sheets out. She'd just put the trays on a cooling rack when someone knocked. Wiping her hands on a tea towel, she opened the door.

Grant stood on her doorstep, holding a sheaf of papers in his hand.

"Hi. Have you got a moment?" He glanced past her, obviously noting the children busy at the table. "It looks as if you haven't."

She didn't want to talk with him, not with the memory of her falsehoods making a heavy ball of guilt in her stomach. But she could hardly say so. She stepped back, holding the door wide.

"That's okay. Come in."

He stepped into the kitchen, sniffing appreciatively. "It always smells good in here."

"We're doing our Christmas cookie baking." She glanced at the kids, then realized Robby had just slid a whole section of dough onto the chair, covering himself with flour in the process.

"Hold on a sec." She rescued the dough, then dusted Robby off. "Let's keep everything on the table, okay?"

Robby nodded, stuffing another piece in his mouth.

She heard a low chuckle from behind her.

"I never knew cookie baking was so hazardous." Grant leaned over to look, keeping a careful distance between himself and the mist of flour in the air. "Maybe you ought to wear masks."

"A little flour never hurt anyone. You can't make cut-out cookies without also making a mess."

She was suddenly aware of her appearance, her sweatshirt dotted with a fine white dust and her jeans probably bearing the marks where she'd wiped her hands. Grant, of course, looked spotless in khakis and a forest-green sweater.

"I wouldn't know about that," he said. "I've never made any cookies."

Immediately three pairs of blue eyes focused on Grant's face.

"You never made Christmas cookies?" Joey sounded incredulous. "Everybody makes Christmas cookies with their mama."

Was she imagining it, or did Grant's face stiffen?

"Not me," he said.

Tacey slid off her chair. She reached out tentatively and tugged at Grant's hand. "You can make my share," she whispered, as if afraid to speak out loud in his presence.

Maggie's throat tightened. Did Grant realize what a generous gift the little girl had offered?

No, of course he didn't. He didn't know that Tacey never voluntarily got within reach of a man's hand. He didn't know how rare something as simple as a quiet afternoon baking cookies was for her.

Grant looked down at the child with surprise and a hint of some other emotion flickering in his eyes. "I don't want to take yours," he said softly.

"We all share." Joey's voice was firm, and he gave Robby a look that dared him to disagree.

Robby nodded. "Share. Mommy says share."

Maggie waited for Grant to make some excuse that would take him right back out the door, but instead he nodded.

"Then I'd like to."

Well, so much for keeping Grant away from the kids. "If you're going to bake, you'd best take off that sweater. Or I have an apron you could wear."

The corner of Grant's mouth twitched. "Think I'll pass on the apron." He peeled off his sweater, revealing a cream button-down shirt. "Will this do?"

She nodded. "At least it's pretty much the same color as the flour. And you can wash it."

What was Grant doing about his laundry? It hadn't occurred to her to wonder. She suspected he wasn't used to doing it for himself.

"That's fine." He unbuttoned his cuffs and rolled the sleeves back. "I'm ready. Somebody show me what to do. Tacey?"

Afflicted with sudden shyness, Tacey shook her head, finger in her mouth.

"It's easy," Joey said. "Just press down with the cutter, like this, and then Maggie will help you put the cookie on the sheet."

"I imagine Dr. Grant can do that for himself," Maggie said.

Grant, head bent as he cut out a reindeer, tilted his face toward her. He smiled, a strand of brown hair falling onto his brow, his eyes crinkling. "I have to have Maggie's help, too. I'd probably break off a reindeer's leg if I tried to do it myself."

His smile had the same effect on her as opening the oven door had. She could only hope he'd think her rosy cheeks were from the baking.

"Maybe I'd better do it then." She cut out a church-shaped cookie. "We wouldn't want the doctor to cause a trauma."

His lips quirked. "You might have to report me to the county medical board."

"What's a tray-mom?" Joey's voice was loud, as if he'd noticed the byplay and didn't like it.

"Trauma," she corrected. "It's an injury."

The boy frowned. "Like when I got my arm broke?"

Her stomach cramped. "Like that," she agreed. None of the Bascoms had ever budged from their story that Joey had broken his arm falling out of the apple tree last spring. She'd had her own ideas about how he'd been hurt, but no proof.

"All ready, Nurse." Grant straightened. "Will you transfer the patient to the cookie sheet?"

Joey grinned as she slid the spatula carefully under the reindeer. "Betcha can't do it, Maggie."

"You're saying that because you know reindeer are the hardest. Just a little more—"

The reindeer's foreleg crumbled.

"Broken," Tacey whispered.

Grant chuckled. "Looks as if we'll have to set the patient's leg."

He reached across the table, his arm brushing Maggie's as he molded the dough back together again. Another wave of warmth swept over her. Really, if the man stayed around long enough, she wouldn't need much firewood for the winter.

"Done." Grant dusted off his hands. "I predict a full recovery."

Joey leaned over to inspect. "It'll break again when we take it off the pan," he predicted.

"The cookie will taste just as good," Maggie said. "Come on, now. Let's get this last tray finished, and soon it will be time to eat some."

Tacey was staring at Grant instead of cutting out her cookies. "Dr. Grant?" Her voice was as soft as a snowflake drifting to the earth. "Why didn't your mommy bake cookies with you?"

Grant was standing so close that Maggie could feel him stiffen at the question. Apprehension rose in her. If he snubbed the child for her innocent words…

He seemed to force a smile. "My mommy didn't like to do things like that."

"Didn't like to do things with you?" Clearly that was beyond Tacey's comprehension. "Why? Were you bad?"

She ought to intervene. Still, what could she say?

Grant's expression hadn't changed, but something lurked in the depths of his eyes that wrenched her heart. What kind of childhood had he had? She'd assumed that silver spoon he'd been born with protected him from hurt.

"No, I wasn't bad." His smile faltered for an instant. "Some people just don't like to do things with kids. You're lucky to have Maggie."

"And Mommy," Joey said quickly. "Mommy always makes cookies with us."

Robby's face clouded. "I want Mommy."

"She'll be back soon," Maggie said quickly, hoping to avert a storm. Robby, the youngest, cried the most over Nella's absence, though all three of them were affected. "Soon. You'll see."

If they weren't convinced, at least they didn't argue the point. They wanted to believe in Nella's return even more than Maggie did.

The children turned their attention back to the cookies. Maggie tried to watch Grant's face without him catching her doing it.

What had just happened? Her neat preconceptions about the kind of life Grant had led had taken a serious jolt. She actually felt a twinge of sympathy for the man she'd thought had everything.

She glanced again at his classic, composed features. Only a little tension around his mouth suggested that he'd been bothered by that exchange, or that he'd said more about himself than he'd intended to.

But he had. He'd shown her a piece of Dr. Grant Hardesty that he probably didn't often show to anyone.

Now how had that happened? Grant concentrated on pressing down the bell-shaped cookie cutter, because he didn't want to look at Maggie.

He didn't let other people know what he was feeling. Ever. All his friends got from him was what was on the surface.

If someone who'd known him since childhood was unwise

enough to mention Jason, he ignored it. He had to. That was the only way he knew how to cope.

Carefully he shut thoughts of his brother back into the secret corner of his mind. Maggie didn't know about Jason, and she never would. As for that little piece of truth about his relationship with his mother—well, she could make of it anything she wanted.

Still, he hadn't expected to blurt that out. He could have deflected the child's question. Maybe Button Gap was having an effect on him. Dr. Rawlins would probably be pleased at that. He wasn't so sure that he was.

"Okay." Maggie transferred the last cookie sheet to the oven and dusted her hands on her jeans. Judging by the looks of those jeans, she'd been doing that all afternoon. "You guys go to the bathroom and wash up while I clean the table. Then you can have cookies."

That pronouncement resulted in a noisy stampede from the room. He could hear their feet thundering up the steps to the second floor.

"What about me?" He held out sticky hands. "Do I get sent upstairs, too?"

Maggie shook her head, smiling. "You can use the sink. I just wanted them out from underfoot while I clean up." She glanced at the kitchen floor. "Although cleaning up might take more time than I have."

He turned on the tap. "You have your hands full with those three, don't you?"

"I'm doing all right."

The thread of defensiveness in her voice made him turn to face her, hands under the stream of water.

"I wasn't criticizing, Maggie. You're a good person, to do so much for a friend."

She studied his face for a moment, as if measuring his

meaning, then shrugged. "People around here take care of each other." She bent to scrub the sticky table surface, her shiny dark hair swinging down to hide her face. "That's just the way it is."

"I see that." He leaned against the sink, drying his hands. Wondering. "Aunt Elly told me you lived with her for a time when you were a child."

Her slim figure stilled. Was she surprised Aunt Elly had told him? Or was she just trying to think of a way of saying it was none of his business?

"That's right, I did." She swung to face him. "My family needed some help. Aunt Elly was there for us."

The words had a ring of finality about them. She clearly didn't intend to say more.

He was surprised at how much that annoyed him. Apparently she didn't feel that his small admission of family frailty warranted any similar confidence from her.

She slid the cooled cookies onto a platter and set it on the table, then got out a pitcher of milk. She hesitated, her gaze fixed on the cookie plate for a moment, then glanced at him as if trying to decide something. The children's feet thumped on the stairs.

"Aunt Elly took care of me," she said. "I'm taking care of Nella's children. I guess I'm doing what she taught me by her kindness. I wish—"

The children came storming back into the room just then, and the fragile moment was gone. Whatever Maggie wished, he wouldn't hear it now, not with three hungry children converging on the table.

Joey grabbed for the cookie platter, his arm dangerously close to the milk pitcher. Robby bumped into him, the pitcher tipped, the milk sloshed and several cookies slid toward the floor.

"Joey!" Grant swung to catch the pitcher before it landed on the floor, too. "You've got to—"

The boy cowered away from him, arms up to shield his face. He stopped, stunned.

Something grabbed his heart and squeezed. Only one thing would make a child react like that. He could hardly breathe for the fury that choked him at the thought of someone harming that child.

He took a breath, forcing himself to be calm. He had to say something that would take that expression of fear off Joey's face.

Maggie beat him to it, catching the boy in a hug. "It's all right. Joey, it's all right, honest. No one will hurt you."

"I'm sorry." Joey's voice trembled on a sob. "I didn't mean to spill it."

"Hey, buddy, I know you didn't." Grant knelt next to him, making his voice soft. "I'm sorry I shouted. I wasn't mad at you. I just wanted to catch the milk before it spilled."

He could see the boy's rigidity ease. Maggie's eyes, wide and pained, met his over the child's head, and she nodded, as if telling him to keep talking.

"Listen, I'm not mad, really I'm not. I was startled, that's all."

Joey slowly unwound himself from Maggie's arms. It seemed to take an effort to look at Grant, but he managed. "Are you sure?"

"Positive." He suppressed the urge to ruffle the boy's hair. He'd better not make any more sudden movements. "Let's have that snack, okay?"

Maggie stood, her hand still on Joey's shoulder. "I have a great idea. You guys can take your cookies and milk in on the coffee table and watch that new Christmas video we bought. Sound good?"

Joey nodded, his face relaxing. "I get to turn it on." He ran toward the living room. The other two children emerged from the corner to follow him.

Anger rocketed through Grant. Was that what they normally did? Cowered in the corner to protect themselves from some adult who was supposed to be taking care of them?

He stalked to the window and stared out past the red geranium on the sill. Dusk was drawing in, seeping down the mountains to cloak the village in shadows.

Behind him, he heard Maggie carrying cookies and milk into the other room. He heard the music of the video start and sensed her return to the kitchen.

When he was sure he had control of himself, he turned to face her, determined to keep his voice below the level of the video from the next room.

"Is that why the mother's not here? Because she abused them?"

He read the answer in the horrified expression on Maggie's face.

"Of course not! Nella's a good mother. She'd never do anything to hurt her children. In fact, she'd take—"

She stopped abruptly, but he knew the rest of it.

"She'd let him hit her rather than the kids." Tiredness laced his voice. He'd seen this way too many times in the E.R., and it still sickened him.

Maggie nodded, glanced toward the door, then stepped a little closer. "The best thing Ted Bascom ever did was wrap his truck around a tree. I don't think you'd find a soul in Button Gap to say any different."

"You're telling me people knew." His hands clenched. "Why didn't you do something about it, if you're all so concerned about each other here?"

She paled. "We tried. Don't you realize we'd try? None of

the Bascoms would ever tell the truth about it. It was always how awkward Nella had been, or how she'd fallen down the steps yet again."

"You still should have called the police."

Maggie rubbed her arms as if chilled. "I did that once. It just made things worse. And the police couldn't do anything when Nella declared up and down that she'd just fallen and Ted wouldn't hurt her. He had her convinced she was nothing without him."

"Social services, then."

If anything, her face went even whiter. "There's no point in your telling me what we should have done. Believe me, we tried everything. I think I'd almost gotten Nella to the point of moving to a shelter when Ted's death made it unnecessary. Now we just have to help them put their lives back together again."

She was right. He knew as well as anyone how often well-meaning efforts failed.

"Sorry. I didn't mean to second-guess you. I know you've been going the extra mile for them."

He clasped her shoulder in what was meant to be a comforting gesture. He wasn't prepared for the overwhelming urge to draw her against him, to soothe away the distress in her eyes.

First the kids. Now Maggie. It seemed Button Gap was getting under his skin in more ways than one.

Could she trust Grant with the truth or couldn't she?

Maggie was still struggling with that question on Friday morning as she filled out yet another of the many forms the county insisted upon. Sometimes she thought the whole clinic would sink under an avalanche of useless paperwork.

The forms were the least of her concerns at the moment.

She let her fingers rest over the computer keys and stared across the waiting room, empty at the moment.

The wide front window gave a gray view of a mostly deserted street. The west wind whipped the flag in front of the post office. It sent a stray newspaper fluttering along like a tumbleweed.

Winter—that was what it looked like. The gray sky suggested snow, and the few people who were out and about had bundled up in winter jackets and scarves. The weather, along with everything else, reminded her of the rapidly passing days. Soon it would be Christmas.

She pressed her fingers against the headache that had been building behind her eyes for the past day. Nella would return before Christmas, surely. She couldn't bear to miss the holiday with her children.

If she doesn't, a little voice whispered relentlessly in her ear, *if she doesn't, what will you do?*

Well, I won't panic, she retorted. *I'll find a way to deal with the situation.*

Which just brought her back to her original question. Could she trust Grant with the secret she hid?

She'd come close to telling him the day before. His sympathy, when he'd realized what Nella and the children had endured, had touched her to the heart. She'd been within a breath of pouring out everything.

Some instinctive caution had held her back. She massaged her temples with her fingertips. Certainly her life would be easier if Grant knew the truth, if he were part of the Button Gap conspiracy.

She didn't know him well enough to be sure of how he'd react. That was the bottom line. Each time she thought she had Grant figured out, he surprised her.

"What are you doing?"

Her hands jerked away from her head. "Nothing. That is, I'm working on the latest statistics report the county office has decided to plague us with."

He nodded, leaning against the desk. "Bureaucrats. They're the same no matter where they are."

That was a featherweight in the balance toward telling him the truth. If he shared her distaste for those who quibbled while others tried to make a difference in people's lives, he might understand about Nella and the children.

She stretched, trying to cover her uncertainty. "We could use someone else in the office just to handle all the paperwork, but that's not going to happen."

"No, they like to keep you on a shoestring, don't they?" He bent a little closer. "How are the kids today? I hope Joey's not still upset."

She found herself turning toward him without really intending the movement. *Get a grip,* she told herself.

"He seems to be fine. Kids are remarkably resilient. At least, I keep telling myself that."

"It's hard to understand how a man could treat his own child that way." His mouth tightened. "As often as I've seen it, I still can't grasp it."

"They're safe now."

He does understand. Surely it's all right to tell him.

She looked up, the words hovering on her lips. But Grant wasn't looking at her any longer. He was staring past her at the computer screen.

"This can't be right." He pointed, frowning at one of the lines she'd filled in. "You've made a mistake."

"Not exactly." Her fingers clenched. She should have closed that file the moment she realized he was standing behind her.

He transferred the frown to her. "What do you mean, 'not exactly'?"

"We've always reported the statistics that way. Doc Harriman figured out a long time ago that the county wouldn't cover the vitamins he ordered for the children if he filled it in as vitamins, so he—"

"Cheated." Grant's tone was uncompromising.

"It's not cheating! He just described it a little differently. If we don't do that, we can't give vitamins to the kids whose families can't afford to buy them. What's more important, a line on a form or a child's health?"

Grant pulled away from the desk and straightened. Every line of his body proclaimed that he didn't accept what she was saying.

"I don't care how you rationalize it, Maggie. It's not the right way. There are other programs that will cover the cost of vitamins."

"Not without pushing families to go through a lot of red tape. Some of them won't do it."

He didn't understand. She'd argued this out a hundred times with her own conscience, but had always come to the same conclusion—the children had to come first.

"That's not our responsibility. We follow the rules. To the letter. Understood?"

She swallowed the argument that wanted to burst out of her mouth and gave a reluctant nod. She understood.

She also understood the answer to the question that had been plaguing her. She couldn't possibly confide in Grant about the Bascom kids.

He might sympathize with their plight, even understand what she was trying to do. But that wouldn't deter him. He'd go by the book. He'd turn them in.

So he couldn't know—ever.

Chapter Six

"Quietly now. Dr. Grant is probably sleeping in, and we don't want to bother him." Maggie followed the children out the door Saturday morning.

Joey leaped off the porch with a shout, followed by Robby. Clearly it was futile to expect three healthy children to be quiet.

She took Tacey's hand and followed the boys, holding the ax close against her side. Actually, she was delighted to hear the Bascoms making noise. They'd been unnaturally quiet for so long that a little ordinary rambunctious behavior could only be a good thing.

This morning, though, she'd like to get well away from the house before Grant was stirring. In fact, she'd be happy if she didn't have to see him again until Monday morning.

Her stomach clenched as she pictured his face the day before when he'd talked about following the rules to the letter. He'd acted as if she were a thief.

The tightness in her stomach seemed to throb. Maybe that was how he saw her.

Well, Dr. Grant Hardesty didn't know everything, even if he thought he did. She beat down the little voice that whispered maybe he had a point.

She was only doing what she had to do to take care of her people. The next time she saw him, maybe she'd just tell him so.

"Good morning. Where are you off to so early?"

Grant stood on the back steps of his side of the house. She'd assumed he was safely in bed, but he looked as if he'd been up for hours, already dressed and shaved.

She swallowed, clearing her throat. But before she could answer, Robby did.

"A Christmas tree!" He bounced up and down, nearly bouncing out of the too-large boots she'd found for him. "We getting a Christmas tree."

It was the first time the four-year-old had voluntarily spoken to Grant. She supposed she should be happy.

"That's great." He glanced at Maggie, seeming to notice the ax, and lifted his eyebrows. "Imitating Paul Bunyan, are you?"

Amazing how that man could make her feel foolish with just a look. "Not exactly. We're going up to Jack White's woods to cut a tree. He offered us one."

Robby stopped at the bottom of the steps. "You wanna come?"

Robby had picked a great time to be friendly.

"I'm sure Dr. Grant has too many things to do today for that." She kept walking. "Come on, Robby."

"Actually, I don't have a thing to do." His voice stopped her. "Maybe I can help."

He'd probably volunteered just to be contrary. She turned slowly to face him.

"You don't need to do that. We can manage."

"But I'd like to. Don't you want me to come, Maggie?" The expression in his eyes told her he knew exactly what he was doing, and exactly what her answer would have to be.

"Fine." She tried not to let her voice reveal her feelings. "We'd be glad to have you."

No, they wouldn't be glad. *She* wouldn't, anyway. Quite aside from the awkward memory of yesterday's encounter, every moment that Grant was with the children was a moment when she had to be on guard. But she didn't have a choice. Making an issue of it would just raise his suspicions.

Grant fell into step beside her, the kids dancing ahead of them. They skirted adjoining backyards and headed for the lane, their feet crunching over frost-crisp grass.

"I'm really not trying to crash your party, Maggie."

A quick glance told her he was watching her with a faintly amused expression.

"Why did you, then?" She may as well be blunt. Nothing else seemed to work with him.

His amusement vanished. "Not from any burning desire for your company, believe me. I thought it would be good to show Joey I really am a friend, not a threat."

So much for being blunt. He'd thrown it right back at her and put her in the wrong, as well.

"I—" She couldn't think of anything she could say to excuse her rudeness. "I'm sorry. That's very thoughtful of you."

It was more than thoughtful. It showed a degree of perception she hadn't expected from him, and that put her off balance yet again.

"He's a nice kid." Grant sounded slightly surprised as he

made the admission. "Given what he went through, I'd have expected more problems."

"Sometimes you can't see the damage." He couldn't know how deeply the subject cut for her.

He watched the kids, frowning just a little. "Isn't their mother due back soon? I thought you said she would be away only a few more days."

That's what she'd said, all right. "Yes, well, she had some family business to take care of."

Nella *had* gone back to the town where her family once lived. And what she was doing might be described as family business, after all. She was trying to find the courage to keep her family together. After years of being convinced she couldn't do anything without her husband, that was a tough battle.

"I hope it won't take much longer."

If there was a question in that, she'd prefer to ignore it. "I'm sure it won't." They'd reached the edge of town, and she waved toward the field that stretched toward the woods. "Up that way, Joey."

He nodded, waved and started off at a run through the frost-touched weeds. Tacey and Robby followed him. Their jackets were bright splotches of crimson and blue against the silvered grass.

Grant put out his hand toward the ax. "I'll carry that for you."

Did he think she was helpless? "No." That came out a little harshly. "Thanks, anyway."

She could sense his gaze on her face as they crossed the brittle stubble, probing as if to question her every comment. She looked firmly away, concentrating instead on the way the slant of December sunlight picked out the blossoms of daisy fleabane and wild asters, dried on the stalk.

"You sound a little hoarse this morning." It was his cool professional tone. "Is your throat sore?"

She cleared her throat. She had no intention of turning into one of Dr. Hardesty's patients, although it would probably be impolite to tell him so.

"A bit scratchy, that's all." She pointed toward the plantation of evergreens dotting the hillside ahead of them. "There are the trees Jack mentioned. He said we could pick any one that's not marked."

The kids were already running between the trees, exclaiming about first one, then another. Grant pushed through a stand of dried goldenrod, its stems crackling. He paused to eye a slightly misshapen Scotch pine.

"Does he grow these for a living?"

She had to smile. "Doesn't look like much of a living, does it? A few years ago, half the county decided there was money to be made in Christmas trees. Anyone with a woodlot started planting them, without thinking about the cost of getting them to market."

"Not a successful experiment, I take it."

"Most of the trees ended up like this, trimmed for a few years, then left to go wild."

"We ought to be able to find one that's not too bad, especially if we trim off the bottom."

That was just what she'd been thinking, but she was surprised that had occurred to him. "I'm sure your Christmas tree is always perfectly shaped."

He shrugged. "The ones I remember as a kid always looked perfect by the time I saw them, anyway. My mother had them professionally decorated."

"Professionally decorated?" The concept boggled her mind. "You didn't trim your own Christmas tree?"

He frowned, then glanced toward the kids. "Hey, guys. Did any of you see one you like yet?"

Apparently she wasn't going to get an answer to that unguarded question. Well, fair enough. She'd certainly evaded plenty of his questions. But what kind of a childhood had Grant Hardesty had, anyway?

Tacey tugged gently at Grant's hand, then pointed. He looked down at her, his face softening.

"Did you find one you like? Show me."

Maggie followed as Tacey led the way past several scraggly pines. She stopped in front of a small blue spruce.

"This one," Tacey whispered. Her eyes seemed filled with stars as she looked up at it.

Joey, joining them, scowled. "I want one that goes clean to the roof. Me 'n' Robby want a big one."

"Believe me, this tree will look a lot bigger when you get it inside," Grant said.

Maggie knew that Tacey had just tugged on his heartstrings. She knew, because she felt the same.

"My ceilings are pretty low," she pointed out. "We don't want to have to cut the top off to get the tree in."

Joey looked unconvinced. She made a point of feeling the spruce's needles.

"I don't know, though. Blue spruce is pretty prickly. Your hands might not be tough enough to trim it."

Joey quickly grasped a branch in one bare fist. "That's nothing," he boasted. "I can trim this one easy as pie. Let's take it."

Over the children's heads, Grant's gaze met hers, softening in a smile. "I guess this is it, then."

Maggie hefted the ax. "Step back a bit."

"Let me," Grant said at almost the same moment.

"I can do it." Her grip tightened on the smooth wood of the handle.

"I'm sure you can."

Grant took a step closer, his body blocking out her view of the children. It was as if they were alone. He closed his hand over hers.

"I'm sure you can," he repeated, his voice lower. "But why should you? Do you dislike me so much that you won't even let me cut down a tree for you?"

Dislike definitely wasn't the right word, not with his skin warm against hers and a hundred messages racing along her nerves straight to her heart.

"I don't dislike you." She was suddenly breathless, and she took a quick inhalation of cold, pine-scented air. She let go of the handle. "I'm just used to doing things for myself."

His eyes, bluer than the December sky, were serious, as if what they talked about was critically important. "It's good to be independent. But like the kids say, you should always share." He smiled then, taking the ax.

Her heart gave an erratic flutter. That wasn't his polite, professional, well-mannered smile. It was considerably more potent.

She took a careful step back. No, what she felt was definitely not dislike. What she felt could be a lot more dangerous than that.

Grant stood at the front window on Sunday, watching as a little parade composed of Maggie and the children crossed the street and entered the house. They'd stood on the corner for a few moments, talking with Aunt Elly. Then the damp chill in the air must have gotten to them, because they'd raced toward the door.

They'd been to church, obviously. It had looked as if everyone in Button Gap went to Sunday services. Everyone but him, that is.

Maybe going to church would have been better than staying in the dingy apartment on such a gray day.

No, probably not. He'd had enough reminders of his grudge against God the night he'd attended the pageant rehearsal.

He toyed with the idea of taking off in the car. The terms of his servitude didn't require that he stay in Button Gap when he wasn't on duty.

But that would feel like running away—from his post, from the unwelcome thoughts of Maggie that had occupied him far too much in the past day.

He frowned out at the now-deserted street. Everyone had headed home for Sunday dinner, probably. A few flakes of snow drifted down from the leaden sky, then a few more.

Joey had been wishing for snow yesterday. He'd talked about it the whole time they were dragging the tree home. He wanted it to snow, and he wanted a new toboggan for his birthday next week.

Well, it looked as if he'd get the snow. As for the toboggan, maybe his mother was taking care of that. Or Maggie.

Every train of thought seemed to lead back to the same place. He turned away from the window, exasperated with himself.

All right, Maggie interested him. Or maybe disturbed him would be a better way of putting it. Admit it, and move on.

It was ridiculous that she was so unwilling to accept any help from anyone. Especially from him. Look how she'd behaved when he'd wanted to cut down the tree. He might have been a mugger, trying to wrest something valuable from her.

Maggie's prickly, determined personality wasn't one he could ever be serious about, but still, she intrigued him. He'd like to see her admit she needed help from someone once in a while.

But probably not from him. He opened the refrigerator door and stared with distaste at the meager contents. He wasn't going to be around long enough for Maggie to learn to depend on him. Another couple of weeks, and he'd be back to his normal life.

He settled for a can of soda, slid into the wobbly recliner and tilted back. He'd concentrate on planning the life he'd have once he returned to Baltimore and started his practice with Rawlins. He should look for a new apartment right away, given how hard it was to find something. Or maybe it was time to consider buying one of the renovated row houses down near the harbor.

By the time he'd finished the soda, the room had darkened so much that he could barely see. A glance out the window told him the reason. The snow had gone from flurries to a steady, dense fall. Already it frosted the shrubs and trees, giving Button Gap a soft, muted visage.

Maybe Joey should have specified how much snow he wanted. Grant reached out to switch on the lamp next to the chair. The bulb came on, then went off. Even as he frowned at it, it came back on again.

Okay, the electricity was flickering. He got up with a protesting squeal from the recliner. He'd better locate a flashlight, in case the power actually went off.

His hand had just closed over the flashlight in the desk drawer when the lamp flickered again, then went out. He waited a moment. Nothing.

Well, all right. He switched on the flashlight. He'd be fine. Bored, but fine.

Then, slowly, his brain identified the grumbling thud he'd heard when the light went out. The furnace. Maggie had told him that the furnace motor was electric. Without electricity, he had no heat.

He was coming back from the bedroom, pulling on a sweater, when he heard someone pounding persistently at the back door. Tugging the sweater down, he opened the door.

Joey had come out without a coat, and he hopped up and down on the porch to keep warm. "Maggie says the 'lectricity is out. Maggie says come over to our place so you won't freeze."

An afternoon in close quarters with Maggie and the three kids. And a fireplace. And a wood burner.

Joey danced. "You comin' or not?"

It was better than freezing.

"You go on back. Tell Maggie I'll be along in a minute."

The apartment was already cooling. He picked up an armful of journals he hadn't had time to read yet. This wouldn't be so bad. Maggie would undoubtedly occupy the kids, and he could immerse himself in the journals. He could make decent use of the time.

Pulling on his jacket, he hurried outside, slamming the door behind him. A step off the porch took him to his shoe tops in snow. He strode across the yard behind the clinic to Maggie's kitchen door, gave a cursory knock and opened it.

"Maggie?"

"Come on in." The croak had to be Maggie's voice, but it sounded more like a frog.

He crossed to the living room doorway, shedding his jacket on the way. He paused.

Maggie sat on the braided rug in front of the fireplace, surrounded by Christmas ornaments and the three kids. The blue spruce they'd cut the previous day occupied the place of honor in front of the window. They'd clearly been spending their Sunday afternoon trimming it.

The room looked like Christmas. Bright cards decorated the top of the pine jelly cabinet in the corner, and a rather crooked red-and-green paper chain swung from the white window curtains.

Maggie didn't look as festive as the setting. She sneezed several times, then mopped her face with a tissue. Her eyes were about as red as her nose, and her usually glossy hair was disheveled.

"I said you were catching something, didn't I?" He picked his way through the boxes scattered on the braided rug to reach her. "Do you have a fever?"

She evaded his hand. "No. It's just a cold."

He touched her cheek. "And a fever. And a sore throat. What have you taken?"

"Nothing." At his look, she went defensive. "I can't take something that will make me sleepy, not when I have the children to take care of."

He glanced at the kids. They stood close together, eyes wary, obviously not sure what to do when Maggie, always strong Maggie, wasn't herself.

"I'll watch the kids. You need to take something right now and get some sleep."

He'd watch the kids? Where did that come from?

Maggie apparently found the suggestion just as incredible. "I'll be fine."

He grabbed her arms and hoisted her to her feet, surprised by how light she was. Maybe her assertive attitude made her seem bigger than she was. He guided her to the couch.

"You won't be fine unless you follow doctor's orders. Do you have something to take, or do I have to go over to the clinic?"

Maggie sank down on the couch, apparently too sick to argue. That alarmed him more than anything.

"Top shelf above the sink in the kitchen," she murmured.

He found the vial, nodded his approval and raided the refrigerator for juice. He went back to the living room to find her curled up, eyes half-closed.

"Here." He stood over her while she downed the pills he doled out, then handed her a glass of juice. "Drink that and relax for a while."

She nodded, tucking her hand under the bright pillow with a little sigh.

He turned to the kids, to find they were all looking at him. A flicker of panic touched him. He couldn't suggest they watch television, not without electricity. What was he going to do with them?

"Why don't you guys sit down by the fireplace and...um, play a game."

Joey shook his head with a look of disgust. "We don't want to play any old game. We want to finish trimming the Christmas tree."

A voice seemed to echo over the years. Jason's voice.

Don't you wish we had a Christmas tree of our very own, Grant? One we could trim ourselves?

He swung toward Maggie, ready to demand she get well and take over.

Maggie slept, her flushed cheek pressed against the patchwork pillow that he'd bet Aunt Elly had made for her. Silky dark hair swung across her face, and one blue-jeaned leg dangled from the couch.

He lifted her leg to the couch, moved the orange juice glass and brushed a strand of hair back from her face. It flowed through his fingers damply, clinging.

A patchwork quilt draped over the back of the couch. He pulled the quilt free, then tucked it around her, moving with the utmost care so he wouldn't wake her. Finally, satisfied that she was comfortable, he turned back to the kids.

He didn't want to do this. But Maggie needed him.

"So, what do you say we finish trimming this Christmas tree?"

Maggie woke reluctantly from a dream in which she had been warm and safe—a child snug in a soft bed, tucked in with love and kisses.

She blinked, coming back to the present. Firelight—yes, the power was off. The room was warm, and the murmur of voices must have made the background music for her dream.

She sniffed, not stirring. Someone must have been cooking on the wood burner. Maybe Aunt Elly had taken over while she was sleeping.

Still reluctant to move, she snuggled under the quilt. Someone had covered her. Someone had tucked her in and told her to sleep. Grant.

She looked toward the fireplace.

Grant sat on the rug in front of the fire, Tacey on his lap, Robby leaning against his knee, Joey sitting cross-legged holding her big yellow mixing bowl filled with popcorn. The old metal popcorn popper she used for camping was propped against the stone fireplace.

"...so Jack and his mother lived happily ever after. The end."

If someone had told her yesterday that Dr. Grant Hardesty would be telling fairy tales to the Bascom kids on her living room rug, she'd have thought they were lying. But this was definitely Grant, even though his face looked softer, somehow, with the firelight flickering on it.

Tacey reached up to tug at Grant's sweater. "A Christmas story," she said softly.

"Yeah, tell us a Christmas story," Joey chipped in. He shoved a handful of popcorn in his mouth.

She wasn't imagining the shadow that crossed Grant's face at that request. Something about Christmas disturbed him at a level so deep, he probably never let it show. Did he admit it to himself?

He ruffled Joey's hair, and for once the boy didn't duck away from a touch. "Why don't we—" He glanced across the room and saw she was awake. "Why don't we see if Maggie needs anything, okay?"

She roused herself to push the quilt back. Those children were her responsibility, and she'd been sound asleep, leaving them to Grant.

"Sorry I slept so long. I'll get up and—"

Grant was there before she could get off the couch. He shoved her gently back to a sitting position on the couch. "No, you won't do any such thing."

She'd have taken offense at the order, but it was said with such concern that she couldn't. It must be the cold that made her feel so tearful. "I'm sorry. I shouldn't have left you with the kids."

He raised an eyebrow even as he touched her cheek and then felt her pulse. "Don't you think I can manage three kids, a power outage and a snowstorm?"

Her gaze tangled with his, and her breath caught. "I think you can manage just about anything you set your mind to."

Joey leaned against the couch and eyed her critically. "You look some better, Maggie."

"Thanks." Although with Grant's fingers on her wrist, her pulse was probably racing. "You guys behaving?"

He looked affronted. "O' course we are. Grant made popcorn."

"A little fast," Grant murmured, and he let go of her hand.

She felt the heat rise in her cheeks. "I'm feeling much better. I didn't realize you could cook."

"Hey, if you want popcorn or soup, I'm your man." He straightened, stretching. "We kept some chicken soup warm for you. You feel as if you can eat some?"

She started to get up and was pushed back again.

"Sit still. Tacey and I are in charge of serving, aren't we, Tacey?"

The little girl actually giggled. Then she nodded and raced to the kitchen. It looked as if Grant had made a conquest.

Of Tacey, she reminded herself quickly. Not of her.

Something remarkably like panic ripped along her nerves, pulling her upright. She couldn't let a momentary gentleness and an afternoon's support make her feel anything for Grant. She wouldn't. That could only lead to heartbreak.

Chapter Seven

Grant shoved another log on the fire and watched as Maggie tucked blankets around the sleeping children. After several stories and snacks, the kids had finally curled up in the nests of blankets she'd created on the living room rug. Thanks to a busy afternoon the tree was trimmed and the ornament boxes put away.

Maggie looked better, and she had things under control. He ought to go back to his own place.

Instead of moving, he settled comfortably into the spot on the braided rug he'd occupied for the past hour, his back against the couch. He stretched out his legs toward the fire.

The power was still off. His apartment would be cold. Maggie might need something.

Those sounded like good enough reasons for staying right where he was.

Maggie glanced out the window at the snowy darkness, then came and sat down next to him. The flush in her cheeks looked natural now, rather than fever-caused.

He put the backs of his fingers against her cheek, just to be sure. Her skin was warm and smooth.

"You okay?" He kept his voice low, although he didn't think anything short of an explosion would wake the kids now.

"Fine." She withdrew a fraction of an inch. "Would you believe it's still snowing out? I'd guess we'll have close to two feet by the time it's done."

"Probably just raining in Baltimore."

She settled back against the couch. "I'll take snow anytime. Maybe we'll have a white Christmas."

Christmas. The holiday was as unavoidable here as it was everywhere else this time of year. A flare of resentment went through him. Why did he have to be reminded?

Maggie seemed to take his silence for assent. She stared into the fire, apparently content for once to sit and watch instead of doing something.

She tilted her head, looking at the battered metal star he'd placed on the very top of the tree. "It looks nice, doesn't it?"

He assessed the spruce. The branches were crooked, and the top tilted a little oddly in spite of his best efforts to straighten it. Half the ornaments were old and worn, the other half homemade.

"Nice," he agreed.

She shot him a look, as if he'd argued about it. "I know it can't compare to a decorator-trimmed tree, but I think it's pretty good."

His brother would have loved the tree, right down to the angels made from paper plates and glitter. The thought of Jason's reaction stabbed him to the heart.

"You have a beautiful tree, Maggie." The thing to do was keep the focus on Maggie and her Christmas, not his. That way was safe. "The kids are crazy about it."

"They are, aren't they?" She smiled in their direction, then got up. "I forgot one ornament."

She took a small box from the mantel, then opened it and removed something. For a moment she held the object protectively between her hands, and then she lifted it so he could see.

A fragile glass angel dangled from her fingers, the flickering light from the fire turning the wings to gold. The way she looked at the angel told him it had a special significance for her.

He got to his feet to look more closely. "Very pretty. It looks old."

"It was my mother's." Emotion shadowed her eyes. "The only thing I have left that was hers."

He touched one wing with a fingertip. "There's a little chip out. If the piece is in the box, maybe I could glue it in place."

"No." Something suddenly pained her face. "I don't have the piece. It was broken a long time ago."

"What happened?" The question was out before he considered that she might find it intrusive.

She shrugged, turning away to hang the angel from a high branch, safe from little hands, he supposed.

"Just an accident."

It must have been more than that, or she wouldn't have that shadow on her face when she looked at the angel's wing. But she clearly didn't intend to share the story with him.

Maggie bent over the enameled coffeepot that she'd put next to the fire to stay warm. "Ready for some more hot chocolate?"

"Sure, why not?" He picked up the mug he'd been using and held it out for a refill. He didn't have the right to push for answers she didn't want to give. He sat back down, letting her choose another subject.

She glanced toward the window again as she joined him on the floor. "I just hope the snow won't keep everyone home from pageant practice this week."

A safe enough subject, he supposed. "How is the pageant coming along? No more disputes about the magi?"

"No." She smiled. "But Pastor Jim used your comments about the magi in his sermon this morning. He said he wanted people to actually listen to the story instead of thinking they know it already."

Being quoted in a sermon had to be a first for him. "I wish I'd heard him."

"You could have come to church."

It blindsided him, coming on the heels of a casual comment he hadn't really meant. He didn't let his expression change, but she probably felt his tension.

"I could have. I didn't."

Let her make of that what she would. She'd probably get defensive. He didn't care. His private quarrel with God wasn't her concern.

"I hope you'll come on Christmas Eve for the pageant. The children would like that."

He couldn't detect anything critical in her voice, but she still might be thinking it.

"Maybe." He made his tone noncommittal. "If I'm still here."

He wouldn't be. His term of service was up that day. He'd be on the road back to his real life by the time the kids began to sing, letting Maggie and Button Gap recede in his rear-view mirror and his memory.

What had possessed her to push him on that subject? Maggie could feel Grant's tension through the arm that brushed against hers. The moment she'd mentioned church, he'd withdrawn.

Well, he'd already made it fairly clear that church wasn't one of his priorities. And that it wasn't any of her business.

Besides, she didn't even want him to stay for the pageant. The sooner Grant left Button Gap, the sooner she could relax and get her life back to normal.

It was definitely time for a change of subject. Past time, really.

"Speaking of holidays, is Joey getting the toboggan he wants for his birthday?" Grant must have been thinking the same thing she was. He nodded toward the window. "Looks as if he'll have plenty of chances to use it."

She glanced at Joey, sprawled on his quilt, his fine blond hair almost white in the dim light. He looked defenseless in sleep, the way a child should.

"I managed to get a snow saucer for him from the church rummage sale. Once I've painted it, it'll be fine." Grant had probably never had a used present in his life, but Joey would appreciate it. "I'm afraid he'll have to share with the other two, though. They only had the one."

"I thought maybe his mother—"

Her hands, clasped loosely around her knees, gripped each other. "Nella can't afford a toboggan."

"Will she be back by Joey's birthday?"

"If she can be."

Lord, please bring Nella home by then. Let her see how much the children need her. Give her strength.

For a moment the silence stretched between them, broken only by the hiss and crackle of the fire. It was oddly comfortable, in spite of the awkward moments.

Well, Grant had things he didn't want to talk about, and

she had her own secrets to hide. As long as they respected each other's boundaries, they could be—

That thought then led to a question. Friends? She wasn't sure that best described their relationship. Colleagues, maybe. At least they didn't have to be adversaries, did they?

Grant shifted, propping one elbow on his knee. In his jeans and white sweater, he should have looked casually at home, but an indefinable something set him apart.

"So tell me, Maggie. What was it like, growing up here in Button Gap?"

She shrugged, thinking of all the things she wouldn't say to him about her childhood. "About like it is now. Small, isolated. Everyone knew everyone else."

"You lived right here in town?"

"No." Her fingers tightened as the image of the old farm-house flashed into her mind, and she forced them to relax. "We lived out of town a couple of miles."

"So you rode the bus to school."

"Yes." When she came. When her father wasn't ranting about the uselessness of educating girls to think they were better than they were.

Grant lifted an eyebrow. "Would you like me to start paying you per word?"

"Sorry." She forced a smile. She'd learned ways of talking about the past that evaded the truth, that made it sound as if she'd had a childhood just like other kids. Why was it so hard to come up with the familiar fantasy for Grant? "Guess I'm just tired."

"Do you want to stretch out on the couch?"

He started to move, but she stopped him with a hand on his arm.

"No, I'm fine." She spread her hands, palms up. "There's not much to tell. I always wanted to be a nurse, but there wasn't enough money for college. So I went to Hagerstown, where I could get a decent job. I took classes at the community college."

"In a nursing degree program?"

"I planned to get into an LPN program. That was all I could afford. But some people at the church I went to took an interest in me. They helped me get scholarship money and made it possible to go for an R.N. instead."

"It sounds as if they were friends."

She nodded, thinking of the college professor and his wife who'd practically adopted her, of the young family who'd given her room and board in exchange for baby-sitting, of the elderly woman who'd paid her tuition when she couldn't possibly have gone to school otherwise.

"They were good friends." Her throat tightened. "I owe them a great deal."

"I'm sure you repaid them when you could."

She shook her head, getting a lump in her throat at the thought of their responses.

"I tried to. They all said the same thing. 'Use that degree to do good.' That's all they wanted."

"So you came back to Button Gap and did just that." He smiled, his eyes warm with what she might almost imagine was admiration. "I suspect those people are proud of you."

Grant's warmth drew her closer, like a flower turning toward the sun. He was only inches away in the quiet room, and the firelight flickered on his strong features and gilded his skin.

She took a breath, feeling as if she hadn't bothered to do that for several minutes.

"That's my story." She cleared her throat. "What about you?"

"How did I end up a doctor, you mean?"

She nodded. *Come on, Grant. Talk about something, anything, that's neutral enough to let me get my balance.*

"Was your father a doctor?"

He made a sound that might have been a laugh if it had had any humor in it. "That's not very likely. My father lives and breathes business. His company is all that interests him."

"I suppose he wanted you to go into business with him, then."

"That was the plan." His lips tightened. "When I decided to take premed, he persuaded himself it was a momentary lapse. I'd grow up and get over it. When I applied to medical school instead of Harvard Business School, the explosion could be heard up and down the eastern seaboard."

"Obviously you got your way." There was more tension in him than she'd have expected over a quarrel with his father that must have taken place several years earlier.

He shrugged. "There wasn't anything he could do to stop me. I had my own money."

The simple sentence defined the difference between them. He'd had his own money. Doors to the life he'd wanted had opened to him, because he'd been able to pay. Could he even imagine what life was like without that?

"Have you and your father made up?"

He tilted his head in a slight nod. "I guess so. We were never close, and that hasn't changed. Maybe he still expects me to walk into his office and take my rightful place at some point. It won't happen."

"No. You already have a partnership waiting for you, don't you?"

"I hope I do." He looked at her, a question in eyes that looked more green than blue in the dim light. "That's the life I want. Is something wrong with that?"

"I wasn't being critical." At least, she hoped she wasn't. "It sounds like a great opportunity. You'll be doing good work."

His smile broke through again. "It's not in a league with Button Gap, I admit. No one there will bring me apple butter in exchange for an office visit." His voice was gently teasing, and he leaned closer.

Did he realize how close he was? She could see the flecks of gold and hazel in his eyes, almost count the fine lines around his mouth.

"You'll miss that," she managed to say.

"That's not the only thing I'll miss," he said softly. And then his lips closed over hers.

For one second she almost believed she could pull back. Then her heart stirred and she melted against him, returning kiss for kiss. She touched his cheek, feeling the faint stubble of beard, the high cheekbone, the curve of his brow. It was as if she'd already memorized how his face would feel and only needed to touch it in confirmation.

His lips moved to her cheek, and he traced a line of soft kisses. "Maggie."

The sound of her name seemed to bring her back to herself. Slowly, carefully, she drew away. Her heart thudded, and her breath came as if she'd been running. Firelight still flickered, the children still slept. Everything in the room was the same.

Except her.

She wanted to make light of it, wanted to say it was nothing, just a kiss, but she couldn't. Even now, the weakness seemed to permeate her very bones.

Weakness. She couldn't be weak. She could never be weak.

She straightened, leaned back, tried to find a way to meet his gaze that wouldn't betray the fact that he'd cut right through all her defenses as if they were butter.

Grant looked at her with a question in his eyes, as if leaving it to her to say how they would respond to this.

"I don't think that was a good idea." She tried for a light touch and feared she failed.

"Right." He pulled back an inch or two, his smile chilling to something impersonal. "We have to work together. No sense complicating things."

That was what she thought herself, so why did it bother her so much when he put it into words? She tried to get her wits about her. This was for the best.

"You'll be leaving Button Gap before long, anyway."

"Speaking of leaving—" he glanced at his watch, then got to his feet "—I think it's time I went home."

"You don't have to go just because—" *Just because you kissed me.* "The power might not come back on for hours."

He shrugged into his jacket. "I'll be fine. A little cold air might be just the thing right now." A few strides took him to the door, and then he paused. "Don't worry about it, Maggie. It was just the firelight."

She nodded, pinning a smile on her face as he went out into the dark.

Just the firelight. She'd like to believe that. She really would.

Grant paused in the clinic's hallway, studying the chart for the next patient. Unfortunately he wasn't exactly thinking about the patient. Maggie's face kept imposing itself on the medical form, looking the way he'd seen it the previous evening with her eyes dark in the firelight.

He'd kissed her. No big deal. It had been a temporary aberration, brought on by the situation. In the cold light of day, they were both quite ready to forget it ever happened.

Something else had come out of their enforced, snowbound isolation. He and Maggie knew each other considerably better than they had before it happened. He wasn't sure yet whether that was good or bad.

He glanced toward the desk, where Maggie was leaning over the counter to talk with someone in the waiting room. She'd had to go through a lot to become a nurse. That protectiveness of hers was an asset, and so was her fierce determination. She'd probably never have succeeded without those qualities.

As for the faith that came through in every aspect of her life—well, it was one more barrier between them. If the God he'd once trusted did indeed exist, He'd have to be satisfied with Grant devoting his life to healing, because that was all he had to offer.

The bottom line was that he'd learned to respect Maggie, even to want her friendship. But it was just as well that they both understood anything else was out of the question. He pushed open the exam room door and put her firmly out of his mind.

Three patients later, he was checking out an elderly man with chronic bronchitis when the exam room door flew open.

"We have an emergency out in the woods." Before he could react, Maggie was handing him his jacket. "We have to go now."

"Wait a second." He frowned. "What kind of emergency? I'm in the middle of seeing a patient."

Maggie gave the elderly man a quick smile. "Harold understands, don't you, Harold?"

The patient was already sliding off the exam table and reaching for his shirt. "Sure thing, Maggie. You folks go on. I'll see the doc later."

As soon as he'd cleared the door, Maggie began filling a bag with supplies.

"The call just came in. A logger, badly hurt, out near

Boone's Hollow. The helicopter can't land anywhere near them, so we'll have to go."

"Any idea of the type of injuries?" He pulled the jacket on, automatically double-checking the equipment she was packing.

She shook her head. "His partner called, badly shaken. Thank goodness for cell phones. It sounds as if his leg is trapped, and he's bleeding heavily. I gave them emergency instructions before I lost the signal."

Maggie's face was grim, and every move was swift and efficient. She'd undoubtedly done this before.

By the time they reached the waiting room, it was already clearing out.

"I'll lock up," one woman offered. Her face was vaguely familiar. One of the pie bakers from the pageant rehearsal, he thought.

"Thanks, Mavis." Maggie just kept moving, apparently confident the woman would handle things.

"I'll start the prayer chain," the woman added. She touched his arm as he went by. "Good luck, Doc." It was oddly like a blessing.

Outside, he started automatically toward his vehicle, but Maggie was already yanking open the door of her battered truck instead.

"We can take mine—" he began, but she shook her head as she stowed the bag behind the seat.

"You don't want to get yours all scratched up, even if it could make it." She patted a dented fender. "She might not look pretty, but she'll get us there."

She slid behind the steering wheel.

He suppressed the automatic desire to question her decision. Maggie knew the way, presumably, and he didn't. He was on her turf. He climbed in next to her.

Maggie took off down the still-slushy street, then turned onto the road that went up the mountain. In just a few minutes the dense woods closed in on them on both sides of the snow-covered road.

Road? Grant braced himself with one hand against the dash as the truck hit a rut. It was hardly more than a track.

He glanced at Maggie. "Sure you know the way?"

She nodded, eyes narrowed as she searched the road ahead. "I used to live in this area. I know every foot of it."

Weak sunshine had melted most of the snow from the streets in the village, but here the mountain loomed over them, casting its perennial shadow. Hemlock branches bowed down with snow slapped the sides of the truck, as if intent on keeping them out. He had a sense of entering a bleak, unforgiving and very alien world.

Nonsense. He shook off the thought. This was an emergency call, nothing more. It hadn't occurred to him that he'd be doing this, but it should have. Out here, they were the first line of medical defense. He looked again at Maggie, and she seemed to feel his gaze.

"What?"

"Nothing." Then, as they slid around a bend, he realized that wasn't true. There was something. "You were right about the truck. You're much more capable of driving this than I am."

The expression in her eyes told him how surprised she was at his admission. Had he really been so arrogant that she thought him incapable of admitting it when he was wrong?

The road narrowed still more, so that the truck seemed to force its way through the overhanging branches. He spotted a broken mailbox tilting listlessly on a post by a lane that was nothing more than a thread through the forest. Davis, it read in faded letters.

"That was where you lived?"

She nodded, her jaw tight with tension. "About a mile hike back."

He whistled. "Your parents must have liked their privacy."

"My father did." She clamped her mouth shut on the words.

He had just enough time to wonder if she'd ever tell him what it was about her past that pained her so when she turned in by another mailbox.

"We're almost there. The patient is Jake Riley, about forty, good general health, no existing conditions to worry about. His wife said she'd post the boy by the lane to show us where they are."

Even as the words were out of her mouth, he spotted the small figure ahead of them, waving. Grant grabbed the medical bag and slid out as Maggie pulled to a stop.

She was by his side almost before his feet hit the ground, it seemed. "Where are they?"

The boy, his face tearstained, pointed to a thick growth of woods. "That way. Hurry. You gotta hurry!"

Grant started toward the trees, adrenaline pumping, his legs churning through the heavy snow. Maggie was right beside him, keeping pace with him. He had a moment's thought for the probable reaction of his hospital colleagues if he tried to describe the situation.

They wouldn't believe it. He hardly believed it himself, but one thing he recognized. He could count on Maggie without question, without doubt. Whatever awaited them, she wouldn't let him down.

Chapter Eight

Blades whirling, the Life Flight helicopter lifted off, carrying the patient to the hospital where a surgical team waited. Maggie tilted her head back to watch it clear the trees, smiling at the spontaneous round of applause from those who watched from the ground.

Thank You, Lord. Thank You.

"He's going to be fine now." Grant held the wife's hands in both of his, his tone reassuring. "Don't worry. They'll take good care of him."

The woman murmured incoherent thanks, then walked away with the neighbor who was driving her to the hospital. The rest of the small group moved, in ones and twos, toward the trucks and snowmobiles that had brought them.

Grant stood watching them for a moment, his expression bemused.

"Where did they all come from?" He nodded toward the plow driver who'd cleared enough space for the helicopter to land. "I thought we were alone in the most desolate place on the planet. Suddenly people appeared out of nowhere."

We're never alone. She wanted to say the words aloud, but she wouldn't, not given the way Grant tensed whenever the subject of faith came up.

"Word spreads fast when someone needs help," she said instead. "One person calls another, he calls another. Anyone who can help just comes."

"In the city, we'd rely on the professionals in a situation like this."

She wasn't sure whether that was an oblique criticism or a compliment. Maybe it was just a statement of fact.

"We're the only professionals out here." She leaned against the truck. "Everyone else helps because they're needed, I guess. Because they know people would do the same for them."

She stamped her feet, feeling the cold for the first time in the past hour. She'd been too busy to notice, but now it seeped through her boots and invaded the space between her hat and her collar.

"We owe them a vote of thanks." Grant raised his hand as a truck spun by them. "He might not have made it without their help."

She looked at him, noting the pinched lines around his mouth and the strain in his eyes.

"He definitely wouldn't have made it without you." A shiver went through her. It had been a close thing, a very close thing. "I couldn't have done it. If you hadn't been here, we'd have lost him."

He caught her mittened hand in a strong grip and held it for a moment. "I wouldn't be so sure of that. You did a good job, Maggie."

"Thanks." Suddenly she didn't feel quite so cold.

She climbed into the truck and started the motor, cranking the heater on all the way. Grant settled next to her, rubbing his hands together as if they'd never be warm. She watched as the last vehicle spun away, then pulled onto the road.

She could feel Grant's gaze on her face.

"I meant that, you know. You're a good nurse."

Most of the time she didn't even think to question that. It was who she was. But sometimes, it felt good to hear it from someone else.

"Thanks." She darted a sideways glance at him. "I meant what I said, too. Your skill saved him."

And his determination. She'd already known Grant was a skilled doctor. She just hadn't seen that fierce will of his brought to bear. He wouldn't *let* the patient slip away. That glimpse into his soul had startled and moved her.

He pulled his gloves off and held his hands out to the warm air streaming from the heater. "Let's just say we can all be proud of what we did today."

She *was* proud—of her people, who'd done just what she'd known they'd do. Of Grant, who'd shown her a passion she hadn't expected.

She took the turn onto the main road. The snow was melting from it now, leaving bare ruts where other vehicles had gone. It was only early afternoon. The whole episode had taken less than two hours, but it felt like a lifetime since they'd raced out of the clinic.

"Okay," she said. "We all did a good job. But if what you did today was the only thing you accomplished during your month here, it would be enough."

His face relaxed in a smile. "We make a good team."

The words repeated themselves in her mind as she drove the rest of the way to the village. *A good team.*

She'd like to believe she and Grant were a team, but she

knew better. Still, if she could ever care enough about some-one to risk marriage, it would have to be with someone who would treat her as a partner. Someone who could respect her independence because he didn't doubt his own strength. Someone like Grant.

Not Grant, she told herself quickly. That was out of the question. But someone like him.

Why not him? A little voice whispered the question in her mind. *Why not Grant?*

She knew the answer to that one. It would never work. They'd both recognized that flare of attraction between them, and they'd both seen that it had to be extinguished.

Well, no. If she were being honest, she'd have to say she hadn't succeeded in extinguishing it. Not when she still felt a little flutter in her heart at the brush of his hands and the curve of his smile.

Controlled, then, she told herself firmly, and tried to ig-nore the faint flicker of hope that teased her heart and re-fused to go away.

Grant pulled his jacket on, fighting the strong inclina-tion to flop down in the recliner and zip aimlessly through the channels. He hadn't realized how tired he was until after they'd treated the string of patients who'd had to be put off for the emergency run.

He zipped his jacket and glanced into the refrigerator. Ev-erything. He was out of everything. That was why he was about to trek to the store instead of relaxing after the long day.

It had been long, but also very satisfying. They'd done good work, he and Maggie. As he'd told her, they made a good team.

Nevertheless, he absolutely wouldn't let himself think of Maggie in any terms but professional. They were colleagues.

Nothing more. He might have given in to temptation for one kiss, but he wouldn't make that mistake again. It wasn't fair to either of them.

The kids were making a racket in the backyard. He grabbed his car keys, swung the door open and took a snowball right in the chest.

The action in the snow-covered yard froze. Maggie, bundled up in that red anorak that made her look like a cardinal, seemed almost as horrified as Joey. The kid's expression was so guilty that it was clear who'd thrown the snowball.

It hurt his heart to see the fear mixed with the guilt in the boy's face. He had to find a way to wipe that out.

He shoved his keys into his pocket and grabbed a handful of snow from the porch railing. "You want a battle, do you?" He packed the ball and threw it, and snow splattered on Joey's shoulder.

Fear faded, and the kid grinned. "You call that a snowball? Where'd you learn how to make snowballs, anyway?"

"It doesn't snow in Baltimore." Maggie rounded a snowball in her bare hands. "Not much, anyway. He hasn't had enough practice. We'll have to show him some snowballs."

"Yeah, show him." Joey scooped up snow, while Tacey and Robby watched, hanging back a little.

"Don't you dare." He gave Maggie a mock-fierce glare. "Just put that snowball down and step away from it."

She wiggled it in her fingers. "Want it? Come and get it."

He charged, taking the snowball in the face and shaking it off as he grabbed her. "For that, you get your face washed with snow."

"Get him." Joey ran at him, pitching his snowball and bending to scoop up more snow to toss.

In an instant, all three kids were pelting him with snow, their shyness forgotten. Ducking, laughing, he managed to grab a handful. He clung tight to Maggie's sleeve as she struggled to break free and managed to get some snow right in her face before she returned the favor.

Breathless, he mopped snow from his eyes, then realized he was holding her too close. Her face was inches from his, her dark eyes bright with laughter, her cheeks flushed. He wanted to kiss her. Again.

He let her go, turning to chase Joey across the yard. But he'd better stop kidding himself that resisting the temptation was going to be easy.

"Enough," Maggie called, laughing as he rolled Joey in a snowdrift, tickling him. "Let's use all this energy to make our snowman and let Dr. Grant get back to whatever he was going to do."

"You wanna make a snowman with us, don't you?" Joey dusted himself off. "It's gonna be the biggest one ever."

He ought to go to the store, get some groceries and watch the news. But his tiredness had miraculously vanished, and he wanted to play in the snow.

"You bet," he said.

Maggie's glance was questioning. "Are you sure about this? You must be tired after the day we put in."

"You, too. But you're doing it." He bent, packing a snowball and rolling it through the deep, soft snow. "Besides, I'm out of practice."

Tacey scurried to help him roll the ball. "Didn't you used to make snowmen when you were little?"

That was probably the most she'd ever said to him, and he discovered that it gave him pleasure to think she considered him safe.

"Well, like Maggie said, it doesn't snow very much in Baltimore, where I grew up."

Her little face wrinkled in a frown. "Why not?"

"Well, it's close to the ocean." Meteorology had never been one of his best subjects. "It's not up high, like we are here in the mountains. We get a little bit of snow, but not usually enough to make snowmen."

"But didn't you ever get to?" Her mournful expression said that she thought he'd been deprived.

He scoured his memory. Suddenly a scene popped up, as clear and bright as if it had happened yesterday.

"I remember one time that I did." He looked down at Tacey, but instead of her face, he saw Jason's. "It was an unusual storm. They'd predicted rain, but it snowed and snowed. My little brother and I got off school because of it, and we decided to build a snowman."

"I didn't know you had a brother." Maggie dusted snow from her red mittens.

He felt the familiar tightening inside him, felt the urge to shut all the doors on his memories and pretend he hadn't said anything.

But that wouldn't be fair to the little girl, who'd brought it up quite innocently. Or to Maggie, who was just expressing interest in him.

"He was two years younger than I am. Jason." After so many years of not saying it, the name felt strange coming out of his mouth.

Maggie got the implication of the verb tense he'd used. He saw the recognition in her eyes.

"You and Jason made a snowman," Tacey prompted. "Was it a big, big snowman?"

"Well, it was pretty big." He measured with his hand. "About this high. Why don't we see if we can make one that big today?"

"We can do it," Joey said quickly. "I'll make this ball really big to go on the bottom." He scuffed through the trampled snow, rolling the ball ahead of him. The other two children ran to help him.

"I'm sorry," Maggie said softly. "I didn't know."

He wasn't surprised at her expression of sympathy. He *was* surprised at the overwhelming urge he had to pour out the whole story.

Do you want to know why I'm angry at God, Maggie? Do you want to hear about a sweet, loving child who didn't have a chance to grow up?

The thoughts burned in his mind. It would be a relief to say them, to let them pour out in a corrosive flood.

But he wouldn't. Saying those things would take his friendship with Maggie to a whole new plane, and it was a place where he never intended to go. Not with Maggie. Not with anyone.

"We'd better help the kids. That's getting too big for them to push."

Maggie nodded, accepting without words that he'd put the subject off-limits. She ran toward the children, her jacket a bright crimson splash against a white backdrop.

He followed. What on earth had possessed him to let his guard down so far? Button Gap seemed to be turning his life upside down.

Maybe it wasn't just Button Gap. Maybe it was Maggie.

"Seems like you're pretty taken with the new doc." Aunt Elly leaned against the kitchen counter the next morning and gave Maggie that look that probed to the bottom of her soul.

"I don't know what you mean." That sounded feeble, even to her. She didn't want to talk about Grant—didn't want to think about how deep her feelings for him might be.

"Oh, I 'spect you do, but if you don't want to talk yet, I'll leave it be."

Maggie shrugged into her jacket. "I'd better get to the office. You sure you don't mind staying with the children this morning?"

"You know I don't." Aunt Elly gave the oatmeal she was cooking another stir, filling the kitchen with such a warm, homey smell that Maggie wanted to sit back down instead of stepping out into the cold. "But, Maggie, how long are you going to go on taking care of those young'uns? Nella should be coming back here by this time."

Maggie paused, hand on the doorknob. As usual, Aunt Elly went right to the heart of the matter. "I thought she'd be back by now." She looked at the older woman, troubled. "I talked to her when she called the kids last night. Asked her. All she could do was cry."

Aunt Elly shook her head, tears filling her eyes. "Poor child. That man beat her down, all right. I know you figure she ought to come back on her own, but maybe that's not going to happen. Maybe you'll have to go after her. You've got a pretty good idea where she is, don't you?"

"I think I do, but I could be wrong." She rubbed her forehead, feeling the tension that took up residence whenever she thought of Nella. "I keep going over and over it, trying to see the best thing to do. If I go after her, I'm afraid she'll never really be sure she'd have come back on her own. Besides, what excuse could I give Grant for taking off?"

"Maybe it's time you told that man the truth."

Maggie suspected her heart was in her eyes. "I don't know. I just don't know."

"Surely you can't think he'd give those children away—not now that he knows them."

"I want to believe he'd understand. I think he can be trusted. But what if I'm wrong? I can't let them be hurt because of my mistake."

Aunt Elly rubbed her hands on her apron. "I know. I know. Well, I'll pray about it. Maybe God has an answer for you about that."

"I hope so." She enveloped the older woman in a quick, strong hug, warmed as always by the feel of Aunt Elly's wiry arms around her. "I'd better go."

She crossed the frosty yard, pausing to smile at the snowman they'd made the day before. She'd provided the carrot and the scarf, but Grant had contributed the Orioles baseball cap the snowman wore instead of a top hat.

The man who'd played in the snow with the children wouldn't turn them in to the authorities. He couldn't. Could he?

Pricked by her unaccustomed indecision, she walked into the office, taking off her jacket as she went down the hall. Grant stood at the desk. He turned slowly, hanging up the telephone.

She looked at him, and her heart turned to ice. His face—she'd never seen that expression on him before. Hard, implacable, determined. He looked at her as if he'd never seen her before. No, worse. As if she'd crawled out from under a rock.

"Hi." She forced a smile. "What's up?"

He gestured toward the phone. "That was Mrs. Hadley. You know her, right?"

Her heart wasn't frozen after all. Instead, it was beating so loudly she could hardly hear her own response. "I know Mrs. Hadley."

"You know her. And I know the truth. Finally." His words dropped like stones. "You're hiding the Bascom kids from social services."

Panic struck then. "You didn't say anything, did you? What did you tell her?"

"Nothing."

She pressed her hand against her chest. "Thank you."

"Don't thank me." He stalked toward her, face bleak. "I will tell her if I don't start hearing the truth from you right now. Why on earth are you hiding those kids? Are you trying to get the clinic shut down?"

"No, of course not." He couldn't think that. "I'm trying to help those children, that's all."

"By hiding them from the authorities? How is that helping?"

"The Bascom kids don't need social services. They already have friends who'll take care of them until their mother gets back."

"Gets back from where?" Grant planted his fists on his hips and loomed over her, looking about ten feet tall. "Where is she, Maggie? How long has she been gone? Why does that Mrs. Hadley think she's run away?"

"I'm not responsible for what Mrs. Hadley thinks." If he'd stop hammering questions at her for a moment, maybe she could come up with an explanation he'd accept.

"Don't dance around it. Tell me the truth. What's going on?"

"All right!" She caught a breath. "It's not what you think. Nella isn't a bad mother."

"No? She's not here with her kids. What kind of mother does that make her?"

"She needed some time, that's all." She shook her head. "Maybe if you stopped shouting at me, I could explain things so you'd understand."

A muscle twitched in his jaw, but he nodded. "Fine. Explain."

Please, Lord. Give me the words.

"You already know the worst of it. Nella's husband abused

her. We tried to help her, but she couldn't seem to break away. When he died, you'd expect her to feel free, but…"

She stopped, shaking her head. She tried to put herself in Nella's mind so she could understand. "I guess after living nine years with a man who dictated her every move, she couldn't think for herself any longer."

"You were trying to help her." There might have been a flicker of understanding in his eyes.

"I was trying to help her," she agreed. "We'd gotten her a job at the café, and Pastor Jim was counseling her. I thought she'd started to turn the corner. Then—"

"She left. Deserted her children." The implacable look was back.

"No, not deserted." She wouldn't believe that. "She left the kids at the clinic early one morning, with a note saying she needed to get her head together, but she'd be back for them. She's coming back."

He was shaking his head even while she spoke, the air between them sizzling with his disbelief. His disappointment in her. "She's gone, Maggie. She's left you holding the bag, and she's gone."

"She'll be back." Why couldn't he see what she was so sure of? "Look, you don't know Nella. She loves those children. She's called and written every few days. She'll come back."

"Wake up." Impatience laced his words. "Even if you're right about the woman, this isn't your responsibility. You shouldn't be taking care of them. Social services is equipped to do that. You're not."

Her temper flared. "I'm doing a good job with those children."

"That's not the point. Let the professionals handle the situation."

"That's what you'd do back in your city hospital, I suppose." She turned away, unable to keep looking at him through her hurt and disappointment. "Pick up the phone and turn them over to a stranger."

"If I didn't, I'd be breaking the law. Like you're doing right now."

She swung back to face him. "I'm not. I'm helping innocent children."

"You're breaking the law," he said implacably. "No matter how you rationalize it. And you're putting the clinic in jeopardy with your actions."

She wanted to deny that, but she couldn't. If the truth came out, it would give the county bureaucrats just the ammunition they needed to close the clinic. She'd known that all along, but she'd believed the children were worth the risk. She still did.

"Look, I'm sorry about deceiving you. But we—"

"We?" The single word cracked like a whip. "How many people know about this?"

She could only stare at him. "Why, everyone. Everyone in Button Gap. Except you, of course."

"Everyone?" Grant looked as if he'd been hit by a sledgehammer. Then his hand shot out to grab hers. "Think, Maggie. That means someone will tell. Someone probably already has told, or that social worker wouldn't have been asking questions."

"No one in town would do such a thing. Button Gap takes care of its own."

"Someone will talk." He let her go, rubbing his forehead as if the sight of her gave him a headache. "They'll close the clinic on my watch."

"Is that the only thing that's important to you? Your precious partnership?"

His mouth tightened. "The only chance is to come clean,

right now." He gestured toward the phone. "You call, or I will."

"No!"

He wouldn't understand. He wouldn't take her word for it. Not unless she told him.

"Maggie—"

"No." She took a breath, tried to speak around the lump in her throat. "You don't see what's at stake. I do. I know what will happen to those children if they get caught up in the system before Nella returns."

"What are you talking about? How do you know?"

She couldn't. She had to.

"I know because I was like them. I know what I'm talking about because I *was* one of those kids."

"You were—"

She forced herself to meet his gaze. "My father abused my mother, abused me, until social services took me away. You'd say Mrs. Hadley was right. You'd say she did what was best for me."

He was processing the knowledge, coping with it, his eyes pained and serious. "She probably thought she did."

"Maybe so." She looked back into the darkness, trying not to flinch. "I just know that my life turned from one nightmare into another. It took me years to climb out. I won't let those children go through what I did. Not for you, not for anyone."

Chapter Nine

Grant tried to absorb what Maggie was saying, but his heart hurt so much for her that it was hard to think straight. *Maggie.* All the pieces of her elusive personality started falling into place like so many toppling dominos.

He should have realized the truth before this—would have, if he hadn't been so preoccupied with his own concerns. He'd known she'd been sent to stay with Aunt Elly when she was just a child. He'd seen her fierce protectiveness toward the weak. Even her brief comments about her father were explained by this one significant fact.

He had to say something. "Maggie, I'm sorry. I didn't realize."

Some of the tension in her face eased slightly, as if she'd been prepared for a blow that she now knew wasn't coming.

"You couldn't have known. People here do, but no one would tell an outsider, any more than they'd tell Mrs. Hadley about the Bascoms."

That was the crux of the situation. Even through his pain

for Maggie, he knew he had to be cautious. He couldn't let his sympathy for her keep him from doing the right thing for those children.

"Maybe so."

He had to admit that she knew Button Gap far better than he ever could. He realized he was standing almost on top of her and eased back a step.

"Will you tell me about what happened to you? About why it makes you so sure you can't bring social services into this?"

Maggie wrapped her arms around herself in an attitude of protection, and for a moment he thought she'd refuse to answer him. Then he recognized that she was only arming herself to say the words.

"I was ten when the county sheriff came." Her eyes grew dark, distant, as if they were seeing that day once more. "My mother had given up trying to protect me by then. He could keep her home, but he had to send me to school, and the teacher saw the bruises."

His mind winced at the thought of bruises discoloring her skin, of the fear that must have lived in her eyes most of the time.

"Mrs. Hadley took me to a shelter. She wouldn't tell me where my mother was or what was going to happen to me. She didn't tell me anything, just left me there."

"You thought you were being punished."

She nodded. "I was. And I thought I deserved it."

Of course she had. Kids always seemed to blame themselves for the miserable things adults did.

"But you went to Aunt Elly eventually."

A ghost of a smile crossed her face. "Aunt Elly wouldn't give up. She kept badgering the county officials until they placed me with her."

"You were happy there."

"Happy?" She considered the question gravely. "Not for a long time. I guess I couldn't believe that she could love and protect me. Not when my own parents didn't."

He reached toward her, and then drew his hand back. She wouldn't welcome a touch at this moment.

"Eventually she got through to me. I started feeling like I belonged. Everyone here knew what had happened, and they were kind." Her lips tightened. "Then Mrs. Hadley took me away again."

"Why?"

She shrugged. "Who knows why that woman does anything? Because she could, I guess."

That didn't correspond to anything he'd experienced with social workers.

"I'm sure you've probably dealt with some wonderful caring people in children's services." Maggie seemed to be reading his thoughts. "But not here. Mrs. Hadley *is* that department, and she runs it like her own private kingdom. She bounced me from one home to another. Every time I started to feel safe, she'd move me again. The only thing I had to hold on to was the faith Aunt Elly had taught me."

If he let himself think too much about that lost child, he could never take action.

"You had a terrible time. But sometimes taking children away from parents is the only way to keep them safe. The Bascom kids—"

"The Bascoms *have* a good mother," she shot back. "My mother lost the will to protect me, if she'd ever had it. But not Nella. She never did. She always tried to protect her children."

How could he put this in a way that wouldn't hurt her? Maybe that was impossible.

"She ran away. You have to face that."

"She's just confused. Nella has a good heart. She'll do the

right thing." Tears filled her eyes. "I can't let her return to find her family broken up. If those children are sucked into the system, she might never get them back. Even if she did eventually, they'd be...damaged."

Like me. He knew that was what she thought, and it grabbed his heart and wouldn't let go.

This wasn't just about Nella and her children. Maggie needed, at some very deep level, to believe that this would work out right for the Bascoms. This was for Maggie's sake, too, to heal that damaged place inside her.

Maybe she sensed that his conviction was weakening. She took a step toward him and put her hand on his arm.

"Please, Grant. Give this a chance. If you don't believe I'm right about the children, talk to them. Get to know them better before you do anything. You'll see that they belong with Nella."

Her grip compelled him to respond. He shook his head, trying to think rationally, but the pain Maggie carried around had fogged his vision.

"I don't know," he said finally. "I don't know if the system would work any better for the Bascom kids than it did for you."

"Then how can you say we should risk it?" The passion in her voice, in her eyes, shook him.

We. If he didn't call the Hadley woman back, right now, he was in this nearly as deeply as Maggie was.

The truth was that Maggie had put him between a rock and a hard place, and any decision he made could lead to the demise of the clinic and probably his partnership, as well. He moved a step away from her, as if that would make it easier.

It didn't. He still felt the pressure of her need to keep the children safe.

He sighed, knowing he couldn't take the easy way out, not now.

"No promises, Maggie. But I won't say anything without thinking it over first and telling you."

Joy flooded her face, but before she could say anything, he shook his head.

"This isn't approval. I still think what you're doing is too risky. But the clinic is already implicated, so I won't act without thinking it through."

Her eyes shone. "Thank you."

"Don't thank me." That probably came out harshly, but he couldn't seem to help it. "I don't know what I'm going to do."

He knew one thing, though. He was letting his sympathy for those kids and his pain for Maggie drag him close to disaster.

"Will you kids please stop stampeding through the living room?"

Three small faces swung toward her, and Maggie saw the apprehension in them. The children were bathed and dressed for bed, and they looked like three Christmas elves in their footed red pajamas.

"It's okay." She shouldn't have snapped at them. It wasn't the children's fault that she still held on to the residue of that confrontation with Grant, like bitter dregs in the bottom of a cup. "I just don't want galloping horses to knock over the Christmas tree, all right?"

Joey nodded solemnly. "We'll be careful."

"Good enough. I'm going to finish up the dishes, and then we'll have a story before bed."

"The Christmas story," Tacey said, and ran to the bookshelf to pull out the tattered Christmas storybook that Aunt Elly had given Maggie years ago.

"Okay. The Christmas story."

Maggie went back to the sink. The black cloud over her head lifted slightly with the memory of that Christmas when she'd begun to feel she belonged with Aunt Elly. She'd actually felt safe for the first time in her life.

She dried the glass milk pitcher carefully and put it in the cabinet. The ordinary routine soothed her, and she tried to look rationally at what had happened between her and Grant that morning.

He knew the truth now, in spite of all her efforts to prevent that. What would he do with it?

At least he'd promised not to do anything without talking to her again. He'd keep his word. She understood him well enough to be sure of that.

Beyond that, she tried to think past his knowing about Nella and the children. She couldn't. She couldn't wipe out the memory of his expression when he'd looked at her as if she were a stranger. She couldn't imagine what he was thinking or planning now.

One fact stood out with perfect clarity in the midst of a fog of uncertainty. Whatever friendship or relationship had been building between them had been shattered to bits. She'd never put it together again.

She gripped the edge of the sink until the pain subsided. She'd already known that a real relationship between them wasn't possible. So she had nothing to grieve over. You couldn't mourn something that had never been, could you?

All she cared about now was what he did about the children. She wouldn't let herself think of anything else. Grant meant nothing to her now but a potential threat to the children. Nothing at all.

A knock at the door set her heart hammering against her

ribs. The kids, playing noisily in the living room, hadn't heard.

Was she going to panic every time someone knocked on her door? Relive the nightmare of Mrs. Hadley coming to take her away?

She steeled herself and opened the door to find Grant standing on her porch.

Her throat tightened. He'd said he wouldn't expose them without telling her first. Was that what brought him?

"Grant." She gripped the doorknob, suppressing the longing to slam the door.

"May I come in?" When she didn't move, his eyebrows lifted. "You invited me to get to know the kids better, remember?"

She could breathe again. He hadn't come to deliver an ultimatum. She stepped back.

"Of course. Come in."

He stamped loose snow from his shoes onto the mat, then slid his jacket off. He'd changed from the dress shirt he wore in the office to a forest-green sweater that made his eyes look more green than blue.

"Is this a bad time?"

"No." She nodded toward the living room. "They're having a game before bedtime. Go on in."

She almost moved to join him, but then knew instinctively that she shouldn't. If Grant were to be convinced that those children belonged with Nella, the kids would have to do it, and without her help. Grant already felt that she couldn't be trusted.

A sliver of pain pierced her at the thought. She turned back to the sink, trying to hold it at bay.

What can't be cured must be endured. One of Aunt Elly's homilies drifted through her mind. True enough. Sometimes a person just didn't have a choice.

She dawdled over the washing up, listening to the noises from the other room. By the sound of things, they'd pulled Grant into playing with the battered board game she'd gotten out for them.

They were all right. She was the one in need of emotional first aid.

Lord, I need some help here. She tried to think how to pray. *Grant knows, and somehow I've got to keep him on our side in all this. Please, show me how to do it. Open his heart to know what's right.*

Grant had a grudge against God. She didn't know how or why she knew that, but she was sure of it.

Open his heart to You, Father. He doesn't seem to know that he needs healing, too. Amen.

Slowly the tension drained out of her. Much as she'd like to think she could do everything herself, she couldn't. God was in control, and she had to believe He'd bring Grant around in His own time.

She moved to the doorway, watching the four of them clustered around the game board. The tip of Tacey's tongue protruded slightly as she clicked her plastic token along the path of the game.

"Five. I won!"

That was the loudest she'd ever heard Tacey speak. Grant's gaze met hers, and she could tell he was thinking the same thing.

He smiled at the little girl. "You won, all right. Good job."

Robby pouted. "I never win."

"Next time." Tacey leaned over to pat his shoulder. "Next time you'll probably win. You'll see."

"Can we play another game?" Joey snatched up his game token.

"Tomorrow." Maggie handed him the box. "Let's put it away for now. It's time for bed."

Did Grant realize what he was seeing? She worried at it as the children put the game away and tidied up the other toys.

Did he understand that children were only considerate and helpful if they had a mother who'd cared enough to instill that? The Bascom kids were a credit to Nella, who'd done a good job with them under the worst of circumstances.

The kids scampered up the narrow wooden stairs, followed by Maggie. To Maggie's surprise, Grant went up with her. She'd thought his interest wouldn't extend to more than a game, but apparently he intended to help put them to bed.

That was good, wasn't it? It had to mean he was trying to see things through their eyes.

All three of them slept in her small guest room—Joey and Tacey in the twin beds, Robby in the trundle bed. The eaves came down on both sides, making the room a cozy nest.

"It's better for Robby to be there," Tacey explained gravely to Grant, patting the trundle. "'Cause sometimes he falls out of bed, and this way it isn't too far."

"That's a good idea." Grant tucked the patchwork quilt around her.

Tacey handed him the Bible storybook. "Do you want to read the story tonight?"

He looked at the book for a moment, then passed it to Maggie. "We'll let Maggie read it tonight, okay? I'll just listen."

She opened the book, her mind scrambling to think of a story that might touch him. Then she glanced at the page. The book had fallen open to the story of the three kings.

Her mind flashed back to that night at the Christmas pageant rehearsal. Perhaps there was a connection between Grant and the rich men who'd brought their gifts.

Open his heart, Lord, she whispered silently.

She couldn't ask for a better audience than the three children to hear the old familiar story. They listened raptly, but Grant's eyes were shuttered, telling her nothing of what he felt.

When the kings had gone home again by another way, she closed the book and put it on the bedside table. "Let's say prayers, now. Who wants to start?"

Tacey folded small hands. "Now I lay me..." The two boys joined in.

"And please God bless Mommy and bring her home soon. Amen."

"Amen," Maggie added softly, and bent to kiss the child's soft cheek.

She moved toward the other bed, smiling as Joey ducked away from her kiss. It was a game they played every night. Joey wanted the kiss, but his manhood demanded that he declare it mushy.

She bent over Robby, then realized that Tacey was holding out her arms to Grant. Maggie's heart twisted. She'd never seen Tacey voluntarily hug a man before. Did he even realize—

Then she saw the sheen of tears in Grant's eyes, and she knew he understood.

She stood, and Grant joined her in the doorway. "You get to sleep now, okay?"

On a chorus of agreement, she closed the door.

Grant didn't speak as they went down the stairs, but the silence wasn't uncomfortable. It was oddly intimate. They might be two parents, planning to spend a quiet evening together after the children were in bed.

She jerked her mind away from that dangerous thought. She couldn't go letting herself imagine anything of the kind. The best she could hope for from Grant was that he wouldn't turn them in.

He stopped in the middle of the living room. He might have been staring at the Christmas tree, but she had a feeling he didn't see it.

Finally he looked at her. "All right. You win."

Her breath caught. "What do you mean?"

"I understand why you feel the way you do about those kids and their mother. I just hope you're right about her. But whether you are or not, I won't turn you in."

"Thank you." She breathed the words, her eyes filling with tears that she tried to blink away. "It's going to work out all right. You'll see."

"I wish I had your confidence." His mouth tightened. "Even with the best intentions in the world, we may not win. You realize that, don't you?"

"I know."

Thank you, Lord.

We, he'd said. In spite of everything, Grant was in this with her. She couldn't ask for more than that.

Grant dug the snow shovel into the layer of fresh snow on the front walk. The additional snowfall hadn't amounted to more than a couple of inches, but it seemed to have made people want to stay home. He and Maggie had cut afternoon clinic hours short when the waiting room stayed empty.

Strictly speaking, he didn't suppose it was his job to clear the clinic sidewalks, but if he didn't, the task would undoubtedly fall to Maggie. She certainly had enough to do.

For a moment he saw her the way she'd looked the previous

evening, her dark eyes shimmering with tears and reflecting the lights from the Christmas tree. He'd wanted to kiss her.

Now where had that thought come from? He'd already decided that was one temptation he wouldn't give in to again. Maggie wasn't the kind of person who'd indulge in a frivolous affair, even if he were so inclined. Her life was wrapped up in her work, her people, her faith and those kids.

So he wasn't going to think about her that way. He'd concentrate on how good it felt to get in some physical activity. Button Gap didn't have a convenient health club, but that didn't mean he had to sit around.

He hefted another mound of snow with the battered old shovel he'd found in the back hall. Amazing how heavy the snow was despite the fact that it looked so light and fluffy. He was actually working up a sweat.

The door to Maggie's place slammed. Joey ran across the porch, used the snow shovel he carried as a vaulting pole and skidded to a stop next to him.

"Maggie says I can help you shovel," he said importantly. "The other kids are too small, but I can help."

"Sounds good."

He tried to think if he'd ever approached a chore with such enthusiasm when he was a kid. Probably not, but then, nobody had expected him to do anything but get high grades and be polite. Joey might be a little rough around the edges, but he had a good heart.

"You know what?" Joey shoveled energetically, sending snow flying. "I was thinking about that story Maggie read last night."

"The three wise men?" He hoped his comments about the number of wise men in the pageant weren't going to come back to haunt him.

"Yeah, those guys." Joey paused, shovel poised. "Seems

like, if they were rich guys, maybe even kings, they should've given Baby Jesus something better."

He tried not to smile. "Better than gold?"

"What's a baby gonna do with gold?" Contempt filled Joey's voice.

"You might have a point there," he admitted.

"What's that frankincense stuff, anyway?"

Joey seemed filled with questions on a subject Grant would prefer to ignore.

"What makes you think I know?" he countered.

The boy's nose wrinkled. "Well, you gotta know stuff like that. I mean, you're a grown-up and a doctor. You oughta know everything."

"Everything is a tall order." He dredged through long-ago memories of Sunday school classes. "I think frankincense was something sort of like perfume. It had a sweet smell. And myrrh is a kind of spice."

"Well, there you go." Joey flung his hands out in disgust. "What would a baby want with stuff like that?"

Grant would have liked to tell the boy to go ask Maggie, but something insisted that Joey deserved an answer from the grown-up he'd asked.

"Those were considered presents fit for a king," he said. "That showed that the wise men understood who Jesus was." And he was certainly the last person in the world who ought to be explaining theology to an eight-year-old.

"Oh." Joey digested that. "You mean like he was God's son."

The kid had a grip of the essentials, anyway. "Yes."

"Well, I still think he'd have liked something else better. Like a red toboggan, maybe." Joey's eyes grew wistful. "A person could go awful fast on a red toboggan, with all this snow."

Baby Jesus hadn't needed a red toboggan, but he suspected he knew who did. "Maybe you'll get one for your birthday or for Christmas."

Joey shook his head and sent another shovelful of snow flying. "No. My mama can't afford something like that. It doesn't matter. I can get on fine without one."

For a moment he was speechless. The child's calm acceptance of what he couldn't have shamed him with reminders of all the expensive toys that had been piled beneath his Christmas tree over the years.

"You wanna know a secret?" Joey leaned close, as if someone might be lurking in the nearest snowdrift.

Grant nodded.

"I'm making something special for Maggie for Christmas. Aunt Elly's helping me. It's a really nice pot holder so she won't burn herself when she takes stuff out of the oven. You think she'll like it?"

He discovered there was a lump in his throat. "I think she'll love it."

"Hey, guys!" Maggie stood in the doorway. "How about warming up with some hot chocolate? It's all ready."

"You bet." Joey scrambled toward the house.

He probably shouldn't. Being around Maggie only seemed to make him do things he'd never expected, like hiding three kids from the authorities. To say nothing of feeling things he'd be better off not feeling. But Maggie was holding the door open, and he found himself following Joey inside.

"You both did a great job on the walk."

Maggie settled the kids around the coffee table with their chocolate, then put a plate of cookies within reach. She tousled Joey's hair, and the boy grinned, then winked at Grant, apparently reminding him to keep his secret.

Maggie went into the kitchen, and he followed, using the sink to wash his hands.

"Would you rather have coffee than hot chocolate?" Maggie lifted the pot from the stove.

"No, the chocolate is fine." He dried his hands. "Smells good."

"You were looking very solemn. I thought maybe you didn't like hot chocolate."

"I was thinking about my conversation with Joey. He has a better understanding than a lot of adults about what it meant for Baby Jesus to be poor and alone."

"I suppose he does." There was a question in her eyes, but she didn't ask it.

"He's making gifts for Christmas." He shook his head. "I honestly think he's more excited about what he's giving than what he's getting."

Maggie considered that, head tilted to one side, her glossy dark hair swinging against her cheek. "That's the way it should be, isn't it?"

"I suppose so. It often isn't." He frowned, knowing he wasn't doing a very good job of putting his feelings into words. "He just made me realize that I've never given anyone a gift that really cost me."

Maggie probably thought he was crazy. He certainly sounded that way.

"Look, I'd like to get something special for Joey's birthday tomorrow. Where can I find a red toboggan?"

Her eyes widened. "Do you mean that?"

"I wouldn't say it if I didn't mean it." He moved impatiently, suddenly wanting to run out and do this. "I know you got a saucer for him, but—"

"That's all right. He'll share that with the little ones, and he'd adore a toboggan. But, Grant, they're awfully expensive."

He shrugged. Maggie's idea of awfully expensive probably wasn't the same as his.

"That doesn't matter. Where can I get it?"

"You'll have to drive down to Millerton. You came through it on your way here. There's a hardware store right on Main Street that would have them. But—"

"Good." He grabbed his jacket. "I'll go now, before they close."

"But it's so expensive," she repeated. Her eyes were troubled.

"Not for me," he said honestly. "That's what I meant when I said I'd never given a gift that cost me. I've never had to sacrifice anything to give to someone else." He caught her hands in his. "Let me do this, okay?"

"Okay." She lifted her face toward him with a smile.

He shouldn't. He was going to.

He drew her toward him and kissed her, feeling the startled movement of her lips against his. Then he let her go and bolted out the door before he could give in to the desire to keep right on kissing her.

Chapter Ten

Grant should be here soon. Maggie glanced at the clock as she forked fried chicken onto a platter. He wouldn't miss Joey's birthday, not after he'd driven down to Millerton the day before for that toboggan.

They'd promised Joey his favorite meal. Aunt Elly bustled to the stove, bearing a plate of sweet corn from her own garden that she'd frozen for winter. Sweet corn and fried chicken—that was all he'd wanted. The birthday cake and presents would probably send him into orbit.

A knock at the door sent Joey racing to it. He flung the door open, and his face fell. It was Grant.

"Hi, Joey." Grant stepped inside, giving Maggie a questioning look.

"Okay, you kids scoot into the other room so we can get this meal on without you underfoot." She shooed them. "It'll be ready in a couple of minutes."

As they stampeded into the living room, Grant turned from greeting Aunt Elly, his eyebrows lifting.

"I think he's been secretly hoping his mother would get here for his birthday," she explained. "That's why he looked disappointed."

Grant's mouth tightened. "She should be here."

"I know." She rubbed her arms, feeling chilled, as if the cold air had come in with Grant. Maybe she'd been secretly hoping that, too. But Nella hadn't come.

"Well, let's get this food on." Aunt Elly wiped her hands on her apron. "No sense fussing over what we can't do anything about."

"Right." Maggie pasted a smile on her face and went to get the chicken. All she could do at the moment was to make sure Joey had a good birthday. She'd worry about Nella later.

After a few minutes of the inevitable last-minute rush, they were all seated around the table.

"Joey, you're the birthday boy." Maggie reached out to him on one side and Grant on the other. "You say the blessing."

Joey, eyes wide at the sight of his favorite dishes, nodded and grabbed her hand. "God-bless-this-food-and-bless-us-Amen." He reached for the chicken.

She started to correct him, but Grant squeezed her hand just then, and she lost track of what she'd intended to say. By the time he'd let go and she could think rationally again, Joey had already passed the platter.

Grant picked up an ear of corn. "This actually looks fresh." He tasted. "How on earth did you get sweet corn at this time of year?"

Aunt Elly smiled, satisfied. "Picked fresh from my garden in August. No more than ten minutes from the garden to my freezer."

"Sure is good." Robby seemed to be wearing butter from ear to ear. "I'm glad it's Joey's birthday."

"Me, too," Tacey said.

Joey dug into his food, and Maggie began to relax. Of course he was disappointed that Nella wasn't here, but it would still be a good birthday. He couldn't help but enjoy himself, especially when he saw the gift Grant had waiting on the porch outside.

They'd eaten their way through the whole platter of corn, most of the chicken and huge wedges of Aunt Elly's double chocolate cake, when someone knocked on the door. Again, Joey darted to answer, hope and caution warring in his expressive face.

"Are you Joseph Bascom?" The deliveryman held a paper-wrapped parcel.

Too awed to show disappointment that it wasn't Nella, Joey nodded.

"Then this is for you." The man handed it over, glanced toward the table and smiled. "Happy Birthday."

"Thank you." Joey shut the door and then turned to them, holding the package in both hands. "I got something. He said it's for me."

"So we see. Do you want some help opening it?" Grant said.

Joey shook his head. As if the question had jolted him out of his wonderment, he plopped down on the floor and ripped the box open.

"Cars!" He took out three small metal cars. "Look, Robby. I got three cars, brand-new ones. And an airplane."

Tacey and Robby hovered over him, awestruck.

"Looks like there's a card," Maggie pointed out, praying it was from Nella.

Joey ripped it open, frowning as he deciphered the words. He looked up finally, and she could see he was fighting back tears. "It's from Mama. She's sorry she's not here. She loves us."

There was a lump in her throat the size of one of the eggs from Aunt Elly's geese. She swallowed. "Of course she does. You know, I think there might be some other presents around here, too."

She went to the pantry and carried out the snow saucer.

"A saucer!" Joey squealed.

Almost before she could put it down, all three children were sitting on it, momentary sorrow gone. Joey wore a grin from ear to ear.

Then it was Aunt Elly's turn to get out the gift she'd hidden when she came in. "Here's something to keep you warm when you play in the snow."

He ripped off the paper and shook out a hand-knitted red muffler. "Wow." He put the muffler around his neck and stroked it. "I never had a birthday like this before. Never."

"Seems as if there's something out here for you." Grant reached onto the porch and lifted in the red toboggan, holding it out to the boy.

If she lived to be a hundred, she didn't think she'd see a better sight than Joey's expression at that moment. Awe, wonder and disbelief chased each other across his face.

"For me?" He reached out tentatively, as if not quite daring to touch it.

"For you." Grant put it in his hands.

"Wow." Joey seemed to have lost the ability to say anything else. "Wow."

Grant looked—

Maggie had trouble classifying that expression. Pleased,

she supposed, that his gift was so well received. But almost ashamed, as well, as if it shouldn't be so easy to make someone so happy.

"What do you think?" Grant ruffled Joey's hair. "You want to take it out in the yard and give it a try?"

All three of the children rushed for their coats, and in a moment the adults were alone with the dirty dishes.

"Well, that boy won't soon forget this birthday." Aunt Elly started to clear the table. "But I reckon he'd give all the presents back if he could have Nella here."

"I know." Maggie picked up an empty platter. "I just wish—"

"If wishes were horses, beggars would ride," Aunt Elly said firmly. "This doesn't take wishing. It takes doing something about."

"I agree." Grant stood up, his palms braced on the table. "You saw Joey's face when he realized his mother wasn't going to come. We have to do something."

She pushed away the sense that they'd both turned against her. They wanted what was best for the children—she knew that. "I know." She rubbed at the ache that had begun in her temples. "I'd hoped and prayed Nella would come back on her own, but I've let it go on too long. I'll have to go after her."

Grant caught her arm, swinging her to face him. "What do you mean, go after her? Do you mean to say you've known all along where she is?"

"Not exactly." Her heart sank. As if everything else wasn't enough, she'd given Grant one more reason to distrust her. "I have an idea, that's all. About a place where Nella used to live. That's where her letters have been postmarked."

"I see." His face had tightened to an impenetrable mask. "You didn't bother telling me that."

She didn't have any response that would make a difference in what he thought.

"I'll go and find her. I'll leave first thing in the morning."

"Good." Grant's expression didn't change. It was still armored against her. "And I'm going with you."

Grant gripped the steering wheel as he waited for Maggie to come back out of the roadside café. They'd closed the clinic for the day and left early. The drive to West Virginia had been done mostly in silence. He hadn't known what to say to Maggie that wouldn't make him angry all over again that she hadn't told him.

The sight of Joey being so brave about his disappointment had ripped through his heart. It was as if being in Button Gap had stripped away his professional barriers, making him vulnerable to the child's pain in an intensely personal way.

He didn't like being vulnerable. Of course he had to care for his patients as a physician, but he'd always kept that solid, professional shield in place. It was the only way he knew to go on functioning.

Maggie came out of the café, juggling two foam coffee cups. He reached across to open the car door for her, and she handed him one.

"No luck," she said, sliding into her seat. "No one there has seen Nella."

He took a sip of the coffee, then consulted the map he'd put on the dashboard. "We'll be in Brampton in another half hour. It looks like a decent-size town. How do you propose we look for Nella?"

He could feel the caution in her gaze. This was the most he'd said to her in hours.

"I thought we'd start with the phone book. Nella's maiden

name was Johnson—unfortunately pretty common, but maybe we'll hit some relatives."

"You're not thinking of just phoning them, are you? If she's hiding, it would be too easy for them to say they hadn't heard from her."

She shook her head. "No, I figure we'll have to go to every address we can find."

"And if that doesn't work?" He had to keep pushing, in case there was something else she hadn't told him.

"The only job Nella's ever had is waitressing. We'll just have to start working our way through the restaurants and cafés."

He started the car and pulled onto the highway. "That could take days." He didn't relish spending his time poking around a strange town, looking for a woman he'd never met. "Maybe we should have called in a private investigator. Or the authorities."

"No!" Her glare singed him. "You agreed to give me a chance to find her first. And if you think this is a waste of your time, you didn't have to come."

"Yes, I did have to come. I couldn't trust you to do this on your own."

The words hung in the air between them like an indictment, and he saw her wince. Well, that was how he felt. Maggie hadn't told him any more of the truth than she'd been forced to, and he'd swallowed every word.

She was silent for so long that he didn't think she'd respond. Then she set her cup carefully into the holder and clasped her hands in her lap.

"I'm sorry. I know I should have told you."

"Yes. You should have." He wasn't in a mood to make this easy for her.

"Why?" She fired the word at him. "You're saying I should have trusted you with Nella's whereabouts. Why? All you've been able to say since you found out about the kids is that I should turn them over to the authorities."

"That's not fair, Maggie. I agreed to wait, in spite of the danger to the clinic."

"That's another thing. I thought you preferred to know as little as possible. At least that way you're not implicated personally."

He clenched the steering wheel, because what he'd like to do was grab Maggie and shake her. "I became involved the minute the clinic did. You know that."

He glanced at her. She was leaning forward, staring out the windshield, as if willing the car to go faster.

"All right, the clinic is involved," she said finally. "But you're asking why I didn't trust you." Her hands gripped each other tightly. "Rely on you. And I guess the answer is that I don't rely on people easily."

"You trusted the rest of Button Gap. Everyone in town knew but me."

"I've known them most of my life. I've only known you a few weeks, and even if—" She stopped, turning her face away from him.

How had she intended to finish that sentence? Even if you kissed me? Even if I cared for you?

He pulled away from that line of thought. It couldn't go anywhere.

"Look, I know how much you care about those kids. I understand why you don't trust the system. But they're not the only ones involved. How will everyone else in Button Gap get along if the clinic closes?"

"That's not fair. Everyone agreed to help."

"Sure they did. But you and I are the professionals. We're the ones who know the rules. If someone gets blamed for this, it will be us. And the clinic." They'd traveled full circle, and it didn't seem they were any closer.

"We won't let that happen." She turned toward him. "For everyone's sake, we have to find Nella. And we will find her."

"I hope you're right, Maggie." He glanced in the rearview mirror to change lanes. "Because here's the exit, and I've got to say I don't feel all that confident."

A few hours later, Maggie's confidence had begun to fade. She tried to pump it up, but it was useless. They were down to the last Johnson in the phone book, and the afternoon was wearing on. If this one didn't know anything, it would be time to start checking on restaurants, and that hope seemed more futile as the hours passed.

Maybe Grant had been right. She glanced at him as he pulled to the curb in front of the cottage listed to a Mrs. Helen Johnson. A private investigator would have done this better, but she didn't have the money to pay one.

Grant did. He hadn't offered, and she wouldn't ask.

He got out. "Are you coming?"

"Of course." She tried to put some energy into her steps as she got out and started up the walk. Grant had been doubtful all along. She couldn't let him guess that she didn't feel so sure of success, either.

She knocked on the door, taking a quick look around. The cottage seemed to sag into itself, as if it had given up a long time ago. She knocked again, and the graying lace curtain on the window twitched.

"Mrs. Johnson?" she called. "Can you come to the door, please?"

She heard shuffling footsteps from inside that moved slowly toward the door. Next to her, Grant shifted his weight from one foot to the other. Impatient.

The door creaked open a few inches, displaying a safety chain and beyond it, a small, wrinkled face topped by scanty white hair.

"What do you want? If you're collecting for something, I can't afford to give."

"We're not collecting for anything, Mrs. Johnson." She tried a reassuring smile. "We're looking for someone we thought you might know. Nella Johnson Bascom."

"Don't know her."

The door started to swing shut, but Maggie got her foot into the space, something in the woman's tone triggering a nerve.

"Think hard, Mrs. Johnson. Isn't Nella a relative of yours?"

Caution flickered in the woman's faded eyes. "Never heard of her."

She knew something. Maggie wasn't sure how she knew, but she did. "Come on, now. I know she came to see you."

"I don't know nothing, I tell you." The querulous voice rose. "Now get away before I call the police."

"Maggie—"

She could tell by Grant's tone that he was picturing them ending the day in jail. He took her arm.

"Just another minute." She leaned close to the door. "Please, Mrs. Johnson. If you won't talk to us, talk to Nella. Tell her that Maggie was here. Tell her that her kids need her. Tell her to come home."

The woman blinked slowly, as if taking it all in, and then shook her head. "I told you. I don't know her."

"Come on." Grant tugged at her arm. "You might want to get arrested, but I don't."

Reluctantly she took her foot from the door. "Please. Tell her."

The door slammed shut.

Maggie bit her lip. "She knew something. I could tell. Couldn't you?"

Grant shrugged as he piloted her off the porch. "Maybe. But you can't force her to talk." He led her down the walk and opened the car door, frowned as if about to say something she wouldn't like, and then shrugged. "Let's go try some restaurants."

Over the next few hours they worked their way up one side of the town's small business district and down the other. Maggie's optimism flagged along with her energy. *Nella, where are you?*

Grant pulled into the parking lot of yet another restaurant.

"This looks like a decent place." He held the door for her. "Let's order dinner while we make inquiries. I think we need to regroup."

The restaurant's interior was warm and candlelit after the chilly dampness outside. Maggie slipped her coat off as Grant consulted with the hostess and showed her the photo of Nella. The woman shook her head.

Grant hung her coat and his on the wall rack as the hostess picked up menus.

"Nothing?"

"She didn't recognize her." Grant touched her arm, maybe in sympathy, as they followed the hostess to a table.

Maggie wilted into the padded chair. "I don't know what else to suggest. I've wasted our time."

"Not necessarily. Maybe you were right about that Johnson woman. She might give Nella your message."

"And I might have been totally off base." She leaned her forehead on her hand.

"You'll feel better when you've had something to eat." He handed her a menu. "Pick something, or I'll do it for you."

"I thought you were only bossy in the clinic." She scanned the menu.

"No, that's my natural state." He smiled, as if he'd somehow gained the confidence she'd lost. "We're not licked yet."

She started to say she wished she could be so sure, but the waitress came to take their order and the moment was gone.

Grant steered the conversation to non-Nella topics while they ate, as if determined to have their meal without arguing. It was only when they lingered over coffee that he gave her a long, serious look.

"You're losing hope, aren't you?"

A lump formed in her throat. "I don't want to. I still hope Nella will come back. She said so in her note. Doesn't that show that she intends to return?"

Maybe it was the flickering candlelight that softened his firm features. He almost looked sorry for her.

"I don't know. You forget, I don't know Nella."

"You know her children. They're a reflection of her. Everything good in them came from Nella. It surely didn't come from that worthless husband of hers."

"They're good kids." He hesitated, making small circles on the white tablecloth with his coffee spoon. "But you have to remember that Nella spent a lot of years in a terrible situation. Maybe she just doesn't have it in her to keep on struggling."

"I don't believe that. I can't." She thought of her mother, and tension gripped her throat.

He dropped the spoon and put his hand over hers, warming her. "I know. Believe me, I hope you're right about Nella. But how much longer can we hope to hide those children from the authorities?"

"We can't give up yet." She wasn't sure anymore whether she was hanging on by conviction or plain stubbornness. "We can't."

"A little while ago you looked ready to."

"As you said, I needed to eat. And I guess, in the back of my mind, I always felt sure I could find Nella if I had to. Not finding her today rocked me."

She pulled out the picture of Nella with the children and put it on the table, as if it might speak to her.

"I can't give up," she said firmly. "Those kids deserve someone who believes."

The server came back with Grant's credit card receipt, and he absently put out his hand for it. "It was a good guess that Nella might be here. We just—"

The woman leaned over, staring at the photo. "Hey, that's Nella Bascom and her kids. Are you folks friends of hers?"

Maggie caught the woman's hand. "You know Nella?"

The server looked taken aback at the intensity in Maggie's voice. "Why? She in some kind of trouble?"

"No trouble," Grant said quickly. "We're friends of hers. I asked the hostess about Nella, but she didn't recognize her."

The waitress sniffed. "'Course not. Lisa, she only works a couple evenings a week. Nella's on days."

"We've been trying to reach her, but I lost her phone number." Maggie tried to keep the tension out of her tone. "Do you happen to know where she is?"

She held her breath while the woman looked her over, then Grant.

"Well, I'd like to help you," she said finally. "Thing is, Nella's not here anymore."

"Not here?" The words seemed to strangle her.

The waitress shook her head. "Manager said she called in yesterday. Said she wouldn't be able to work anymore. Said she was leaving town."

Maggie sank back in the chair, vaguely hearing Grant ask another question or two. No, the woman didn't know where Nella had gone. She'd just left, that's all.

She'd left. Maggie tried to believe that meant Nella was on her way home, but somehow she couldn't. Nella had gone. There was no place else to look. She'd failed.

Chapter Eleven

Grant just sat for a moment, trying to decipher the expression on Maggie's face. In spite of her brave words, she looked nearer to defeat than he'd ever seen her.

He ought to be relieved, in a way. Their quest for Nella had failed, and Maggie would have to admit that there was nothing left to do but turn the whole situation over to the authorities and try to salvage what remained of the clinic's reputation.

He wasn't relieved. Frustrated, upset—but not relieved. How could he be, when the children's future hung in the balance along with that of the clinic?

He scribbled his name on the credit card receipt and vented his frustration by shoving his chair back. "Let's go. We can't do anything else here."

Maggie didn't move. Maybe she was numb, but in an odd way it made him angry. He'd rather Maggie fought him than sit there looking lost.

She let him help her on with her coat, let him take her arm as they went to the car. She got in, and he slammed the door with a little unnecessary emphasis. He felt her gaze on him as he got behind the wheel and turned the key.

He didn't attempt to pull out. He frowned at the heater, which was making a brave effort to put forth something besides cold air, then transferred the frown to Maggie. She was huddled in her coat, hands tucked into her pockets.

"I don't suppose there's any chance Nella's on her way home."

Maggie's shoulders moved slightly. "I'd like to think that. But if she left yesterday, where is she?"

He discovered he was looking for something hopeful to say, as if he and Maggie had traded places. "If she took the bus, she wouldn't make the time that we did driving."

"Even so, she'd surely have gotten there by now." Maggie massaged her temples. "And if she had, Aunt Elly would have called. She has my cell phone number."

He bounced his fist against the steering wheel. It didn't help. "We've wasted the day, then."

"You didn't have to come along." A little of Maggie's spirit flamed up. "I didn't ask you to."

"That's not the point." He knew perfectly well he'd volunteered to come. He wasn't sure he wanted to admit his motives for that, even to himself. "The point is, we're both involved in breaking the rules now, and we haven't gained a thing."

"Sometimes you have to break the rules."

"It doesn't pay." Didn't she see that? "You bent every rule there is, and we're no further ahead. You could lose your job. Don't you understand that?"

She looked at him then, her mouth twisting a little. "I understand. It's already happened to me."

"What are you talking about?"

"My first job after I graduated." Her eyes looked very dark. "A man brought his wife into the emergency room. He said she'd fallen down the stairs. She hadn't."

"Did the woman tell you the truth?"

"At first she did. I reported it, of course. But before the cops arrived, the husband came back with flowers, told her how much he loved her, how sorry he was."

It was a familiar story to anyone who'd worked in an E.R. He knew how it ended. "She backed down and refused to prosecute."

Maggie's hands clenched together. "She was ready to go home with him. It would have been the same thing all over again, and next time she might die."

"I know." He put his hand over hers. They were cold, gripping each other. "But you did the right thing. If she wanted to leave—"

"I didn't let her." She looked at him defiantly. "I said her X-rays had shown a problem and talked an intern into ordering more tests. By the time it was caught, the police had arrived. Once we could tell her that he was locked up, they were able to get the truth."

He looked at her steadily. "And what happened to you?" He knew the answer to that one, too.

"I lost my job." Her lips trembled momentarily, and she pressed them together. "It was worth it."

"Maggie—" What could he do with someone like her? "You know as well as I do that she probably turned around and went right back to him as soon as she was out of the hospital."

"At least I gave her a chance."

"You sacrificed your job. Now you're probably going to pay the same price again. Don't you see that—"

He stopped. She wasn't answering. She couldn't.

Maggie—determined, stubborn, always strong Maggie—was crying. Tears spilled down her cheeks without a sound, and she made no effort to wipe them away.

"Maggie."

Softer this time. Then he put his arm around her and drew her against him so that her tears soaked into his shoulder.

"It's okay." He patted her gently, as he'd seen her pat the kids. "You've done everything you could."

She let out a shuddering breath that moved across his cheek. "I failed."

"You didn't. You did your best." He tried to think of something else encouraging to say, but he couldn't. Maggie was crying in his arms, and he couldn't find a way to comfort her.

Because the truth was that she probably had failed. Nella probably wouldn't come back. The children would end up in foster care.

And Maggie? He stroked her back, feeling the sobs that shook her.

Maggie needed so much to be the rescuer instead of the victim that she could lose her way entirely if she didn't save Nella and the children. And there didn't seem to be one thing he could do about it.

Even if the organist hadn't been playing "Adeste Fideles," Maggie would have known it was the Sunday before Christmas. It was in the air—the scent of the pine boughs on the chancel rail, the scarlet of poinsettias banked in front of the pulpit, the rustle of anticipation. She might be the only person in the sanctuary who wasn't consumed with excitement over the approach of Christmas.

All she could feel was dread as she glanced at the three children sitting in the pew with her. How long? How long until social services snatched them away?

She'd put Joey on her right, experience having taught her it was best to sit between him and Robby if she was to have a semblance of control during the service. Joey was on the end, taking advantage of this position to crane around and gape at each person who came into the sanctuary during the prelude.

She touched his shoulder, turning him toward the front, and he grinned at her, eyes sparkling. Her heart clenched.

Don't let me fail these children, Lord. Please, don't let me fail.

But how could she expect God to pull her out of this situation? She was the one who'd gotten into it, so sure she was right and that Nella would come back on her own. She'd betrayed the secret to Grant. And she'd been so weak as to break down in front of him.

She should never have let that happen. Excuses came readily to her mind—she'd been exhausted, stressed, worried about Nella. But she couldn't lie to herself, and certainly not in the Lord's house.

She'd grown to care too much for Grant. She'd never intended to, and she hadn't even seen it coming. She'd been blindsided by the emotion. When had her initial dislike changed to grudging respect, and respect to liking? And liking to love?

Love. She forced herself to look unflinchingly at the word. She'd fallen in love with him.

Nothing could possibly come of it, even without the complication of the Bascom kids. They were far too different for that. But she loved him.

Worse, she'd shown him everything there was to know about her. He could use it against her.

But he hadn't.

All the way home from West Virginia on Friday night she'd waited for that, and it hadn't come. During office hours the day before, she'd been keyed up every moment for him to confront her about Nella and the children. He hadn't.

Instead, he'd been considerate. Kind. Almost as if he felt sorry for her.

Robby wiggled next to her, and she put her arm around him. He snuggled close, resting his head against her side, and her heart hurt again.

Grant probably did feel sorry for her. He'd *be* sorry, too. But she suspected that wouldn't stop him from calling social services first thing Monday morning.

The prelude ended, and the organist played the first notes of "Joy to the World," the opening hymn. As she opened the hymnal, Joey leaned perilously far out into the aisle.

She grabbed him, glancing back to see what so attracted him, and her breath caught.

Grant. Grant had come to church for the first time since that night at the Christmas pageant rehearsal.

Before she could think what that might mean, he'd started down the aisle. As he passed them, Joey reached out to grab his arm.

"Sit with us, Doc." What Joey thought of as a whisper was loud enough to be heard all the way across the sanctuary. "We have room."

Grant sent her a questioning look, as if asking permission.

Everyone was watching them. She could hardly deny him a seat. She managed a smile and slid Tacey and Robby over to make room. He sat down, Joey between them on the worn wooden pew.

This shouldn't be worse than being alone with him at the clinic. After all, he could hardly bring up any painful subjects while they were worshiping.

Still, she fumbled for the hymnal page, her fingers suddenly clumsy. She was just thrown by the unexpectedness of it, that was all. What had led him into the service this morning?

"'Joy to the world, the Lord is come.'"

Voices sang out. Grant grasped the edge of her hymnal, holding it between them, and her vision blurred. What was he doing here?

The hymn ended on its triumphant, ringing note, and a rustle went through the sanctuary as the congregation sat down. She fixed her gaze firmly on Pastor Jim.

She would not look at Grant. She would not wonder why he was here, or what he was thinking. But she couldn't help being aware of his every breath, no matter how she tried.

She managed to keep her eyes fixed to the front until the Old Testament reading. Pastor Jim had chosen the passage from Isaiah.

"'For unto us a child is born, unto us a son is given.'"

Powerful emotion swept her at the words. That linking of the most intimate, personal love of a parent for a newborn child with the advent of the Lord of all creation—how could anyone not be moved by that?

Something, some infinitesimal tension emanating from Grant, pulled her attention irresistibly. She turned, just a little, so that she could see him.

He was struggling. Probably no one else in that sanctuary could guess at the emotions surging under his calm exterior, but she knew. It was as if they were connected at the most basic level.

Something was wrong between Grant and the Lord. She'd known that since the night of the pageant rehearsal. She didn't know what, and she didn't know how, but that inner warfare was coming to a head.

Please, Lord. She didn't know how to pray for Grant, but she had to. *I hold Grant up to You, Father. You know the secrets of his soul. Touch him. Heal him.*

Through a jumble of emotions she tried to listen to the rest of the sermon. Her mind seemed able to pay attention at one level while all the time, underneath, a constant stream of prayer went on. *Touch him, Lord. Please.*

The service flowed on to its close. Pastor Jim raised his hands in the benediction, then paused, holding the congregation with his smile.

"And whatever you do, don't forget to be here tomorrow night for the pageant. It wouldn't be Christmas Eve without each and every one of you."

She rose automatically, shepherding the children into the aisle. Grant let them pass and then moved close behind her. She felt his hand on her back, guiding her toward the door. His touch sent a tremor through her. Longing, need, apprehension, all jumbled up together, leaving her knees weak.

She managed to smile and speak as she walked up the aisle, hoping she looked normal enough to everyone else. Pastor Jim shook hands with each of the children. As they scrambled down the steps, he took Maggie's hand in both of his.

"Everything okay?"

Apparently she wasn't looking normal, at least not to someone as observant as Pastor Jim.

"I'm fine."

He pressed her hand. "If you need me, you know I'm here for you."

"I know," she said softly.

She stepped through the doorway. A damp wind swept down the street, bringing a promise of snow. She shivered, pulling her coat around her.

Behind her, she heard the pastor greeting Grant, sounding as relaxed and friendly as if Grant attended every Sunday. If Grant felt embarrassed, his response didn't betray it.

"You're coming to the pageant tomorrow night, aren't you?" Pastor Jim was at his most persuasive. "Maggie and the children have worked so hard on it."

"I'll try," Grant answered evasively.

She started down the steps. Joey had found a patch of snow left on the church lawn and was busy packing a snowball.

"Joey." Her voice contained a warning.

The boy looked at her, grinned and dropped the handful of snow.

"We'd better get on home and fix some lunch," she began, then stopped when Grant touched her arm.

She glanced up and found her gaze trapped by his.

"Do you have a minute?" His voice was firm and determined, as if he'd made a decision and intended to carry it out, no matter what.

Something chilled inside her. "Not really. I was about to fix lunch for the children."

He frowned. "Can't Aunt Elly watch them for a while?"

"I don't—"

"I'll be glad to take care of them." Aunt Elly, unfortunately, had heard. "Joey, Robby, Tacey, come on with me. You can play outside after you have lunch and change your clothes."

Before she could think of another excuse, Aunt Elly had tramped off, chasing the children in front of her.

She straightened her shoulders and managed to look Grant in the eyes. "What is it?"

"Let's take a walk." His face was grim. "I have something to tell you."

Her heart seemed to stop. Only one thing Grant might have to say would put that look in his eyes.

Grant could see Maggie's fear in the way she braced herself, as if preparing for a blow she knew would fall. That reminder of the abuse she'd suffered from her father dented his confidence, and for an instant he questioned himself.

He was doing the right thing—no, the only thing possible. In these circumstances, with the children's happiness at stake as well as the future of the clinic, he couldn't see any good solutions.

He could only do what his training had taught him to do. He had confidence in that, at least.

That didn't make it any easier to take a step that would cause Maggie pain. His heart clenched again. She'd endured so much already.

They'd covered most of Main Street without speaking. Still without saying anything, they turned as if in silent agreement onto the lane that wound toward the woods. They'd come this way before, with the children, in search of that lopsided Christmas tree.

Last week's snow had gone from the roads, but it still lay in patches in the fields and the woods. Maggie tilted her head to look at the leaden sky.

"You'd better warm up your shovel. It's going to snow again."

He followed her gaze. The clouds didn't look any worse than usual to him. "How do you know?"

"I just know." Her lips twitched in what might have been an attempt to smile.

"Button Gap will have a white Christmas, then."

Two days until Christmas. Would he still be here? He'd been going over the question in his mind. Technically, his stint at the clinic lasted until the end of the week, but the volunteer doctor coordinator had given him the option of leaving to spend Christmas with his family.

Not that he had any intention of doing that. Christmas in the Hardesty mansion wasn't something that would warm the cockles of anyone's heart.

Still, he could leave. No one would blame him. He didn't have to let anyone know he was back in the city until the holiday had safely passed.

"I realized I never thanked you for going to West Virginia with me."

Maggie's voice sounded oddly formal, as if she had practiced saying that. Or maybe she was just trying to distract him from what she must know he intended to say.

"It was no problem."

The ironic thing was that he didn't need any distracting— he was distracted enough already. The thing he had to say kept tying his tongue in knots.

No. That wasn't what tripped him up. Each time he looked at Maggie, he found himself thinking instead how incredibly dear to him she'd become in such a short time. He wanted to stop dead in the road, pull her into his arms and kiss away the tension and fear in her dark eyes. He wanted to hold her close and feel her hair like silk against his cheek.

He wouldn't. But he wanted to.

All right, he had feelings for Maggie. Their footsteps scuffed along the gravel lane in perfect tempo, as if they'd been made to walk side by side.

But a relationship between them would never work. It was not just that they were too different. Lovers could surmount that difficulty.

They wanted different things out of life. That was what it came down to, and that was why they'd only hurt each other if they tried to build a relationship.

If everything about the Bascom children came out, if the clinic were closed on his watch, he might lose the partnership with Dr. Rawlins. He faced that. He'd deal with it. That wouldn't change the kind of life he wanted, nor the kind of life Maggie needed.

Say it. Tell her.

"Maggie—"

"I was surprised to see you in church today." She rushed into speech as if to stop him. "You don't usually come."

"No."

He couldn't explain to Maggie what he led him into the sanctuary that morning. No, not led. Drove. Something drove him there, in spite of every intention to the contrary. He couldn't explain, because he didn't know himself.

He only knew that a battle was going on inside him, as if some part of himself that he'd buried a long time ago had risen up and demanded attention. He realized Maggie was waiting for more of an answer than his curt negative.

"I thought I'd like to hear Jim's Christmas sermon, that's all. He's a nice guy."

"He is. Does that mean you're leaving before Christmas?"

"No." Sometime in the last few minutes that seemed to have been decided for him. He wouldn't be a coward. He'd stay and face the consequences of what he had to do. "I owe the clinic the rest of the week. I'll work out my days."

Tell her. Just say it.

He stopped abruptly, catching her hand and turning her to face him. He didn't want to look at her, but he owed her that much, at least. He'd have to watch the fear in her eyes change to hate.

He pushed the words out. "I'll let the kids have Christmas with you. The day after, you have to call social services. If you don't, I will."

Chapter Twelve

She was losing.

Maggie leaned against the kitchen sink, staring out the window through the steam created by her breath. Snow. As she had predicted, snow was falling. It was December the twenty-fourth, and they would have snow for Christmas.

And the next day, Nella's children would be scooped up by social services. She might never see them again.

She frowned at the bird feeder on the hemlock branch. A scarlet cardinal shared seed peacefully with three chickadees and a pair of nuthatches, until a blue jay swooped in, scattering the other birds.

She'd have to send Joey out with more seed. He loved that job.

Soon Aunt Elly would come tramping cheerfully through the snow to watch the children while she went to the clinic. It might have been any ordinary day. It would be, if she didn't know what was going to happen as soon as Christmas was past. The knowledge hung on her, weighing her down until it was an effort to move.

She should have known that this would be the end of it, from the moment Grant found out the truth about the kids. She'd thought her heart couldn't hurt any more, but thinking about Grant brought a fresh spasm of pain.

Father, help me deal with this. Please, help me see the way.

She tried to cling to the hope that some miracle would take place, bringing Nella home for Christmas. Hope seemed to be in short supply right now.

Please, Father, give me a sign. Give me something to assure me that Nella will come back. She rubbed her forehead, reminded of too many Biblical characters who'd asked God for a sign because they lacked in faith. *I believe, Lord. I just don't know what to do—about the children, about Nella, about Grant. Show me.*

She stood still for a moment, trying to listen, and then pushed herself away from the sink. If an answer were forthcoming, it hadn't jumped into her mind yet. Maybe she'd best get on with her work, and trust God to deliver His answer in His time.

The children were awfully quiet. That couldn't be good. With a vague sense of foreboding, she walked into the living room.

The kids weren't there. But her mother's glass angel lay shattered on the floor beneath the Christmas tree.

She knelt, reaching carefully for the pieces. Maybe she could—

No, she couldn't. No one could put this back together again.

A tidal wave of grief threatened to drown her, and she choked back a sob. Her last tangible tie to her mother was gone.

What if God is showing you that the same is true for those children? You did ask for a sign, didn't you?

She stood quickly, shaking off the fragments of glass as she shook off the treacherous thought. No, she wouldn't let herself believe that.

"Joey, Tacey, Robby, where are you?" She raised her voice. They had to be upstairs.

A small, scraping noise from the floor above said she was right.

"Come on down here. I just want to talk to you." Surely they knew by this time that she didn't talk with her fists, the way their father had done.

Another small sound, and then came reluctant footsteps. Tacey and Robby crept down the stairs. They halted at the far edge of the braided rug, not looking at her.

"Where's Joey?"

No answer.

She crossed to them and knelt. "Come on, guys, I'm not mad. I just want to know what happened to my angel. Did Joey knock it off the tree?"

Tacey gave an almost imperceptible nod. "He didn't mean to," she whispered.

"Sweetie, I know that. Where is he?" She glanced up the stairs. "Joey? Come on down, okay? I'm not mad at you."

Nothing.

She trotted up the steps, apprehension knotting her stomach. It took two minutes to search the small upstairs. Joey wasn't there.

She hurried back down, her imagination racing ahead of her. "Tacey, you need to tell me. Where is Joey?"

The child didn't answer, but she looked toward the rack where Joey's jacket should have hung. It wasn't there, and his boots were missing.

She grabbed her own jacket, then swung to look at the

other two. "You stay here, all right? I'm going to get Dr. Grant to stay with you."

They nodded, eyes wide.

She yanked the door open. The toboggan was gone from the porch. She hurried down to the yard. Joey must have left while she was upstairs dressing. She could make out small tracks, almost obliterated already by the steadily falling snow.

"Joey!" She took a breath of cold, wet air. "Joey! Answer me!"

The back door of Grant's apartment swung open. He held it wide with one arm. "What's wrong? Why are you shouting for the boy?"

She ran toward him, heart pounding. "Is Joey with you? Have you seen him?"

Grant stepped onto the porch, shaking his head. "Not this morning. Why all the fuss? He probably just came out to play in the snow."

"Then where is he?" She spread her hands toward the empty yard. "He knows he's not to go out of the yard without permission."

Grant lifted an eyebrow. "Aren't you overreacting a bit? He was probably excited about the snow and wanted to try out his toboggan. It wouldn't be the first time he forgot to ask permission for something."

"This time is different." Her sense of foreboding intensified. "He apparently knocked my angel off the tree and broke it. Maybe he was scared. He slipped out of the house while I was upstairs."

That superior look was replaced by something that might have been concern. "I'm sorry about your angel. I know how much it meant to you. But still, he might just be hiding around the house."

"You always like the easy answer, don't you?" That probably wasn't fair, but it was what she felt. She swung around, torn by the pull to run in several different directions at once. "I better see what I can get out of the other two."

She couldn't ignore Grant's quick footsteps behind her as she hurried back into the house. Heedless of the snow she tracked in, she bent down, hands on knees.

"Tacey, I need to know where Joey went. Come on, now. You have to tell me."

Tacey's lips trembled, and she pressed them together, shaking her head.

She felt Grant's hand on her shoulder, and for a fraction of a second she wanted to lean into that strong hand.

No. She couldn't. Grant had already shown he wasn't on her side. She had to do this herself.

Then Grant knelt next to her. He reached out to draw Tacey into the circle of his arms.

"Tacey, honey, you have to tell us where Joey is. I know you probably promised him you wouldn't say, but it's snowing hard outside, and he could get lost. It's not wrong to break a promise if it means helping someone else."

His voice was soft, gentle, wringing Maggie's heart. "You know, don't you?"

Tacey nodded slowly. "He was afraid. He didn't mean to break the angel."

"Sweetie, I know. I'm not mad." Maggie brushed a strand of hair back from the child's forehead. "Just tell us where he went."

Tacey sniffled, then rubbed tears away with the back of her hand. "He thought you'd be mad. He took his toboggan. He said he was going to find Mommy, and he wouldn't come back until he did."

The words hit her like a blow. Maggie pressed her hand

to her chest, as if that might ease the pain. Joey, out in the snow somewhere, searching for his mother.

She scrambled to her feet and ran to the phone.

"What are you doing?"

Grant was up, too, striding across the room to her.

"Calling Aunt Elly to stay with the kids." She punched in the numbers. "I have to go look for him."

"You can't do that alone."

"No." Fresh pain swept her heart. This was one thing she couldn't do alone. "I'll get help."

"I'm going, too." His tone was uncompromising.

"Fine." She wouldn't take the time to argue. She hung up. "Aunt Elly doesn't answer, so she must be on her way. If you want to help, stay here until she comes. Then put on your warmest clothes and come to the church. We'll organize the search from there."

She didn't give him time to answer, just grabbed her cell phone and heavy boots and ran for the door.

Help. She had to have help. The thoughts kept time to her running feet. *Please, Lord. Please.*

Grant was right. This was one thing she couldn't do alone.

He'd never have believed a bunch of volunteers could organize so fast. Grant stood at the back of the sanctuary, watching as the fire chief assigned duties. Judging by his clothing, the man was a barber when he wasn't setting up a rescue, but he seemed cool and in control.

They weren't just fast, they were efficient. They might be volunteers, but they operated as smoothly as any professional unit he'd ever seen.

The sanctuary was crowded with people, summoned by the church bell that had stopped pealing only moments ago. But it didn't matter how full the room was. His gaze was pulled to Maggie, only Maggie.

She stood at the front, close by the communion table on which they'd spread a large-scale map of the township. Her face was tense, her body rigid. She was hurting, but she wouldn't give in to it. Not Maggie. She'd never give in.

The chief went rapidly through the grid, assigning areas. Those with snowmobiles would search the woods. Others would take the streets and roads.

Grant thought of the miles of forests on the mountains, and his fists clenched. If the boy had gone that way, what chance did they actually have of finding him, especially in this snowstorm?

Pastor Jim stepped forward. By the look of his clothes, he intended to be one of the rescue party, but he clearly had something to say in his pastoral role first. He raised his hands, and the sanctuary grew quiet.

"Friends, let's pause for a word of prayer."

Heads bowed throughout the room.

"Eternal Father, we know that You see everything. You know where Joey Bascom is right now. We ask that You be with him, keeping him safe, and with us, leading us to him. Amen."

Amens chorused through the sanctuary, and people moved quickly toward the doors, lining up in twos and threes. As they went out, several older women bustled in, carrying tureens and coffee urns. Clearly everyone in Button Gap had a role when things went wrong.

Grant fell into step with Maggie as she hurried toward the door. She shot him a quick, questioning look.

"You have an idea which way he's headed, don't you?"

She shrugged, trotting down the steps toward her truck. He kept pace with her.

"Don't you?" he repeated.

"I might."

"I'm going with you."

"You should stay here. You might be needed." Her voice shook a little on that. If Joey was hurt, she meant.

"I can be reached on the cell phone."

"I don't want—"

He caught her arm, turning her to face him, frustration and fear warring inside him. "Face facts, Maggie. I know you want to do everything by yourself, but you can't. If you do find him, you'll need someone along to help. Like it or not, I'm going with you."

He could see emotion surging beneath the surface, but she set her mouth and nodded. She jerked a nod toward the truck, and he scrambled in.

She whipped down the street, then turned onto the narrow back road they'd taken the day they'd gone to help the injured man back in the woods. The windshield wipers fought against the thick, wet snow—huge flakes that piled up swiftly and would hamper the search.

"Why do you think he came this way?" If he didn't pump her, he didn't think she'd say a word.

"We were out by my family's house one day in the fall. I pointed out the logging trail that went over the mountain." Her face lost a little more color, if possible. "He'd know we'd look along the main road. I can't be sure, but it's worth a try."

Poor Maggie. She had something else to blame herself for. "You couldn't imagine these circumstances. It's not your fault."

"It's my responsibility."

The truck skidded as she took a bend too fast, and she fought the wheel. He grabbed it, helping her regain control.

"Take it easy. We can't help him if we smash ourselves up."

If she heard, she didn't acknowledge his words. She seemed to force the truck on by sheer willpower, barreling through the thickly piled snow. He braced his hand against the dash, sure they'd end up smashed against a tree, but she kept it going somehow.

If they didn't find Joey safe... He couldn't begin to see all the ramifications of that. Plenty of lives would be smashed then, that he knew.

The truck barreled along, its cab a warm cocoon protecting them from the storm. They reached the turnoff to the house where she'd once lived. The dilapidated mailbox still hung from its post, but the lane was drifted shut.

She hesitated, gunning the motor, and he grabbed her hand.

"Don't, Maggie. We'll need the truck usable if we find him. We'll have to walk in."

She held out against him for a moment, and then she nodded. "You're right."

She turned off the motor and slid out of the cab. He followed suit, slogging around the truck.

Maggie stared at the narrow lane. "What if I'm wrong? He may not be anywhere near here."

He spotted faint traces in the snow. "Look. The toboggan could have made those marks."

She looked doubtful. "It could have been an animal." She pulled out her cell phone, then shoved it back in her pocket. "We'd better find out for sure before we call people off any other area."

Nodding, he pulled his collar up and struck into the lane. He sank to above his knees at the first step. "It'll be slow going."

"I know." She was right behind him, her face set and determined.

He struggled on a few more arduous steps, apprehension growing. Maybe those had been animal tracks.

"How could he possibly have gotten through this? It's so deep, I can hardly make it."

"He could." Her voice was thick, as if with tears. "He's a strong little kid, and he had a head start on us. It wouldn't have been as deep an hour ago." She choked back a sob. "I have to believe that. I have to."

He reached out to grab her hand, pulling her through the deep drift. "I know." He sought for anything that would comfort her. "He's smart, too."

Maggie nodded, but her eyes were bleak, almost dead.

She won't survive if we lose this child. Who was he talking to? The God he wasn't sure he believed in anymore? *You have to help.*

God hadn't saved Jason. What made him think He'd save Joey?

She had to pull herself together. She couldn't give in to her fear.

Help us, Father. Help Joey. Your children need you so desperately today.

Grant's hand gripped hers, pulling her along through the deepest of drifts. Maybe that was part of God's answer. She hadn't wanted Grant with her today. She would have come alone if she could have.

And that would have been wrong. She couldn't do this alone.

Thank You. I wish Grant and I could at least be friends, but even if we can't, thank You for sending him with me today.

"Wait." Breathless, she caught Grant's hand with both of hers. "There's the logging road." She nodded toward the cleft in the trees, barely perceptible in the thick snow.

He frowned. "Are you sure? It doesn't look like much."

"I'm sure." A shiver went through her, not entirely from the cold. She knew every inch of this terrain. "I don't see how he could have gone that way, not without leaving a trace."

Grant pointed down the lane toward the house. "There. Doesn't that look like the marks the toboggan would leave?"

She didn't want to go down that way. She had to. "It could be. Joey knows where the house is—what's left of it, anyway. He might have gone there for shelter."

Grant's fingers tightened on hers. She felt the reassurance of his grasp through her thick gloves, warming her.

He knew how she left about the place. How could he not? Pointless, now, to try and disguise her fears or anything else from him.

"They that wait upon the Lord shall renew their strength." The promise from Isaiah echoed in her mind, and a fresh spurt of energy propelled her forward.

"Let's go."

Again Grant forged ahead, pushing his legs through the deepening snow. If not for the track he made breaking the snow, she might not have made it.

They struggled around the bend, and the house loomed ahead of them. Or maybe *loomed* wasn't the right word for something that was tumbling down into itself as if from the sheer weight of unhappiness it had seen.

"Joey!" She coughed a little on the intake of cold air. "Joey, are you here? Answer me!"

The snow seemed to muffle her call, and nothing else broke the silence.

"Joey Bascom!" Grant added his voice to hers. "Where are you?"

He looked at her, eyes questioning. "It doesn't look disturbed, and it definitely doesn't look safe. Maybe we're on the wrong track."

"No." Improbable as it was, a sense of certainty swept through her. "He's here. I know he's here."

"Maggie—"

She pushed forward, closer to the place she'd never wanted to see again. "We have to check. We can't come this far and just walk away."

He followed her, and she felt his doubts. Did he think she was clinging to straws?

He brushed past her, leaning forward to peer into a broken window. "The whole roof is down, Maggie. There's not much shelter."

"He's here." She scrambled forward to grab at what had been exposed by Grant's movement. "Look." She pulled the toboggan free of the snow.

In a moment Grant had pushed away the rotted door and climbed into the house. He reached back a hand for her.

"Here, but where? Joey!"

He wasn't saying the thing he feared. That Joey didn't answer because he couldn't. That they were too late.

"The root cellar." She shoved past him, heading for the old summer kitchen. "He could shelter there." She had, more times than she cared to remember.

She yanked at the door, then stumbled down the three steps, jerking the flashlight from her pocket. "Joey?"

"There." Grant jumped down the steps, rushed to the side wall where a whole section of shelves had fallen. Beneath the shelves—

"Joey!" She couldn't breathe as she stumbled across to him. He was so still, so white. *Father*—

Grant dropped to his knees, shoving the wooden shelves out of his way.

She dropped next to him, and she had to fight to hold the light steady on Joey's face. "Is he—"

Grant's hands moved swiftly and surely over the child's body. Then he looked up, and his smile blazed. "He's breathing."

"Thank God." Her tears spilled over, but she smiled back at him, feeling an instant of perfect harmony, perfect gratitude. "Thank God."

Chapter Thirteen

Grant turned his attention firmly to the boy. That was the thing to do—think of him as any anonymous patient who'd been brought into the emergency room. Don't think of the little boy whose eyes had filled with wonder at the sight of that red toboggan. That way lay weakness, and he couldn't afford to be weak.

He cleared the debris carefully away from the child's shoulder and head. The arm lay at a bad angle.

"Looks like a dislocated elbow." He ran his hands along the boy's arms. "I don't think there's a break, but I'd like to see an X-ray."

Maggie was checking pulse and respiration. "Vitals look good. If he's been unconscious—"

She didn't finish that sentence, probably because at that moment Joey's eyelids flickered and opened.

"Maggie," he whispered. "Doc." He managed a smile. "I was asleep. I dreamed you came."

"Looks like your dream came true." Maggie touched his

cheek gently. She sounded perfectly calm, as if they hadn't been hovering on the razor edge of disaster a few moments earlier.

"You'd better call this in." His voice was sharper than he intended it to be. "We'll need some help getting him out of here."

She sent him a questioning look, then nodded and moved toward the steps as she pulled out the cell phone. As he checked the child over carefully, he listened to the joy in her voice.

Maggie was happy. Resentment knifed its way into his thoughts. Had she forgotten so quickly why they were in this mess? If Jason—

He stopped, appalled at himself. This wasn't Jason. He looked at the boy, and for a moment the face in front of him wavered. It almost looked like his brother's face from so long ago.

No. What had made him think such a crazy thing? This was Joey.

Maggie came back, slipping the phone into her pocket. "They'll be here in a few minutes." She smiled at Joey. "We'll have you snug and warm in no time."

He touched the child's forehead. "I can't figure out why he's not colder than he is. He's been exposed to the weather for hours."

Joey wiggled a little. "It's not so cold in here. I remembered what Maggie said about the root cellar."

He glanced at her, lifting his eyebrows. "Root cellar?"

"We always kept vegetables in the root cellar in the winter. It's underground, so it stays at an even temperature. Joey was pretty smart to remember that."

"You were pretty smart to realize he might be here." He sat back on his heels, trying for a normal tone of voice. He wouldn't think about that moment when he'd confused Joey with his brother. Nor about his anger with her for getting them into this mess to begin with. He'd stay coolly professional.

Something changed in her face, just for a second. "I used to hide here."

Joey might think she meant as a game. He knew better. Maggie was talking about hiding from her father.

The images battered at him—Maggie cowering in a dirty corner. Maggie shivering, waiting for the door to burst open. He tried futilely to push the thoughts away. He seemed to have no emotional barricades left. He hated that.

The roar of a snowmobile motor broke the silence. Someone shouted from outside, and Maggie hurried up the steps.

"Here," she called. "We're here."

In moments the tiny cellar was filled to overflowing with people, pushing out all the ugly images.

"We brought the rescue truck, Doc." The barber/fire chief carried a litter down the steps. "We can put the litter on one of the snowmobiles to get him out to it."

He started to say they'd better carry the litter, and then remembered their struggle through the knee-deep snow to get here. The man was right. That would be safer.

"Good." He reached for the kit, but one of the volunteers already had a neck collar ready to put in his hand. "We'll immobilize his neck and arm first."

It was reassuring to have familiar equipment at hand, comforting to go through the familiar movements. He could block out those moments when he'd seen his brother's face on Joey. When he'd seen a small Maggie cowering in the corner, weak and afraid.

In minutes they were ready to transport. Willing hands seized the litter and bore it gently to the waiting snowmobile. The motor purred. The driver moved off slowly and carefully with his precious cargo, several volunteers walking on either side.

He started to follow, but someone hustled him onto another waiting snowmobile. How had they all gotten here so quickly? The once-deserted area around the derelict house teemed with people, all trying to do something to help.

His snowmobile driver roared through the woods, apparently feeling no need to go slowly with him. He dismounted at the emergency truck and pulled open the rear door. Before he could do more than glance inside, another snowmobile roared to a stop next to him. Maggie got off, lifting her hand in thanks as the driver swung around.

"I want Joey taken straight to the nearest hospital," he said. "We'll ride with him."

Maggie shoved wet bangs out of her face. "That's not a good idea."

His jaw tightened until it felt as if it would break. As usual, Maggie seemed to think she knew better than he did.

"This is no time to worry about someone finding out about the Bascoms."

She blinked. "That never entered my mind." She lifted her hands. "Look around. The snow hasn't let up—if anything, it's worse. The chopper won't fly in this, and the roads are bound to be bad. Jostling him along forty miles of slippery roads isn't going to help a dislocated elbow."

"He needs more sophisticated care than we can provide."

Was that the reason? What was wrong with him, that he'd let his professional judgment be hampered by this place and these people?

Maggie looked at him gravely, as if she knew what was going on beneath the surface.

She couldn't know. No one could.

The snowmobile with the litter pulled up. All he could see was Joey's small face as they lifted him into the van. Joey's face. Not Jason. Joey.

Maggie stepped closer. "Grant." She lowered her voice. "He really is better off at the clinic."

He didn't want this. He didn't have a choice. He gave a curt nod and climbed into the back of the van.

Maggie paused outside the clinic door a few hours later, taking a breath, lifting an almost wordless prayer. Joey had been treated with Grant's usual skill, and he was safely tucked up in bed with Aunt Elly in attendance and half the village running in and out bringing food or offering to watch the other children. Crisis over, she should be able to relax.

But she couldn't. Aside from every other worry, something was wrong with Grant. She'd felt his tension, so strong it vibrated through the room the entire time he'd taken care of Joey. Felt it, but not understood it.

Help me, Lord. I don't know what's going on within Grant. Show me how to help him.

She opened the door and went inside.

Grant stood at the desk, his head bent, hands braced on its surface. He'd changed into dry slacks and a gray sweater, and he should have looked warm, dry and relieved. He didn't.

Please, Lord.

"Joey's tucked into bed and nearly asleep. One more story from Aunt Elly should do it."

Grant turned his head to look at her, and the inimical expression in his eyes nearly stopped her heart.

"Why are you looking like that?" The question came out involuntarily. "He's all right. You should be happy."

"Happy?" His voice rose, and he took a step toward her. "I don't see much to be happy about in this situation."

"But he's all right," she repeated, not sure what else to say. Was he still worried that Joey needed more sophisticated care than they could provide? "You did everything they'd have done if we'd taken him to the hospital. He couldn't have received better care than you gave him."

"That's not the point. Don't you see that we can't be responsible for these children? Today should have made you face reality. Don't you realize that Jason could have died out there?"

For a moment she could only stare at him. "Joey. Not Jason." Then, as if a curtain had been pulled back, she knew. "Jason was your brother."

He looked gaunt suddenly, as if all the life and strength had been drawn out of him. "Joey. I meant Joey."

She'd asked God how to help him. Perhaps she was hearing the answer.

"Joey reminds you of your brother, doesn't he?"

"No." His mouth tightened. "They're totally different."

"Externally, maybe. But something about Joey still reminds you of him." She took a step, closing the gap between them, and put her hand on his arm. It felt like wood beneath her fingers. "Tell me, Grant. What happened to Jason?"

His face was so rigid it was a wonder he could move his lips. "He died. Childhood leukemia."

Her heart hurt for him. "I'm so sorry."

"That was a long time ago. It doesn't have anything to do with what's happening now."

"Maybe it shouldn't, but it does." A certainty that could only come from God pushed her on. "For some reason, you relate to Joey in the way you did to your brother. And you don't want to."

"No, I don't want to!" His reserve broke, so suddenly that the wave of emotion nearly knocked her off balance. "I can't.

I can't be a decent doctor if I let myself see Jason in every child I treat."

He tried to turn away, but she tightened her grasp, holding him. She couldn't let him retreat from this. Once he went back behind those protective barriers, he'd never come out again.

"You can't be a decent doctor if you're afraid to care."

"You sound like Dr. Rawlins. That was why he talked me into coming here. He thought I'd find some passion for my patients here." His hands clenched. "He thought Button Gap would make me open up. It's just shown me I was right all along."

"No." She wanted to shake him, as if that would make him see how painfully wrong he was. "You can't shut yourself off from people because you're afraid to lose them the way you lost your brother."

He whitened. She'd probably gone too far, but she couldn't stop now.

"You can't live that way, Grant." Her voice went soft, almost trembling with her need to reach him. "No one can."

His mouth curled in a mirthless smile. "Sure they can. My parents have been doing it for years."

"What do you mean?"

"My mother uses her social whirl, my father uses his business. They haven't felt a thing since the day we buried my brother."

She'd thought she already hurt as much as she could for him, but that revelation sliced into her heart. They hadn't felt a thing for him, the child they had left. "Who comforted you?" Not his parents, that was clear.

"I didn't need comforting. I don't need it now. I just need to—"

"What? Stop caring? Stop grieving? You can't shut other people out of your life."

He probably hadn't ever truly grieved for his loss. How could he, when his parents had blocked themselves off from caring? Her heart wept for him.

He shook her hand off, his face a mask of denied pain. "Leave it alone, Maggie. You're not exactly an advertisement for relying on other people yourself."

She felt as if he'd hit her. She caught her breath and fought to be honest, knowing only honesty could possibly reach him.

"Maybe so. I've been so determined not to be weak, like my mother was, that I couldn't accept help."

Why couldn't you be strong, Mama? Why couldn't you protect me? She struggled for control.

"Don't you see, Grant? That's something taking care of those kids made me face. I had to have help, and I got it. Button Gap didn't let me down—not when I was eleven, and not today."

"You belong here," he said stubbornly. "I don't. In a few more days, I won't have Button Gap. I'll be back in my real life."

"Back to helping people only when you can do it from a safe distance? Back to letting your white coat insulate you from caring?"

"That's my choice."

They'd come full circle. It *was* his choice.

"You're right." She clasped her hands to keep from reaching out to him. He didn't want her touch. "You can go straight back into that hard, cold shell of yours. It'll keep you safe from anything raw or painful. You can just go on blaming God."

A tiny muscle twitched in his jaw, the only sign a living human being existed behind the mask he wore. Maybe she'd probed the sorest spot of all.

"If God is there, He could have saved Jason." Implacable. He couldn't give an inch.

God alone knew the answer to that hard question. He knew, too, how much she'd struggled with it. Why did the innocent suffer? Maybe everyone had to deal with that one alone.

"God is there." Tears stung her eyes. "I don't know why your brother died, but I know God was there, holding him in His hands. I know God is ready to help you deal with it, if you'll let Him."

His face was closed and barred against her. "I don't want Him to. I don't need help. Not from Him. Not from you."

He grabbed his jacket and slammed his way out of the clinic. The door seemed to close on her heart.

She'd tried. She'd failed. Grant was lost to her for good. Worse, she was afraid he was lost to the only One who could help him.

By the time he stopped reacting and started thinking, Grant realized he'd walked to the edge of the village. He hadn't bothered to zip his jacket, and the cold air seemed to permeate his very bones.

He zipped the jacket, pulling the collar up. He should go back. The snow had stopped falling, finally, but dusk was drawing in. This was no time to be out on a cold, lonely lane in the middle of nowhere.

He didn't want to go back. Didn't want to see anyone, speak to anyone. He particularly didn't want to see Maggie.

Maggie.

He shoved his fists into his pockets and looked up at the dark mountainside. His anger flared again, white-hot. How dare she say those things? She should be grateful to him instead of attacking him.

Maggie wouldn't see it as an attack, of course. She thought

she was helping, as if taking a scalpel to his soul could possibly help him.

He'd spoken the truth, and she hadn't been able to take it. She couldn't accept the fact that he'd chosen to live his life cut off from God.

Maggie didn't understand. She didn't know what it was like, how he felt...

Didn't she?

Shame burned into him. Maggie was probably the only person who knew what he felt. She was certainly the only one he'd revealed anything to in years.

And Maggie couldn't be accused of having life easy. After what she'd gone through, how did she even manage to get up in the morning, let alone carve out a full, useful life for herself?

He knew the answer she'd give if he asked her the question. The one she called Father had brought her through it. She didn't see why the same didn't apply to him.

Because I can't forgive You.

The thought, coming from somewhere deep inside him, shocked him with its bone-deep honesty. Maybe he'd been kidding himself about a lot of things, but that, at least, was true. He hadn't forgiven God for taking Jason.

Those last days, with nurses taking over the house and running their lives—the images flooded in upon him. They hadn't let him see Jason. He'd curled miserably behind the drapes in the hall window seat, where he could watch the door to Jason's room, waiting for a chance to sneak in and see him.

The last day had been like this one—snow in the air, and the dusk drawing in early. Shadows had filled the hallway, as if they waited, too.

Save him. He'd gone beyond tears, beyond bargaining, beyond demanding. All his prayers had come down to those two words. *Save him.*

Now he glared up at the darkening sky, not sure whether he was the hurting boy or the grown man. *You took away the person who meant the most to me. What do You want from me now?*

There wasn't an answer now. Any more than there'd been an answer then.

Maybe it was better not to believe God existed. Then, at least, he'd have known there wasn't any hope.

The cold seeped through the soles of his boots, into his bones, into his soul. He turned, looking back toward Button Gap.

Lamps were on now, glowing warmly in windows. The strings of Christmas lights on the tree in front of the post office blinked red and green, and the stained-glass windows of the church gleamed like jewels against the white snow that blanketed the village.

Above, the mountains loomed dark and cold, but the first star made a pale point of light.

He exhaled, watching his breath form steam in the air. Still. Silent. Nothing moving, nothing speaking. Nothing touching him. He was as cold and isolated as the star.

Something floated toward him through the dusk. The notes of the piano, then the treble of children's voices.

"'Silent night, holy night, all is calm, all is bright...'"

It was Christmas Eve. The children were practicing for the pageant that would begin in another hour.

Maggie would be there, directing them and smiling as if nothing had happened. She probably expected him to walk in and take his place in the pew, pretending everything was normal.

He couldn't.

You don't have to stay. The thought formed without volition.

No one expects you to work out the week. You can pack and go. You never have to think of Button Gap and Maggie again.

Even now he couldn't convince himself that he'd dismiss Maggie from his thoughts so easily. But he could leave.

He started walking, his footsteps making little sound on the snow-packed lane. He'd pack and leave. He didn't have to go to his parents' house. He could hole up in a hotel somewhere until the holiday was safely over.

You can go straight back into that hard, cold shell of yours. He hadn't managed to get Maggie's voice out of his head yet. He'd have to try harder. *You can let your white coat insulate you from caring.*

Leave me alone. He didn't know if he was speaking to Maggie or to the God he wasn't sure he believed in. *Just leave me alone.*

Chapter Fourteen

"'Bless all the dear children in Thy tender care, and fit us for heaven to live with Thee there.'"

The final notes of the old carol died away, and the children looked at Maggie expectantly.

"Wonderful." She managed to smile. "That's perfect. Just you sing it that way in the performance, and everyone will absolutely love it."

People were already filtering into the pews, talking softly so as not to disturb the rehearsal. They didn't mind that they'd see and hear the same thing again in half an hour. This was part of Christmas for them.

"Okay." She clapped her hands. "You can go and get your costumes on now. Mind, no running. I don't want any broken angel wings."

Released, the children scrambled off the chancel steps, toward the helpers who had costumes spread out over the pews. For a second she could breathe. She could think.

Maybe it would be better not to have time to think. In

only a moment of quiet, the pain surged back out of hiding, ready to sink sharp teeth into her again.

"'And fit us for heaven, to live with Thee there.'"

Grant's brother had lived those words the children sang so cheerfully. Surely God's hands had been around him, safe and comforting, in those last minutes.

Grant had been the one left alone and uncomforted. A fresh spasm of pain gripped her, tinged with guilt. She'd been so judgmental of him when they'd first met.

Forgive me, Lord. You know how often I fall into that same sin. You must be tired of hearing me confess it.

She'd thought she knew who Grant was—wealthy, privileged, taking his easy life for granted and perfectly willing to use a month in Button Gap to get something he wanted.

She hadn't been willing, or able, to look beneath the surface for the pain that lived there. She, of all people, should know how often a calm exterior could hide a raging grief. She'd been there most of her life, and her own shield had been hard-won.

She hadn't bothered to look for what Grant was hiding until life, in the form of the Bascom family, had forced both of them into sharing things they'd otherwise never have told each other. Now she knew him all the way through.

She understood his pain. And he wouldn't let her do one thing to help him with it.

She squeezed her eyes closed, shutting out the kaleidoscope of children, costumes, Christmas tree, chattering adults.

Help him, Father. I can't. I wanted to, but he wouldn't let me. He's going away, and I can't do anything to make a difference.

Cold certainty gripped her. Grant would go away. He might be on his way already.

Please, Father. I've lost any chance I had.

She struggled to see her way through the days ahead. She'd

do what she had to do—try to help the Bascoms, try to keep the clinic running. She'd keep putting one foot in front of the other, and one day, unlikely as it seemed right now, she'd be happy again.

Be with him, Lord. Hold him in Your hands.

That felt like a benediction, but with it came some small measure of peace. She'd done everything she could. The rest was up to the Father.

Aunt Elly slipped an arm around her waist. "Are you okay, child?"

She took a shaky breath. She hadn't told Aunt Elly yet. She hadn't told anyone, but she'd have to. They wouldn't understand why Grant wasn't here for the pageant.

"I'm all right. But Grant—" Her throat closed.

Aunt Elly squeezed her. "He's fighting something, isn't he?"

She nodded. "I wanted to help. I'm afraid I just made things worse. He's probably packing to leave right now."

"Have you turned it over to God?"

Had she? Maggie searched for any reservation, any self-interest clouding her prayers for Grant.

"Yes," she said finally. "I have."

"That's all we can do, then." She pressed her cheek against Maggie's. "Have faith, Maggie. Maybe you planted the seed that will make a change in his life. We're not always called to see the harvest, you know. Just to be faithful in planting the seed."

Aunt Elly had certainly done that in her own life. Now it was up to Maggie to do the same.

"I know." Her smile felt more genuine. "Well, let's get those children dressed. What have you done with Joey?"

Aunt Elly pointed to the front pew. Joey, nestled in a pile of cushions, reclined like a sultan, his arm positioned carefully in its sling. He was a little pale, but he grinned when he saw her looking at him.

"You didn't think we'd be able to keep him away, did you? He says he's going to make sure the substitute king does it right."

She actually felt like laughing, something she'd thought it would take years to accomplish. "He'll probably scare the poor kid into making a mistake, more likely."

"It's going to be all right." Aunt Elly sounded sure of herself. "It always is."

"True enough." No matter what mistakes anyone made, the pageant still always announced its eternal truth to hearts willing to hear it. "I guess—"

She stopped, realizing that a hush had fallen over the sanctuary. The door swung to with a clatter.

She turned, looking toward the back of the sanctuary to see who had come in. Looked, identified and felt her heart freeze in response.

Mrs. Hadley, the county social worker, stood just inside the door. Gus Foster, looking harassed and reluctant but official in his deputy's uniform, stood beside her.

Mrs. Hadley didn't look harassed or reluctant. She looked triumphant.

The children—

From the corner of her eye, Maggie saw Evie Moore drop an angel gown over Tacey's head and sweep Robby behind her with a deft movement.

Brave, but futile. Maggie's mind scrambled for ways to get the children out, even as she recognized the impossibility of it all. Joey, immobilized in his nest of cushions, couldn't be hidden, and Mrs. Hadley's eagle eye had probably already identified the other two.

Help. She couldn't seem to manage anything else in the

way of a prayer, and Mrs. Hadley was advancing down the center aisle like a Sherman tank, flattening anything and anyone that dared to be in its path. *Help!*

"Margaret Davis." The woman rumbled to a stop dead center. "I thought it would be you."

"Mrs. Hadley." It was a sign of recognition between enemies, as if flags dipped before a battle. "Have you come for the pageant?"

The woman swelled. "I've come for the Bascom children, as you well know. You've been hiding them from me."

Not from social services, Maggie noted, even as her mind ran this way and that, searching for a way out. For Mrs. Hadley, this was personal. Was the woman still trying to assert her authority over the rebellious eleven-year-old Maggie had once been?

"I don't know what you mean."

Maggie felt Pastor Jim move up next to her. She sensed the rest of Button Gap arranging itself behind her. It was a good sensation.

Unfortunately, that support wouldn't be enough. Mrs. Hadley had brought the law with her. Gus didn't want to be here—that was clear from his hangdog expression. He had better things to do with his Christmas Eve. But he'd do his duty, like it or not.

Mrs. Hadley's eyes were small and mean behind her wire-rimmed glasses. She hadn't changed, it seemed to Maggie, in the past two decades. She'd gotten a little grayer, a little meaner, a little fatter.

Maggie had once looked at her bulk and seen a mountain of a woman, terrifying in her power. The power was still there, but she wouldn't allow herself to be terrified any longer.

Mrs. Hadley sent a commanding glance toward Gus. He shifted uncomfortably and cleared his throat.

"We're here to pick up the Bascom kids." There was an apology in the look he gave Maggie. "Seems Mrs. Hadley's office has some information that Nella Bascom ran off and left those kids."

"Ran off?" Maggie raised her eyebrows, trying for a composure she didn't feel. "Just because Nella went on a trip doesn't mean she deserted her children."

"Certainly not." Pastor Jim waded in. "Nella left her children in Maggie's care when she had to go away for a while. There's nothing wrong with that."

"That's what I've been saying." Gus looked relieved at the pastor's intervention, undoubtedly seeing it as a way out of a situation he disliked. "Nothing wrong with that."

"Nothing wrong?" Mrs. Hadley gave him a contemptuous look. "You'd take anything these people said as gospel and use it as an excuse not to do your duty."

Gus stiffened. "I don't need nobody telling me how to do my duty. If the woman deserted her kids, I'll help you take them in. But seems like we've got a dispute about that."

"Nella asked me to take care of her children while she was away. I said yes." Maggie hoped she sounded as if that would be an end to it.

"If that's the case, where is she?" Mrs. Hadley fired the question like a dart. "If you're taking care of her children for her, you must know where she is."

"She had to go back to West Virginia." She chose her words carefully. "She has family there."

"That's right," Aunt Elly chipped in. "We all know Nella's family's from West Virginia."

Mrs. Hadley dipped into her bag and pulled out a cell phone. She held it out to Maggie with a malicious gleam in her eyes. "Then you know how to reach her. Call her, now.

If she tells me what you're saying is true, I'll leave it alone. For the moment."

There was the challenge. Mrs. Hadley would only make it if she felt sure Maggie couldn't do just that.

And she couldn't. *Oh, Nella. Why didn't you trust me enough to tell me where you are?*

The cell phone waved in the air between them. Mrs. Hadley's air of triumph grew. Her tongue snaked out to moisten her lips, as if she tasted victory.

"Take it." Aunt Elly's voice was soft in her ear. "Call Grant. We need him."

Just the sound of his name was an arrow in her heart. *We don't,* she wanted to say. *We don't need him. He walked away from us. He's leaving.*

Is that really the reason? The question dropped quietly into her mind. Is that the reason, or is it because you don't want to admit you need him?

Her instant response told her the truth. Grant didn't need her. She didn't want to need him. She couldn't rely on him.

But she had to.

Grant slammed the back of the SUV on all the belongings he'd brought with him to Button Gap. He was ready to go. There was nothing to keep him here any longer.

He glanced toward the church. It must be time for the pageant to start. Maybe it was already under way. All of Button Gap would be gathered there. He was the only holdout.

Well, he wasn't part of Button Gap. He never had been.

His cell phone rang, a shrill, imperative summons. For an instant he was tempted to ignore it. He couldn't.

He snapped the phone open. "Hardesty."

"Mrs. Hadley is here." Maggie's voice was a whisper—a

frightened whisper. "Come to the church. Please. We need you." A slight hesitation. "I need you."

"Maggie?"

The connection was broken.

He stared at the phone, then turned to stare at the church. Mrs. Hadley was there. Maggie needed him.

He could slide behind the wheel and drive away. He didn't have to be involved in this. The roof was falling in on Maggie's scheme, and all he had to do was drive away.

He couldn't, any more than he'd been able to ignore the call. He couldn't shut Button Gap out of his life, like it or not. Not yet.

He jogged across the street toward the church. Maggie had called him. Maggie had asked for his help.

That was the strangest thing. Maggie—determined, fiercely independent Maggie—wanted his help. She'd actually put away her pride and asked for help.

Could he give it? He paused at the foot of the church steps, gripping the railing.

He'd told himself all along that calling social services would be best for those children. He'd let himself be manipulated into the conspiracy to hide them, knowing all along that he shouldn't.

Now it had been taken out of his hands—out of all their hands. Mrs. Hadley was there. Presumably she knew about the Bascom kids. What should he do, even if he could?

Isn't this for the best? With a sense of shock, he realized he was speaking to the God he'd been trying so hard to ignore. *Isn't turning those kids over the right thing? They're not my responsibility.*

Why not? The voice seemed to whisper in his heart. *Why aren't they your responsibility?*

Because when I looked at Joey, hurt and helpless, all I could see was my brother. I can't take responsibility for them, don't You see that? What do You want from me?

All of you. The answer rang through him. *All of you. Not just your skill as a doctor. All of you.*

He bent over, his breath coming as if he'd been running. The cold air seared his lungs. He couldn't. He couldn't give in, couldn't trust. He'd trusted God with Jason, and look what had happened.

Jason is safe in God's hands. That was what Maggie's message had been, and the words resounded, refusing to leave him alone.

If that was true, how could he go on using his brother as a reason not to take responsibility for another child?

He straightened slowly, looking at the church door, feeling its pull. Quickly, without letting himself think of possible consequences, he ran up the steps, pulled the door open and ran inside.

Chapter Fifteen

Grant stepped inside the sanctuary and paused, assessing the situation. The pews of the small church were filled with people. All of Button Gap had come to spend Christmas Eve watching the children's pageant.

Instead, they were seeing a pageant of a different sort.

Maggie stood at the front of the sanctuary, the deep red of her sweater making the pallor of her face more pronounced. Pastor Jim, next to her, had distress written across his countenance.

The woman opposite them looked ready to take on all comers, hands planted on her hips, brows drawn down, eyes glinting behind her glasses. Next to her, the deputy sheriff he'd met before stood representing the law, no matter how reluctantly. The battle lines were drawn.

For a moment it seemed to Grant an epic battle between good and evil. He shook off that fancy and started down the aisle at a deliberate pace. No one here was evil. They were just people trying to do what they thought was right. Maybe that was even more frightening.

Take it slow and easy, he told himself, aware that most of the people in the sanctuary were watching him now, as if a new fighter had entered the arena. Knowing Maggie's penchant for charging into situations, this one had probably already escalated too fast, too far.

The best thing he could do was calm the rhetoric and get some sort of delaying movement. Maggie had turned this woman into a monster in her mind, but surely any social worker worth her salt couldn't really want to take the children away on Christmas Eve.

Maggie, confronting the woman she considered her enemy, looked as strong and determined as a crusader ready to die for her cause. Then she glanced toward him, and he saw the pleading in her eyes.

He faltered, almost losing his place in the open pain of that look. Maggie needed him.

Mrs. Hadley, apparently alerted to his presence by the shifting of attention in her audience, swung ponderously to face him, too.

"Grant." Maggie's voice was strained, held calm, he was sure, by sheer effort. "This is Mrs. Hadley."

Then, apparently realizing she should have done it the other way around, she blinked. "This is Dr. Grant Hardesty, the physician who's working at the clinic this month."

He nodded, sizing the woman up. Solid, entrenched, sure of herself—she reminded him of a parade of bureaucrats he'd dealt with in his professional life. He didn't detect any of the fierce passion for the underdog he'd seen in other children's advocates.

All of that passion came from Maggie. Mrs. Hadley stood

secure in her authority and her rules and regulations. She wouldn't back down easily.

"I don't know why you wanted to call him." Mrs. Hadley dismissed him with a glance. "The only thing that matters is that you don't know how to reach those children's mother. That gives me every right to put them in foster care." She swung on the deputy. "Do your duty, for once in your life."

"Just a moment." Grant's words, quietly spoken, had enough steel to bring a quick appraising look from the deputy. "I'd like to know what's going on here."

"What interest is it of yours?" Mrs. Hadley snapped.

The question, rude as it was, went right to the heart of the situation. If he admitted his involvement, that would spell even more trouble for the clinic, probably dooming his chance at the partnership. To his astonishment, that didn't mean as much as it had just a day ago.

All of you. The words echoed in his mind. *I want all of you.*

He'd been so sure that his future was his own to determine. Admitting that it wasn't brought an amazing sense of freedom, and with that feeling came the knowledge of how to play this situation.

He swung on Maggie. "Well, Ms. Davis, what's going on? Perhaps you'll be good enough to explain."

Pain flashed in her eyes at his curt tone. Then she seemed to recognize the incongruity of his question. Her eyes widened. Her lips twitched, as if she held back an unguarded remark. Then she turned away, her hair swinging down to hide her face.

"I don't know what Mrs. Hadley is doing here." She managed to produce a sulky tone that was a perfect counterpoint to his arrogant doctor routine.

He should have known she'd instantly grasp what he

wanted. After all, wasn't that how they'd worked together through every crisis of the past month?

"Try to explain," he said condescendingly.

He sent a covert glance toward the social worker. Her faint smile suggested that she liked hearing him put Maggie down. He had to control an anger that was surely irrational, since that was just the reaction he wanted.

"She seems to think Nella Bascom has deserted her children. We've tried to explain that we're just taking care of them while she's away, but Mrs. Hadley won't listen."

He paused for a beat, then turned toward the woman, raising his eyebrows. "I think that's perfectly clear. What seems to be the problem?"

Mrs. Hadley's face tightened until she looked like an angry bulldog. "It's a nest of lies, that's what's wrong. Those children belong under my supervision."

"I can't imagine why you feel that's necessary. They've been under the care of a physician and a nurse, not to mention the minister and half the town." He paused, letting that sink in. "Why would we need you?"

There was an approving stir in the congregation. Someone said a resounding Amen.

Mrs. Hadley's face flushed. "No one here knows where Nella Bascom is. You can't deny that. I gave Maggie a chance to call her, and she couldn't do it."

"Naturally not." Please, let this be true. "How can anyone reach her when Nella is en route to Button Gap for Christmas?"

"You expect me to believe that?"

He shrugged. "It's immaterial to me what you believe."

An approving flicker in Gus's face alerted him. The deputy, he'd guess, might weigh in on their side if he could give him a reason.

"The fact is, it's Christmas Eve," he continued. "Even if you had a reason for suspecting someone was breaking the law, I can't imagine any good social worker would try to snatch children away from a safe situation on Christmas Eve."

"I knew I'd find them in church on Christmas Eve if they were here." Her arrogance was tinged, for the first time, with defensiveness.

He raised his eyebrows. "Really." Two syllables to express doubt. "That hardly seems a reason to me for such drastic action."

"That's what I've been saying right along," Gus said. "We ought to let this go till after Christmas."

The woman's flush deepened alarmingly. "I didn't ask for your opinion."

Gus hesitated, probably weighing his desire to go home to his family against the Hadley woman's political clout. He needed something to push him over the edge.

Grant pulled out his cell phone. "Something was mentioned about calling Nella Bascom," he said pleasantly. "I'm afraid I can't do that, but my speed dial does connect with the home phone of John Gilbert, senior partner in Gilbert, Gilbert and Hayes. He handles the legal affairs of the Hardesty Foundation. I'm sure he wouldn't mind disturbing—" He paused, turning to Gus. "By the way, who's the county judge?"

Gus grinned. "That would be Layton Warren."

"I'm sure my attorney wouldn't mind calling Judge Warren on Christmas Eve, if necessary, to obtain an injunction preventing you from removing the children pending a hearing." He raised the phone. "Shall I make the call?"

The sanctuary was hushed. It felt as if no one so much as took a breath. He sensed, quite suddenly, the wave of prayer flooding the room from all those souls sending up the same petition at one time.

Mrs. Hadley was as pale now as she'd been ruddy before. Her mouth moved twice. Then she spoke.

"That won't be necessary," she said in a strangled tone.

"No, indeed," Gus said promptly, taking her arm in a firm grip.

Grant could breathe, but he couldn't relax yet. "I'm glad we're in agreement. I'm sure none of us wants further unpleasantness." Grant dropped the phone back into his pocket.

"Guess we've held up the Christmas pageant long enough." Gus nudged the woman toward the door.

For a moment Grant thought she'd stage a comeback. Then she seemed to sag into herself. She allowed the deputy to propel her to the door.

Gus paused, touching the brim of his hat. "Merry Christmas, folks."

Grant caught the sound of Maggie's sigh of relief, so soft no one else could have heard it. He wanted to turn to her, sharing the moment.

But even if they hadn't stood in full view of the entire village, that probably wasn't a good idea. His own emotions ran too high, and he could only imagine what she might be feeling.

They'd saved the Bascom kids for the moment, but nothing was resolved between them. That was the bottom line.

He'd better be perfectly sure he knew what he wanted before he said one more word to her.

There'd been a moment when she might have said something to Grant—tried to express her feelings. Then the organ started to play, the children filed into their places and the opportunity had passed. Maggie, kneeling next to the front pew, motioned the shepherds to close their eyes in feigned sleep before the angels startled them awake.

God, breaking into ordinary lives and making them different. Making them new.

Was that what was happening to Grant? She couldn't think of anything else to account for the extraordinary change in his attitude.

Grant, the person who'd pushed all along to turn the children over to social services, had instead walked into the sanctuary and taken on the system he'd claimed to rely upon.

Walked in? Maybe that wasn't quite the right explanation for Grant's appearance.

The angels popped out from behind the chancel rail, waking the shepherds. Mary Jo Carter's blue jeans peeked from the hem of her white gown, adding an interesting contrast to her angel costume. Someone should have caught that before the performance started. Her, probably. But she'd been a bit preoccupied, hadn't she?

She'd called Grant. In that moment of crisis, when she'd faced something she couldn't handle on her own, she'd called on him for help.

Maybe that wasn't as surprising as she thought. Maybe she'd been moving in that direction throughout the past month, as their lives had become more and more entwined.

He'd come—that was the significant thing. He'd answered her cry for help, and he'd saved them.

She had no illusions about that. If Grant hadn't appeared just when he did, the Bascom kids would be on their way to spending Christmas Eve in foster care. No one else would have succeeded in stopping Mrs. Hadley. He'd thrown his power and influence into the mix, and that had swung the balance to their side.

What was it going to cost him?

The organist hit the opening chords of "The First Noel," and the congregation rose to join the children in the carol. Under cover of the movement, she glanced back to the center aisle.

Halfway back, Grant shared a hymnal with Aunt Elly. He could have left. He could have walked right out the door behind Gus and Mrs. Hadley, but he hadn't. She wasn't sure what that meant.

He'd been willing to risk the partnership he wanted for the sake of the children. He could still lose, and so could they. If Nella didn't come back, Mrs. Hadley would undoubtedly be seeing the judge the day after Christmas. The resulting clash might end with the clinic closed and Grant's partnership destroyed.

Why had he taken that chance?

Not because of me, Lord. I know that. Have You found a way into his heart?

The shepherds, sneakers showing beneath their robes, had found their way into the stable to kneel before the manger. The sheep, provided by Dawson Carter from his flock, gazed at them benignly. Her throat tightened.

These people—her people—probably understood as much as anyone about this familiar scene. They lived close to the land, too. They knew what it was to stand in a barn on a cold winter's night and feel the warm breath of the animals, patient in their stalls.

The kings, surprisingly stately in their makeshift finery, moved toward the manger. Their presence pricked her.

God had not kept His revelation only for the poor and humble. The rich and powerful had been invited to that stable, too.

She glanced at Joey, half expecting tears, but he watched

the kings with a critical eye, apparently ready to pounce on any mistake.

The pageant moved to its timeless conclusion, and the organ sounded the final carol. As always, it was "Away in a Manger." The children's voices piped in the first chorus, and her tears spilled over. She let them fall, unashamed.

As the congregation joined in the second verse, she looked again toward Grant. He sang with the rest, and his eyes shone with tears.

Has he resolved his quarrel with You, Father? Has he found his way through his grief?

If he had, then Grant was whole again. She couldn't ask for more than that.

She couldn't, no matter how much she wanted to. She'd never really believed there could be anything serious between them, but she'd gone and fallen in love with him anyway.

Well, she'd deal with it. He'd go back to Baltimore, and she'd deal with that, too. Knowing him, loving him, had helped her move past some of her private demons. She'd be a better Christian for having loved him.

Her gaze drifted over the faces of her friends—no, her family. She loved them. They loved her. With all their faults, they'd never let her down. They never would.

Someone moved, drawing her attention to the very rear of the sanctuary. Her breath caught in her throat.

Nella. Nella had come home for Christmas.

Chapter Sixteen

Maggie's heart was so full she couldn't speak a word. She could only watch as others realized Nella was there. A wave of joy seemed to pulse through the sanctuary, uniting them.

Willing hands pushed Nella toward the front, with people patting her, hugging her.

Maggie grabbed Tacey, who was nearest to her. "Look." She pointed. "Look who's here."

Nella stepped clear of the crowd. Tacey and Robby were a blur of movement as they rushed into her arms.

Maggie started toward Joey, but Grant reached him first. He scooped the boy up and carried him to his mother.

Following them, Maggie saw the expression on Grant's face as he put Joey into Nella's arms. The guarded look had vanished from his eyes. Anyone who looked could see the loving person Grant was inside, and he didn't seem to care.

Thank You, Father. Somehow the thought that he would leave didn't hurt quite as much, because she could see beyond her own personal pain. *You used us to reach him. No matter what he does or where he goes, he'll be a better person and a better doctor for having been here.*

"Maggie." Nella reached out to embrace her, squishing Tacey between them in a joyful hug. "Thank you. Thank you."

She looked tired and thin, but her hazel eyes shone with a peace that transcended the external. Nella looked like a person who'd been through fire and come out with a new sense of who she was.

"We're glad you're home." Maggie gestured toward Grant. "This is Dr. Hardesty."

"I already told her," Joey said importantly. "I told her how Dr. Grant took care of me."

"I'd heard about the doctor. My aunt told me you folks came all the way to West Virginia looking for me."

Maggie shook her head, remembering the elderly woman who'd shut the door in her face. "She did a good job of telling us she'd never heard of you."

"I was worried." A flush rose in Nella's pale cheeks. "Guess about now I'm feeling pretty ashamed of how I acted. I don't know why you went on trusting me."

"Because we knew you'd do the right thing." Maggie squeezed her.

Nella wiped away a tear. "I figured I wasn't a very strong person. But knowing you—" Her glance seemed to gather in the whole village, pressing around her. "Knowing all of you had faith in me, well, I guess that convinced me I should have faith in myself."

"You have friends here," Pastor Jim said. "We won't let you down."

"Probably Mrs. Hadley would still say I can't make it, if I have to depend on other people."

"Mrs. Hadley isn't human enough to understand." Maggie realized she could think of the woman now without her childhood fear. "We all need help sometimes." Did Grant understand what she was saying? "Sometimes we just have to learn how to ask for it."

Nella's smile trembled on the verge of tears. "I won't be the person I was in my marriage. Not ever again."

For an instant Maggie seemed to see her mother's face, and the last faint bitterness slipped from her heart.

She did the best she could, Father. I see that now. Thank You that Nella found herself before it was too late for her and the children.

"Thank you, all of you." Nella's whisper seemed to penetrate the farthest reaches of the sanctuary. "God bless you."

Pastor Jim cleared his throat. "That sounds like a benediction to me. God bless us all. And now—" his smile broke through "—I happen to know that a birthday cake for Jesus is waiting downstairs. Let's celebrate."

Maggie was caught in a flood of goodwill as people moved toward the stairs. As she reached the last pew, Grant caught her arm.

"Come outside with me for a minute, Maggie." His eyes were very serious. "I have something to say to you."

Goodbye.

The word pierced her heart. Grant's time in Button Gap had come to an end. He wanted to say goodbye.

She wanted to run downstairs, hide in the crowd and pretend this wasn't happening. But she wouldn't be a coward about it.

She nodded, and they stepped together out into the starlit, silent night.

How did he say what he needed to say to Maggie? His heart was so full he felt as if he'd choke when he tried to speak.

They walked down the few steps to the sidewalk. Button

Gap lay still around them, its lights flickering bravely against the blackness of the mountains looming above.

Maggie's head was tipped back, and he realized she looked, not at the mountains, but at the sky. It was a paler gray, spread with the crystal light of countless stars. The village's Christmas lights were a simple imitation of the real thing.

"Do you ever wonder what it was really like?" Maggie's murmur barely touched the silence.

"I know," he said as softly. "It was like this. Dark, quiet, seeming lonely, but filled with good-hearted people who are open to miracles."

"You see that now?" She made it a question.

He turned, so that they stood facing each other. He wanted to take her hands, but wasn't sure he should. Not yet.

"Yes." He took a breath, trying to find the words. "You know what I was doing before I came here. I was trying to deny God's existence, as if that would make my grief easier to control."

"That doesn't work." Her voice was gentle. "I know. I tried. You can't box up pain and pretend it's not there."

"I might never have faced that if I hadn't come here." He looked inward, probing for the truth. "Jason knew God was with him every step of the way." He had to smile in spite of himself. "He's probably been bugging God ever since, wanting to know when He planned to make me recognize the truth. That was Jason."

It was the first time he'd been able to say Jason's name without pain—the first time he could smile in remembrance. Suddenly memories flooded through him in a tidal wave. Happy memories—things he'd locked away with the pain of Jason's death.

"As long as I couldn't deal with Jason's death, I couldn't remember his life." He did reach for her hands then. Hers were cold, but warmed to his touch. "You've given him back to me, Maggie."

"Not me. The Father did." Starlight reflected in her eyes. "He used me, and I wasn't a very willing tool."

"You can think of Him as Father, in spite of what your own father did."

"Aunt Elly helped me see that I could either let my past destroy me or I could let God use it to make me stronger. Seeing Him as a true Father was a big step forward for me."

She had a way of putting matters of faith into the simplest of terms. Once he'd have thought that naive, but no longer. Now he understood the strength and power of that.

"I almost let Jason's death destroy who I could be. I thought I was handling things better than my parents, because all they could do was give money in his memory. I thought giving my talent to healing was enough."

"But it wasn't."

She deserved to hear all of it.

"No. It's not enough. I realized tonight that God doesn't want the little pieces of me I've been willing to give. He wants all of me." He took a breath, letting the certainty settle deep inside him. "So that's what He's getting."

Joy lit Maggie's face, and her hands gripped his. "I'm glad. You'll be a better doctor for it, I promise you. When you go back—"

"I'm not going back."

Maggie's eyes widened. "Your partnership—surely that won't be a problem now. You can explain."

"I don't want to explain. I want to stay here." He smiled. "I might not be the doctor you'd have chosen for Button Gap, but I think I'm the one Someone Else picked."

"You can't give up everything you've wanted professionally."

"Maggie, listen. It's not giving something up when you've found something you want more. I want to be here. I want to be an important part of people's lives in a way I never could somewhere else. Button Gap needs me, but I need Button Gap just as much. It makes me whole."

Hope battled doubt in her expressive face. "The county can't afford a full-time doctor. It's been hard enough to get them to fund the clinic."

He smiled. "Oddly enough, I don't need the county's salary. As a matter of fact, I think I can convince the family foundation to provide us with a better facility. They like giving away money."

"You'd actually do that? You won't be sorry sometime down the road?"

He knew the answer to that one. "I'll never be sorry. This is what I want."

The church bells began to chime. Maggie looked up at the starry sky, as if hearing their echo in the stars.

"It's midnight. Merry Christmas, Grant."

He reached into his jacket pocket for the gift he'd been carrying around all day. He held it out to her.

"Merry Christmas, Maggie."

The crystal angel dangled from his fingers, glinting with reflected starlight.

He heard the sudden intake of her breath. She took the angel in both hands, and tears shone in her eyes. "It's beautiful."

It was time to say the rest of it, and he was absurdly afraid she might not give him the answer he longed for.

"I love you, Maggie Davis. Will you be my partner and my wife?"

The bells fell silent, as if the world waited with him for

her answer. Then he heard the voices ringing out from the church. "'Joy to the world, the Lord is come...'"

Maggie's face reflected that joy as she stepped forward into his arms. "I love you."

His lips claimed hers, and his heart filled with the certainty that he'd finally found his way home for Christmas.

Epilogue

"Let's put the angel toward the top of the tree." Standing on a step stool, he smiled down at Maggie. "Just to be on the safe side."

She glanced at the table, where Nella and Aunt Elly were helping the children string cranberries and popcorn together. "Good idea." She held the crystal angel up to him with a small, private smile. "I want this one to stay whole."

"Right." It had been a year since he'd given Maggie the new angel—a year of changes beyond measure in all their lives. He put the angel carefully on one of the topmost branches and watched it reflect the tree lights.

"I could come up and help you."

"Absolutely not." He stepped down from the stool and put one arm around her, then gently stroked the smooth, round curve that was just beginning to show. "I don't want little Jason or Emily to take any tumbles."

Maggie leaned against him and put her hand over his. "The

baby is fine. Leave it to a doctor to worry ten times as much as a normal father."

Changes, he thought again. Beautiful, blessed changes for all of them.

"Aunt Maggie, can I pat the baby, please?" Tacey danced over to them, her small face flushed with the excitement that only Christmas could bring.

"Sure you can." Maggie made room for the small hand.

Tacey wasn't withdrawn any longer, and Robby no longer looked around in apprehension when he laughed. As for Joey—he'd zoomed to the top of his class in school, determined to become a doctor, just like the person he now called "Uncle Grant."

With the completion of the new clinic, thanks to the Hardesty Foundation, the old building had been remodeled into two comfortable homes. Nella, proud of her position as the clinic office manager, lived with her children on one side, while he and Maggie would bring their new baby home to the other.

Maggie nestled her head against his shoulder as she looked at the nearly finished Christmas tree. "It's beautiful, isn't it?"

He dropped a kiss on her cheek. "It's beautiful. Just like everything else in my life now."

"Really?" She smiled at him teasingly. "You mean you like taking care of the whole county practically single-handedly? Taking payment in jars of jelly and cuts of venison? Crawling out of your warm bed to deliver a baby in the middle of a cold winter's night?"

He cradled her cheek in his palm, wondering at the love that seemed to grow stronger every day.

"I love every bit of it. Even the venison." He bent his

head, his words for her alone. "God gave me everything I ever wanted when He brought me to Button Gap. He brought me home."

★ ★ ★ ★ ★

THE TWINS' FAMILY CHRISTMAS

Lee Tobin McClain

To Kathy, Colleen and Sally, who helped me brainstorm this story,
and to Bill, for research assistance and emotional support.
You guys are the best.

For now we see through a glass, darkly; but then face to face: now I know in part; but then shall I know even as also I am known.

—*1 Corinthians* 13:12

Chapter One

You can do this.

Lily Watkins forced a smile as she carried the last of her photography gear into Redemption Ranch's Cabin Four and then came back out onto the small front porch. "Honestly, I'm fine being alone on Christmas," she said to her aunt. Which was true; at twenty-six, she'd already spent a fair number of holidays alone. "It'll be peaceful. Just what I need to finish my project."

The harder task would be to find out whether her fallen comrade's kids were being mistreated by their manipulative, cruel father. Doing that, according to her army therapist, might bring her some measure of peace.

She just had to figure out how to investigate the status of Pam's kids without losing her cool.

"I know several people in town who'd love to have you join them for Christmas dinner." Aunt Penny pulled out her phone. "Want me to make some calls?"

She *did* need to go down into the town of Esperanza Springs, talk to people, in order to find out the truth about Pam's husband and kids. But Christmas dinner wasn't the time to do that. And although she needed to make new friends and get on with her life, she wasn't likely to settle here in Colorado.

"No, thanks," she said. "I appreciate the offer, and I appreciate your letting me stay. The place is lovely, and I've been so busy. I'll enjoy a little solitude, to be honest."

To her relief, her aunt, who owned the ranch for struggling veterans and senior dogs, didn't put up a fight. "You're doing me a favor, too, taking on that other little photography project I mentioned. Anyway, the cabin's nothing fancy, but the scenery is nice."

"It's gorgeous," Lily agreed, looking out toward the snow-covered Sangre de Cristo Mountains towering over the wide, flat valley where the ranch was situated. "I can't wait to explore."

"One of our older veterans will be here over the holidays, and a couple of volunteers will stop by to take care of the dogs. They can help you with anything you need."

"I'll be fine." Lily smiled at the older woman. She was glad to have reconnected with Penny; they didn't know each other well, since Lily had grown up across the country, but in their few interactions, the older woman had always been down-to-earth and kind.

"I admire you, going back to school as a veteran and working so hard at it. And I'm thrilled you're using our ranch for your capstone project. Who knows, it might get us some great PR." She hesitated and then spoke again. "I've always regretted not doing more for you when you were a kid. Your mom wasn't the easiest to live with, and holidays stressed her out. No wonder you'd just as soon spend Christmas alone."

Lily waved a hand. "I wasn't any too easy to live with, either. I was wild."

"I know, I heard the stories." Her aunt chuckled, and then her face got serious again. "Just one more concern, and then I'll stop mother-henning you. Your car isn't really made for Colorado roads. The weather's nice now, but I saw where we might get some freezing rain tonight, in front of some snow."

Lily bit her lip, glancing over at her old car. Having spent the past year in Phoenix—and the years before that in the Middle East—she'd lost the knack for driving on icy roads. But she had to be able to get into town to investigate Pam's husband. That was the key reason she was here.

Penny patted her shoulder. "Long John—that's the vet I mentioned—can arrange a ride for you if you want to go down to town for Christmas Eve services."

"Thank you." It *would* be tough to miss church on Christmas Eve. "I might just have him do that."

"Good." Penny turned toward her car, and Lily walked with her into the frosty cold. "While you're enjoying some mountain solitude, I'll be with my daughter and grandson out east." She gave a wry smile. "I wish I could invite you to join us, but my daughter and I have a shaky relationship. Say a prayer that we'll all get along, will you?"

"Of course." Lily understood family problems all too well. She hugged the older woman. "I hope you have a wonderful time."

"I'll try." Penny got in her car, started it up and waved. Halfway down the short driveway, she stopped and lowered the window. "I forgot to tell you the name of that family you're to photograph. It's Carson Blair, one of our local pastors, and his twin six-year-olds. They'll be staying up here for the week." She raised the window and was off.

Lily stared after her aunt's car as the name she'd thrown out so casually whirled tornado-like through her head.

Carson Blair? She was doing family photographs of Carson Blair?

Pam's husband and kids were staying up here at Redemption Ranch?

The thought practically made her hyperventilate, but maybe it was a good thing. If they were staying here, it should be easy to do some quiet investigating.

She owed it to Pam. Paying that debt might help Lily move on.

She just had to make sure Carson didn't discover the awful truth about Pam's death.

Carson Blair whistled as he turned his truck into Redemption Ranch, a mere ten miles from his home in Esperanza Springs, but worlds away from his too-busy life. His last-minute plan to spend Christmas week up here was an opportunity to fill his daughters' hearts while they were off from school, let them have plenty of Daddy time. He would preach the Christmas Eve service tomorrow night, but that was all. Canceling the few other events and closing down the building meant that everyone—the secretary, the janitor, the committee members and volunteers—could do as he was doing: focus on their families.

Coming early to the ranch also let him escape the numerous invitations a single pastor got for Christmas parties and dinners. He loved his congregation, but spending time with their big, happy extended families was a painful reminder of the life he'd hoped his girls would have, but that he hadn't been able to provide.

He had to admit that he probably wouldn't have made this Christmas getaway happen without his friend Penny's urging. She knew he needed a break. But she'd also given him a small side job: watch out for another cabin resident here for the holidays, Penny's niece, who'd been struggling with her readjustment to civilian life. Apparently she'd had formal counseling through the military, but Penny thought that Carson, as a pastor, could offer a different type of support.

"It's worth a try," the older woman had said. "And she's a beautiful woman. You might enjoy her company."

Carson had bitten back the uncharacteristically sharp retort that had formed in his mind: *Yeah, but will she enjoy mine? Pam didn't.*

He *really* needed a vacation from failed efforts at matchmaking.

"Just don't mention I asked you to talk to her," Penny had gone on, oblivious to Carson's inner dialogue. "She's independent."

He didn't like deception, but if it was the only way this woman, Lily, would open up, he supposed he could comply with Penny's request.

He pulled up to Cabin Two and turned to wake up the twins, both asleep in the back seat after a sugar-laden holiday party in their kindergarten class. Their identical faces were flushed, their long eyelashes resting on chubby cheeks. His chest tightened. Despite the sad ending of his wife's life, the weaknesses of his marriage—the weaknesses he'd had as a husband—his daughters were the wonderful, God-given outcome.

"Wake up, sleeping beauties," he said quietly, giving a light pat to Skye's arm, then to Sunny's.

"Is it Christmas?" Sunny jerked upright.

"Presents?" Skye asked, yawning.

Carson chuckled. His girls did know the true meaning of Christmas, but preachers' kids were like anyone else's when it came to gifts.

"Christmas is in two days," he reminded them. "We're at the ranch now, though. We're going to do some sledding, and play with the dogs, and do puzzles by the fire. Let's get our stuff into the cabin."

"Yay!" Sunny cried, and both girls scrambled out of their booster seats.

But as Carson opened the truck door, Long John McCabe, one of the gray-haired veterans who lived at the ranch, came toward him, his walker bumping over the dirt path at an alarming pace. "Change of plans," he said. "Willie's cabin had a plumbing leak, so you can't stay there. We're putting you up in Cabin Five."

Carson shrugged. "Sure, that's fine. We'll be a little farther away from you, but we can bundle up and come visit."

"Long John!" Both girls spilled out of the truck and ran to hug the older gentleman, carefully, as they'd been taught. "We have a present for you," Skye added.

"It's a—" Just in time, Sunny slapped a hand over her own mouth.

"I might have a little something for you two girls as well." Long John reached a shaky hand down to pat Skye's head, then Sunny's.

"I'm going to pull the truck down to Cabin Five so we can unload," Carson said. "Girls, hop back in."

"But we want to go pet Rockette," Skye complained.

"And see Mr. Long John's Christmas tree," Sunny added, then looked up at the older man, her forehead wrinkling. "Do you *have* a Christmas tree?"

"If you don't," Skye said, "you can come see ours, when we get it set up."

"Maybe you can come help!" Sunny suggested. "Daddy, can he?"

"I'm fine. I've got a little Norfolk Island pine in a pot." Long John chuckled at the girls' enthusiasm and waved Carson toward the row of cabins. "Go ahead, get unpacked and settled. I'll entertain these two for half an hour, maybe fix 'em some hot chocolate."

"Can we, Daddy?" Skye pleaded.

Carson drew in a breath to say no, not wanting to put Long John to the trouble, but just in time, he caught the eagerness in the older man's eyes. Long John didn't have any kids or grandkids of his own, and his worsening Parkinson's disease made it difficult for him to get out.

He glanced over at Long John's cabin and noticed an accessibility ramp in front, its raw, light-colored wood a contrast to the old cabin's dark hue. That was new.

"You girls can visit," he said. "But behave and do what Mr. Long John says."

"Yay!" Sunny ran toward Long John's cabin.

"Wait!" Skye called sharply after her twin. She walked beside Long John at a sedate pace, glancing over her shoulder to make sure that Carson had noticed her considerate behavior.

He had, of course, and he gave her a thumbs-up. It was such a blessing, these older veterans becoming a part of his girls' lives. The twins had no local grandparents, but these men filled the gap, just as the girls filled a gap in Long John's life.

He let the truck glide down the road to Cabin Five. Got out and opened the back hatch...and stopped.

At the cabin next door, kneeling to catch a photo of the sun sinking over the Sangre de Cristos, was the most beautiful woman he'd ever seen.

Well, the second-most beautiful. He could never forget his wife's glossy golden hair, her sparkling eyes. He'd never stopped loving her, even through the arguments and the emotional distance and the absences.

He'd never *thought* he would notice another woman. But he was sure noticing this one.

Was *this* Penny's niece? If so...wow.

Clad in worn, snug-fitting jeans and a blue parka, the blonde was focusing so closely on what she was doing that she paid him no attention.

Not that a woman who looked like that would pay someone like him any attention. Pam—popular, fun-loving Pam—had been the amazing exception, the girl a former nerdy weakling would never have expected to attract.

"Daddy!" Sunny's voice sounded behind him, out of breath and upset.

He turned to see her running toward him, covering the rocky dirt road at breakneck speed. "Slow down, sweetie! What's wrong?"

"Daddy!" She hurtled into him and bounced back, grabbing his hand. "Mr. Long John is hurt!"

He dropped the bags he was carrying and turned toward Long John's cabin. "Where's Skye?"

"She's sitting with him. Come on!"

Carson ran beside her, their breath making fog clouds in the cold air. He should never have left the girls alone with a man in Long John's condition, even if he *had* seemed fine just a few minutes ago.

Running footsteps sounded behind him, then beside. "Which cabin?" the blonde woman asked. She was carrying a large first aid kit, and she lifted it to show him. "I overheard. Might be able to help."

"First one in the row." He gestured toward it.

"Daddy... I can't...run any...more." Sunny slowed beside him, panting, so he stopped to pick her up as the woman jogged ahead.

Now he could see Long John sitting on the bottom porch step, Skye beside him. The older man was conscious and upright, which was reassuring. When the blonde woman reached him, she knelt, spoke and then started pawing through her first aid kit.

Carson reached the trio a moment later and swung Sunny to the ground. "What's going on? Everyone okay?"

"I'm taking care of him," Skye said, patting Long John's arm.

"That you are, sweetie." Long John reached as if to put an arm around her and winced.

"I wouldn't move that arm just now, sir," the blonde woman said. Something about the cadence of her words spelled military. So this most likely *was* Penny's niece.

"Good point." Long John looked ruefully up at Carson. "I'm okay, it's just the Parkinson's getting worse. Affects my balance sometimes. I hit the edge of the porch wrong and went down. Bumped myself up and got a nasty splinter."

"He was spozed to use the ramp," Sunny explained, "but he didn't think he needed it."

"What's Parkinson's?" Skye asked.

"It's a disease that affects your muscles." As Long John went on with a simple explanation, Carson breathed a sigh of relief. His girls were okay, and Long John was, too, from the looks of things.

Penny's niece—Lily, her name was—had Long John's arm out of his parka and was using tweezers to remove the splinter. Once that was done, she swabbed the older man's hand with something from a clear bottle.

When she glanced back and saw Carson watching, she frowned and nodded toward the porch. "This porch isn't in great shape, especially for someone with mobility issues."

Carson nodded. "They've been gradually upgrading their structures here, as money permits. Looks like this place should move to the top of the list." The struggling ranch was getting back on its feet—they all hoped—but it would take time to recover from the embezzlement it'd suffered earlier this year.

Meanwhile, while Carson was here, he'd try his hand at shoring up Long John's old porch.

"Good idea." Lily gave him a brief smile and he sucked in his breath. No woman would ever be as beautiful as Pam, but this one, with her slim figure and short, wavy hair and lively eyes, came close.

Not that he was interested.

And certainly, not that she would be.

Carson focused back in on the conversation among Long John and his daughters.

"Could I get that disease?" Sunny was asking.

"Not likely," Long John said. "I was in a place called Vietnam, and spent a lot of time around a fancy weed killer called Agent Orange. The doctors think that might be why this happened." He waved a hand at his body. "But don't you worry. They don't use it anymore."

"I'm sorry." Skye patted his arm again, and Carson smiled.

A matching smile crossed Lily's face as she looked at the little girl comforting the old man. "There you go, sir," she said to Long John. "All patched up."

"Can I help you get inside?" Carson asked.

"Just a hand to stand up," Long John said. "Think I'll take it easy, watch a little TV. Your hot chocolate will have to wait until another day," he added to the girls.

"That's okay," Skye said, and then nudged her twin.

"That's okay," Sunny said with considerably less enthusiasm.

Carson helped Long John up on one side while Lily steadied him from the other. Once he was on his feet, he gestured for his walker. "I'll be fine from here," he said.

"But we want to see Rockette!" Sunny protested.

Bless her. That would give Carson the excuse to make sure

Long John was settled inside. "We'll just visit for a minute," he said.

So he followed Long John up the ramp, the girls eager behind them, Lily bringing up the rear. Once inside, he stood ready to help the older man into his chair, but it was obviously a move he'd made many times before and he did it smoothly.

The girls joyously patted big, gray-muzzled Rockette, who licked their faces and then flopped to the floor with a big doggy sigh that made them both giggle. They settled down beside the patient old dog, patting her head and marveling over her soft ears.

"Can I make you some coffee?" Carson asked Long John, moving toward the kitchen area, basically one wall of the cabin's main room. He noticed a single bowl, glass and spoon in the dish drainer.

"Don't touch the stuff, but thanks." Long John had the remote in hand, flipping channels.

"You let us know if you need anything." Carson turned to usher the girls out and realized that Lily wasn't there. Sometime while he'd been getting Long John settled, she must have slipped away.

Sure enough, when they got outside, he saw her up the road, walking rapidly toward her cabin.

Which probably meant she didn't want to socialize. Penny had said she was independent.

But he'd promised to reach out to her. He'd get his things unloaded and then pay a little visit, do an informal assessment of his quiet neighbor.

Lily heard the little girls' voices from a distance behind her and practically ran up the steps of her cabin. She went inside and shut the door.

Pam's husband and her twins. Seeing them had tugged her

emotions in ways she didn't expect. Especially those adorable, energetic little girls who were the image of their mother.

What a family Pam could have had…if only she'd survived.

But Lily needed to focus on the future rather than wallow-
ing in regret. She needed to gather her strength and find out
if Carson was, in fact, an abusive bully. The least she could
do for Pam, since she couldn't turn back the clock and change
what had happened, was to check on her children and make
sure they were okay.

They'd seemed more than okay, but appearances could be
deceiving.

She went to the window and watched as the man and the
little blonde twins carried things into the cabin next door.

Hearing the laughter of the children, punctuated by some
booming laughs from *him*, made loneliness squeeze Lily's stomach, but she straightened her back and drew in the deep,
cleansing breath she'd learned about from her army therapist.
She deserved to be lonely.

Because the father-daughter fun outside didn't make up for
what was missing from the picture: a mom. Beautiful, mysterious Pam, who hadn't gotten to spend nearly enough time
with her husband and kids in the years before her death.

Don't dwell on what you can't change. Lily looked away from
the trio's good spirits toward Long John's cabin. She'd seen
the undecorated Christmas tree, the single strand of lights
around the porch railing, the pizza box beside the trash can.
All of it spoke of a man alone, and Long John wasn't in such
good shape.

Having a trained medic—her—up here over the holidays,
when the older man was likely to be cut off from his support
system, might be a blessing. Something God had planned. It
was another way Lily could make up for her past.

When she looked back at the little twins, they were building something out of rocks, possibly a house for the bright collection of toys on the ground. Normally, she didn't understand kids—they were aliens to her. But these girls' serious, intent faces made her smile. They were focused on fun, just as kids should be.

Fun. It wasn't something she'd thought a lot about. No time. She'd joined the army at eighteen, gotten trained as a medic and then a combat photographer, done pretty well for a poor girl from a rough background. After that, college on the GI Bill at an accelerated pace.

Everyone told her to slow down, but she didn't want to. Slowing down gave her the time to think.

It wasn't until she heard the knock on the door that she realized the girls' father was nowhere in sight.

As she went to answer a second knock, she glanced through the window.

Carson Blair stood on her front porch. Her heart thumped, and she inhaled a bracing breath. She'd wanted to investigate the man, to make sure he was treating Pam's girls well.

It looked like the opportunity had just fallen into her lap.

Chapter Two

Carson waited for the mysterious Lily to answer his knock, wondering at his own intense curiosity.

The pastor part of him had noticed the sad, distant look in her eyes. There was some kind of pain there, and it tugged at his heart. He'd try to establish at least an initial connection. There was plenty of time to do more probing, as Penny had requested, within the next few days.

He also wanted to get a better look at her, and honesty compelled him to ask himself why. Surely not because he found her attractive? He did, of course—he was human, and she was gorgeous—but gorgeous women were not for him. He wanted to marry again, if God willed it; his girls needed a mother, and his own work as a pastor would be enhanced if he had a wife ministering at his side. Not to mention how long and lonely winter evenings could be when you didn't have a partner to talk to and love.

But this woman wasn't a prospect.

The door jerked open. "Can I help you?" came a voice out of the cabin's dimness. A voice that wasn't exactly friendly.

"We didn't have the chance to introduce ourselves. I'm Carson Blair. Just came by to say hello, since it looks like we're going to be neighbors over the holiday."

"Pleased to meet you." Her voice didn't sound pleased. "I'm Lily. What brings you to the ranch? Penny mentioned you live nearby."

Her interrogation surprised him—in his counseling role, he needed to find out about her, not vice versa—and it made him feel oddly defensive. "My daughters and I are looking for a peaceful Christmas, away from our daily stresses and strains."

"Your girls are stressed?" She came forward into the light, standing on the threshold. Her wheat-blond hair seemed to glow, and her high cheekbones and full lips were model-pretty.

So were her big, slate-colored eyes. Eyes that glared, almost like she had it in for him.

He took a breath and reminded himself of that old counseling cliché: *hurt people hurt people.* "I guess it's just me that's stressed," he admitted, keeping his tone easy and relaxed. "Busy time of year for a pastor. But the girls are thrilled to be up here with Long John and the dogs."

Her face softened a little. "It *is* nice up here. Good feel to the place."

"Yes, there is." He paused. "Say, Penny mentioned that you're a photographer. And that she'd asked you to take some family photos of us as a Christmas present."

"That's right. When are you available?"

Noting that her body language was still tense, Carson decided that this wasn't the time to work out details. Besides, she wasn't inviting him in, and her short-sleeved shirt and faded jeans weren't cold-weather gear. She must be freezing. "We can figure that out in the next day or two. Meanwhile, if you need anything, I'm right next door."

He turned to go down the steps when two blond heads popped up next to the railing. "Hi," Sunny, always the bolder of the two, called out to Lily. "What's your name?"

Carson walked halfway down the steps and stopped in front of his curious girls. "I think Miss..." He realized he didn't know her last name. "I'm sure our neighbor is busy right now."

"Whatcha doing?" Sunny slid under the wooden rail and climbed the rest of the way up the steps. "Can we see your cabin?"

Skye, easing up the stairs behind Sunny, didn't speak, but it was plain to see that she was equally interested.

"Girls." He put a hand on each shoulder. "We don't go where we're not invited." Watching the pouts start to form, he added, "Besides, we've got unpacking to do, and then some dogs to meet."

"Dogs!" they both said at the same time, their curiosity about the lady next door forgotten.

"Unpacking first," he said, herding them down the steps. But as he turned to offer an apologetic wave to their neighbor, he thought her stance on the porch looked lonely, her eyes almost...hungry.

The next morning, Lily shivered in the bright sun, looked at the newly slick, icy road out of the ranch and had a crisis of confidence.

Could her ancient, bald-tired Camaro handle the trip into town?

If not, could she handle staying up here without coffee?

The lack of caffeine had left her head too fuzzy to figure out how to investigate her surprise neighbors, and there was no coffee or coffee maker in the cabin.

She could go to Long John or Carson to see what she could borrow, but she didn't want to open up that kind of neighborly relationship with Carson, not when she was trying to ascertain his suitability as a father. And she'd heard Long John say that he didn't drink coffee.

Her caffeine-withdrawal headache was setting in big-time. So she had to go, and now, full daylight with the sun shining, was the right time, rather than waiting until later when it was likely to snow. And when all the shops would be closed for Christmas Eve.

Because most people wanted to be with their families.

You're not an orphan; you're just making a choice. Her father was still living, and he would have certainly taken her in for Christmas. If she could find him, and if he had a roof over his head. And if he was sober.

But in all the years she'd spent Christmas with her parents as a child, she couldn't remember one where he'd made it through the holiday without heavy drinking. There was no reason to think that now, with her mother gone, this year would be an exception; the opposite, in fact.

And while she hated to think of her father being alone, she knew he probably wasn't. He was probably carousing with his buddies. He was the friendly type and had a ton of them.

The image of her dad's jolly face brought an unexpected tightness to her throat.

"It's her!" came a high, excited shout.

"Hey, Miss Neighbor!"

The two childish voices let her know she'd stood reflecting too long. She turned, and the sight of the twins—*Pam's twins*—coming toward her made her heart turn over. Clad in identical red snow jackets, black tights and furry boots, they could have been an advertisement for Christmas family joy.

And she couldn't make herself turn away from them, even

though she should. She'd keep it brief. "Good morning, la-dies," she said, kneeling down to be at their level.

They slipped and slid to her with the fearless footing of chil-dren accustomed to snow and ice. "Where are you going?" one of them asked.

Lily studied her. "Are you Sunny?" She'd noticed that Car-son had gestured toward the twin in the lead when naming them yesterday.

"How did you know?" Sunny asked, eyebrows lifting high.

"Nobody ever does, at first." The other little girl studied her, head cocked to one side.

"Just a guess," she said, smiling at them. Man, were they cute.

Man, did they look like Pam.

"Where are you going?" The quieter girl, who must be Skye, asked.

"Down to town," Lily said.

"Us, too!" Sunny sounded amazed. "Daddy sent us out to play so he could look over his sermon in peace, but as soon as he's done that, we're going down into town, too."

Oh, right. Pam's husband was a preacher. According to Pam, it was a cover-up for his abusive ways.

"Is your dad pretty strict?" she asked the twins. And then she wished she could take the words back. It wasn't fair to ask the girls to tattle on their father. If she wanted to know some-thing, she would discover it by observation, not by grilling these two innocents.

"What's strict?" Sunny asked.

"She means, does Daddy make us behave." Skye glanced back at the house. "He tries to be strict, but we don't always do what he says."

Lily was dying to ask what kind of punishments he meted out, but she didn't.

Didn't need to, as it turned out.

"When we don't do what he says," Sunny said, "we get a time-out."

"Or an extra chore," Skye added.

"Yeah, we have lots of chores!" Sunny spread her arms wide and nodded vigorously, the picture of childhood overwork. "We have to make our beds *every* day."

"And put the silverware in the drawer." Skye frowned. "Only, here at the cabin, we don't have a dishwasher. So Daddy washed our dishes last night, himself, and put everything away."

Lily waited for a continuation of their onerous list of chores, but it didn't come. Either the list was limited to two not-very-challenging tasks or their attention had drifted elsewhere.

Meanwhile, she had better get going before Carson the ogre came out of the cabin. Even though she needed to check on Pam's twins, she didn't want to get sucked into even a superficial friendship. Not when she had secrets to keep. "It was nice talking to you girls," she said, getting into her car and starting it up.

The girls still stood next to her car, and Sunny's lips were moving, so she lowered her window.

"Maybe we'll see you in town," Sunny said.

"That would be...fun," Lily said. *Not.* She would drive down to town, get the coffee and coffee maker she needed now even more desperately than before—her headache was getting worse—and then drive back up and hide out in her cabin for the duration of Christmas Eve.

Spending the holiday by herself seemed a little bit lonelier after talking to Skye and Sunny, but Lily pushed the feeling away. She put the car into gear and started cautiously down the icy road.

The car picked up speed on the incline, and she hit the

brake reflexively. The car fishtailed a little, even though her pace was slow. Her heart beat faster, and her hands on the cold steering wheel were slick with sweat. If she went off the road, who would help her?

You're tough; you're a soldier. She just had to remember that you braked gently in icy conditions.

She gathered her courage and took her foot off the brake. The car started moving again.

There was a shout behind her, and when she looked into the rearview mirror, she saw the two little girls running after her. That wasn't safe. What if they got too close and the car went out of control? She braked, harder this time, and the antilock *tick-tick-tick-tick* didn't stop the car from sliding sideways. It stopped just at the edge of a two-foot dropoff. Not deadly, but… She put the car into Park and got out just as the girls reached her.

"We saw your car slide and we told Daddy!" Sunny said.

"And he said you could ride to town with us." Skye looked up, her brown eyes round and hopeful. "We have a big truck."

"Oh, no, it's okay." She walked to the front of her car, and it was, in fact, okay. About three inches from being not okay, but okay.

She looked back toward her cabin and saw Carson Blair striding toward them, flannel-shirted and boot-clad and looking nothing like any preacher she'd ever seen.

More like a lumberjack.

Weren't there social media sites and photo calendars about good-looking lumberjacks?

She shoved *that* ridiculous notion away, her face heating as Carson reached them.

"Everything okay?" He patted each twin on the back and then walked around to look at the front of her car.

"It's fine," she said.

"But her car went sliding. Like a sled!" Sunny demonstrated with a complicated hand motion.

Carson nodded. "I like the rear-wheel-drive Camaros," he said, tapping the hood, "but they're not the greatest on snow and ice."

"I didn't think of that before I came," she admitted. "Not much snow in Phoenix. But it's no big deal for me to get to town," she added while her body cried out for caffeine.

"Daddy's a good driver," Skye said earnestly.

"You should come to town with us!" Sunny was wiggling her excitement, which seemed to be her normal state of being. "You could come to church!"

"Oh, I..." She trailed off, part of her noticing that the girls seemed enthusiastic about church and life in general, nothing like abused children were likely to be.

"You're welcome to join us," Carson said. "We're picking up a couple of things at the hardware store and then going to church for Casual Christmas Eve."

That made sense of Carson's lumberjack attire and the girls' outdoorsy clothing. "Are you staying until midnight? Because I can't...can't do that." *Can't deal with you and your girls for that many hours in a row.*

Carson waved a hand and smiled, and he went instantly from good-looking to devastatingly handsome. "I scored this year. Got the afternoon service, and the other church in town—Riverside Christian—they're doing the evening services." He held out his hand. "Come on. I'll drive your car back up, and you can ride into town with us."

His comfortable, take-charge manner both put her at ease and annoyed her. It was nice to think of someone else driving on the slippery roads—and it was *really* nice to think of coffee—but she didn't know Carson. Or rather, she only knew *of* him, and none of what she'd heard from Pam was positive.

Besides, she didn't want to be that wimpy woman who needed a man to drive her around.

His hand was still out for the keys, but she held on to them.

A smile quirked the corner of his mouth. "If you want to drive it back up yourself, go for it," he said, "although I've been itching to get behind the wheel of a cherry-red Camaro since I was seventeen."

She suspected it was a ruse to make her comfortable letting him drive and help her save face. Okay, that was nice of him. She handed him the keys.

Carson was glad they ended up taking Lily to town. Beyond Penny's request, he found himself curious about the shy photographer. She said she was working on a college project, and he had surmised from all the camera equipment that it involved photography. But that was all he knew.

He was about to ask when she turned to him. "So, how long have you and the twins lived in this area?" she asked.

"We moved here when they were born," he said. "We've always lived in Colorado, various parts, but a job opened up here at just the point when we were ready for a more stable life. How about you? Where are you from?"

"Most recently, Phoenix." Lily didn't elaborate but instead asked another question. "Do you like the job?"

He got the odd feeling she was trying to ask him questions to deflect attention from herself. "I do. It's a wonderful church and community. Not without its problems—there's a lot of poverty—but people are good-hearted here. It's an old-fashioned community. Neighbors look after neighbors." Great. He sounded like his grandfather, hearty and wholesome and focused on his own small town. Not fun and exciting.

Pam had always criticized him for being boring.

But how could he not be? He'd grown up on the straight

and narrow, with strict parents. Now he was a pastor and a frazzled single dad.

What chance did he have to be full of scintillating conversation, when his biggest social activity all season had been helping at the kids' classroom holiday party?

"And how about you girls?" Lily turned in the seat to look back at them. "How do you like your town?"

"There's an ice cream store," Skye said matter-of-factly, as if that were the feature that determined the worth of a town.

"And our teacher, Ms. Garcia, is so nice." Sunny launched into her favorite theme. "She brings her dogs to school sometimes. And when we told her we want a dog, too, she said one of her dogs is having puppies!"

Not this again. "If we ever did get a dog," Carson said, "we would get one from the shelter. Not a puppy."

"That's okay, Daddy," Skye said. "We like all dogs. We don't have to get a mala… Mala…"

"Malamute?" Lily glanced over at Carson. "A malamute puppy would be adorable, but a lot of work. And hair."

"Exactly." Carson turned the truck onto Esperanza Springs's Main Street. "Look at the decorations, girls," he said in an effort to distract them from their dog quest.

It worked. Even though it was early in the afternoon, it was a gray enough day that the streetlights had lit up. The town resembled a Christmas card scene.

"So beautiful," Lily murmured, leaning forward and staring out the window, elbows on knees.

"You said you live in Phoenix?" he asked.

"Yeah." She wrinkled her nose. "We have Christmas decorations, but where I live, they tend to be giant inflatable cartoon characters and lights wrapped around the trunks of palm trees. This is prettier."

Carson pulled the truck into a parking space just down from

the hardware store. Across the street, the Mountain High Bakery was doing a surprisingly brisk business—people picking up their Christmas desserts, no doubt. In front of La Boca Feliz, Valeria Perez folded the signboard and picked it up, shaking her head at an approaching couple with an apologetic smile. Closing down for the day: good. That meant Valeria would be able to attend church with the rest of her family.

"Oh, wow, look!" Sunny bounced in her seat. "Mrs. Barnes's new dog has reindeer antlers on!"

"Can we go pet it, Daddy? Can we?" Skye leaned forward to beg.

"In a minute. Get out on Lily's side." He came around and opened Lily's door. Growing up as the only child of older parents had certainly had its drawbacks, like making him into a total nerd, but at least he had learned old-fashioned manners. His women friends always praised him for that. Usually in the process of making it clear that he was just a friend, no more.

And why did that matter? He automatically held out a hand to help Lily down from the high truck seat. He didn't look at her, not wanting her to read his thoughts.

Once he'd helped her down and dropped her hand almost as fast as she pulled it away, he opened the back door of the truck. The girls tumbled out and rushed to Mrs. Barnes, an older member of the congregation known for pressing other church members into service doing things they didn't want to do. At a ranch fund-raiser last summer, she had come to meddle but had ended up falling in love with one of the senior dogs. Now Bosco plodded slowly beside her, indeed sporting a pair of light-up antlers.

"Girls," he warned, a hand on each one's shoulder. "Make sure you ask Mrs. Barnes if it's okay to pet Bosco." He knew it was, but he also wanted the twins to practice safety around other people's dogs. Plus, he knew that Mrs. Barnes enjoyed talking about Bosco, reveling in the attention and status her dog brought her. Indeed, several other people had already clustered around to admire the dog in his costume.

"Dogs sure do a lot for people," Lily said, closer than he had expected.

He looked at her and saw that a smile tugged at the corner of her mouth.

"Oh, no," he said, mock-serious, "you're not going to throw me under the bus. I am *not* getting a dog."

She raised mittened hands, laughing openly now. "Did I tell you to get a dog?" she asked innocently.

Her cheeks were flushed in the cold, and strands of blond hair escaped from the furry hood of her jacket. Her lips curved upward, and her wide eyes sparkled, and Carson's heart picked up its pace.

Time to get businesslike. "The hardware store is right there," he said, gesturing toward Donegal's Hardware. "Come on, girls, let's leave Mrs. Barnes to her errands. We have a few of our own to do."

"What are you buying, Miss Lily?" Sunny tucked a hand into Lily's.

Not to be outdone, Skye took Lily's other hand.

They walked ahead of Carson, and the sight made his heart lurch.

Maybe this was a very bad idea. Carson didn't need the girls getting attached to some model-perfect photographer who would be here only a few days. He'd noticed that they tended to be drawn to young women, probably because they missed their own mother. They'd been four when she died, so their memories were patchy, but despite Carson's best efforts to be both mother and father, some part of them knew what was missing in their lives.

"I'm buying coffee and a coffee maker," Lily said, "because I love coffee so much, and there isn't one at the cabin."

"You're like our daddy!" Skye tugged at her hand. "Daddy isn't very nice if he hasn't had his coffee."

Lily laughed back at him, and he couldn't keep his own mouth from lifting into a smile. Their eyes met.

Color rose into her cheeks, and she looked away, and then the girls tugged her into the store.

Inside, tinsel and ornaments hung from the ceiling and Christmas music played. Long lines of customers waited at the two front registers, some holding wrapping paper and others bags of salt. Two men both approached the last snow shovel in a rack, and then one waved his hand in good-natured defeat. "You can have it," he said, "if you'll come over and shovel my walks when the snow starts."

"Deal," the other man said, laughing.

Lily and the twins had disappeared, so Carson took advantage of the opportunity to pick out two boxes of ornaments. They had a few, but not enough to make even their small artificial tree look as colorful as six-year-olds demanded.

Of course, Carson ran into several of his parishioners, and by the time he'd greeted them, Lily and the twins emerged from the back of the store. "Success!" Lily said, holding up a box with a coffee maker in it.

"And I have something for you." With a fake-gallant gesture, he poured her a paper cup of free, hardware-store coffee and handed it over.

"You're my hero," she said, taking the cup and inhaling appreciatively. She took a sip and her eyes met his.

He started to feel giddy.

When they reached the counter with their purchases, Marla Jones, the cashier, reached over the counter to shake Lily's hand. "So you're Penny's niece? Penny told me you were staying up at the ranch."

Lily's smile was a little shy. "I'm just here for a few days, to photograph the dogs. My senior project."

"You know," Marla said, "I'd like to talk to you about going back to school for photography. I'd really like to finish my degree, but I'm worried that I'm too old."

"You should! It's been a great experience for me. And there are lots of older students at colleges these days."

"Do you mind if I get your number? It's Liliana...what was your last name?"

"Watkins," she said.

Shock exploded like a bomb in Carson's chest. He must have made some weird sound, because she glanced over at him. When she saw his reaction, her eyes widened, and she turned quickly away.

The clerk rang up Lily's purchases, still chatting, and then punched her number into Lily's phone. Meanwhile, all the implications slammed into Carson. Lily was Liliana Watkins? Pam's party-happy roommate? The one with all the boyfriends? He shook his head, but he couldn't shake the pieces into place.

Why was Liliana at the ranch? Was she here to dry out? To bring a message from Pam? Most important, was it safe for his girls to be around her?

His eyes narrowed. Had Penny known the connection between Lily and Pam when she'd asked Carson to check on her?

Lily grabbed her purchase and her change, gave a quick, artificial smile to Marla and then hurried toward the door.

He wasn't letting her escape. "Hey, wait up," he called after her as he handed cash to Marla.

Lily hesitated, then turned.

Carson took his change and strode over to where she was standing. "I need to talk to you later, after church," he said.

"Okay." She looked pale, but she didn't ask him why. For some reason, that angered him.

The girls were calling to him, talking to Marla, collecting his bags. "I'd like to get some information from you, *Liliana*," he said, keeping his voice low, "about Pam."

Chapter Three

A short while later, Lily stood in the foyer of the small church while Carson talked to a parishioner, and the girls excitedly greeted their friends.

Anxiety twisted her stomach. He knew.

Carson Blair had obviously just realized that she'd been Pam's friend and roommate, and now she had to decide how to deal. And she had to figure it out soon, before the church service ended.

Just the fact that she hadn't said anything when she'd met them made her seem guilty of wrongdoing. She should have copped to the truth right away. Should have smiled easily and said, "Hey, what a coincidence, I think I knew your wife."

But she'd kept quiet. How was she going to explain that?

Out of all the things he was likely to think and wonder about, one was the most worrisome: Did he know she'd been right there with Pam at the end? How much did he know about his wife's death?

"Come see our costume!" Little Sunny tugged at Lily's

hand, bringing her back to the present. They walked farther into the small, white-adobe-fronted church building. Evergreen boughs emitted their pungent aroma, and a large Christmas tree dominated the corner of the lobby. Adults talked and laughed and hung up coats while kids ran around. From the sanctuary, a choir practiced a jazzed-up version of "Hark! The Herald Angels Sing"; the music stopped midline, there was some talk and laughter, and then the group sang the same line again and continued on.

"Over here!" Skye beckoned, and Sunny tugged, and Lily followed them down a hallway to a classroom where barely organized chaos reigned.

"We're two parts of a camel," Skye explained. "I was the front in the dress 'hearsal last week, so Sunny gets to be the front today." The contraption they held up made Lily smile; someone had affixed a brown sheet to a horse-on-a-stick, and a complicated arrangement of pillows made for the hump. Two holes allowed the girls' heads to stick up through it, creating visibility and a very odd-looking camel.

"Can you help them into it?" a young woman, obviously pregnant, called over her shoulder. She was kneeling, trying to place a flowing head covering over a shepherd boy who kept trying to twist away. "I'm Barb, by the way," she added.

"Um, sure." Lily knelt beside the twins and, despite their confusing instructions, got the costume situated on them. Immediately, they began prancing around, running into another child just as Carson appeared in the doorway.

"Skye! Sunny!" He lifted his hands in warning. "Slow down."

"Daddy!" They rushed over and struggled to embrace him, their camel costume twisting askew, as if they hadn't just parted from him ten minutes before.

Wow, he was handsome. And she'd felt a spark between

them earlier, in the street, when they'd teased about getting a dog.

What was *that* all about? Getting attracted to Pam's husband was just plain wrong.

"You look great." He hugged them both quickly and readjusted their costume. "I want you to go over there and sit with the others until it's time to come out and do your show." He guided them toward the calmest corner of the room, where several other child actors milled around.

"I'm sorry things are so wild, Pastor Blair," Barb said. "I'm trying to get everyone dressed, but it's hard. We'll be ready when it's time."

"Isn't Missy here?"

She shook her head. "Her little one's sick. But I'm sure I can handle it."

"If you tell me what to do," Lily heard herself say, "I can help."

"Thank you!" Carson gave her a smile that warmed her to her toes, and then someone called him from behind. He turned toward an agitated-looking acolyte who was holding a broken candle. He spoke to her gently, and they walked off down the hall.

"I'd appreciate your help." Barb gave her a harried smile. "If you can just keep the kids entertained while I get these last couple dressed, and help me get them to the sanctuary, we'll be good."

Keep kids entertained? How did you do that? She wasn't a mom or an aunt, and she didn't have many friends with kids.

As she looked at them, her mind a blank, the group began to nudge and push one another in the small, crowded room.

Inspiration hit. "All right, we're going to take pictures," she said, pulling out her phone. "First, everyone stand up."

Like well-practiced models, they instantly struck poses, and she snapped several photos.

"Now everyone look sad."

They giggled and tried to do it without success.

"Now individual photos. Quietest kids go first."

They continued doing photo sessions, and Lily actually got some good shots that the parents would love, including candids of the kids who were still being helped into their costumes.

What seemed like only a few minutes later, a gray-haired man appeared in the doorway. "You kids are up next," he said, and the children shrieked and lined up, following Barb's harried instructions.

Once they got to the front entrance of the sanctuary, several other adults appeared to direct the children, and Barb gave Lily a quick half hug. "Thanks for giving me a hand. You can slip in and watch, if you'd like."

So Lily did, strangely warmed by the opportunity to help out.

The sight of the girls galumphing up the aisle, Sunny grinning and waving while Skye tried to hold the camel costume in place, made Lily's breath catch.

Pam would've found the camel costume hysterically funny. Lily could almost hear her friend's rollicking laugh that usually ended in an undignified snort. It would have created a disruption in church, but Pam would have enjoyed that, too, rebel that she was.

If only she could be here. If only things had gone down differently those last days before she'd died.

Lily swallowed hard and made herself focus on the service. But the past seemed determined to intrude. As she watched the children perform their nativity skit, breathed in the scent of pine boughs and candles, and sang the familiar carols, her own long-ago memories flooded in. Church attendance had been a spotty thing in her childhood, but for a stretch of several years, a neighboring family had taken her along to a Christmas craft workshop, where she'd enjoyed a few hours of contented concentration, making wreaths or pot holders or Styrofoam ornaments. Christmas music had poured out of speakers and people had been friendly and kind. For those short periods, she'd felt a part of a larger whole.

This seemed like the kind of church that would welcome a lonely child into their midst.

Maybe if she'd kept up her church attendance, she wouldn't have gone down the wrong path.

When the skit ended to enthusiastic applause, the children left, and Carson stood in the pulpit. He looked around as if meeting each individual's eyes. Was it her imagination, or did his gaze linger a little longer on her face?

"Did you know that Jesus was an outsider?" he began, and then continued on to preach a short but apt sermon, inviting everyone to recommit themselves to Christ, incarnated in the world, during this season.

He was a talented speaker, and Lily found herself thinking about the state of her own soul. She believed, read her Bible somewhat regularly, but she *did* feel like an outsider among religious folks. Her past had gone from isolated to wild, and while she'd straightened herself out overseas, with the help of a couple of Christian friends, she'd never found a church where she really belonged.

People in the congregation listened attentively, some smiling, others nodding. Carson seemed to be well respected.

And his kids obviously adored him.

So Pam's assessment of her husband was at least incomplete—she'd portrayed him as mean and abusive. She'd also said that he put on a good show, of course, and maybe that was what was happening tonight. But as the service ended and she watched Carson greet people by name and ask about their families, she couldn't detect even a note of insincerity.

It looked like he was going to be busy for a while, and the twins were still working on a craft in the Sunday school classroom. So Lily took a cup of hot apple cider from a smiling teenager and wandered off toward the small church library.

She didn't browse for long before the woman watching over the library struck up a conversation that ended in an invitation for Lily to come for Christmas dinner. Even though she turned it down, the offer lifted Lily's spirits. Then the clerk from the hardware store came over and started talking photography. Before she knew it, she was sitting in a small grouping of chairs, eating cookies and listening to a trio of women venting about how stressed they felt from Christmas preparations and expressing envy for her single, unencumbered state.

Yes, this was how church should be. Friendly and open and welcoming.

If she settled in a place like this, this was the type of church she'd want to attend.

"Lily." There was a touch on her shoulder, and she turned to see Carson's serious face. His interruption made the other three women exclaim about the time and get up to join the thinning crowd, collecting coats and children and heading out into the late-afternoon light.

Lily's heart thumped in a heavy rhythm as Carson sat down kitty-corner from her. She looked around the church lobby, desperate for a distraction, an excuse to escape. Why hadn't she used the church service as a time to figure out what she could say to this curious, grieving husband?

What could she say that wouldn't devastate him?

"When I heard your full name, I realized that you were Pam's roommate," he began. "That surprised me. Did you come to Esperanza Springs because of Pam? Is there anything you can tell me about her?"

Lily shook her head rapidly. "I didn't realize you all were here. At the ranch, I mean," she added, to keep from lying. "I'm just here to photograph the dogs for a project I'm finishing up. And to take your family pictures, remember? The gift from Penny." She was blathering.

And all of it was to deflect his interest away from her real purpose: to check on his daughters, for Pam.

His head tilted to one side, and there was a skeptical expression on his face. He opened his mouth to say something more.

"Pastor! There you are. I have a little gift for you and your girls." A curvy woman with reddish hair thrust a container of cookies into Carson's hands.

"Thank you, Mariana." Carson's smile looked strained.

"I don't believe we've met." Mariana fixed Lily with an accusing glare.

"I'm sorry," Carson said. "Mariana, this is Lily, one of Pam's friends."

"Pleased to meet you." Mariana sounded anything but. "We all wanted to get to know Pam, but she was never around."

"I'm glad to meet you, too," Lily said in a weak response. She'd never thought about Pam's career from her hometown's point of view. It *was* odd that Pam had spent most of her leaves traveling, rather than being home with her family.

Mariana had just sat down when a teenage voice called from the doorway. "Mom! Let's go!"

"Kids." With a heavy sigh, Mariana stood, waved and walked toward the door.

Now the lobby area was almost completely empty, and parents were coming out from the back hallway with young children in hand. If Lily could only stall...

"Listen, we don't have much time," Carson said, "but I also

know you won't be around long. That's why I'm really eager to talk with you about Pam. Do you know the circumstances of her last days?"

Lily blew out a sigh. "Didn't they contact you? Usually the army is good about—"

"Yes, they contacted me and gave me the official version," Carson interrupted. "But you and I both know that the official version isn't the whole story. What was her state of mind, what had she been doing beforehand, that sort of thing."

Exactly what Lily didn't want to talk about, couldn't bear to talk about. "I think I hear your girls," she said desperately, standing up.

"Is there something I should know?" Carson stood, too, and stepped closer.

"No." He most definitely *shouldn't* know what had happened. It would only add to his unhappiness. "No, there's nothing you should know. I'll be outside." She spun and hurried toward the door.

Why had she done that? Now he would know there was something she wasn't saying. It would be so great to be a good liar, to be able to smile and tell Carson that Pam had spent her last moments thinking of him and her girls. That she'd been happy and content until the horrible accident had happened.

But Lily was a bad liar, and the pretty version was far from the truth.

She pushed open the door and walked out into a sunset world of cold and whirling snowflakes.

Almost an hour later, after a neck-tensing drive to the ranch in whiteout conditions, Carson gratefully pulled his truck into the driveway between Cabin Four and Cabin Five. He got out and came around to find Lily already opening the door for the girls.

"Yay! Snow!" Sunny called. "C'mon, Skye!"

But Skye was clinging to Lily's gloved hand. "Can you come in our cabin? We put out food for Santa every year."

Worry stabbed at Carson. Skye seemed to already be getting overly attached to Lily.

Lily smiled down at Skye. "That's such a nice offer, but I'd better not," she said without offering an excuse. "Run and see if you can catch a snowflake on your tongue!"

Distracted, Skye danced toward her sister, tongue out.

Carson handed Lily her package from the hardware store. "Let's finish our conversation later, or tomorrow," he said, by way of warning her that their talk wasn't over.

She'd obviously not wanted to discuss Pam, and possible reasons why were driving Carson crazy. Pam had been highstrung and intense, not without her problems and issues. Lily might know something about Pam's death, or her last days, that would shed some light.

Had she also known that Pam was pregnant again?

Even the thought of it stabbed at his heart. Carson had begged her not to go back into the army, to stay home instead. She could have easily gotten a discharge or at least a desk job. But she'd refused. She'd loved the excitement of being overseas. She'd said she wanted one last adventure before she really settled down.

The strong implication being *settled down with her boring old husband.*

But she'd promised to be careful and to tell her commanding officers about the pregnancy, and she'd assured him she wouldn't be assigned to any dangerous missions.

So how was it that she'd died from enemy fire?

The loss he'd faced had been double: his wife and his unborn child. To get over it, to move forward with his life, he needed more information, and the army's official materials hadn't satisfied him.

"Thanks for the ride," Lily said. She headed toward her cabin, then turned back. "Merry Christmas."

"Same to you." He watched her walk, straight-backed and lonely-looking, toward her cabin to spend the rest of Christmas Eve, and Christmas, alone.

He guessed people might feel sorry for him, too, but at least he had his girls. A true blessing.

"Daddy! Come here!" The twins were jumping up and down on the cabin's porch, and Carson hurried to them, concerned that even their slight weight would cause the old porch to cave in.

But when he got there, the porch was sturdy and intact, and the twins waved a large red envelope.

"Read it, Daddy, read it!" Sunny said.

He opened the envelope and read, in shaky handwriting: *You are cordially invited to a Christmas Eve dinner in Cabin 1. Banjo music included.*

He chuckled. He'd planned to serve the girls canned soup and grilled cheese tonight, waiting until tomorrow to attempt to cook the turkey and potatoes he'd bought, but a real, full dinner would be far preferable. And behind the cheerful wording of the invitation was the obvious: Long John wanted the company.

"What does it say?" Skye asked.

He knelt and read it to the girls, earning squeals of excitement.

"Let's put our things away first," he said, "and then we'll head down to see Mr. Long John."

"Let's go now!" Sunny held up the package containing the ornaments they'd bought at the hardware store. "Because Mr.

Long John doesn't have any decorations for his tree, and we can put ours on it."

"Good idea." There was no point in getting the girls out of their coats just to put them on again. He stowed the rock salt he'd bought on the cabin's porch and followed the girls through the snow to Long John's cabin.

As they climbed the porch steps, there was a rustling sound behind them, and Carson turned and saw Lily approaching, carrying a big shopping bag.

"Yay! He invited you, too!" Sunny jumped up and down.

Carson's heart picked up its pace. Not because of her slender figure and pretty, flushed cheeks, he told himself sternly. Only because he saw the possibility of having his talk with her sooner than he'd expected.

Long John opened the door, and his weathered face broke into a big smile. "What do you know, Rockette, we've got company!"

The dog lumbered to her feet, let out a deep "woof" and nudged at the twins, making them giggle.

Lily smiled down at the scene. "Dogs are such a gift. They make everyone happy."

"You folks didn't need to bring anything," Long John said as he ushered them into his cabin. "I mean this to be my treat, and a chance for you to relax. Come on, hang your coats right on that rack."

Carson turned to help the twins with their jackets and saw that Lily was already unzipping Skye's. He helped Sunny out of hers. Convenient. Two girls, two adults.

"We brought things to decorate your tree!" Sunny cried, twisting free of her jacket and hurtling over to the bag they'd brought. "See, look, there's orderments!"

"*Ornaments*, right, Daddy?" Skye asked.

"Why, they're right pretty," Long John interrupted with a

wink at Carson. "But I would hate to use up the decorations you planned to put on your own tree."

"Go for it," Carson said, at the same time that Skye said, "It's okay." Both girls hurried over to Long John's waist-high, potted Norfolk Island pine.

"Thank you for inviting me," Lily was saying to Long John. She didn't hug him, but she clasped both of his hands.

"I'm just glad you all could come," the older man said, "because I've cooked up enough food for a battalion. I'd be hard-pressed to eat it all myself."

"I brought things to make cookies," Lily said. "If you'll let me mix up the batter and start them baking before dinner, the girls can decorate them afterward. Or take them home to decorate, if the party winds down."

"This party isn't winding down until midnight!" Long John said indignantly.

Lily lifted an eyebrow and tilted her head to one side, the corners of her mouth turning up. "You think you can out-party me? Game on."

She was obviously just joking, but Long John chuckled as he patted Lily's arm, and Carson's heart warmed. He hadn't been sure Lily really wanted to join in the gathering, but she was entering into the spirit of it, being kind to the girls and to Long John.

Long John led Lily to the kitchen area, showing her where things were and opening pots to stir them. A sweet-tart smell, ham baking, filled the air. The girls took turns placing ornaments on the little tree, for once not one-upping each other, but having fun together.

Unexpectedly, Carson's eyes prickled with tears.

This was what he'd wanted for his girls. A warm family Christmas. And if the family wasn't one of blood, well, that didn't matter. What mattered was the caring in their hearts.

He let his eyes close, to keep the tears from spilling, but also to offer up a silent prayer of thanks.

Later in the evening, Lily wiped frosting from the twins' faces, then attempted to clean up the multiple splatters on the kitchen counter. In front of the fire, Long John plucked at his banjo while Carson strung lights on the little Christmas tree.

"Daddy! Mr. Long John! Come see our cookies!" Sunny crowed.

"They're soooooo beautiful," Skye added, admiring the two colorful platefuls.

Lily bit back a laugh. Piled high with frosting, plus sprinkles and colored sugar they'd found at Long John's friend's house next door, the lopsided cookies wouldn't be considered beautiful in any standard sense.

The twins' happy faces, though, made up for any imperfections in the cookies they'd decorated. And the fact that Lily had found a way to help these motherless girls—Pam's girls—have a little more Christmas joy opened a corner of her heart that had long ago closed down.

"Now ain't those the prettiest cookies ever," Long John said, leaning down to admire them. "Do I get to sample one?"

"Choose mine! Mine are on that plate!" Sunny begged.

"Mine are these," Skye said, pointing to the other plate.

"I think I'd like to try one of each," Long John said diplomatically, and a moment later Carson did the same.

"This is the best Christmas ever," Sunny said, and Skye nodded solemnly.

At that, Lily's good warm feelings drained away. This was most assuredly *not* the best Christmas the twins had ever experienced, nor Carson, either. Because Pam wasn't here. She looked uneasily at Carson and caught the stricken expression on his face.

"I don't think I'll make it until midnight after all," she said quickly. "I'm going to head back to my cabin. Thank you for your hospitality." She gave Long John a quick hug and then knelt and did the same for the girls.

Sunny yawned hugely and leaned into Carson's leg, while Skye ran to get Lily a cookie to eat later. Long John scooped ham and vegetables into a plastic container and insisted she take the leftovers along for Christmas dinner tomorrow.

"I'll walk you back," Carson said as she shrugged into her parka.

"No need. You stay with your girls."

"Then I'll watch from the porch to make sure you get there safely," he said, plucking his own parka from the hook.

She couldn't think of an argument against that, so she hurried out onto the porch. And gasped.

Snow blanketed everything—the trees, the fence, the cabins. There had to be six or eight inches.

"Whoa." Carson came to stand beside her, tapping at his phone. "Snow's not letting up anytime soon," he said, holding up his weather app for her to see.

She blew out a sigh. "All the more reason for me to get settled inside. Thanks for driving me to town and…and for sharing your girls."

A small smile tugged at the corner of his mouth. "Thank you for entertaining them. They loved baking cookies." Suddenly, his gaze grew more intense. "They don't remember, but they did it with their mom, too."

"I know. She talked about it." Lily swallowed hard and started down the porch steps, picking her way carefully, but as quickly as possible.

"Lily," he said, and she turned. "Since it looks like we'll be snowed in, I'll stop over tomorrow to make sure you have everything you need," he said.

"Oh, you don't have to—"

"And," he interrupted, his voice decisive, "so we can finish our conversation about Pam."

Chapter Four

The next morning, Carson checked the cinnamon rolls in the oven, inhaling the rich, sweet smell, and then pulled out the hot chocolate mix. So the rolls were from a refrigerator tube and the cocoa was instant. The girls wouldn't care.

He paused to look out the cabin window. The sun was just starting to share its rosy light, illuminating the snowy mountains in the distance. He closed his eyes for a moment's thanks to the Creator: for the majesty outside, for the girls still sleeping in the loft upstairs and, most of all, for the Christ child who'd come into the world to save and bless them all.

He heard a rustle and a giggle upstairs and refocused on his cooking duties. He wanted to make this the best Christmas possible for his girls. Being here at the ranch, away from his computer and work tasks so he could focus on his girls, was a step in the right direction. And last night at Long John's house had been a good start to the festivities. Long John's funny songs and joke-telling had kept the girls laughing, and they'd loved playing with Rockette and decorating Long John's little tree.

And Lily! The way she'd helped the girls decorate cookies had given them such a good time. They'd talked about it, and her, until he'd tucked them into bed around midnight.

The pretty, cryptic woman had held Carson's attention, too. What motivated her to be so nice to the girls and to Long John?

And what did she know about Pam?

Her eyes had looked troubled both times Carson had brought her up. Why?

Was it something so bad she didn't want him to know, or had Pam made her promise secrecy?

Unfortunately, he had an idea of what the secret might be.

He heard another giggle and then some whispering. He poured water into the cups holding instant cocoa mix and pulled the cinnamon rolls out of the oven just in time, then snapped open the little container of sugary frosting and started slathering it on the hot rolls.

His mother's cinnamon rolls had been homemade, yeasty, buttery. He hadn't known how good he'd had it when he was a kid. But now, looking back, he could recognize that his parents had done their best to make Christmas festive and fun for him, even though, as the only child of only children, he hadn't had other kids with whom to share the holiday.

"Daddy!" The wooden ladder from the loft clattered alarmingly, and then the twins galloped across the cabin and flung their arms around him, nearly knocking him over in their enthusiasm.

"Merry Christmas!"

"Did Santa come?"

"Can we get in our stockings?"

"Let's open presents!"

He laughed, wiped his hands and knelt to hug them. "Merry

Christmas, sweeties," he said. "I want you to eat a cinnamon roll first and we'll have a prayer and a little cocoa."

"Daddy!"

"And then, if you cooperate, we'll dig into the stockings."

They groaned but obediently sat down at the little table and held out their hands for a prayer. Carson thanked God for Christ, and their friends, and their family—quickly—and then helped them each to a cinnamon roll.

"These are good, Daddy!" Sunny said through a way-too-big bite.

Carson decided not to correct table manners on Christmas morning. He was just glad to get a little breakfast into the girls before the gift unwrapping madness began.

Of course, considering that they had candy galore in their stockings, he probably should have fixed something without quite so much sugar for breakfast.

But it was Christmas. He took another cinnamon roll himself. He'd work it off shoveling snow later today.

After the girls dumped out their stockings and gleefully examined all the candy and little windup toys and tiny bottles of scented shampoo and lotion and hand sanitizer, it was time for presents.

"Do we *have* to take turns?" Sunny asked.

"We always take turns!" Skye frowned at her sister. "And I think it's *my* turn to go first."

Carson grabbed a candy and put both hands behind his back. "Whoever guesses which hand has a peppermint in it goes first." After Skye guessed correctly, he averted Sunny's fuss by picking out two identical packages. "She'll go first *after* you both open these at the same time."

They ripped eagerly into the gifts and then raved over the pretty, fancily dressed dolls. They'd stretched Carson's budget, but he hadn't been able to resist after seeing the twins' longing faces when they'd shopped in Colorado Springs earlier this month.

While they examined each feature of the dolls and compared their outfits, Carson picked up an ornament one of the girls had knocked off the tree. When he saw which one it was, his heart twisted a little. It was a plastic ball made from a photo: him, Pam, and the girls as babies, all dressed up for Christmas.

He missed that family feeling. Missed the Pam of those days, when she'd been in love with being a mom. In love with him, at least a little bit.

Before she'd gotten restless with the whole package.

Maybe someday he'd be over the feelings of inadequacy and ready to move forward, find a new mom for his girls. Because no matter how happy they seemed now, rummaging under the tree for the next gift, he knew they needed a woman's influence and warmth.

So did he, if the truth be told.

"Open yours, Daddy!" Sunny cried as she handed him a clumsily wrapped gift.

"No, mine!" Skye held out a similar package, but then her face grew thoughtful, and she pulled it back. "You can open hers first," she said, "since I get to open my package first."

"Nice, honey."

"I'm nice, too!" Sunny looked indignant. "I didn't fuss about her getting to open her gift first!"

Yes, Carson could use a partner just to help him handle the mathematics of making sure two little girls got equal time, gifts and love.

He ripped open the tube-shaped package and unrolled a cloth banner, a felt reindeer head with handprints for antlers. "I made it, Daddy," Sunny explained, fitting her hands over the handprints. "Those are my hands. And our teacher said the parents would be happy because our hands would never be the same size again."

"They're gonna grow much bigger," Skye explained. "Here, open mine."

He did, then exclaimed over the slightly neater reindeer Skye had produced, watched her show him how the antler-handprints fit her hands.

"Look on the back, look on the back!" They said it in unison, laughed and fist-bumped each other.

Carson turned both banners over and read the poem out loud.

"This year my hand is little,
But one day, when I'm tall,
This reindeer will remind you
Of the time when I was small."

His throat tightened, and he reached out to hug his daughters to him, one in each arm. "Thank you for the reindeer banners," he managed to choke out. "They're the best gifts I've ever gotten."

It was true. And he needed to remember to embrace this moment, not focus on the past or the future. This Christmas, at Redemption Ranch when the girls were six, would never happen again. One day, he'd look back and long for the sticky kisses and chocolaty handprints and excited bouncing of his twins, who were growing up at a way-too-rapid pace.

He cleared his throat. "Two more gifts for each of you," he said. "Skye, you first."

So Skye ripped into her art set. And then Sunny squealed over her remote-control car. And they both expressed dutiful enthusiasm for their third packages, containing warm winter outfits. It wasn't the extravagant set of gifts some kids got, he knew, but he'd done what he could, within his budget.

Besides, he liked to keep the focus on the real meaning of Christmas.

He stood to get a garbage bag for the wrapping paper scattered all over the floor and realized both twins were looking at him expectantly. "Go ahead," he said, "you play with your new toys. I'll clean up."

"Where is it?" Sunny asked.

"Where's what?"

"The puppy!" they both yelled.

He looked at them, confused. "What puppy?"

"He's joking!" They both hurled themselves at him, tugging his hands. "Daddy, stop joking! Where is it?"

He was getting a really bad feeling. He sank to his knees on the ground, still grasping their hands. "Hold on a minute," he said. "There's not a puppy."

Skye was the first one to realize he was serious. He could tell, because her eyes welled up with tears.

Sunny glanced at her twin, read the expression on her face and started beating her fist against Carson's chest. "There *is* a puppy! There *is*!"

"No, there isn't." He caught Sunny's fist in his hand as a heavy sensation settled around his heart. "No hitting. I don't know where you got the idea you were getting a puppy, but it's not true."

Skye turned to Sunny, hands on hips. "You *said*."

"Miss *Lily* said. And Krissy Morgan's getting a puppy, and her daddy isn't even very nice, so I thought—"

Lily had told them they were getting a puppy?

"Our daddy isn't nice, either," Skye stated. Then she sank to her knees and buried her face in her hands.

"We wanted a puppy," Sunny said, big tears rolling down her face. "We really wanted a puppy."

Carson pulled them both into his arms, his chest aching. "Sometimes we don't get everything we want," he said, trying to soothe them even as the words rang hollow in his own ears. Looking over their heads to the candy wrappers scattered across the floor, he realized that the crash from their sugar high wasn't helping things.

You're the worst father ever.

Pam's words, yelled in anger and quickly retracted, still rang in his ears. He looked at the ceiling. Right now, his angry wife seemed just about right.

Which didn't mean he could lash out or give up. He was the grown-up. "Look," he said, "I'm going to go make us some eggs. Sunny, you can come help me while Skye washes her face, and then you can trade places. After we've had some real breakfast, we'll play a board game or build a snowman."

He went into the kitchen, Sunny trailing mournfully after him. As he got out eggs and broke them and then let her beat them with a fork, he berated himself. He should have realized they'd be hoping for a puppy. It was what they'd been talking about for weeks.

He should have sat them down and talked seriously about what was realistic, rather than just saying "no" and letting his refusal be laughed off.

"I'm sorry you were disappointed, kiddo," he said when Sunny handed him the bowl of beaten eggs. "What are you going to play with first, your doll or your car?"

"I don't care," she said sulkily, but then she added, "Probably the car."

He set butter melting in a pan and then told Sunny to go wash her face. "Send Skye in to help with the toast while you get cleaned up," he said, realizing belatedly that he should have had her wash her hands *before* cooking. Oh, well. Priorities.

A moment later, Sunny came back into the kitchen. "Hey, Daddy."

"Yeah." He turned down the heat and poured the eggs into the frying pan.

"I can't find Skye," she said.

Lily headed down the road that cut across the ranch. It was the only spot where the walking was easy, since some Good Samaritan had already been through to plow the foot and a half of snow that had fallen last night.

She shouldn't have even glanced in the window at Carson and the girls, but their cabin had been lit up like a theater. A theater showing the perfect family Christmas. The girls ripping open their packages, and Carson's hug when he'd opened his; lots of smiles and laughter. The way Christmas should be but rarely was, especially in her experience.

Then again, Carson and the twins didn't have things perfect: missing from the picture was Pam.

And her absence was Lily's fault.

She pushed away that thought and tramped along, her ancient boots crunching on the packed snow and ice. If she stayed here, she'd need to get some new ones.

But what was she thinking? She wasn't going to stay here.

She looked out across the wide-open spaces. The air was so clear that the distant mountains seemed to be cut out of cardboard, so crisp and distinct were the edges of them against the blue sky. The snow sparkled bright, making her wish she'd remembered to bring her sunglasses along. But who would have thought you'd need sunglasses in the dead of winter? Lily associated them with hot Phoenix sun.

Her breath made clouds as she debated whether to go back

and get her sunglasses. It would be more comfortable. And why not? She had nothing else to do on Christmas Day.

No self-pity, she warned herself as she turned to climb back up the road. *Plenty of people have things a lot worse than this.* She'd get her sunglasses and take a nice long walk, then go inside and eat the leftovers Long John had pressed on her last night. In the afternoon, she'd get busy on her project of photographing the dogs. It would be good for them to get the extra attention, and good for her to get a big chunk of her project done. Unlike people, dogs weren't busy with family activities on Christmas—at least shelter dogs weren't.

When she got closer to her cabin, she heard a sound, like a kitten crying. She walked faster, craning to see.

A flash of bright pajamas. One of the twins, huddled by her front door. What in the world?

She ran the rest of the way to her cabin and picked up the little girl. "Honey, you're not wearing your coat! Let's get you back home."

"Can I come in your house?" she asked, sniffling.

"For a minute." It wasn't a bad idea to get a blanket to wrap around the child before carrying her back over to Carson's house. "You're Skye, right?"

The little girl nodded and sat obediently on the couch while Lily found a fleecy blanket to wrap around her. "Does your father know you're here?"

She shrugged.

"He must be worried sick about you. Let's get you back over there." She picked the child up and carried her out onto the porch.

"I wanted a dog so bad." Skye buried her head in Lily's shoulder. "But we didn't get one."

Lily's heart ached as the little girl clung to her. Christmas disappointment was the worst when you were a kid.

"I thought maybe *you* got us a dog," Skye said as Lily shifted her to her opposite side to shut the front door. Man, six-year-olds were heavy.

"You thought what?" she asked absently.

"I thought maybe you got us a dog, because you said..."

Lily closed the cabin door, shifted Skye into a more secure position and started down the steps, careful of her footing. "What did I say?"

"You said, dogs are gifts. And we thought that meant..."

"Oh, honey, no!" Lily's stomach twisted and she hugged the child closer, still walking toward the cabin next door. "I meant dogs are a gift from God, such wonderful companions, but I didn't mean that you'd get a dog as a Christmas present." Trust a child to be literal that way.

Skye buried her head in Lily's shoulder and shook with a couple more sobs as Lily approached the other cabin.

The door burst open, and Carson came out, bundled up, with Sunny right behind him. "Skye!" he cried when he saw her and Lily. He rushed forward and took her from Lily's arms. "Where did you go? I was worried!"

"She was on my porch when I got back from a walk," Lily said. "I wrapped a blanket around her, but she's still shivering." Like she could tell this experienced parent anything about his daughter.

He was already turning back to his cabin. "Let's get you inside."

Lily stopped and watched the trio head into Carson's cabin. Her work was done. She'd get her sunglasses and go back to her walk, which now felt even more solitary.

Had she really made the girls think they'd get a puppy? How awful. Chalk it up to her inexperience with kids. Head down, she turned back toward her cabin.

"Lily!" It was Carson's voice.

She pretended she didn't hear. Cowardly, but she didn't want to be berated for her mistake.

There was the sound of crunching footsteps, and then a small, cold hand clasped hers.

"Daddy wants you to come over to our house," Sunny said, smiling up at Lily. "Will you?"

"Oh, honey, I…"

"He wants to say thank you. And you could look at our new toys. Please?"

No human with a heart could turn down the childish plea in those round eyes, that sweet face. "I'll come over for a few minutes," she said. She'd pay a little visit, confess to Carson about her unfortunate choice of dog-related words yesterday, and ooh and aah over the girls' toys. And then she'd get on with her hike.

Inside the little cabin, Carson sat in a big chair next to the fire, holding Skye. He smiled up at Lily, his eyes crinkling at the corners. "Thank you for helping Skye," he said. "Won't you stay and have some scrambled eggs with us?"

"Oh, I couldn't, I—"

"Have too much else to do?" His eyes were too observant.

"Maybe I do," she snapped, and then felt awful for it. "I'm sorry. I… Sunny mentioned wanting me to see their new toys, but I don't want to intrude on your family Christmas."

"Look at my doll!" Sunny thrust it into Lily's arms. "Come on, help me change her clothes. I got three outfits for her, in the box. Skye's doll only has two, but one of them is a fancy ball gown, so it costed more."

"She's beautiful," Lily said, running her fingers over the doll's furry snow jacket. "Look, her eyes are the same color as yours. And they open and close."

"And her hair's pretty. I'm going to try to keep it pretty,

cuz my other doll's hair is a mess. I washed it with soap, and I wasn't supposed to."

As Sunny prattled on, Lily slipped out of her coat and helped the little girl change her doll's clothes while covertly observing Carson. He was talking seriously to Skye, and she could catch a few of the quiet words. "Careful" and "no leaving without me" and "I was worried."

No yelling, hitting, even scolding. Just a caring, concerned parent.

Pam had been wrong about her husband. How had she been so wrong?

Soon Skye wiggled off her father's lap and came over to join them. Lily glanced back and saw Carson head for the kitchen area. So she looked at Skye's doll and helped with her wardrobe change as well, and pretty soon they were involved in a game of pretend.

"I want a dog!" Sunny made her doll say, poking at the other doll with a stiff, outstretched arm.

"No!" Skye batted the doll's hand away with her own doll. "You can't have one."

"Why not?"

"Because you don't help your daddy enough, and he's busy, busy, busy." The words were spoken by Skye in an adult inflection that made Lily smile a little.

"I'll help more," Sunny's doll said. "I'll clean the floor and take out the garbage and cook—"

"You're not allowed to cook," Skye's doll said, pointing her plastic arm at Sunny. "You're too little."

"*You're* too little!" Sunny's doll cried.

Lily put a finger to her lips. "Quiet dolls get more attention," she said, having no idea where it came from. "And any-age doll can pretend cook, right?"

Both girls frowned thoughtfully. "Then," Skye said, "can we pretend get a dog?"

Oh, boy. Lily didn't want to say the wrong thing again, but both pairs of eyes looked at her expectantly. Amazing how little kids thought adults knew everything.

"Your dolls might be able to get a pretend dog," she said carefully, "as long as you know it's not real. And as long as you don't use it to torture your daddy."

"What's torture?" Skye asked, just as Carson came over from the kitchen area.

Lily looked up at him, afraid she'd really said something wrong, but he just lifted an eyebrow.

"I was exaggerating," she said to the girls. "I only meant that you shouldn't use your pretend dog to bother your father and beg for a real one all the time." She leaned forward and beckoned the little girls closer and whispered, "Bugging him probably won't work at all, but if he sees you play nicely with your pretend dog and do your chores, maybe he'll change his mind."

"Yay!" Both twins jumped up and danced around. "We're getting a dog, we're getting a dog."

"No, I didn't mean—" Lily looked desperately at Carson, whose forehead was wrinkled, the corners of his mouth turned down. "Girls, that—what you're doing right now—that's bugging him and torturing him." She blew out a breath and looked at Carson. "I'm just digging myself in deeper and deeper. I'd better leave while you're still speaking to me."

He chuckled ruefully. "You may as well stay. I have way too much cheesy scrambled eggs for the three of us. And toast, and fruit."

The smells coming out of the kitchen made Lily's stomach growl audibly. "If you're sure."

"I'm sure," he said, giving her a half smile. "Just, please, let's change the subject from dogs, okay?"

"Of course. I'm sorry. I think something I said yesterday was what gave them the impression that they were getting a dog. I'm really sorry. I said 'dogs are a gift' and…"

"And they heard what they want to hear. Welcome to six-year-olds." He clapped his hands. "Girls, I want you to wash your hands and then come to the table. You can show Miss Lily where to wash her hands, too. We all need a little breakfast before we decide what to do with the rest of our day."

After they'd stuffed themselves on breakfast food—including cinnamon rolls left over from their earlier meal—Carson cleared his throat to get the girls' attention. "Let's everyone say one thing they'd like to do on Christmas," he suggested, and Lily nodded approval of his parenting skills. In her own family, no such open communication had happened; the adults had done what they wanted—usually involving drinking—and Lily had taken refuge in drawing and books and, one year, the camera Aunt Penny had sent her in the mail. That wonderful gift had impacted her career decisions both in the military and after.

"I want to go sledding!" Skye cried.

"I want to build a snowman," Sunny said.

They all looked expectantly at Lily. "Ummmmm… I want to go take pictures of the dogs in the barn, for my school project."

"No more dogs," Carson groaned.

"I'm sorry!"

Lily clapped her hands to her mouth as the girls chanted, "The dogs, the dogs!"

She'd done it again. She was causing more trouble in this family.

And this was just superficial stuff compared to what she'd

done to Pam, the girls' mother, Carson's beloved wife. "Hey, listen, I'd better go," she said, and stood. "Thank you for the breakfast."

"Don't go, Miss Lily!" Skye said.

She high-fived each of the girls. "I've got a hike to take, and you've got a snowman to build!" She gave Carson a quick wave, grabbed her coat and headed outside.

She needed to escape before she made more trouble for Carson. And before he roped her into talking about Pam again.

Chapter Five

"Wait!" Carson stood and followed Lily, stopping at the cabin door.

Still on the porch, she turned. She looked over her shoulder, biting her lip, her blue coat bright against a background of diamond-crusted snow.

"I didn't mean you should leave. Visiting the dogs isn't a bad idea." He couldn't believe he was saying that.

But he didn't want Lily to go, and when he examined his reasons, he wasn't entirely sure what they were.

One of them, he reminded himself firmly, was finding out more about Pam's death. Because Carson needed to move on. As the girls got older, he was realizing just how much they needed a mother's touch; witness their clingy behavior toward Lily. Their concerns and issues were getting more complicated, too. He needed a partner in parenting.

The undeniable tug he felt toward Lily reminded him he might need a partner's love and companionship for himself, too.

"I want to go visit Long John and see how his Christmas

is going," Carson said, directing the comment to both Lily and the girls, who were now pressing against his sides. "And then we'll do a little sledding and snowman-building, and then we'll see." He reached out toward Lily, an automatic welcoming gesture.

At least, he thought that was all it was.

She looked at his hand and then at him, and a flush rose to her cheeks.

What did *that* mean?

"We'd be honored if you'd stay and spend more time with us," he said.

The girls pushed their way past him and out the door, tugging at Lily with their surely very sticky hands. "Stay! Play with us today!"

Yes. They needed for Carson to find them a mother figure, and soon. They were attaching themselves to Lily way too much, too soon, and he shouldn't be encouraging it.

After he'd found out what he wanted to know—and tried to offer her some counseling and support, as he'd promised Penny he would—he'd create some natural distance.

And then this Christmastime at the ranch would be over, and they'd go their separate ways.

He shook that thought away as Lily looked searchingly at him. "If you're sure, I'll visit with you for a little while," she said, her voice hesitating. Obviously, she was uncertain of her welcome.

Or was she hiding something? What did she know about Pam?

Thoughts of his wife's flirtatious behavior with other men crowded in, even as he tried to push them away. Had Pam been headed for an assignation with a lover when she'd blundered into enemy fire? Did Lily know something about it, and was she just too kind to tell him?

"Come on, girls—coats and boots and hats and mittens before we can play in the snow," he said, and the flurry of getting them and himself ready, of pulling saucer sleds out of the truck and finding a suitably safe hill for sledding, helped to clear his thoughts.

The safest hill they found sloped down from Long John's cabin, so Lily and Carson stood at the top and watched the girls race each other on their plastic sleds, squealing. Long John came out on his little back deck and waved, but declined their invitation to come down.

"I'm taking it easy today," he said. Code for his Parkinson's acting up, Carson suspected.

"Are you sure?" Lily smiled at the older man. "It's a beautiful day. We can come up and help you."

"No, thanks. I'm just going to stay inside and watch my birds." Long John gestured toward the seed-and-peanut-butter pinecones he'd hung all around the porch. Nuthatches and warblers darted and flew around them.

Long John waved and went inside. A moment later he appeared in his chair by the window, where he could watch his birds and the girls, too.

"He's good at making a life for himself," Lily said thoughtfully. "We could all learn something from him."

"That's true." They walked over a few feet to where there was a big rock to perch on. A couple of ponderosa pines loomed behind them, and Lily looked up. "They're so beautiful," she said. "I love the green against the blue sky and the snow."

A bit of nature lore emerged from somewhere in the back of his brain. "Smell the trunk of the tree," he urged her.

"*Smell* it?"

He nodded, and gamely she walked up to the trunk and sniffed. Her face lit up. "Butterscotch?"

"Or vanilla. It's the only tree that smells like cookies."

"That's so cool!" Her cheeks were pink and just for a minute she looked carefree and delighted.

Carson couldn't take his eyes off her.

She flushed and looked away. Then she frowned up at Carson. "Hey, I'm sorry I contributed to that mess with the dogs. I shouldn't have even mentioned dogs to the girls. I hated to see them so upset."

"They've rebounded quickly." Carson gestured toward the twins as they reached the top of the little slope, tugging their plastic sleds, and then plopped down together to slide down the hill again. "Don't blame yourself. I feel bad about not getting them the present they really wanted, but the truth is, I'm hard-pressed to manage our home life already. Taking care of a puppy is beyond me."

"You seem like you're doing a great job."

"Thank you." He hesitated as a natural way into a difficult conversation came to him. "Did Pam say anything to you about how I was as a father?"

Lily looked at him quickly and then looked away. "Not really," she said, her voice uneasy.

"How well did you and Pam know each other?" he pressed. "From what she said, you were pretty close." In fact, he'd gotten a completely different impression of Lily from Pam than how she was now. Pam had made it sound like she was a drinker and partier, wilder even than Pam herself.

The woman beside him didn't match that description at all. Could she have changed that much? Or had Pam been wrong?

"Miss Lily! Come sledding!"

"Okay!" Lily slogged through the snow toward them without a glance back at Carson, which left him wondering: What would have been her answer to his question?

★ ★ ★

Later that afternoon, Lily sat wrapped in a snug fleece blanket in a comfortable chair in her cabin, trying to read a Christmas book.

The picture on the cover, a snow-covered Victorian home all decorated for Christmas, matched the sweet story, and normally she'd have been swept away. But her eyes kept drifting to the window and the scene outside.

Carson and the twins were building a snowman, laughing and shouting. They'd gotten one giant ball on top of the other to form the snowman's body and now were rolling a smaller ball for the head.

She watched Carson kneel to help the girls pat more snow into place. He was a good man, a good dad. When he'd asked her how well she and Pam had known each other, what Pam had said about him, she hadn't wanted to tell him. Still didn't.

It was hard to understand why Pam had misled her so badly. Why had Pam wanted her to think she had an abusive husband? Was it possible that Carson used to be that way? After all, Lily herself had done a 180-degree turnaround in the past few years. Maybe Carson had, too.

But watching his gentleness with his girls, noticing the way he interacted with Long John and his parishioners, it was simply impossible to imagine that he'd ever been the bully of Pam's vivid stories.

Maybe she *should* tell him the truth. Was it worse to mislead someone, or to knowingly hurt them?

This morning, the opportunity to ride a sleigh down the hill with the girls had come as a welcome interruption. When Carson had approached her again, she'd pleaded cold and work and gone inside.

But it bothered her. She and Pam had started out so close.

Notorious for being the most party-happy females on the base, they'd spent a lot of time together in all sorts of conditions.

Which made the way things had ended even worse.

And if there had been a sense of betrayal between Lily and Pam, how much worse would Pam's final actions feel to Carson, her husband?

Lily should have found a better way to handle the whole situation. Should have sat down in a friendly way with Carson and told him, "Look, here's what Pam said, here's what happened."

Lily couldn't figure out a way to do that without hurting Carson in the process. And a selfish part of her didn't want to admit her own role, to destroy forever the warm way he'd looked at her.

A knock on the door, followed by a high, piping "Miss Lily!" pulled her out of her low thoughts.

She hurried over and opened the door, and the sight of Sunny and Skye made her smile. "Hi, girls! How's the snowman coming along?"

"He's getting real big!" Skye said, pointing.

"But we need help," Sunny added. "Do you have a carrot for his nose?"

She looked over their heads to where Carson was shoveling, but he didn't glance their way. Did he know the girls were here? Had he encouraged them to come?

"I do have a carrot," she said slowly. "Come on inside and I'll get it for you."

They came inside but stayed on the mat by the door. "Your cabin is a lot like ours," Skye said. "And you like to read, too, just like Daddy!"

"Does your dad read to you?" she asked as she pulled a couple of carrots from her refrigerator.

"Uh-huh. Right now, he's reading us a Christmas book

called *The Story of Holly and Ivy*, about a little girl who doesn't have a family."

"It's sad," Skye said, "but Daddy promised us it will have a happy ending. Will you come out and help us finish our snowman?"

Lily made a pretense of washing the carrots while she pondered. She wasn't exactly enjoying her solitary time in the cabin, and she'd been watching the progress of the snowman with interest. It was beautiful and sunny out, and she'd love to get a little more fresh air.

And company, she realized. Seeing Carson and his girls made her aware of the family she didn't have.

But she didn't need to get any more involved with them. Didn't need to hear any more of Carson's questions, nor struggle more to conceal the truth.

She turned toward the girls, and the sight of the two eager faces swayed her resolve to stay inside. "Here you go," she said.

"Won't you come?"

Inspiration hit. "I'll bring my camera," she said, "and take some of the family photos I'm supposed to do. We'll do some today and some tomorrow. That way, we'll have different lights and clothes."

And she'd have a barrier between herself and Carson. The camera could be a friend that way, giving her something to do and allowing the right amount of distance from people.

She pulled on her coat and mittens and boots and followed the girls outside, inhaling the fresh, cold air. Notes of pine and spruce added to the holiday feeling, and sun sparkled off the snow.

You couldn't doubt the existence of God when you saw His amazing handiwork.

She picked up Skye and let her poke the carrot in for the nose, noticing that she had a tiny mole on her cheek. Then she lifted up Sunny to put in the chocolate-cookie eyes Carson had brought out. This close, she could see that Sunny had a tiny scar in her hairline.

So they weren't identical, and Lily felt satisfied knowing that she could tell them apart, even if they were sleeping.

Although, why would that be of interest to her? It wasn't as if she were going to be involved with this family after the holidays.

"So they talked you into coming out again?" Carson's deep, friendly voice behind her danced along her nerve endings.

She held up her camera like a shield. "I thought I'd get some of the family photos done today," she said, "if that's okay with you."

"We're not exactly dressed up for the occasion," he said. "I ought to at least comb their hair. And mine," he added, forking fingers through his already mussed hair.

Lily shook her head. "You're all rosy and active and happy. These will be great pictures. We'll do dress-up clothes by the fireplace tomorrow."

"If you're sure." He looked at her just a little longer than was necessary.

She broke her gaze away and studied her camera, making small adjustments, taking deep breaths. It must be the season that was giving her these odd feelings about Carson. She wasn't one to get all fluttery around a man.

Carson tied a scarf around the snowman's neck and then lifted the girls, one in each arm, to place his hat. Lily snapped photo after photo as they laughed and adjusted it. She could tell already that these would be a delight, much more appealing than anything posed.

"Come here, Miss Lily, let Daddy take your picture with us!"

Lily glanced at Carson to see him looking at her with his

head cocked to one side. Was he thinking that it was inappropriate for her, a stranger, to be in a photo with his girls? Or that he'd like to see it?

He held out his phone. "I'll just use this," he said. "Your camera looks too high-tech for me."

So she knelt beside the snowman, one girl on either side of her, and let him take pictures. As the girls laughed and mugged for the camera, she couldn't help joining in. They were irresistible, these two sweethearts.

"Did you ever make snow angels?" she asked them.

They both frowned and shook their heads. "Show us how!"

So she lay down and moved her arms and legs, showing them how to make angels in the snow. Then she helped each of them do the same.

"I'm going to call my angel Miss Lily!" Sunny said.,

Skye looked thoughtful. "I'm going to call mine Mommy," she said, "because our mommy would think they were pretty. Only, she can't see them, because she's in heaven."

The words made Lily's breath catch, and she glanced at Carson. His mouth had twisted to one side as he studied her and the girls.

Grief and shame pushed at her, but she didn't get to wallow in her feelings, not when there were little girls to watch out for. She knelt and gave Skye a quick hug, then reached to have Sunny join in. "Your mommy just might be smiling from heaven to see your snow angels," she said, "and that's nice you're naming yours after her. But it's sweet you named one after me, too."

Both girls clung on a little longer than she expected and she felt her chest tighten. Such dear children. They shouldn't have lost their mother. *Oh, Pam, why did you do what you did? How could you leave your girls motherless?*

"Why don't you make two more snowmen? Little ones, twin kids," Carson suggested.

"Yeah!"

"Will you help?"

"I wonder if you can figure out how to do it yourself, now that you've had some practice?" Carson asked.

Hmm. Good parenting, or a desire to talk to Lily apart from the girls, especially now that Pam had figured so prominently in the conversation?

She supposed it was inevitable, so she brushed snow off her jacket and went to stand beside him. For a moment, they watched the girls argue about how to get started, and then Lily heard a sharp tapping, like a rapid drum. "What's that?" she asked.

He looked around and then pointed. "There," he said.

"Where?"

He came closer so she could look along his arm to his pointing finger, and she caught a whiff of his spicy aftershave. "See the bird?" he asked.

She saw it then, a small black, gray and white creature with a bright red spot on its head.

It seemed to notice them, for it stopped drilling, cocked its head and offered a quiet *pik-pik-pik-pik*.

"Downy woodpecker," he volunteered.

She studied him. "How come a pastor knows so much about the outdoors?" she asked.

He laughed, a little self-consciously. "I was an only child. Spent a lot of time outdoors with my grandpa, and he taught me the names of the trees and the birds." He laughed. "Pretty geeky, huh?"

"I think it's cool," she said. "When I was a kid, Aunt Penny sent me this deck of card-like things, birds of the Plains. I went all over my street and the fields nearby, trying to identify stuff."

He smiled, started to say something, shook his head.

"What?"

"We have some things in common. Things Pam and I didn't."

She didn't answer, afraid to walk onto that dangerous ground.

"You know," he said as the girls worked together on twin snowmen, "Pam made some mistakes. I know that."

She held her breath. What did he mean?

"You wouldn't be hurting her memory if you told me she had a boyfriend, and that somehow contributed to her getting shot."

She stared at him.

"I wasn't what she wanted. She told me. I wasn't exciting enough for her."

Lily blew out a breath. On the one hand, she knew what Carson was talking about. Pam had been a seeker, never satisfied with what she had, always wanting more.

But Carson was such an amazing man. How would any woman married to him want someone else?

Yes, Pam had been a flirt, and it had made Lily uncomfortable because Pam was married. But she'd never taken it far, and she'd laughed when Lily had questioned her actions. "I'm married, not dead!" she would say.

It had bothered Lily even more toward the end of Pam's time. When Pam had been drifting further and further away from Lily, when their lives had gone such different directions.

Once Lily had started studying the Bible, she'd realized that sins of thought and feeling counted, just like sins of action.

Raising those ideas with Pam, though, had been the beginning of the end of their friendship.

Carson was looking at her with calm expectation. How could a husband be that calm about the notion that his wife might have cheated on him?

"I mean, look at today," he said. "My girls wanted a puppy, and did I get them one? No. Because I'm boring and no fun, just like Pam said."

"Not true," she said firmly. "You know what you can handle and what's right for your family." She hesitated, wondering how much to say. But at least she could reassure him on one score. "She didn't have a boyfriend, Carson. If she had, she would've told me."

"I just keep trying to understand it," he said. "She wasn't supposed to be in the line of fire. And you knew… Did you know? She was expecting a baby."

"What?" She stared at him, his words echoing crazily in her ears.

Pam had been expecting a baby?

Expecting a baby.

A new wave of guilt washed over her, stealing her breath. By not saving Pam, Lily had deprived this family of a precious new member.

She knew, as a Christian, she was forgiven. *But for this, Lord? How can I be forgiven for this?*

"You didn't know?"

She shook her head. That made everything so much worse. "Look," she said desperately, "I'm so sorry. Sorry for your loss." She blew out a breath. She was going to lose it here. "It's been great to hang out with you guys, but I'm getting cold, and you need to spend time as a family. Take care, Carson." She gave him a little wave and headed off toward her cabin.

After his conversation with Lily—and her abrupt departure—Carson felt like the girls needed some quiet time. And

Carson needed some advice on how to get the truth out of Lily. You and Rockette up for a visit? he texted Long John.

Come on over, was the reply.

Moments later, the girls were settled in front of a Christmas movie with the ever-patient Rockette while Long John and Carson, bundled up, examined the splintered porch.

They talked beams and nails and braces for a few minutes, and then Carson dived in. "What would you do if you wanted to know something and you knew somebody knew about it, and they wouldn't tell you?"

"Sounds like a puzzle." Long John's forehead wrinkled as he studied Carson. "Is this about Lily?"

How had the older man guessed so quickly? He nodded. "Uh-huh."

"I'd ask myself why. What could that person stand to lose?"

Carson shook his head. "I can't imagine. I've told her I understand that Pam was...or rather, that she wasn't..." He bit off the sentence.

Compassion spread over Long John's face. "I'd also ask myself," he said, "if I really wanted to know whatever truth that person was hiding."

Did he? "Yes," Carson said, "I think I do. I need to know so I can move on."

Long John picked up a handful of nails and began to sort them by size. "You sure you're not the one running away?" he asked. "If you've made this a barrier to getting involved with anyone else, well..." He didn't look at Carson but laid the nails down in a line, neat despite the Parkinson's tremor in his hands.

"I just..." Carson started pulling the rotting board from the porch, using the claw of the hammer. "If you've been married and it didn't go well, you ought to take a look at what happened. Especially when there are two little ones involved in any mistakes you might make."

"True enough," Long John said.

They were silent for a couple of minutes, Long John handing him nails as he moved down the new board, hammering. Then the older man said, "Sometimes, you have to turn to the Lord. Ever think about that?"

The words hit Carson like a hammer bigger than the one he held in his hand. "You shouldn't have to tell me that. Some preacher I am." He ought to be counseling Long John, not the other way around.

"Sometimes the doctor needs a doctor," Long John said. "You're young. Maybe too young to realize that moving on from what's hurt you in the past isn't always a matter of finding out every detail."

"But I want to know." Carson pounded in a nail with punishing force. And then another one. And then he glanced up to see Long John watching him steadily.

I'm angry, he realized. *But at whom?*

The sound of a car engine and tires crunching on snow were a welcome distraction. A big SUV pulled to a halt and one of his parishioners, Minnie Patton, climbed out.

Carson's heart sank a little, but he overcame it quickly. "Hello, Minnie," he called.

"The last thing I need is a visit from General Patton," Long John muttered beside him.

Carson swallowed a smile. He knew a number of church members called Minnie "The General," and it wasn't only because of her surname.

"I heard you were up here alone," Minnie said to Long John as she opened the back door of the SUV.

"He's not alone, Minnie," said a voice from the passenger

seat. Beatrice, Minnie's younger sister, was a sweet woman who rarely got a word in edgewise.

Minnie pulled a large casserole dish from the back seat. "You shouldn't be out here in the cold," she scolded as she approached Long John.

"And Merry Christmas to you, Minnie," Long John said with a hint of sarcasm in his voice. "I'm going to say hello to your sister." His glance at Carson was eloquent: *save me.*

Carson watched as Long John greeted Beatrice, who lowered the window with a smile. Even from here, Carson could see the scarf that covered Beatrice's bald head, her pale, thin face. Chemo had been hard on her, and not the least of it was that she'd had to move in with Minnie.

As she looked up at Long John, though, Beatrice's eyes sparkled, and her thin face curved into a smile.

Carson shoved down a sigh as General Patton—Minnie—approached. "Merry Christmas," he said, shaking her hand.

"It would be merrier if you were down in town instead of up here vacationing like a man of leisure," she said. "What if someone in your congregation falls ill?"

The ones who need love the most are the hardest to love. "If someone from the church has a problem, I'll come down to town, of course. Let me help you with that casserole."

"I'll take it inside," she said, turning to block him from taking it from her. She was obviously planning to go in the house. Which presented its own set of problems, because the girls very distinctly didn't like Miss Minnie. Carson couldn't blame them; no one liked being called "poor little motherless things."

"Long John," Carson called, still standing in Miss Minnie's path, "what would you like us to do with this casserole?"

"Well, obviously," Minnie said, "I'm going to take it inside and heat it up and dish it out." She looked back at Long

John, and for the first time, hesitancy came into her voice and manner. "If you'd like, John," she said, "I could stay and eat with you."

Long John glanced down at Beatrice, reached for her hand and squeezed it. Then he came over to where Minnie and Carson were engaged in a standoff, him blocking the way to the house and her trying to get past him, and both of them trying to smile.

"Minnie," Beatrice called, her voice gentle, "it's getting colder. I think we should head on home."

"But—"

Long John took the casserole dish. "Thank you kindly," he said. "I'll enjoy this tonight and for the rest of the week. For now, though, I'm going to take a nap."

Minnie turned to Carson as if to get his support.

"I'm sure you understand Long John's need to rest," he said gently. "It was kind of you to bring him food. The true spirit of Christmas."

She narrowed her eyes and tilted her head as if trying to gauge his sincerity. Then she turned her palms up, spun and marched back to the SUV.

Carson and Long John waved to Beatrice and then watched the two women drive away.

"Close call," Long John said. Then he winked at Carson. "Sometimes it's the quiet ones who have something to offer. You remember that."

Carson lifted an eyebrow. "Something going on with you and Beatrice?"

"I wish," Long John said. "Maybe I was referring to our new friend Lily. Penny tells me your first wife was the dramatic sort. That Lily, though, she has a lot going on underneath."

Carson didn't answer. What could he say?

"You're not the only one who has things to deal with in the past," Long John persisted. "At least according to what Penny told me, Lily has had it rough."

That made Carson wince. He'd been so preoccupied with Lily's secrets about Pam that he'd neglected to offer her the pastoral counseling Penny had requested he do.

As he headed inside to collect the girls, he resolved that he'd make progress toward that before the day was out.

Chapter Six

As the sun set on Christmas Day, Lily walked toward her cabin, tired but feeling better.

Photographing the dogs for her school project had been fun. She'd posed one of the dogs near an old tractor in the barn, and another on a plaid blanket she'd found. Two big dogs, a black Lab and an Irish setter mix, had gotten in a play fight when she'd let them out into the fenced area. She'd taken photo after photo, knowing they'd look amazing against the snow with the mountains in the background.

Keeping busy with the dogs had helped to distract her from the news that Pam was pregnant when she'd died. That was what her therapist said to do when the past threatened to overwhelm her. Distract, and think about something else, something positive.

She'd memorized a Bible verse from Philippians about that, during her darkest days, and now she recited it in a whisper. "Whatsoever things are true, whatsoever things are honest, whatsoever things are just, whatsoever things are pure, whatsoever things are lovely, whatsoever things are of good report; if there be any virtue, and if there be any praise, think on these things."

Right now, the lovely things in her mind consisted of the hot bath she planned to take. The novel she'd read until she dozed off.

A lot of people were facing cranky kids and a big mess right about this time on Christmas. Lily, on the other hand, had pleasant time to herself. She'd revel in it and push away the sad information about Pam and the tug she'd felt toward family life, courtesy of Carson and the twins.

As she passed Long John's cabin, the front door burst open and Carson emerged. He was carrying a sleepy-looking Skye and had Sunny by the hand.

"You sure you want to take them along?" Long John was asking from the doorway.

"I think it's best." Carson's voice was tense, and when she looked more closely at his face, she saw deep vertical creases between his brows.

He glanced over at Lily, gave a quick, distracted wave, and then his phone buzzed. He held it to his ear and talked in short bursts, his forehead wrinkling tighter.

Something was wrong. As Carson hurried the girls toward their cabin, Lily stayed behind, looking up at Long John. "What happened?"

Long John leaned on his porch railing. "Someone from the church tried to take her own life today. She's in the hospital, and the rest of her family is having trouble coping."

"Oh, how awful!" Lily's chest ached for them. "On Christmas. Wow."

Long John nodded. "The family called Carson, and of course, he's going down to pray with them."

"I wonder if there's any way I could help. Maybe I can watch the girls for him."

Long John shook his head. "I offered, but he says he's going to take them down. They'll visit with their friend—this woman, she has a little boy, Gavin, who's six—while Carson talks to the husband and grandparents."

Lily sucked in a breath. Exposing the twins to a situation that was hard for adults to understand just didn't seem right. She waved to Long John and then hurried after Carson, reaching him as he was ushering the girls into the car. "Hey, hold up a minute."

"Emergency with one of our church families." He closed the truck's back door as the girls strapped themselves in. "I have to get to town."

"It's about that." She stepped in front of him as he headed for the driver's seat. "Long John told me what happened. If being at the hospital will upset the girls, I'd be glad to watch them up here."

He forked fingers through his hair. "I'd love that, except that the girls overheard some details, and they're insisting on going. It's their friend's mom, you see. And they...well, because of Pam, they tend to get sort of anxious in any kind of family emergency, and they don't like to be away from me. I just..." He threw up his hands, looking frazzled. "I just think it's better I take them."

"Then let me come," Lily said impulsively. "I can watch out for them, feed them, whatever you need." She owed Pam's family any help she could offer.

His eyebrows lifted. "You'd do that for me?"

"Of course."

A little bit of the tension eased from his shoulders. "That would be great."

So they headed to town, Carson driving smoothly and

safely, but fast. He allowed the girls to watch a movie in the back of the vehicle, apparently a rare treat, and they both wore headphones and were soon rapt.

"So, can you tell me what happened?" she asked after ascertaining that the girls were engrossed and not listening.

He shook his head. "This is a family that's been having some hard times," he said. "She lost her job, and she's been separated from her husband for a while. Money was tight this Christmas and…well, for some people, the holidays aren't happy." He sighed. "Honestly, I don't understand it myself. But I'll provide what comfort I can."

"That must be hard," she said while her mind raced. "Is she all right?"

"She's going to be. But it's hard for her family," Carson said. "I've only been in this situation a few times before, but I know people tend to blame themselves."

"They do." She felt like Carson was talking to her directly.

He swerved to avoid a branch lying on the road and then turned the car away from Esperanza Springs. "This is a regional hospital that serves several communities here. I'm not too familiar with it, but hopefully, they'll have a playroom or something for the kids to do."

Once out of the car, the twins clung to Carson, and Lily saw what he'd meant about unusual situations scaring them. Gone were the confident little girls who'd run all over the ranch. In their place were scared, nervous, teary kids.

Carson located the family in the waiting room and then turned to the twins. "I'm going to need to talk with the grown-ups for a little while," he said. "You can say hello, and then Miss Lily will help you and Gavin find somewhere to play quietly."

The little girls nodded, eyes wide.

Inside the small, dim waiting room, a gray-haired couple

who must be the poor woman's parents, and a distraught-looking man—her estranged husband, maybe?—stood talking while a little boy hunched over a phone game in the corner.

Lily watched as Carson waded in. With his quiet questions and a hug for the older couple, he changed the atmosphere in the room.

Lily's heart squeezed, watching him. He'd confided to her that he didn't know what to do, and yet he was acting sure of himself, just what people needed in a pastor.

But while the adults' tension noticeably decreased with Carson's words, the children's didn't. The little boy abandoned the phone he'd been playing with and ran to bury his head in the man's leg, confirming Lily's impression that this was the boy's father. Sunny and Skye clung to Carson's hands.

Time to take action. She stopped a passing aide. "Is there a play area for children who are visiting?"

He shook his head. "The only thing we've got is an area for the siblings of patients in our children's ward."

"Could the kids play there for a little while?"

"You'll have to ask the nurses in that area."

Lily thought about it. Lots of the hospitalized kids were most likely home for Christmas, along with their siblings. And this situation was unusual, an emergency. A little boy desperately needed a distraction.

She went back into the waiting room and sat on the edge of a chair, gesturing to the twins. "Skye, Sunny," she said. "Would you like to go exploring? We can stop and get some hot chocolate in the cafeteria." She didn't want to promise them a play area if one wasn't forthcoming.

"Okay." Both girls nodded, but they also seemed reluctant to let go of Carson.

She beckoned them in, as if to listen to a secret. "Go talk

to Gavin and ask him to come," she said, "while I speak to his daddy."

They nodded and hurried over to the little boy while Lily introduced herself to Gavin's father. She explained what she was doing and where they'd be, so intent on helping that she forgot that she was a stranger in this community and inexperienced with kids.

The distraught father looked down at his son, who was now asking if he could go along. He lifted his hands, palms up. "Okay, um, sure, if Sunny and Skye are going."

As she turned to shepherd the children out of the room, she felt a hand on her shoulder. Carson. Heat rose in her face as she turned. "Thank you," he said, his eyes crinkling as they looked directly into hers. "That's just what they need."

Okay. She officially had a crush on this man. "You have my cell number, right?"

"Give it to me," he said, and she typed it into his phone.

He squeezed her hand briefly as he took the phone back, and Lily's heart rate accelerated.

They found the playroom, and when Lily explained the situation to a passing nurse, she readily opened it. Soon the children were oohing and aahing over the new-to-them toys, and Lily had a chance to think.

She really, really liked Carson. She had to acknowledge it now. But that just made things more complicated.

Because what if the unexpected happened, and he wanted a relationship with her? What if they got involved?

She'd have to tell him the truth about Pam and what had happened. Even she, who wasn't especially experienced with or good at relationships, knew that having a secret like that at the center would destroy anything they attempted to build.

But telling him would hurt him terribly. Even worse than she'd initially thought, given that Pam had been pregnant.

Lily watched the twins help their friend put together a race-track for some little plastic cars.

Pam should have tried harder.

As soon as she had the judgmental thought, she pushed it away. Pam must have been going through so much pain. And yes, she'd masked it with lots of partying—partying that, Lily realized now, had put her unborn child in jeopardy—but pain was pain, and Lily knew from her father that drinking was more of a symptom than a base problem. It was a way to self-medicate.

Poor, poor Pam.

If only Lily had paid more attention, tried to find ways to help her.

Pushing away her own dark thoughts, Lily focused on the children playing at her feet and realized that little Gavin was running over a small plastic figure with his race car, over and over.

"Gavin, stop!" Skye put out a hand to protect the battered figurine.

"No!" Gavin pushed her hand away and ran over the doll again.

"You're hurting her!" Skye started to cry.

That got Sunny's attention away from her own race car. "Gavin, quit it!"

Lily sank to the floor in the midst of the children. "Hey. Let's play nice with the cars."

"This lady doesn't want to be alive," Gavin insisted, running his car into the doll again.

Out of my depth here. Why had Lily thought she'd be able to help this poor child? "Hey, Gavin," she said, "let's go see what we can cook on the stove. What's your favorite food?" She waved an arm to the plastic kitchen set.

"Don't wanna cook," Gavin said, turning his back to all of them.

Skye and Sunny looked more distressed.

"Girls," Lily said, "I'm going to give you a job. Please cook a pretend meal for all four of us and set the table. Gavin and I are going to talk a little, and then we'll come eat whatever you've fixed for Christmas dinner."

"Okay," Sunny said doubtfully. "Come on, Skye."

"He was hurting my doll," Skye said, hands on hips.

Lily gave her a stern look and pointed at the stove. To her amazement, it worked.

The girls occupied, she turned back to Gavin, who was still banging his car into the doll. She was no psychologist, but she'd had some bad Christmases and some childhood struggles. "Christmas wasn't much fun this year, huh?" she said, picking up a car and running it aimlessly along the track.

"No!" He banged the doll hard with his car.

"I guess that makes you mad," she said.

"Mommy didn't get me any presents," he said, his lower lip out. And then suddenly, big tears welled up in his eyes. "I yelled at her and she almost died!"

Her heart constricted as she realized that he was blaming himself. Should she hug him, pull him into her arms? But she barely knew him. She reached out and patted his arm instead. "Sometimes grown-ups do things that are hard to understand," she said, "but what happened to your mom isn't your fault."

"I yelled at her a *lot*," he confessed, more tears rolling down his cheeks. "And then she went into her room and shut the door and then the amb'lance came and took her to the hospital."

Hard to argue with a six-year-old's concept of cause and effect, but she had to. "I yelled at my mother sometimes," she said. It was no exaggeration; she'd been awful as a teenager.

"I feel really sorry about it, but parents understand. Kids are allowed to get mad."

There was a rustle beside her, and Skye came and knelt beside Gavin, patting his back. "I yelled at my daddy two days ago," she said. "And Sunny yells at him *all the time*."

"Did he die from it?" Gavin asked, gulping through tears.

"No. He's strong."

"Kids yelling never makes adults die," Lily said firmly. "And your mommy is going to be okay. There are good doctors here who will help her feel better."

"Aunt Biddy said I might have to go away," he whispered, looking anxiously at Lily.

Lily felt like throttling Aunt Biddy. "Do you ever stay with your daddy?" she asked.

He nodded. "Wednesdays and Saturdays," he said.

"Hmm. Do you ever stay longer with him, like if your mom is sick?"

He nodded. "When Mommy was going to have a baby, I stayed with him a lot. But then she didn't have a baby after all."

Oh.

A miscarriage. Hormonal fluctuations. Christmas. Her heart went out to the poor woman who'd been in enough pain to overdose on pills.

"Maybe you'd stay with your daddy again for a while," she said, thinking of the man who'd agreed for her to bring Gavin down here. He'd seemed kind and concerned. But she didn't want to promise Gavin anything. You didn't make promises to kids unless you could keep them.

"When our mommy was gone at Christmas," Skye volunteered, "we made her cards."

Bless the child. "Let's go eat our pretend Christmas dinner," Lily said, "and then we'll make cards for your mom. I bet that will cheer her up a lot."

"Okay," Gavin agreed, and went gamely over to the table to partake of the plastic food Sunny had arranged.

A short time later, she heard the sound of a throat clearing at the half door, and Lily looked over and saw Carson. Since the children were occupied at the little table, she went over to stand by him. "How are things going?"

He ran a hand through his hair, mussing it. "Not great. She's stable, but the rest of the family is struggling to understand what happened." He nodded toward the children. "Looks like you did a better job with them than I did with the adults."

"I'm sure that's not true."

"I have a hard time with this particular issue," he said. "Especially talking to the survivors. Even the attempt is such a slap in the face to them."

Lily's stomach turned over. "Sometimes," she said, because she felt like she needed to say something, "people think their families will be better off without them."

Carson gestured at the children. "How could any mother think her child would be better off without her? How could Hannah—" He gestured toward the other wing of the hospital. "How could she plan to leave her son alone in the world?"

Lily let her head drop and stared at the floor. "I don't know, Carson," she said. "I just don't know."

He hadn't done enough, Carson berated himself as he exited the hospital behind Lily and the girls.

The three of them swung their linked hands, and Carson was torn between enjoying the fun they were having, worrying about the girls' attachment to Lily and wishing he were better at helping people dealing with such an incomprehensible situation.

A group of carolers approached the nursing home next door, and Carson recognized several of them from his church. So did the girls. "Can we go see Renee and Jackson?" Sunny asked, poised to run.

"If you walk on the sidewalk," he said.

The girls took off, walking rapidly, and he watched until he could see that Jackson's mother had greeted the girls and waved at him.

Lily stood beside him. "You okay?" she asked.

He shrugged. "Wish I'd done a better job in there," he said. "I had a hard time finding the right words, either for Hannah or her family. Like I said, it just doesn't make sense to me. How could a young mother with everything to live for try to take her own life?"

Lily's throat worked as she looked at him, distress obvious on her face. He wasn't impressing her, but he couldn't seem to stop himself from confiding. She was such a good listener.

"The truth is, ministers are just people," he continued on, because it helped to talk about it all. "Good at some things and not at others. Some are great preachers but can't do counseling. Some do beautiful funerals. Some are great with the sick, others with kids."

"You seem like you're good at most things."

That she thought so made him happier than it should, so he pulled himself back to earth. "Not what went down in there."

"How'd you leave the situation with them?" she asked.

He reflected. "Actually, her husband, who's been estranged, seems to want to help her, maybe even try to save their marriage. I think the potential loss of her hit him hard. As well, the impact it would have on his son."

"That's good," she said. "And I'll bet you set up counseling for the woman, right?"

He nodded. "Not just now, but into the future awhile."

"Then those are some good outcomes," she said. "Maybe their marriage will pull through." She thought a minute, then added, "My parents had a whole lot of ups and downs, but they stayed together until the end. Marriage isn't easy."

"True," he said. He paused, then added, "Pam and I... I don't know if she told you, but we had our share of problems."

She opened her mouth and shut it again.

He was about to say more when the carolers started yelling for his attention.

"Hey, Pastor C!" Jessie Malton called. "Why don't you join us?"

"Yeah, come sing!" another added.

Carson glanced over at her, then lifted his hands, palms up. Truthfully, he'd welcome the chance to be in a situation where he felt more comfortable and competent. He walked over toward the carolers, Lily trailing beside him. "What are you guys doing? Where are you headed?"

"Singing at the nursing home," Vance Richards said. "We could use your baritone."

"Can we go, Daddy?" Skye tugged at one of his hands, making puppy-dog eyes up at him.

"Please?" Sunny did the same.

He glanced over at Lily. "Do you mind staying in town a little longer? It might be fun for the girls."

And help them forget the sadness of the hospital.

She nodded, smiling her understanding. "It's fine, just as long as I'm not expected to carry a tune."

They followed the group inside, and as everyone got organized and lined up the kids, he found himself off to one side with Lily. He touched her arm. "Look," he said, "I'm sorry I've been talking so much about Pam. I didn't mean to push you to tell me every detail of your friendship. I feel like I haven't been much of a pastor to you."

She waved a hand. "You have no obligation to me."

Conveniently ignoring his comment about Pam, but he

wasn't going to focus on that anymore tonight. He did wonder, though, why she was so dismissive of her own needs and concerns. If he got the chance, he'd follow up with her.

For now, they followed the carolers into the rec room, where a large Christmas tree stood in the corner. Residents, some in wheelchairs, others helping to decorate the tree, looked up and waved. One man who was slumped in a chair, apparently asleep, lifted his head at the excited voices of the children.

The staff wore Santa hats and reindeer antlers, and several of the residents sported Christmas sweaters. Above the sound of a woman's rattling coughs, Carson heard violin music and looked toward the corner of the room where a frail, elderly man played with beauty and grace.

There were the usual nursing home smells, and he watched his girls to see that they were doing okay, weren't going to blurt out something rude. But they seemed a bit in awe of the new environment, and the scent of pine branches predominated as they moved farther into the room, near the large live Christmas tree.

They sang several carols, and the elders and some of the staff joined in. Carson glanced over at Lily and was pleased to guess from her gentle smile that she was enjoying the moment as much as he was.

Even in the face of all the pain they'd seen at the hospital, there was Christmas joy to share.

After half an hour, the carolers broke up into smaller groups and visited residents who couldn't leave their rooms. Lily and Carson ended up together—okay, because he angled for it—visiting several patients too ill for the children's noise and energy. They took turns reading the Bible and praying with individual residents, and it occurred to Carson: Lily was someone he'd like to minister with. She was so calm, so attuned to the needs of others.

As they strolled out into the hall, now quiet and deserted, he put a hand on Lily's arm. When she turned, her face was bright, her eyes aware. And he'd never seen anyone more beautiful.

He felt such warmth, for his girls and for Lily, too. He didn't know what to do with all his feelings.

"I know you were Pam's friend," he said, "but I'm starting to see you as more. That was…" He gestured back toward the rooms they'd visited. "That was good to do with you."

Her cheeks went pink and she nodded. "I liked it, too."

He glanced up and down the deserted hall and then turned toward her, taking her face into his hands. "A Christmas kiss?" he asked.

She didn't refuse. Her eyes shone like jewels as she looked up at him.

He drew her close and kissed her.

Chapter Seven

The nursing home sounds, the realization that it was Christ-mas, thoughts of the twins...everything faded away as Carson kissed her. Lily's heart pounded as the feelings swept and swirled inside her.

After an hours-long moment, he held her shoulders, lifted his lips from hers and touched her face with one finger, his warm, kind eyes just inches away from hers. "Ah, Lily," he said. "Lily, what have you done to me?"

Her lips curved into a smile as she savored the tenderness between them. No thoughts, just warm feelings. So this was what people wrote songs about; this was what made the music swell in romantic movies. "I don't take credit. It's you doing this to me."

At the end of the hall, the *clink* of a cart and a staff member's cheery greeting at the door of a resident's room alerted them that they weren't alone anymore. Carson took a step back. "I hope that was okay," he said, his eyes still intent on hers. "It was more than okay with me."

Lily's breath felt shallow, and her heart pounded out a jazzy rhythm. How was she supposed to answer his question? And yet the kiss had been wonderful, and she wanted him to know it. She let herself nod, let herself smile.

His eyes flickered down to her lips, and she drew in a breath. This was happening fast.

Too fast. She drew in another breath as reality pushed back in.

This was Pam's husband. Lily didn't deserve to enjoy his kiss.

Confusion washed over her. She didn't want to even think about what it all meant, but she knew she'd have to. "We should find the others," she murmured.

"We should." He draped an arm around her shoulders as they turned toward the lobby, and again Lily's breath caught.

Being close to Carson felt like the fulfillment of every romantic dream she'd ever had. She let herself lean into him, relishing the heartfelt emotions swimming through her.

And yet. And yet.

She couldn't let herself forget that this was Pam's husband. Pam was dead, but she, Lily, had to keep Pam's secret so as not to hurt Carson and the twins.

"Are you okay?" he persisted, his breath warm on her ear.

"I... I *guess* so, but... I have to think about all of it." She glanced up at him. "I'm not sure it's a smart thing, letting in those feelings."

His face seemed to fall. He straightened, putting distance between them. "That's wise. I should think, too. I'm supposed to be counseling you, not kissing you."

She stared. "Counseling me? Why?"

"Because Penny wanted me to..." He broke off.

She stopped and turned to face him. "Penny wanted you to what?"

"Oh, nothing. It's nothing. Just…get to know you. Befriend you, and see if there was anything I could do to help you."

She put a hand on her hip. "Did that include kissing me?" But almost immediately, her indignation turned into embarrassment. It was like that time when the teacher in her new fifth-grade class had assigned two girls to "make Lily feel at home." Forced friendships hadn't worked then, and they didn't work now.

"Hey." They were almost to the lobby now, the sound of voices and music penetrating the private space they'd been in. "What rabbit hole are you going down?"

She shook her head. "Nothing. It's fine."

"It's what I said, isn't it?" He smacked his own forehead. "What a smooth operator I am, huh? I kiss this beautiful woman, and it doesn't take but five minutes before she's wishing she'd never met me."

He was being funny, self-deprecating, but it almost sounded like he believed his own story. That couldn't be, though, could it? Surely Carson had confidence in himself, as attractive and charming as he was.

"I didn't kiss you because of what Penny asked me to do," he said. "That was my very own idea. Maybe not a wise one, in retrospect, but I can't say I regret it."

They were about to walk into the lobby, and she turned to him, putting a hand on his arm to stop his forward movement. "Look, Carson…that was lovely, but…you're right, it probably wasn't wise. We should go home as soon as we can, and maybe keep a little distance."

So I don't blurt out the truth to you.

His lips pressed together, and his posture stiffened. "You're still doing the rest of our photography session tomorrow?"

Oh, no. She'd forgotten about that obligation. "Right," she said. "It shouldn't take long, and then…"

"And then you'll pull away again?" He leaned closer. "Lily, I'm sorry if I wasn't as smooth as I should have been, and I'm really sorry if I've in some way offended you or hurt your feelings. That's the last thing I want. But—"

"Daddy!"

"Miss Lily!"

The twins came running and flung themselves on Lily and Carson, practically quivering with excitement.

"Come see our craft we made!" Sunny begged, tugging at Lily. "I made one for Daddy, and Skye made one for you."

Lily's heart seemed to swell inside her chest as she let Sunny tug her over to a low table. On it, reindeer made of Popsicle sticks and glitter sat drying.

Conflicting emotions flooded Lily's consciousness.

She wanted this. Wanted the excited kids and the messy crafts and the handsome man who cared for her.

But she didn't deserve it. All of this was Pam's, not hers. And if Pam couldn't have it, then no way should Lily. She needed to back off. For her own sake, for Carson and for the girls.

It would be a whole lot easier if she didn't have a photo shoot with them tomorrow.

The next morning, after she'd procrastinated by cleaning her already immaculate cabin and checking her email and social media multiple times, Lily gathered her photography equipment and headed over to Carson's cabin.

Her nerve almost faltered on the way there.

She'd spent the night tossing and turning, thinking alternately about how wonderful it had been to kiss Carson and how weak and vulnerable she'd felt afterward. Especially when she'd learned that Penny had asked him to check on her and counsel her.

Carson was the kind type and would do his duty by anyone in need. No, he wouldn't consciously decide to romance the lonely female veteran next door, but on some level, maybe that was what he had had in mind.

How humiliating. Best to get this photo shoot done and over and hurry on out of there. Protect herself. Stay in her cabin and with the dogs and refocus on why she was here.

And the reason for that had changed. She knew, now, that Pam had been wrong about Carson, that he was a wonderful father for his girls.

Which made Lily's unhappy knowledge about Pam's last days even worse. Hurting someone like Carson seemed unforgivable. She couldn't let it happen. She couldn't let the little family get any more embedded in her heart.

She had just one more obligation: a photo shoot with them as a way of paying her rent.

She needed to make more progress on her senior project. She was here to photograph dogs, not kiss a man.

That was what men and romance could do to a woman—take her off course. Make her dependent and weak, as her mother had been.

Carson opened the door, dressed in a flannel shirt and jeans, and the circles under his eyes suggested he hadn't slept any better than she had.

But they didn't detract from his rugged good looks. Her mouth felt too dry to speak.

"Let me help you," he said, immediately reaching for her things. "I would have carried that stuff over here."

She shrugged but handed him her lighting screen and lens bag. Then she followed him inside, where a delicious bacon smell and two pajama-clad little girls drew her like a magnet.

The twins jumped up and hugged her, their warm, sticky hands clutching, their faces bright. Then they both let go and settled back down to their bacon and pancakes.

She'd interrupted their breakfast, which made her feel awkward and out of place. "I'm sorry," she said to Carson. "I can see you've been sleeping in. I should have texted first. We can wait until later. I thought, with little ones..."

"That we'd be up early? Usually, yes, but yesterday was pretty busy and a late night. Want some breakfast?"

"No, it's okay," she said, watching Sunny pour an excessive amount of syrup over her flapjacks, turning the butter into a cloudy pool.

"Are you sure?" He lifted an eyebrow, his lips quirking into a smile. "I'm not exactly a master chef, but I do good pancakes."

"They're *super*good," Sunny said through a big mouthful.

"Sunny. Manners." Carson's correction was gentle, tinged with laughter.

And that was the problem with Carson and his girls—they were impossibly tempting. "All right, you talked me into it. I'll have a plate. Everything looks and smells so good."

"Right here." Skye patted the chair beside her.

And just like that, she was a part of the family again.

The problem being, that was exactly what she shouldn't be. And a sleepy, stubbly Carson who'd kissed her like he meant it last night was hard for her to resist.

Not to mention his adorable girls, whom she was coming to care for more with every hour she spent with them.

Not good.

Carson handed her a plate and then leaned back against the counter, forking a hand through his hair in what she was starting to realize was a habitual gesture. Possibly a sign he was stressed.

"Aren't you eating?" she asked him.

He shook his head. "I will later. I like to get the girls fed and settled first."

And get chores like me out of your way. "I was thinking—oh, wow, this is so good—anyway, I was thinking we could do a few shots in front of the fire, and some others by the Christmas tree. It shouldn't take long."

"Should we wear our Christmas dresses?" Skye asked.

"Hmm." Little girls in fancy dresses were always adorable. "What do you think, Dad? Do you want casual family photos or dressed-up ones?"

Instead of answering, Carson went over to the Christmas tree and pulled off an ornament. He showed it to her. "That's the last family photo we had made," he said. "It's a little, I don't know, stiff?"

Lily studied it while her heart pounded. Carson, Pam and the twins as babies. Their pose was definitely artificial, with Pam leaning forward behind a seated Carson while the twins sat, each on a knee.

But Pam was smiling with what looked like real happiness. So was Carson.

The photo nagged, pounding in her own role in Pam's death, a role she was too cowardly to describe to Carson—especially when it would mean causing pain to him and the girls. "You want something more laid-back?" Her voice sounded breathless.

"I think so," Carson said as he began carrying empty plates to the sink. "We're really not a dress-up kind of family. Even at church, most weeks, the girls go casual. I do, myself, when I can get away with it."

The twins were conferring. "We want to wear our dresses," Sunny announced. "Please, Daddy?"

"How about a compromise?" Lily pushed back one of Sunny's stray curls, and when the little girl let her face linger in Lily's hand, leaning against her, Lily gave her a little hug before letting go.

These girls needed mothering, badly.

Or maybe it was Lily who needed to mother. "Let's do casual pajama pictures by the Christmas tree, and then some fancy ones by the fire."

"But Daddy's not wearing his pajamas," Skye objected.

Lily glanced at Carson, who was busying himself at the sink, and saw color rise up his neck. "I think daddies can just wear jeans and a shirt," she said quickly. The last thing she needed was for Carson to change into pajamas.

That, she definitely couldn't handle.

"And he could put his bathrobe on over them. That's what he does when it's cold, anyway."

"Perfect." Lily helped wipe the twins' faces and brushed their hair while Carson fetched a robe and straightened up around the small tree. Lily set up several shots and asked them to talk to each other naturally, which they mostly did, although Sunny kept mugging for the camera with a big fake smile.

Finally, Lily got one shot with both girls looking up adoringly at Carson and knew it was perfect.

"Okay, next the fancy ones." She wanted to get this over with as soon as possible, because watching Carson and the girls through the camera lens, seeing the kind of family she'd always dreamed of—and the family Pam should still be a part of—simply hurt too much.

"Will you come help us change?" Skye asked, leaning against her.

"Yeah, will you?" Sunny ran over and started tugging at Lily's hand, nearly knocking her camera to the floor.

Carson frowned. "I'll help. Leave Miss Lily be." Setting boundaries, obviously. He was the daddy. She was just the visiting photographer.

The twins seemed to recognize that he wasn't kidding, because they moved away from Lily and followed him up to the sleeping loft without a backward glance.

And that was as it should be. They were the family, and she wasn't. The sounds of the girls giggling and Carson's deep baritone in response, scolding and laughing, were not for her.

She breathed deeply and focused on the artistry of light and filters and angles, and by the time they came down, she'd arranged rugs and logs and a wooden chair in front of the fire, making a cozy background.

It took only a few minutes to get all of them smiling and being their attractive selves, especially when Lily thought of silly questions to ask them or told them to think about their favorite Christmas memories and share them. All three visibly relaxed, and Lily felt accomplished, pleased that she was able to capture their good looks and love for one another.

"That's it," she said, "unless you can think of another angle or pose."

She was talking to Carson, but Sunny answered. "Now you should be in the picture," she said, coming over to stand beside Lily.

"No, honey." Lily patted Sunny's shoulder and then refocused on the meters on her camera to avoid looking at anyone. "I have to take the pictures, not be in them."

"Can't you set a timer like our teacher does?" Skye was beside her now, too. "We really want you to be in the picture!"

Lily looked over at Carson and saw the same concern in his eyes that she was feeling. The girls were getting too attached to her, if they were trying to include her in a family photo again today. And the trouble was, she felt the same way about them. Combine that with the fact that Lily herself was getting pretty attached to Carson, especially after kissing him, and they were creating a recipe for disaster.

"No," she said, without being able to think of an excuse.

"I can't. I'd better not. Your pictures are best with just you and your daddy."

Big tears welled up in Skye's eyes. "Don't you like us?"

"Of course I do!" Lily knelt and embraced both girls. "You're great girls, and I like you a lot. It's just that today we're doing family pictures. And I'm your friend, but I'm not in your family."

Carson cleared his throat. "I'll take a picture of you three on my phone," he said. "There's no reason you girls can't have a Christmas-tree picture with your new friend Miss Lily, too." He looked at her, concern creasing his brow. "Unless she doesn't want that."

Oh, boy. They were walking on eggshells here. "I'd love to have another picture with the girls." And she would. She would treasure it, always remembering this Christmas on the ranch and the feeling of belonging she had gotten here, however briefly.

So she lifted her face and tucked a girl under each arm and they all smiled for the camera, and Carson took several pictures. And Lily tried not to pretend that they were her girls, and Carson was her husband, and they'd spend the future together as a family.

When he was done, the girls both hugged Lily tight, and her eyes got a little teary. "I'd better go," she said. Even as she started to gather her equipment, she felt her heart sink. Maybe this was the last time she would see Carson and the girls. They had had this excuse to be together, but it was over. Soon, they would leave the ranch and go back to their normal lives in Esperanza Springs. And Lily would go back to her normal life. She'd finish her degree, as planned, and then go live...somewhere. Wherever the road took her; wherever she could find a job.

Suddenly, that didn't feel exciting and adventurous, but lonely.

She shoved her arms into her coat and gathered her bags. Carson had gone back into the kitchen area, washing dishes. The girls were whispering up in the loft.

"I'm taking off, girls," she called up to them. "Have a fun rest of the day."

Carson wiped his hands on a dish towel and took a few steps toward her. "Thank you so much for coming over and doing this for us," he said. "I never have enough pictures of myself with the girls. It was a really thoughtful gift for Penny to think of, and kind of you to do."

"I'll get you proofs as soon as I've taken a look at them." She wanted to touch them up, and maybe, just maybe, she was hanging on to a shred of hope of seeing the little family again.

The girls came clattering down the ladder, practically tumbling over each other, smiles creasing their faces. "We have an idea," Sunny said.

"Uh-oh," Carson said, rolling his eyes, but smiling at the same time. "Sounds like trouble. What's your idea?"

Both girls turned to Lily, holding hands. They walked up to her, close, and looked up, their faces sweet and engaging. Then Sunny looked over at Skye. "Ready?"

Skye nodded.

Both girls took deep breaths and then turned to Lily and recited: "Will you be our new mommy?"

Chapter Eight

You had one job to do: counsel a troubled young woman. And instead, you kissed her.

And now your girls want her to be their mommy.

Later the same day, Carson walked away from Long John's cabin toward the barn where the dogs were housed. Long John had been happy to have the twins visit for a little while. And Carson had been glad for them to focus on someone other than Lily.

Even now, two hours after that awkward moment when the girls had asked Lily to be their mother, he was beating himself up.

Why had he let their relationship with Lily go so far?

He knew why, though: because in some ways, Lily was perfect for them. She was so sweet, kind, good with the girls. She was beautiful, innocently attracting Carson's interest without even a hint of provocative clothing or behavior.

Nonetheless, she was hiding things about Pam, and Pam's death.

And in the end, a woman like Lily would never go for a man like him. She'd started to back away almost the moment after he'd kissed her.

Sure, being in the mountains was fun for now, an adventure to a woman raised in the flatlands, but that would go stale soon. He'd seen it happen with Pam.

And when she got tired of this place, of him, of the girls, she'd leave. Well, that was her right. But what he had to do was keep a distance, avoid building the connection any further.

The potential for hurt was so great. His girls didn't need another loss in their lives.

He didn't need it, either.

He had to cut this relationship with Lily off, fast. A little pinch now was better than a huge, painful break later.

A sharp *CHEW-EE, CHEW-EE* sounded from a fence post, a bright-eyed songbird seeming to call Carson away from his own thoughts and into the world of nature. Obedient, Carson looked out over the wide-flung fields to the Sangre de Cristos, white against the sky's intense blue.

He sent up a prayer of thanks for the beauty of this place and for being able to stay here over Christmas with his girls.

He needed to think more about his blessings and less about Lily.

Christmases had been simpler when he'd been married and the twins had been small. The girls hadn't had difficult expectations to fulfill, as they had this Christmas.

Man, he'd screwed up. They'd really, really wanted a dog.

If they'd had a mother, maybe she would have seen that and helped him figure out how to manage it. As it was, he'd been busy and scrambling and not paying enough attention, obviously. Single parenting was an ongoing challenge.

But had it really been that much easier when Pam was here?

When he remembered the two of them together at Christmas, his first thought was of her discontent. She'd always wished for parties and shows and bright lights, things that he, a country pastor, hadn't been able to provide. Even before the twins had been born, he hadn't been able to take some fancy trip at Christmas as she'd wanted to. One, because he couldn't afford it, and two, because he had to preach on Christmas Eve.

And three, honestly, because he didn't want it. Didn't want to get on a plane to go somewhere else and party the season away. He'd preferred to stay at home.

Boring, Pam would say.

Man, had they been ill-suited.

And it had contributed to Pam's problems, her increasing unhappiness. Surely he, trained in pastoral counseling, should have been able to help his own wife. But he hadn't. Hadn't realized how serious the situation was getting. Hadn't known how to stop the flood of her angry emotions and moods.

Hadn't been able to stop her from running away from him and the girls, albeit in the guise of military obligations.

He reached the kennels at the same time a truck pulled in and parked. Jack DeMoise jumped out, then opened the rear door to extract his year-old son.

"Thanks for coming up on the day after Christmas," Carson said to the veterinarian.

Jack shrugged. "Nothing else to do. Glad you were here to open the place up for me. When the ranch volunteers let me know that old Bella was having trouble, I wasn't sure how I'd get into the barn to see her."

Carson opened the door and they walked inside to the

sound of loud barking, greetings from a plethora of dogs who all could use more attention than they normally got.

"Mind holding Sammy?" Jack asked.

Carson reached out and took the one-year-old into his arms, cuddling him close. Sammy's back was stiff and arched, his tiny hands on his ears.

"Those dogs are loud," Carson agreed with the baby, pitching his voice low and pacing, bouncing him gently. "They'll quiet down soon."

And it was true; their woofed greetings were already dying down, and the child settled, too.

Wish I could have another child.

And where had *that* thought come from? Pam hadn't wanted more children—honestly, hadn't initially wanted the twins; they'd been a surprise—and since her death, he'd had his hands full taking care of the girls. Normally, he didn't have an ounce of attention to spare to the idea of maybe having another child; witness his obliviousness to his daughters' expectation of a puppy. Besides which, thinking of a third child evoked painful thoughts of the unborn child who had died with Pam.

Now having another child would involve remarrying, obviously a complicated proposition.

Focus.

He watched as Jack knelt before Bella's cage, studying her before going in. He looked back up at Carson. "Man, those volunteers are great. They keep this place clean. Helps prevent disease."

Carson sniffed and nodded, appreciating that the place smelled like disinfectant rather than the many other odors a group of dogs could produce.

"And they're sharp," Jack added. "They noticed Bella's problem quickly."

"Which is what?"

Jack undid the lock on the cage and eased in, soothing the big black dog as he knelt before her. "Aside from neglect and being thirteen years old, with parasites and some mammary tumors…she seems like she has an ear infection." He nodded at her. "See how she's pawing at her face and ear?"

Carson nodded. "What can you do for a dog who's that old?"

Jack studied the dog, his face thoughtful. "Quite a lot, actually. An antibiotic should wipe out this infection, and then we'll take on the tumors if need be. They're probably benign. What she really needs, though, is some tender loving care for her golden years."

"Is she likely to get adopted?" Carson stooped to look at the dog. "Akita, isn't she?"

"Uh-huh. And there are people who have open hearts for these hard cases." He glanced up at Carson. "Thanks for holding Sammy. You look like a natural with him."

"I love babies. If things were different, I'd like to have another," Carson admitted. To preclude Jack's asking questions, he asked one of his own: "How about you? Any urges toward another child?"

Jack snorted. "I worry about this one too much. I couldn't handle another." He ran his hands over the dog. "Don't know how you managed as a single dad with two."

"Wasn't easy, but at least they were older when we lost Pam. You had Sammy alone almost from the beginning." He thought back over what Jack had said. "What do you mean, you worry about him too much? Is something wrong?"

Jack sighed, his forehead creasing. "Seems to me he's too quiet. Doesn't react the way I'd like to see." He frowned. "The last nanny thought he might be on the spectrum, but I can't get a doctor to corroborate it this early."

"Wow. I'm sorry, man. That's a lot for you to handle alone."

"Alone's how I'm going to be." Jack shrugged and continued his examination of the dog. "Never mind about me. What's going on with you? Heard you and your girls aren't up here by yourselves."

Carson glared. "No, we're not. Long John's here, too. In fact, that's where the girls are now."

Jack chuckled. "Heard there was someone even prettier than Long John."

Carson blew out a sigh. "Word does travel fast in a small town."

"When General Patton and Mrs. Barnes are involved, it does." Jack grinned. "Word on the street is, you like Penny's niece."

Now, who had said that? "I do like her," he revealed, "but that doesn't mean I'm getting involved with her." Even as he said it, he realized he was fooling himself. What had that kiss meant, if not involvement?

"Why not?" Jack shoulder-bumped him as they walked to the front of the barn. "Don't you ever want someone to share your life?"

"Do you?"

"I'm different," Jack said, "and we're talking about you."

"I'd like the companionship," Carson admitted, "and I'd like a mom for my girls. But…" He sighed. "I didn't exactly do a bang-up job at marriage before. And I'd hate to have the girls learn to care for someone, then lose them."

"You can't let one bad marriage ruin you for the institution," Jack argued.

Carson noticed that he didn't dispute the idea that Carson's marriage had been bad. Did everyone in town know it, then?

"Everyone's not like Pam," Jack went on, pretty much confirming the notion. "Take this Lily, for example. Sounds like she's a nice person. Why don't you ask her out? Give dating a whirl."

"It's not that easy!" Carson thumped the wall, too hard, to push a loose board back into place. "Especially with someone like Lily. She's first class, man. Gorgeous, big heart, talented…"

"What, you're holding out for a loser?"

What could he say to that? Carson waved a hand to indicate he was done with the conversation, but Jack's words echoed in his mind. As he watched the man administer a shot to Bella, he had to admit he was mixed up inside.

He couldn't claim that he felt nothing for Lily. In fact, he'd kissed her and loved it. It was the first time he'd been drawn to anyone since Pam.

It wasn't just the kissing, either. Lily was fun and funny and kind, warm and natural with his girls, with passions for photography and dogs that made her interesting.

But Lily was keeping secrets. What's more, he'd pledged to counsel her, not romance her, and he was doing a shoddy job of that.

And all of that was aside from the fact that a man like Carson just wasn't appealing or exciting enough for a woman like Lily, not long-term.

The door to the barn burst open, and there was the woman in question—with a twin holding either hand. He got to his feet, shifting the baby to his other arm. "You girls were supposed to stay with Long John," he scolded, not looking at Lily.

"We saw her walking by, and we wanted to come, and Long John let us," Sunny said.

"I'm sorry," Lily said. "I was coming to figure out my next photo session with the dogs. I didn't know whether to say yes, but they pleaded so hard…"

Jack chuckled. "Just imagine when they're teenagers."

"Dr. Jack!" The twins ran to him, clearly delighted. The fun-loving veterinarian was a favorite with them. "What are you doing here? Did you find a puppy for us?"

"He's not here for that." Carson sighed, feeling over-whelmed.

"It's fine." Jack introduced himself to Lily—now, why had Carson forgotten to do that?—and then invited the twins to watch as he finished up Bella's care. "Puppies are nice," he told them as he manipulated the old dog's back legs, checking her joints, "but there are dogs who need homes more. Puppies will always find a home. It takes a special family to love a dog like Bella."

"*I* could love her," Skye said. "She's pretty."

That was a stretch, but more power to Jack if he could steer the girls toward a senior dog. If Carson ever did give in to their pleas for a canine companion, it would be for one who really needed a home.

And who was calm, and didn't chew up shoes, and was house-trained.

But he didn't want a dog, he reminded himself. And he didn't want his girls getting any more attached to Lily, either. Didn't want to get more attached to the woman, himself. Didn't want to watch the way she put an arm around each girl as all three of them knelt in front of Bella's cage, listening to Jack explaining that you needed to be careful even around nice dogs, that you shouldn't get between a dog and its food.

It seemed to him that Jack was leaning too close to Lily, smiling at her a little too much. Heat rose in Carson's neck. Was the vet hitting on her?

Carson started over, but just in time, he caught himself. He had no right to feel possessive about Lily.

Annoyed, he walked toward the front of the barn, the part that served as an office, hoping to get a grip on himself.

Instead, he saw a bulletin board. The left-hand half was covered with photos of dogs who needed homes, while the right-hand half displayed families who'd already adopted a senior dog. Lots of happy-looking people, some of whom were friends of his.

If Carson were any fun at all, he wouldn't have disappointed his girls at Christmastime. He'd already have gotten them a dog, if not several pets.

But Carson wasn't any fun. Just ask the girls' mother.

In the couple of minutes it took Carson to compose himself, Jack got Bella from the cage and walked her outside, Lily and the girls following along. The girls giggled and clucked at the dog, and she turned and slurped one twin's face, then the other—she was basically the same height that they were.

Lily looked on, laughing with delight. The way her face lit up...

She glanced over, saw him watching and flinched. "I have to go," she said quickly, and headed away from the barn.

Automatically, Carson walked her to the gate.

Behind them came the sound of Sunny's high, clear voice: "Daddy doesn't want us to talk about this," she was saying to Jack, "but me and Skye want Miss Lily to be our new mommy."

Lily glanced at him, distress written all over her face. It matched the distress in his own heart.

He couldn't let his girls get hurt again.

When they got to the gate, he opened it and held it for her, shifting Jack's baby to his other arm. "Listen, Lily," he began.

"I'm sorry," she said at the same time.

They both stopped. Looked at each other, and their gazes tangled.

Best to do this quick. "Lily," he said, "you're a great person, but it would be better if you'd stay away from me and the girls."

Chapter Nine

The next day, just after Lily had cleaned up from the healthy lunch she'd forced herself to eat, she looked through the window and saw Carson walking out the door of his cabin.

Instantly, she was flooded with embarrassment and hurt.

It would be better if you'd stay away.

She didn't normally dwell on the times she'd felt unwanted: tiptoeing around her parents' arguments, trying to make friends at a new school, being assigned as the only woman in a work unit overseas.

But somehow, being told to stay away by Carson—from him *and* those sweet little girls—hurt a hundred times more.

She couldn't give in to the despair that threatened her, though. She had to make every effort to keep it at bay.

She dried her hands and went over to the spot in front of the fire where Bella, the old Akita, lay on a soft blanket.

Step one, when you were feeling bad: help someone else.

She rubbed the dog's ears for a few seconds, earning a feeble tail wag, and then grabbed her laptop and settled in at the little kitchen table.

Starting her online course early would keep her plenty busy, keep her mind from going places that wouldn't do her any good.

She'd just opened the welcome video from the instructor when there was a knock on her cabin door.

Her emotions stampeded out of the place she'd corralled them, because it couldn't be anyone but Carson.

She stood and drew in a deep breath. She'd send him away.

As she crossed the cabin, there was another knock. "I'm coming!" She grabbed the door and flung it open, but didn't step back for him to enter. "What can I do for you, Carson?"

He winced. "Could I come in and talk for a minute?" His eyes were concerned, studying her.

"Are the girls all right?"

"Yes, of course! They're down in town, at a party for one of their friends."

"Then what do you need?"

He sighed. "It would be easier if I could come inside."

Don't you know you're killing me? She opened the door and stepped to one side, arms crossed.

He closed the door behind him, rubbing his hands together and stomping the snow from his boots. Then he looked at her, his dark eyes sorrowful. "I've hurt you when I was supposed to help you. I'm sorry."

"I'm fine."

"It's not your fault my girls tend to get attached too easily. Probably, it's my fault."

"Happens a lot, does it?" The moment she said it, she wished she could take it back. But she'd thought her connection with his girls was at least a little special.

"No," he said slowly. "They do tend to enjoy being around

women, and to cling to their teachers. But the way they've latched onto you...no, it's never happened before, quite like this. They've grown so fond of you that they want to make it permanent. In fact, they're quite annoyed with me that I don't see the light."

She waved a hand. "Kids."

He blew out a breath. "I'm botching this apology. I think you're a very appealing woman—you can probably tell—and if things were different, I'd—"

"Don't, Carson. There's no need. I'm not interested in a relationship." She looked away, not wanting to see the relief on his face. "Anyway," she said, "it's nice of you to check on me, but I'm fine. I have coping mechanisms." She gestured toward the open laptop computer, the fire, the dog.

His eyes skimmed from one to the next, and then to her face. "Give me ten minutes to talk with you and I promise I'll get out of your hair."

There seemed to be no other option, unless she wanted to be outright rude. She gestured toward the couch and sat in the armchair kitty-corner from it. "Something to drink?" politeness made her ask.

He waved the offer away. "What made you take in Bella?" he asked.

"I wanted to help." She slid to the floor and reached out to run a hand along the dog's bony back. Bella thumped her tail and licked Lily's hand, and Lily's heart twisted.

"She needs help, from the looks of things."

Okay, she could spend their ten minutes talking about Bella. It was probably better that way. "According to Jack," she said, "Bella was tied to a tree for years. You can see how worn away the fur is around her neck. And she has tumors from never having been spayed. She needs to regain strength before she can have surgery to have them removed. I figured, at least for the couple more days I'm here, I can give her some extra attention and love."

He looked from her to the dog and back again. "You put me to shame," he said quietly. "Here I've resisted getting a dog, and you're not even in the area for but a few days, and yet you're reaching out to an animal that needs care. I admire you for that."

She felt her cheeks heat at the unaccustomed praise. "I get as much out of it as Bella does. Right, girl? You're good company." Bella was keeping her from over-the-top sadness about how she'd started to fall in love with the idea of family, represented by Carson and his girls, an idea she was pretty sure she'd never get to realize herself.

"So," he asked, his voice sounding falsely cheerful, "you were in touch with Jack about this? Is that how you came to take the dog in?"

She looked up at him, confused by the tension in his voice. "Yes. Is that against the rules?"

"No. No, of course not." He shook his head and then rested his cheek on his clasped fists, leaning forward, staring out the window. "Jack's a good guy."

Lily felt her eyebrows draw together as she tried to puzzle out what Carson was saying and what he really meant. If she hadn't known better, she'd have thought he was jealous of her having contact with Jack. But that didn't make sense on any level.

"Listen, Lily," he said, "I've been remiss. I'm a pastor, and Penny wanted me to talk to you about your, well, your issues with the war and maybe even other stuff in your past. She didn't want me to tell you she'd put me up to it, but I let that slip, so I might as well be open about it now."

This again. Nothing like making her feel even more screwed up than she was. "You don't need to do that. I'm fine. Really. The military has good counselors, and I've taken advantage of that when I've needed to."

"Why do you think Penny wanted me to talk to you, then?"

Lily shrugged, but she knew, and as long as she'd given Carson ten minutes, she might as well tell him just to pass the time. "Penny is my mom's sister. She knows my mom wasn't the strongest person in the world, and that my dad has…issues."

"What kind of issues?"

"He's an alcoholic. Nowadays, he's addicted to opiates, too." The simple words choked her a little, surprisingly, and she clamped her mouth shut.

"That must be hard to deal with," Carson said.

She nodded and drew in a breath. "Sometimes."

"Like at Christmas?" he probed. "Where are your parents now?"

Lily cleared her throat. "Well, Mom, she…she passed away last year. My dad's in the Kansas City area, I think. Last I heard."

"You're not in touch?"

She shook her head. "Not much." Then, to cover up how guilty she felt about that, she shot him a glare. "Are you judging me? Believe me, I've tried to help him at various times, even though he made my mom's life a nightmare, and even though all he wants from me is money for booze and drugs. He won't admit he has a problem, though, and until he does—"

Carson held up a hand. "Whoa. I didn't mean to accuse you of anything. I'm sorry you've had to deal with all of that, and the last thing I would do is judge you. You've built a fine life for yourself."

Lily looked briefly around the cabin. "Yeah, with a stray

dog and nowhere to go on Christmas. Some life." The bitter sound of her own voice shocked her and she clapped a hand over her mouth. "I didn't mean that! I have a lot of good things going for me."

"You're a kind person who's trying to improve her lot in life by getting a degree, and you still have room in your heart to help others," he said quietly. "In my book, that's a fine life."

She shrugged. "We all do what we have to do." She wanted to add a compliment to him—that he'd lost his wife and was managing to do a lot of good in the world despite that tragedy—but she was afraid it would come out wrong.

And she didn't want to bring up the subject of Pam.

"You never fell into drinking or drugging yourself?" His voice sounded elaborately casual.

She raised both hands like stop signs. "I didn't say that. I made my share of mistakes." Remembering some of her escapades, during her teen years and even her early twenties, made her blush and shake her head. "I was a wild child. That's why Pam and I…" She trailed off. Why had she brought up Pam?

"Why you partied together?" Carson didn't sound disapproving.

Lily hesitated, then nodded. "I'm not proud of the way we acted, Carson. I wasn't comfortable with it even back then. And now that I know better, I'm even more ashamed."

"There's no condemnation in Christ," he said lightly. "Did she talk about our marriage?"

Lily blew out a sigh. Carson was obviously obsessed with finding out exactly how Pam had felt about him at the time of her death. How was she supposed to handle this? "A little."

"Did she tell you we had problems?"

She'd *told* Lily that Carson was an abusive husband, but that was obviously a lie.

What had been Pam's agenda, with all the lying?

Bella, bless her, chose that moment to stand up, her limbs shaky, and limp toward the cabin door. "I have to help her." Lily hurried across the cabin to open the door, and then she guided Bella down the steps. "Take your time," she muttered to the dog. Maybe Carson would forget his question.

After a moment, Carson came out the door and stood on the porch. "I guess I had my ten minutes and more," he said.

"Yeah." Lily forced a little laugh. "I should get back to work on my online course."

"I understand." He trotted down the porch steps and then stopped beside her. "Listen, Lily, I was wrong, and rude, to tell you to stay away. While you're up here, you're welcome to spend time with me and the girls."

She shook her head quickly. "I don't want them to get attached to me. I'm only staying a couple of days longer."

"I'll talk to them," he said firmly. "It'll be a good lesson for them, and…and pleasant for all of us, if you'd care to spend time together. As friends," he added quickly.

"Right," she said. "Friends."

Later that afternoon, Carson accepted Long John's offer of a hammer and nails and headed outside to continue the work on the cabin's porch.

His girls stayed inside the cabin with Long John…and Lily.

Carson blew out a sigh. He'd had a serious conversation with the girls over lunch, reminded them that Lily was a friend, not a potential new mother. Explained that if they kept making her uncomfortable by talking about her joining their family, she wouldn't be able to hang around with them.

They'd hastily agreed not to bring it up, said they understood, but Carson had his doubts. Still, when they'd seen Lily walking Bella outside, he'd allowed them to go out and say hello. It turned out they'd begged her to bring the big dog to Long John's to meet Rockette when they went over to visit. They'd developed a fantasy that the two dogs could be best friends.

Oh, well. It was better than the fantasy that Lily could be their mom.

Better than his own fantasy that Lily could be some kind of romantic partner to him.

He ran his hands over the ramp, inspecting the spot that had broken. If he could just shore it up with a couple of two-by-fours, it wouldn't look perfect, but it would be safe. Safe, at least, for now.

He was measuring boards when his phone buzzed. He checked the lock screen and smiled.

Finn Gallagher was the ranch manager and was fast becoming one of Carson's good friends; in fact, in November, Carson had performed the marriage ceremony for Finn and his new wife, Kayla. The two had gone through a lot, both separately and together, but now they were deliriously happy, and so was Kayla's son, Leo, who'd found a true father figure in Finn.

"How's the south?" he greeted Finn, and they talked for a little while about Kayla's friends whom they'd visited before Christmas, and Finn's big family of brothers, with whom they'd stayed for the holiday itself. Apparently, Leo was having the time of his life with his new cousins, and the family had even welcomed Shoney, their blind and deaf cocker spaniel, as an honored visitor.

"So how's the ranch?" Finn asked, and Carson was able to report that the dogs were fine, that he was fixing Long John's porch and that his girls were keeping the older man company.

"Is that other guest doing okay?"

"Lily? Yeah."

"Great." Finn didn't pursue the subject; obviously, he wasn't in the gossip circuit.

Which, perversely, made Carson want to confide. "She's an...interesting woman."

"Oh?"

"My girls have really taken to her."

"That's good," Finn said, "because from what I've heard, it sounds like Pam wasn't really there for them. Or for you."

Finn's words, so blunt and matter-of-fact, echoed oddly in Carson's ears.

He'd spent so much time beating himself up about being a bad husband that he hadn't really considered Pam's adequacy as a wife and mother. And that was okay; it was good to be nonjudgmental, right?

But he had to admit that Finn was right. Pam had spent most of her time overseas, even after the girls were born. Especially after the girls were born, even when she'd had the option to take a job stateside.

She'd had many great qualities, but she hadn't been enthusiastic about motherhood.

Nor about being a wife.

And while he could blame himself for the latter, he could never blame his lovable girls for their mother's lack of interest. They'd done nothing to deserve her neglect.

A tiny voice inside him whispered that maybe, just maybe, he hadn't deserved that, either. Maybe her lack of interest in him and the girls had more to do with her issues than with Carson's inadequacies.

"You still there?" Finn asked. "Hey, I shouldn't have said that. Sorry."

"No, it's fine. You might have a point."

And Carson had some more thinking to do. They talked

a little longer, and then Finn rang off, saying he'd see Carson in a few days.

And that reminded Carson that this interlude alone on the ranch, with Long John and Lily and the girls, would come to an end. They'd be back into their busy lifestyles. Lily would be gone.

The thought brought a big bank of mental black clouds, so he was grateful to hear Long John thumping out of the house, using his walker to get to the porch.

"Haven't made much progress, have you?" Long John asked, ragging him. "You getting paid by the hour or something?"

"If I could have some…" Carson broke off. He'd been about to make a joke about how it would be nice to have some help, but Long John just wasn't able.

The older man seemed to know what Carson was going to say. "Believe me, I'd help if I could. I hate being all crippled up."

"I know you would. You do a lot for me, including watching out for the girls. Are they okay?"

"Having a lot of fun with Lily and the dogs." Long John paused. "You know, you and I both have some problems in the past, but I think it's about time we tried to overcome 'em."

"Yeah?" Carson stayed focused on leveling a board and sliding it into place.

"Yeah. You need to get over that wife of yours. Face the truth about her. Deal with it."

Not again.

Long John was right, and Finn was right. Carson had things to work on. But he didn't necessarily want the older man's advice right now.

He focused on the other man. "I know what problems I have. What about you?"

Long John leaned a little closer. "Truth is, I'd like to ask someone out, but with my limitations..." He waved a hand at his walker.

"Is it Penny? I don't know that you should pursue her." Carson knew that both Long John and his friend Willie had a good-natured rivalry about the woman who owned the ranch. "She's still hung up on what happened with her husband. I don't think she's ready."

"I know that. That's not who I meant."

"Who, then?" He grinned. "Minnie Patton?"

Long John snorted. "She does make a fine tuna fish casserole, but no. Close, though."

Then Carson remembered. "Minnie's sister?" Long John had seemed to enjoy chatting with her.

Long John rubbed his grizzled chin and nodded. "Yep. She's a real sweet woman."

"I think you should do it. Ask her out. What can you lose?"

"I could ask you the same question," Long John said, neatly turning the tables. "You have some limitations yourself, but why let the past ruin the present for you?"

Carson *didn't* want to talk about Pam. "I'm not the most exciting man on the block," he said. And then he remembered Finn's off-the-cuff remarks about Pam. Maybe the lack of fun had been more about her restlessness than a personal trait of his.

"You need to deal with your past," Long John said. "Really face what happened with your wife and in your marriage."

Carson nodded. "You're probably right."

"That young woman in there might need just exactly what you have to offer," Long John said. "Maybe she's what your girls need, too. The good Lord works in mysterious ways."

"It's possible," Carson said. Then, figuring he had enough deep stuff to think about, he changed the subject.

They chatted easily about sports, the weather, fishing.

Until suddenly, there was growling, barking and a loud cry from inside the cabin.

Chapter Ten

At the sound of dogs snarling and girls screaming, Lily spun from Long John's refrigerator, where she'd been getting drinks for the twins. She ran toward the sitting area as the door opened from outside.

Rockette and Bella stood stiffly, several feet apart, Bella gulping down a treat, Rockette growling.

Behind them, both twins wailed.

"What happened?" Lily cried, running to Skye as Carson burst through the door and ran to Sunny.

"Bella bit me!" Sunny sobbed, clutching her hand to her chest. "Daddy, she bit me!"

Carson pulled Sunny into his lap. "Did you see what happened?" he asked Lily.

Lily shook her head, feeling two inches tall. "I'm so sorry. I was getting them something to drink." What had she been thinking, leaving two little ones alone with two big dogs? "I'm so sorry, I should have been watching them more closely. Skye, honey, are you okay?"

"I am, but Sunny's not," Skye sobbed.

"Let me see your hand," Carson said, his head bent over Sunny, cuddling her close.

Sunny held it out, and they all leaned forward to see… nothing. "Where does it hurt, honey?" Long John had come in behind Carson, and now he sat down on the edge of his recliner to better see the damage, or non-damage.

Sunny pointed to a spot on her hand, and when Lily leaned forward, she saw a tiny speck of pink. No broken skin. Relief bloomed in her chest.

In Lily's lap, Skye gulped away her tears and leaned forward to study her twin's hand. "I can't see anything."

"I think you're going to live," Carson said, the tension gone from his voice. "The skin isn't broken."

"I felt her teeth!" Sunny insisted. "Why did she bite me, Daddy? I thought she was nice!"

"Because you were teasing her with treats," Skye said. "Remember, Dr. Jack said to be careful with dogs and their food."

"I was just playing a game," Sunny said, an expression of annoyance replacing her tears. "I wanted to see which dog could get the treat first." She held her hand up in the air to demonstrate what she'd done.

"Big mistake, honey," Carson said. "Did you learn your lesson?"

"They're bad dogs!" Sunny frowned at Bella. "Especially you. Bad dog!"

"They're just doing what dogs do naturally," Long John said. "In the wild, back in the wolf days, they'd fight over every morsel in order to survive and feed their young."

"And Bella's been hungry a lot, from what Dr. Jack said," Carson added. "She's probably extra worried about getting enough to eat."

"I should never have brought Bella over," Lily said. "I wasn't thinking about how she might compete with Rockette for food. They were getting along so well, but I shouldn't have left the girls alone with them, even for a minute." She didn't dare look at Carson. He must think she was the worst person ever, putting his precious girls at risk.

"It's my fault," Long John said. "I should have stayed in here to help you. These two are a handful!" He put a hand on each blond head.

"Look, I'm the one responsible for the girls. I'm sorry to leave you in charge like that," Carson said. "You couldn't have known what would happen."

Grace instead of blame. It was a new experience for Lily, and her heart melted.

"It's not Miss Lily's fault." Sunny scrambled out of Carson's lap and scooted over to lean on Lily. "She told us to be careful and gentle."

Lily sat, one girl on her lap and one beside her, her heart contracting painfully. She'd always claimed she didn't understand kids, was in no hurry to have her own, but these two had effortlessly won her heart.

She'd started to care for these girls as if they were her own. Any little hurt they had, she seemed to feel herself. She wanted to take care of them and comfort them and love them.

But they were Carson's girls, not hers. Carson's and Pam's. What right did she have to feel anything for them?

After Carson had left with the girls, Lily hesitated near Long John's door, her hand on Bella's collar. She hadn't wanted to go with Carson and the twins, impose herself on them, feel more attached. But she also didn't feel like being alone.

"I'd be obliged if you'd fix me a cup of tea," Long John called from his recliner.

"Sure!" Relieved, Lily hung her coat back up, went over to the kitchen area and turned on the kettle.

"Fix one for yourself, if you'd like," he said. "I'd welcome the company."

Something in his tone sounded artificial. Why was he encouraging her to stay? She marched over and faced him, propped a hand on her hip. "Are you just being nice?"

"Welllll…" He drew the word out, smiling a little. "I *would* like the company. But I think you've got something on your mind. If you want to talk about it, I'm available. Free and confidential," he added, a twinkle in his eye.

She couldn't help smiling back at the older man, and a couple of moments later she was sitting on his couch, two steaming mugs of tea on the table between them.

"So what's been on your mind, little lady?" He sipped his tea and gave an appreciative sigh.

On the floor, Rockette echoed it. Bella was nosing around the edges of the room.

The "little lady" label might have irritated her from some men, but not Long John. "Too much," she admitted. The situation with Carson and the twins had her head spinning with confusion, her heart raw and aching.

Tell him about Pam.

The idea seemed to come out of nowhere, but all of a sudden she wanted a sounding board. "You meant it when you said confidential?" she asked.

"Absolutely."

She took a sip of tea and then wrapped her hands around the cup. "I… Something happened when I was in the service."

He nodded and raised an eyebrow.

"I… This woman, another soldier…" Saying Pam's name, revealing her identity, seemed too scary. "A friend of mine, she and I had an argument. There was a lot that happened… Anyway, she was furious at me." She waved her hand, not wanting to go into the whole complex story. "But the end result was, she ran out of our guard hut and purposely got herself shot."

His bushy white eyebrows came together. "She make it?"

Lily shook her head. For just a moment, she relived the scene: Pam running off toward the oncoming vehicle. Lily's own shouts and those of their two fellow soldiers. They weren't supposed to leave the hut, but to stick together and inspect each vehicle entering their compound.

Lily remembered the *rat-tat-tat* of gunfire. Pam had stopped as if running into a glass wall. Her body had curled in on itself and then collapsed.

The other two had rushed after the fleeing vehicle. But Lily had gone to Pam. "When I got to her, she was already…gone," she said. And then her throat closed and her eyes burned and she couldn't say any more.

"And you blame yourself."

Lily nodded.

They sat for a moment, staring into the fire. And then Long John spoke. "When I was in 'Nam, I left a buddy in the jungle."

"How do you mean, left?"

"Turned tail and ran," he said. "Saved my own life."

From what she knew of the older man, she thought there was probably more to the story. "Was he down?"

Long John nodded. "Down, and in pretty bad shape. Felt like I had a choice—lose him or lose both of us." He spread his hands. "It dogged me for a couple of years, that I didn't choose right. Any grunt in the movies or on TV would've stuck around, even if just to bring his body home."

"Life's not like the movies or TV."

"No, it's not."

They sat in silence for a couple of minutes, but Lily was

curious. Finally, she asked, "You said it bothered you for a couple of years. How'd you get over it?"

Long John stared into the fire. "Ever hear that expression 'confession is good for the soul'?"

"Uh-huh."

He turned his head and propped it on his folded hands, facing her. "I went to his twin brother, who also served. Told him the whole story."

"Wow." That had taken courage. "Was he angry?"

"Slugged me hard enough to break his own hand." Long John shrugged. "Can't blame him. Rick might've had a chance, if I'd been able to stay with him or drag him out of there. I was honest about that."

"Did his twin end up forgiving you?"

Slowly, Long John nodded. "He did more than that."

"What do you mean?"

Long John gestured toward the window. "You ever hear me talk about Willie? Guy who lives next door?"

A shiver danced up and down Lily's spine. "He's your best friend."

"Uh-huh. And he's Ricky's twin."

"Wow."

"Having him forgive me made all the difference."

"Makes sense." And it gave her food for thought.

She *would* feel better if she could confess what she'd done, already *did* feel better having told Long John. If she could tell Carson...

"Something to notice," Long John said. "You listened to me tell you the thing that, to me, is the most awful failing of my life. And you're still sittin' here. You didn't run off thinking I was a horrible person."

"No, of course not!" Lily studied him. "You had to make a terrible choice, and you did the best you could."

"Same goes for you, too," he said. "Are you supposed to never argue with anyone, just do what everyone says, on the chance that they might go self-destructive on you?"

"Noooo," she said cautiously.

He leaned forward, sipped some more tea. "And yes, we're our brothers' keepers, but we can't stop them from taking any risk. My buddy, he bucked orders by heading into that swamp. I couldn't stop him from doing that. Willie says he was always reckless that way."

She nodded. When she looked out the window, she saw that the sunset was turning the tops of the mountains to red flame. "I should go," she said, collecting their empty teacups and putting them over on the dish drainer.

"You think about what I've said now."

She shrugged into her coat. "I will." Impulsively, she leaned over and kissed the old man's dry, bristly cheek. "Thank you for helping me think it through." As tears came to her eyes, she hurried out of the cabin with Bella.

She'd never known her grandfather, and certainly her father hadn't been a helpful influence. But Long John, today, felt like the grandfather she'd never had.

Not only that, but his words had lit a fire in her.

Tomorrow, she needed to tell Carson the truth about Pam.

The next afternoon, Carson was washing lunch dishes when there was a knock on the door. He dried his hands and glanced out the window.

Lily. Warmth spread through his chest and he walked double time to the door. Opened it and felt his mouth curve into an automatic smile.

"Hi," she said, her voice tentative. "Can I come in a minute?"

"Sure!" He beckoned her in. "The girls are working on

some mysterious project up in the loft, and I'm all alone down here."

Had that sounded pathetic?

No, because she smiled back at him—nervously, true, but it was still a smile. "That's good," she said. "I wanted to talk to you about something."

"If you're worried about Sunny and the dog bite, she's fine," he said. "She had a dream where she was a little dog fighting with a big dog—"

"Oh, no! That sounds scary."

Carson laughed. "Not for Sunny. The little dog got the big dog a leash and took him for a walk, and then they became best friends." He grinned, remembering Sunny recounting the dream. "I don't actually know how much of it was a dream and how much an embellishment, but it seemed to make her feel better."

"It *was* my dream!" Sunny called from the loft. "Hi, Miss Lily."

"Hi, sweetie," Lily said, and they both smiled up at the rosy face that peeked over the loft railing.

"I can't come down because we're doing something *very important.*"

"Come on, Sunny!" Skye called from the back of the loft area. Skye was his responsible one, always keeping her twin on task. He hoped that would translate into schoolwork when they got older.

"You can see it later, Miss Lily," Sunny promised. "But it's a secret from Daddy." Then she disappeared and her footsteps clattered across the floor above them.

Carson reached to help Lily take off her coat, chuckling. "They've been whispering and working for the past couple of hours. I think it's a late Christmas present. Come on, let me get you some coffee."

"That sounds good." She followed him into the kitchen area and leaned one hip against the counter.

She looked so pretty in slim-fitting jeans, a sweater and a vest. Outdoorsy, makeup-free, a natural beauty.

He wanted to talk more to her, learn about her. After his conversation with Long John, he was feeling increasingly certain that he wanted to get to know her better. And more hopeful that something might come of it.

"How's Bella?" he asked instead of leading with something deeper right away. Lily was skittish, like a wild animal. He had to approach getting closer in the right way, the slow way.

"She's doing fine. I'd like to think she feels bad about what happened with Sunny, but truth to tell, I think she's forgotten all about it." She sighed. "I scolded her all the way home, but she just looked up at me with her tongue hanging out."

Carson could picture it, the pretty young woman lecturing, the dog laughing up at her. "How's her recovery?"

"I think she's doing great. Jack, the vet, he's coming up to look at her tomorrow."

Jealousy pushed into Carson's consciousness. Of course Jack was coming up to check on Bella. Probably to check on Lily, too. Check *out* Lily.

And what was it about the gentle woman standing in his kitchen that brought out his caveman instincts? He wanted her for his own.

He carried their mugs of coffee to the table, put them down and pulled out a chair for her. "Listen, Lily," he said, "after you leave the cabins, where are you headed?"

"That's a good question." She kneaded her hands together. "I'm almost done with my degree, and I don't have any real ties aside from finishing that work."

"You have your aunt Penny, right here. Ever think about

sticking around this area?" Carson felt heat climb up his neck. He had no right to ask her a question like that.

She didn't seem to take offense. "I do love it here," she said. "Esperanza Springs is a really nice town. I've liked everyone I've met here, and it's so pretty."

"Do you like the snow?"

"Mostly." She held out her boot, showing him how the sole was flapping loose. "I obviously need to get new boots, and I wouldn't mind a warmer coat, but I do like it. Listen, Carson—"

What kind of a jerk was he, letting her freeze like that? "Sit tight. I'm going to get you some slippers."

He climbed halfway up the ladder. "Coming up, girls," he said.

"No, Daddy, you can't!" they said together.

"Then throw me down my slippers, will you? And a pair of my big warm socks from my suitcase."

Little feet clattered, and then socks and slippers soared out of the loft, one slipper hitting him on the head.

"Now stay down there," Skye lectured from the top of the ladder. "We're not finished yet."

"Okay, okay." He backed down the ladder, collected the footwear and went into the bathroom to grab a thick bath towel. Then he knelt in front of Lily. "Give me your foot."

"Oh, no, it's okay, you shouldn't…"

He ignored her protest, took her foot into his hands and gently pulled off her broken boot.

Her feet were delicate, pink and cold. He wrapped the towel around her foot and rubbed it dry. His hands wanted to linger, make this into a full-blown foot massage, but he knew better. *Remember, skittish.* He pulled a sock over her foot and fitted the slipper onto it.

He glanced up at her face. Her cheeks were pink, and when their eyes met, she blushed more deeply.

Quickly, he repeated the treatment on the other foot, trying to keep his movements businesslike rather than romantic. As soon as he'd put the second sock and slipper on her, he put her damp boots and socks in front of the fire. He took a moment to arrange them carefully, so he could calm his own racing pulse.

He was less and less immune to this woman. Physically and emotionally, yes, but spiritually, too. He wanted to take care of her.

If he were honest with himself, he hadn't done the best job of serving Pam. He'd meant well, but he'd been a little selfish, too young to look at their life from her point of view.

Next time, he'd do better.

Serving Lily that way would be an honor and a joy.

He walked over to the table and sat. She met his eyes and then looked down at her coffee cup, but he'd seen the uneasiness on her face. Should he keep things impersonal or try to go deeper?

He went with his gut, touched her hand. "I was asking you about where you might settle for a reason, and I need to say it before I lose my nerve."

"Before you... Okaaaay." She took a sip of black coffee, watching him over the rim of the cup.

"If you were to stay around here awhile," he said, "would you consider going out with me?"

She set down her mug too hard, making coffee splash onto the table.

Automatically he grabbed a napkin and wiped it up. Then he met her eyes again, a sinking feeling inside.

She hadn't answered. She didn't want to go out with him and was figuring out how to say so.

No woman as pretty and talented as Lily would want to date a small-town pastor, tied down with a couple of demanding kids. Why would she, when she could date anyone she wanted to?

Jack DeMoise, for example?

"You don't have to answer that," he said quickly, scrubbing at the table with the soggy napkin. "I didn't mean to put you on the spot. Of course, you have other things to think about besides dating, especially since you're basically just here on vacation—"

She put a hand over his. "Carson."

The throaty sound of her voice sent a heat wave through him, despite the cold day. Man, he had it bad. He was probably showing that, too, by the way he was acting. And he knew, had counseled his parishioners in job-hunting or dating situations, that desperation was never appealing.

Her hand was still on top of his, and he looked up to meet her eyes.

"I like you a lot, Carson," she said, "and I like your girls a lot, too."

"But..." He tried to say it in a joking way, to soften the blow to his own ego. "There's always a 'but.'"

"Yes, there is," she said, looking at him seriously. "There's something I need to tell you first."

Chapter Eleven

Lily looked at Carson's dear face and tried to hold on to her reasons for telling him the truth.

She thought of Long John, who'd confessed his wartime sin and not only felt more peace, but had built a lifelong friendship with the person he'd confessed to.

Carson was offering a relationship, or at least the start of one. But a relationship without honesty would never work.

And she was starting to think that maybe, just maybe, she was worthy of love and could be loved. That she could build a community and a life in this cold but warmhearted place.

"It's about Pam," she blurted out before she could lose courage. But then she did lose courage, her heart pounding hard and fast like some tribal drum.

He smiled at her, his face gentle. "What about Pam?"

She drew in a shaky breath. "It's…not good."

He reached out and covered her hand with his. "Lily, whatever Pam did, it's no reflection on you."

But he didn't know what she'd done to cause Pam's death. "Carson, shortly before Pam died, I—"

"Miss Lily, Miss Lily, come and see!"

"And help us!"

Carson squeezed her hand. "Just a minute, girls," he called upstairs.

"Daddy, you can't come! You stay down there!"

"Come on, Miss Lily, you have to help us now!"

The girls' voices were loud. She looked at Carson.

She should get this confession out of the way. She'd started; she'd come this far.

But no way could they have a real conversation with the girls clamoring for attention upstairs.

"Go ahead," he said. "We can talk later. Maybe tonight." His voice was full of promise.

Oh, how she hoped that promise would remain once he'd heard what she had to say.

She smiled and walked by him and climbed the ladder to the loft. Carson stood behind her, always protective, there to catch her if she fell.

His kind, compassionate nature made her hope that he'd be able to understand what had happened. He'd learned forgiveness, had modeled it, in his years of being a pastor. She hoped it would apply to her.

She reached the top, and immediately the twins rushed to her. "Miss Lily, come see what we made Daddy!"

She went over to the bed, where the girls had laid out a large poster board. On it was a dizzying array of photographs and drawings, ribbons and medals and...

Medals?

Then she saw the headline: Our Mommy.

She looked more closely at the photographs. Pam was in every one.

"Wow, this is…really something." Lily swallowed hard at all the images of her friend: with the girls, in her uniform, with Carson.

"It's for Daddy," Skye explained. "'Cuz we listened to Mr. Long John saying he needed to get over her."

"Deal with her," Sunny corrected.

"And face the truth about her."

"And then he could move on, and maybe we could get a new mommy!"

"Oh." As Lily's legs went jelly-ish, she sat down on the bed beside the poster to look at it more closely and try to collect herself, getting a little wet paint on her wrist in the process.

There, in the center of the poster board, was an official-looking paper. She leaned forward to read it.

DISCHARGE UNDER OTHER THAN HONORABLE CONDITIONS.

Her heart thumped painfully. "Where did you get this?" she asked the twins, who'd started arguing over who had to clean up some spilled glue.

"Oh! That came in the mail," Skye said.

"So we hid it away with all our Mommy stuff before Daddy could see."

"Because sometimes papers that look like that make Daddy sad."

Lily swallowed. "How long ago?"

The twins looked at each other. "A long time," Sunny said.

"Maybe when we were five," Skye added.

"We have a big box of Mommy things. We stopped at home for it yesterday, when we went to town for the birthday party, 'cause we knew then we wanted to make this."

"And we sneaked it outside. We told Daddy it was toys." Skye frowned. "Do you think that was a bad lie, Miss Lily?"

"What?" Lily had been barely paying attention to the twins'

explanations, because she was trying to understand the situation and figure out what to do.

The twins couldn't read the dishonorable discharge, obviously; it was full of military jargon, words too big for them to understand at six. They thought the paper was a good thing.

Carson certainly wouldn't.

Right after Pam had died, Lily had talked to a superior officer about whether Pam's discharge would have been effective immediately, such that her family wouldn't get military benefits. They'd figured out that since Pam's death had come only hours after the discharge meeting, it wouldn't have been official yet.

In her limited conversations with Carson, Lily had realized that he didn't know about the discharge. She'd guessed, had hoped, it had never been processed.

But here was the paperwork to suggest otherwise. One of those mix-ups that tended to happen in a giant, form-heavy organization like the US Army.

If, as she suspected, Carson didn't know, then there was a whole layer of information he'd need to come to terms with, in addition to the way Pam had died.

He wouldn't like it, not any of it, not one bit.

"Can you help us carry it down to Daddy?" Sunny asked. "It's still a little wet from glue, and we don't want to mess it up."

Could she do that? Deliver the bad news with her own hands?

"Girls, I'm not sure this paper will make Daddy happy," she said, pointing at the discharge letter.

Their faces fell. "Why not?"

How did you explain something like that? "It's complicated," she said weakly.

"Should we take it off?" Skye asked.

"If we take it off, it'll rip, because we put that on first," Sunny said. "Why do you think it won't make Daddy happy, Miss Lily?"

The sound of footsteps on the ladder forestalled her from any impossible answer she might make. "What's going on up here?" Carson boomed in a comical, read-aloud voice.

"Daddy, you can't look! Because Miss Lily thinks you won't like it!"

"I think he will," Sunny said stubbornly. "And Miss Lily is mean for saying he won't."

Carson's head and then the rest of him appeared at the top of the ladder.

Lily looked at the twins' faces and then at Carson's. Whatever she said, whatever she did, someone would get hurt.

"I think your daddy will love your gift because of the work you did," she said, looking at Carson, trying to telegraph to him that he needed to school his reaction. "Even if some of the things on it are a surprise, or make him a little sad, he knows you girls are trying to make him happy."

"And get him ready for our new mommy," added the irrepressible Sunny.

"Sunny. I told you not to talk about that." Carson climbed the rest of the way up the ladder and walked over, ducking his head to avoid hitting it on the loft's slanted roof.

"Ta-daaah!" Sunny cried, and after a second's pause, Skye echoed her twin's words.

A smile curved Carson's lips as he looked down at the poster, and Lily tried to freeze that smile in her head, to remember how kind and happy he looked.

She had a feeling she wasn't going to see that expression on his face again.

And sure enough, his smile faded as he saw the topic of the

poster. "Our Mommy," he read aloud, and looked from one twin to the other.

"Because you have to face it," Skye explained. "Mr. Long John said."

He put an arm around her shoulders, and then Sunny came to his other side, and all three bent over the poster.

"See, there's the time she took us to the playground," Sunny said.

"And here's when she cooked us a birthday cake."

The girls prattled on, pointing out various photos with an emphasis on themselves.

Lily saw the moment when Carson read the military paper, because his shoulders stiffened. "Other than honorable… Where did you girls get this paper?"

Skye glanced nervously back at Lily. "Does it make you too sad, Daddy?"

"Where did you get it?" he repeated.

"It came in an envelope, and we hid it," Skye said, her voice shaky. "But not to be bad. We just thought papers with that picture—" she pointed at the official army insignia "— sometimes they make you sad. We didn't know you needed to *face* it."

He nodded and patted Skye's shoulder, his lips pressed tightly together. Then he looked up at Lily. "Did you know about this?"

She looked into his dear, hurt eyes and nodded. "About the discharge, yes." The last word came out in a croak, pushing through her tight throat.

He opened his mouth to ask another question and then looked down at his daughters, both watching him, both faces concerned, Skye's scrunching up toward tears.

"I love the thoughtfulness and caring you put into this gift," he said, his voice a little husky. He knelt down and pulled them both close.

His wrinkled forehead and downturned mouth, as he looked at Lily over the heads of the little girls, told another story.

He was confused and upset, of course. He was learning something terrible about his wife.

It still wasn't the worst thing, though.

He stood and clapped his hands. "I'm going to take this downstairs where the light is better, so I can look at it more," he said. "And then I'm going to take you girls over to see Long John, because he told me Rockette is getting lonely."

"Yes!" Sunny pumped her fist.

"Are you mad at us, Daddy?" Skye asked.

He put his hands on Skye's shoulders. "No, of course not. It's a very caring gift." He kissed her forehead. "Now, clean up a little and then we'll hurry over to Long John's."

"Okay!" Skye rushed over to where Sunny was already stuffing paper scraps into a trash can.

Carson looked at Lily. "I need to talk to you."

She couldn't tell him the truth. But now she couldn't *not* tell him.

Lily watched Carson walk up the road toward Long John's cabin, a twin on either side, holding their hands. It was a picture of idyllic family happiness, etched against the blue sky and the mountains.

But Lily knew Carson well enough to see the unusual rigidity of his shoulders.

He'd invented that planned visit to Long John. He was going to come back here and demand to know everything.

It would start with the discharge and go on from there. And when he found out the whole truth about Pam, he'd be furious at Lily for not telling him right away. Worse, he'd be devastated.

She shouldn't have kept the secret, but how could she not when the whole thing was her fault in the first place?

She'd never been able to navigate the complicated waters of her parents' relationship, keeping them both happy and providing the buffer they needed, being there when they wanted her and away when they didn't.

She'd been a difficult child, as her mother had so often told her.

This past week, immersed in the mountains and in the culture of Esperanza Springs, she'd started to feel different about herself. The acceptance from Carson, the uncomplicated affection of the twins, the joy of a Christmas that had started out lonely and ended up warmly connected—all of it had begun to work a change in Lily. New birth, new life, fitting for the Christmas season.

But it had all been a facade, because she *wasn't* reborn. She was the same old messed-up Lily.

Only now the consequences were devastating, and every minute brought closer the time when more people would be hurt.

How could she cut the pain? How could she make it at least a little better for Carson and the girls?

She squinted out the window. The little family was almost to Long John's place now, two colorful specks with a tall, dark figure between them.

In less than a week, they'd come to mean so much to her. The trusting little girls, the funny, warm pastor…the way they'd accepted her into their circle, cared for her…it was all she'd ever wanted.

Maybe she could tell Carson the truth in a way that would

make him understand. Maybe she could explain part, but not all, of the details of Pam's death, sparing him the worst of it.

But knowing Carson, how observant he was, he'd know there was more and would insist on the truth. And it would break his heart.

Did she have the right to break his heart?

Did she have the strength to do what was necessary to avoid breaking it? To sacrifice her own happiness for his?

The three figures had disappeared from sight. They had to be inside Long John's cabin by now, which meant that Carson would be striding back any minute, insisting on an explanation that would devastate him.

She rushed to the kitchen table, found pen and paper, and composed a note. Prayed a quick apology for lying, and hoped she was right that the damage to Carson and the girls would be minimized by the act.

Then she ran to her cabin, threw her belongings into her suitcase willy-nilly and carried them to the door.

Bella whined, looking mournfully up at her, seeming to know something momentous was going on.

The sight of the dog's concerned face released the tears Lily had been fighting off. She knelt and wrapped her arms around the big, bony dog. Bella licked at her cheeks, gently wiping her tears.

Oh, how she wanted to take Bella with her. But the dog was too old and frail to make the trip, especially since Lily's destination was uncertain. Better to leave her here in the warm cabin as she'd originally planned.

She'd asked it in the note, and so Carson would take care of Bella. Lily trusted him for that.

Her throat impossibly tight, she picked up her bag, slipped out the cabin door and closed it behind her. Minutes later she'd started down toward the highway, wiping tears with the backs of her cold hands.

Heading to Arizona, simply because she had nowhere else to go.

Carson marched back to the cabin at military pace, almost a jog, fueled by anger and confusion and pain.

Pam had been other-than-honorably discharged?

He didn't want to believe it. It didn't make sense. He and the girls had received the survivors' benefits. Nobody at the VA had said anything about a discharge, let alone a dishonorable one.

Halfway there, his steps slowed.

Unpleasant facts were pushing their way into his consciousness. The things a couple of friends had said about Pam's behavior overseas. Her impatient mentions, during Skype calls, of meetings with commanding officers, of mix-ups about whether she was allowed to go off base or not.

Pam's thrill-seeking personality, the behaviors that had gotten her in trouble stateside, had been at odds with the discipline required of soldiers.

Lately, he'd realized how far from perfect Pam had been as a wife and mother. She'd had serious flaws. But if she'd also gotten into trouble as a soldier—trouble significant enough to lead to a bad discharge—was there nothing good to say about her?

The pedestal on which he'd placed his beautiful wife, already cracked, began to crumble into pieces.

Shying away from those thoughts, his mind settled on Lily. On her sad, knowing face as she'd admitted that, yes, she knew about the discharge.

No wonder Lily hadn't wanted to talk about Pam! She'd

been hiding huge pieces of the puzzle. Why, he couldn't understand. What did Lily stand to gain from lying to him?

A light snow was starting to fall. He looked ahead toward his cabin and suddenly was filled with a bursting desire to know the truth, the whole truth, about Pam's last days and her death. He practically ran up the steps, flung open the door. "Lily! I want some answers."

But she was nowhere in sight.

He hunted quickly through the main room and then climbed the ladder to the loft. No Lily.

So she'd gone back to her place.

No way was he letting this slide. He'd go over there, right now.

On his way to the door, he looked down at the table and saw a paper that didn't belong. Picked up the hastily scrawled note.

Carson, I'm sorry, but I've decided to leave the area. The isolation and lack of cultural resources bother me, and I feel that you and the girls are getting too attached to me when I'll never be able to return the feelings.
Regards,
Lily
PS: Could you please put Bella back in the kennel for me?

He stared at the cold note and tried to reconcile it with the woman he knew.

No "give my best to the girls"?

"Regards"?

It didn't sound anything like Lily, but it was undeniably her handwriting.

Maybe he hadn't known her at all. His legs suddenly weak, he shrugged out of his coat and sat down. Lily's complaint about the region was far too familiar. It was what Pam had

said at first, before the real problem surfaced: *he* was too boring, too tame, too upright.

*But being boring has its strong points, Pam. Like, you don't get
in so much trouble that you're dishonorably discharged from the armed
forces.*

He couldn't figure it out. Was Lily just trying to escape a
difficult conversation, or did she feel the same way Pam did?

He looked out the window, his stomach knotting. He tried
to focus on the beautiful faraway mountains that had been here
before his petty human problems and would be here after.
Tried to connect with the divine force that had made them.

Why, God, why?

He'd started to think Lily's coming here showed God's
hand, that the Lord had brought them together for a reason,
healing for both of them and for the girls. The Christmas Eve
celebration in Long John's cabin, when she'd helped the girls
decorate those cookies that were even now blaring their colors
and sparkles from a plate on the table. The way she'd smiled
as she'd photographed his little family, as they'd watched the
girls speed down the hill on their sled. The compassion in her
eyes as she'd leaned over an injured dog.

It all flashed before him and was gone in an instant, replaced
by the cold, almost mocking words of the note before him.

He read it again, and this time he realized something else.

She'd said she was leaving. Was she already gone?

He half stood and looked over toward her cabin. Through
the snowflakes, he couldn't see any lights.

Her car was gone.

She was gone.

Chapter Twelve

Lily clenched the steering wheel and peered through the snow, making her way down the lonely mountain road toward the busier highway that would take her home.

Or what passed for home. Funny, even though she'd spent only a week in Colorado, she had the feeling she was *leaving* home.

The car slid a little on its nearly bald tires, tires that had seemed perfectly fine in the desert Southwest. She sucked in a gasp and tapped the brakes lightly, and the car came back into line.

Had she made a terrible mistake, writing that awful letter to Carson? Not just abandoning him and the girls and poor sweet Bella, but doing it in a cold, uncaring way that would definitely sever any relationship that was left between them?

No, because knowing Carson, knowing the way he cared for others, he'd come after her if she didn't cut him off completely. Not because he loved her, specifically, but because he wouldn't want any person to be at risk in snow like this.

He loved people, all people. It was his nature, and it wasn't fake and insincere like some men, even pastors, that she'd met in the past. His generosity and concern for others went heart-deep.

But he wouldn't be able to love her, not after what she'd done. She'd seen the look of betrayal on his face, just hearing about the discharge. Well, what would happen if he learned the whole truth?

He'd put part of the blame on himself, of course, and that would make him miserable.

But he'd also blame Lily, and rightly so.

Pam had certainly laid the blame at Lily's feet. *Some friend you are! You threw me to the wolves! It's all your fault!*

The horrible memories came rushing back and she fumbled for tissues. She swiped at her eyes and then grabbed a half-frozen water bottle and took a drink, trying to calm herself, to force the ugly pictures out of her mind. She couldn't allow herself an emotional breakdown now, on a snow-covered road.

She needed to think of something else.

She noticed the paint smear on her wrist, and immediately her mind was cast back to the twins' eager, adorable faces.

The sob that rose from her chest made her buck forward, and instinctively she hit the brake to slow down, making the car fishtail.

Just like it had the first morning she'd been here, when the twins had come running down to offer six-year-old advice and assistance.

They were so dear. Such sweet, good little girls. Fun-loving, with a hint of Pam's mischief and a bigger dose of Carson's kindness.

She'd never see them again.

She swallowed hard, clenched her jaw. *Get it together; you can do this.*

For the tiniest second, she caught a glimpse of Pam's despair. When you felt like you'd lost everything, when it seemed that no one cared, when to go on living meant a bucketload of pain and no one to help you deal with it, when you'd hurt the ones you loved... Yeah. It made at least a little sense.

Lily glanced toward the dropoff on the left side of the road.

No. She sucked in deep breaths and focused on the narrow, slippery highway in front of her. She couldn't let herself wreck and freeze and die out here.

She had to believe God had some kind of a plan, even if it felt as blurry and hazy as the low-visibility air in front of her.

She gripped the steering wheel tighter, navigated around a curve. Lost traction.

Her car skidded sideways, and she tried to steer into it, braking as lightly as she could, hands suddenly sweaty on the wheel.

There was a jolt, and then the car did a sickening nosedive, bumping Lily's head forward to the steering wheel, back against the headrest and then forward again.

Help, Father!

Carson paced his cabin, trying not to look at the note he'd let flutter to the floor. Trying to pray.

He should probably just go get the girls. Oh, they were fine; Long John had said they could stay as long as he needed, and they'd been settled in to watch a gentle nature show while cuddling with Rockette.

It was Carson who needed them this time, not the reverse. So that he could focus on what he was good at: being a dad. Forget about Lily.

Maybe he should go after her.

The inaudible nudge felt completely familiar to Carson. He'd experienced it before.

She doesn't want me, Father. She made that perfectly clear. He even gestured at the note on the floor, as if God needed to be reminded of the truth.

She'd sure acted friendly, though. She'd seemed to like Carson for who he was, had seemed content with small-town life, had seemed to love hanging around the cabin with him and the girls.

How did her note fit in with that? Had her contentment and enjoyment all been fake?

He slammed a fist against the wall. She'd deliberately misled him, which was bad enough, but she'd also gotten his girls involved. Put their hearts at risk, when she of all people should understand how vulnerable they were, having lost their mother.

They'd be devastated when they learned that Lily had gone away.

He should never have let them get close to her. *He* shouldn't have gotten close to her. She wasn't worth it.

She wasn't.

There came that inner nudge to go after her, again.

"No!" He shouted the word aloud, then felt like an idiot. Anyone looking in at him would think he was flat-out crazy.

He knew the truth, though. His craziness didn't consist of walking around by himself yelling and hitting things. It consisted of getting involved with the wrong woman, not just once, but twice.

A gust of wind whipped around the cabin, making a lonely whistle.

Against his will, an image of Lily driving alone through the winter weather formed itself in his mind. She didn't even have good boots, and she wasn't comfortable driving in these slippery, whiteout conditions. If she went off the road…

Carson blew out a sigh and looked out through the increasingly heavy snow toward the spot where Lily's car should be.

Even if she'd had the skill and comfort level, she wasn't equipped for snow driving. Her vehicle wasn't made for it. She probably didn't even have a blanket in the car, let alone a shovel, gravel, water, snacks. Things any rural Coloradoan wouldn't need to be told to carry along, but she wasn't from around here.

And night would fall early at this, the darkest time of the year.

Arguing with himself, he started coffee brewing. Then he texted Long John, got back into his coat and boots, and stuffed a blanket, extra socks and mittens into a backpack.

He poured the fresh coffee into his big thermos and stuck that in the pack, too. If he *did* catch up with her, she'd need it. She loved her coffee.

Minutes later he was on the slick, icy road, making his way carefully around the bends. No other vehicles in sight. People knew better than to drive in weather like this.

Lily didn't, though. And while he'd started his rescue trip berating himself as a fool, now he was glad he'd come.

She'd withheld information, made him angry. But she was a fellow human being who needed help, and for whatever reason, God had put him in a position to help her.

He was steering around a particularly tight curve when he saw the back end of her car, poking up out of the roadside ditch. His heart gave a great leap. He found the next safe spot to pull off, got out with his backpack of equipment and rushed to her car.

She wasn't in it.

Lily's face stung with the cold, and her feet were blocks of ice.

Had she made a mistake, leaving the car?

Of course you did, came a familiar, critical voice from inside. *Always causing problems. Never in the right place. Making trouble for everyone.*

She rolled her eyes. *Thanks, Mom. I needed that.*

Thing was, her winter wandering might *not* cause trouble for anyone. Who would know she was gone, who would care, now that she'd cut off her ties with Carson and the twins?

But Aunt Penny would care. Long John would care. If she thought about it, a few friends from her university program would care, and a couple of army buddies. Even her father would care, if he were sober enough to be aware of her absence.

Would anyone get to her in time, though, if she were reported missing? By the time her car was found, she'd likely be a stick of ice.

All the more important that she reach her destination. She'd remembered this area from her drive up here, and she knew there was a small cluster of cabins on a lake visible from the road. She'd thought it looked so cute and welcoming.

If she could just reach those cabins, she could find help or at least shelter. And that would be better than staying in her less-than-airtight, not-that-reliable car that had quit running and wouldn't turn on again.

The trouble was, she could barely see through the blizzard-like whiteness, and it was getting increasingly difficult to trudge through the snow in her loose-soled boots. Twice, she'd fallen, and now she fell again. This time, it was harder to get back up.

She tried to feel God's presence. Never had she needed Him so badly. For emotional survival and physical, too.

Was that a building ahead? She got to her feet and squinted toward the dark shape, stomping her feet and rubbing her hands together. When she realized it was one of the cabins, she ran toward it, slipping and stumbling in the snow, praying for a friendly reception.

But when she got there, the cabin was cold and empty.

Carson strode as fast as safely possible in the shin-deep snow. The path Lily had broken was filling in quickly, and he was terrified of losing her.

What kind of a person would leave the warmth of her car and strike out across a windy field in a snowstorm? Didn't Lily know she was putting herself, as well as anyone searching for her, at risk?

He tried to work up more righteous anger. Inconsiderate, that was what it was. She was thinking of herself and not of others. Maybe that offhanded note she'd left on the table represented the real her, and if so, once he found her, he'd take her to the nearest airport and deposit her there, no problem.

Yeah, right.

He plunged forward through the deepening snow and then realized he was off her path. Panic gripped him as he scanned the surrounding whiteness, but he floundered back and picked up her trail again. Where was she going? Was she headed to that abandoned miners' camp that served as an unofficial shelter for local hunters?

What would she do once there?

He wished he didn't care about her so much. But he did. The thought of her out here alone—or encountering a sketchy, drunk group of hunters—made him move faster.

He had to admit the truth; he'd fallen hard for her.

And as he thought about Lily, as memories of their short-but-intense time together flashed through his mind, he knew she'd felt something, too.

She'd certainly seemed to care. To enjoy what he had to offer, and he *did* have something to offer. He wasn't an urban sophisticate or an international playboy, but those types wouldn't suit Lily. She was country to the core.

And if he found her, he was going to tell her so.

He made out the shape of the cabins through the sideways-blowing snow and was relieved to see her footprints led in that direction. If she'd gotten inside to safety, she'd be all right. Cold, wet, uncomfortable, but all right.

And once he got her thawed out, he'd demand an explanation of what she knew about Pam and why she'd hidden the truth.

Suddenly, a familiar fragrance met his nostrils.

Woodsmoke? Here?

And there was light inside one of the cabins. Maybe someone was staying here after all, and he could only hope that, if it were a hunter, it was a friendly rather than a dangerous one.

He practically ran the last few steps to the door, pounded on it and then flung it open.

And there, sitting cross-legged in front of a roaring fire, was Lily. Relief overwhelmed him, and he automatically looked skyward, breathing out a silent "thank you."

"Carson!" She sounded shocked. "How…how on earth did you find me? And why…" She trailed off, her head cocked to one side.

He scanned the cabin—rudimentary, dirty and empty but for her—and then stood in the doorway, staring at her. "You're fine!" he accused at last. Which was a ridiculous thing to say, and the annoyance he felt was ridiculous, too. But he'd fought his way here through the storm, thinking she'd be desperate and half-dead.

Apparently, she wasn't as helpless as he'd thought her to be.

She rose gracefully to her feet. "I'm not *fine*," she said. "I'm still thawing out. And it looks like you need to do the same."

"How'd you build a fire?"

She gave him a tentative smile. "There were matches and wood here. I was a Girl Scout for a couple of years. Could you close the door?"

He pulled it shut behind him, and the roar of the wind quieted.

He shucked his coat and knelt beside his backpack. "We have some talking to do," he said. "And knowing you, it'll go better if you have coffee."

"You brought *coffee?*"

The delight in her voice just about undid him. He liked bringing pleasure to this complicated woman.

He pulled it out and poured her a steaming cup. When he offered it to her, her hands, pink and cold-looking, curled around it. "Thank you," she said. "Oh, Carson, I shouldn't have run away."

He busied himself with pulling the remaining supplies out of the backpack. "That note," he said.

"Was a lie," she admitted immediately. "The first I've ever told you, and I'm sorry."

"Why did you do it, Lily? Why would you say those things if they weren't true?"

She took a sip of coffee. "I was trying to protect myself from your anger," she said. "And trying to figure out how to tell you something."

"What kind of something?" he asked, although he had a pretty good guess.

"The truth about what happened to Pam." She bit her lip. "You're going to hate me for it, Carson, so I'd just about decided to write it in a letter. But now that you're here..." She swallowed convulsively. "Now that you're here, I'll have to tell you in person."

The firmness in her voice and resolution in her eyes took him aback, almost as much as the cozy fire had done. Now that she was willing to talk, Carson felt an odd reluctance to hear what she had to say.

She drew him toward the fire. "Sit down," she said, indicating the floor beside her. "What I'm going to tell you, you'll want to be sitting down."

Something about her tone made the hairs on the back of his neck rise, and he paused in the act of sitting on the dirty, rough-hewn floor. "We should get out of this storm. You can tell me later."

"I'll lose my courage," she said. "It's not going to get that much worse in half an hour. Please, just listen."

He sank the rest of the way to the floor. "Okay. So first off, why didn't you tell me about Pam's dishonorable discharge?"

She closed her eyes for a moment, then opened them again and looked straight at him. "It wasn't even supposed to happen," she said. "When Pam…was killed, I knew she'd just been meeting with our CO about her status. They said in that situation, since the meeting had only happened that day, they'd let it go. She died before being officially discharged, so it kind of didn't count." She shook her head. "But you know what a big bureaucracy the army is. Some paperwork must have gotten started and nobody canceled it."

He had to force himself to stay calm, not to jump up and yell at her. "You had all these discussions with other people about Pam's death, and you couldn't tell the details to me, her husband?"

"There's a reason—"

"I don't get it, Lily. I thought you were a good person. Thought you were starting to care for me and the girls, but how could you care when you kept this big—this *huge*—piece of information from us?"

She blew out a breath, glanced up at the ceiling and then leaned forward. "Look, I'm going to tell you exactly what

happened," she said. "I think you'll understand then why I
didn't want you to know."

A sick feeling formed in the center of Carson's chest, and
again he had the desire to get out of there, not to hear what
she had to say. He even looked out the small cabin's window,
saw the growing darkness and opened his mouth to tell her
they should leave instead.

But she started speaking rapidly. "You heard about some of
Pam's run-ins with military authority, right? How she kept
getting in trouble, was confined to base, stuff like that?"

"Some of it." He was ashamed to admit that he didn't know
much about that, just a few hints he'd picked up. It was one
of many indications that his relationship with his wife hadn't
been the best.

But if she was going to be honest, he would, too. "Truth
is," he said, "Pam didn't like to tell me about things like that,
because she knew I'd scold her. I wanted her to be careful
and take care of herself, not run around. And I was jealous.
I could guess she wasn't doing those kinds of things alone."

Lily cocked her head to one side. "She wasn't unfaithful
that I knew of, Carson. That wasn't the problem."

Something tight he'd been carrying in his chest loosened
up. "Then what happened?"

"She was out looking for adventure, excitement. She said
army life was boring."

That sounded like Pam.

"And she was doing a lot of drinking. Even some drugs."

"She was pregnant!"

"I didn't know that. Maybe she cut down when she found
out."

"Don't placate me!" He'd kind of known Pam didn't want
the baby, but this sealed it.

She looked at him with misery in her eyes. "Things came

to a head a couple of weeks before, well, before she died. Investigators came and talked to me about what I'd observed, as her roommate, and… I told the truth."

"What do you mean?"

"I told them the things that led to her dishonorable discharge." She bit her lip. "Showed them her stash of drugs, gave them her diary. Carson, I caused her death."

"What do you mean?" He imagined Pam's sense of betrayal at having her secrets revealed. Lily had been a close friend. Still, to say that had caused her death seemed extreme.

And wait: Pam had had a stash of drugs?

"She was furious, because the evidence from me was part of what led to her discharge." Her hands were twisting together. "I've rethought my conversation with the investigators over and over, and I can't figure out what I could have done differently. She was going out high, see, and of course she had her weapon. It was so dangerous, and she wouldn't listen to me. I'd thought about reporting her myself, but before I could make that decision, the investigators came to me."

Carson's stomach twisted to think of Pam that way. Desperate enough to do drugs; cavalier enough to put other soldiers—and her baby—at risk.

Deceptive enough to hide the whole situation from her husband. All those "I'm fine" video calls, her cheerful smiles and jokes and songs for the girls.

All of it a lie, apparently.

"I'm so sorry, Carson. I never wanted to get her in trouble."

He looked at her distressed face and believed her. "It sounds like you did what you had to do."

Lily swallowed. "On the day she died, Pam came running out to the guard hut where I was working. She was furious, yelling and waving her arms around. She told me I'd betrayed her and was an awful friend. She was raving."

Carson nodded slowly. "I've seen her like that a few times. I just can't believe they let her leave a discharge meeting and go out on her own in that state."

"The whole base was crazy. Reports of suspicious vehicles everywhere had come up, real sudden. So after her board meeting they put a junior guy in charge of Pam."

Carson could imagine how that had played out. Pam's mixture of charm and determination, even her beauty, could have flummoxed an inexperienced soldier.

He looked back at Lily to see her eyes filling with tears. "She told me that I'd ruined her life," she choked out. "And then she opened the door of the hut and ran out into the road, just as a suspicious vehicle we'd been watching for all day came into view. We'd gotten warnings about this vehicle, and we were all yelling for her to come back and get down, but she refused. She just walked right into it."

"She must not have known."

Lily bit her lip. "She *did* know."

"But if she knew how dangerous it was, then…" He trailed off as what she was hinting at pushed its way into his mind.

He looked at Lily, hoping she'd have another explanation.

"I'm sorry, Carson," she said, "but she did it on purpose. She ended her life on purpose."

"No." He was shaking his head, shaking the words away. "No, she wouldn't have done that."

"Right before she ran out of the hut, she handed me a note."

A great stone pushed down on him. "What kind of a note?"

She swallowed and didn't answer. "She put it in my hand and told me not to tell anyone, to keep that private at least, not to betray her again." She put her face into her hands and let out one gulping sob. Wiped her eyes on her sleeve and looked up. "Then she went out into the line of fire."

Everything in him pushed away the notion. "You must have

misunderstood. She wouldn't do that. Not to the girls. And she..." He couldn't go on, but he couldn't stop the thoughts and realizations, either.

She'd been pregnant with their third child. "I can't believe that."

"I have the note."

He stared. "You have a note and you didn't tell me?"

She nodded. And then, unbelievably, she fumbled in her coat, pulled out her wallet and opened it. Extracted a small piece of paper and handed it to him.

Tears were running down her face, but he couldn't spare sympathy for her. Instead, he read it aloud. Just three lines.

You destroyed my life.
I can't face what they're going to do to me.
This is on you.

Pam had purposely walked into enemy fire. She'd destroyed their baby. As well as abandoned Carson and, worse, the girls.

He let his head sink down into his hands. The thoughts, the words were too much.

His whole world was darkness.

Chapter Thirteen

Lily watched Carson's shoulders hunch in, his head resting in his hands. She couldn't see his face, but she knew that he was distraught beyond words.

He'd hate her forever for this.

"I'm so sorry," she said, wanting to blurt out the words before he shut down entirely. "If I hadn't told the investigators all I did, or if I'd responded better when she came to the guard hut so upset…"

But he wasn't listening. He didn't need to hear her details or apologies. He was devastated, just as she'd known he would be.

If only she'd never come here, he would never have had to know the painful truth.

Why couldn't she have had the strength to turn him away when he'd arrived here tonight? Why had her heart leaped with happiness? Selfish, selfish, selfish.

She went over and sat beside him. Not touching him, but shoulder to shoulder. She looked into the fire, now dying down a little, and tried to talk to God.

By the time Carson stirred from his slumped position, the sky outside had darkened. Lily had finished her coffee, and she'd found the blanket in his pack to drape around his shoulders. She'd wandered the cabin and found a spot where there was intermittent cell phone reception, and had texted Long John that Carson was safe and with her.

She was poking at the fire, trying to get a few last flames out of it, when she felt him looking at her.

His face was sunken. He looked like he'd aged twenty years.

Oh, Pam. "I'm sorry I couldn't prevent her death. So sorry. And I'm sorry I kept the truth from you." Inadequate words, obviously, but the best she could do.

She felt hammered by the events of the day. And by the crushing sensation that she'd let Pam down, let Carson down, let the twins down.

And the pain in Carson's face gutted her. Hurt her as if it were her own.

He pushed himself to his feet, his motions jerky, and studied her. "I've got to get out of here."

She stood, too. "Of course."

"I'll take you wherever you need to go, as long as it's away from the ranch and me and the girls."

She'd expected this, but his words still cut like blades.

"Can I drive you somewhere?" His voice sounded like a parody of the kind, helpful pastor.

Drive her somewhere. Help her to leave.

She'd been headed south with the idea of driving back to Phoenix, but that wasn't going to work, not with her car in a ditch.

And yet she couldn't go back to the cabin.

She had to get far, far away, both for her own sake and for Carson's.

A plan formulated in her mind, and she spoke up as soon

as she thought of it. "Could you take me to the bus station in Trinidad?"

"You want to take a Greyhound bus in a snowstorm?"

No, she didn't want to, it was killing her, but if she was going, she had to do it fast. "If you can't, it's okay. I'm sure I can get someone in Esperanza Springs to take me, if you can run me back there."

"I'll take you." He stood abruptly. "But we should get moving. The roads won't get any better. What are you doing about your car?"

His businesslike attitude hurt, but it was for the best. "I think I can call someone to tow it. Maybe even donate it, if it can't be fixed."

"Sure." He nodded. "I'll put out the last of this fire. Gather your things." His voice was stern, impersonal.

She couldn't bear for him to be like this, couldn't bear for their connection to be entirely gone. "Did...did you get Bella back to the kennel?" The thought of the poor old dog had been hovering at the back of her mind. Bella didn't understand all this human drama; she just wanted a quiet place to rest and be loved.

Didn't they all.

"I haven't had time to move Bella," he said, still in that detached tone, "but I'll take care of it."

Don't be like that, she wanted to scream. *Be your old self with me.*

But that old self was gone. She'd killed it with her deceptions and mistakes.

She bundled up and then helped him haul in snow to make sure the fire was out.

"You ready?"

No. "Sure."

"I'll break a path. Walk behind me."

It was the most miserable walk of Lily's life. She followed Carson, never taking her eyes off him, trying to memorize the set of his shoulders, the slight hitch in his gait she'd never noticed before, maybe an old sports injury. The curl of hair that peeked out beneath his cap when he turned to check on her, make sure she was still there.

The hour-long ride to the little town of Trinidad was miserable, too. Carson turned on the radio, but it was mostly static. No good as a distraction. He drove expertly, not overly fast but not creeping along.

By the time they pulled into the small truck stop that housed the bus station in Trinidad, Lily already had her hand on the door handle. "You can just drop me off at the front door," she said.

"I can't just leave you here in the middle of nowhere," he said in a tone that brooked no reply. "I'll come in."

If he sat with her for the hours it would probably take for a bus to arrive, she wouldn't be able to bear it. And neither, from the looks of it, would he; he was just offering to stay because he was a protector and a gentleman to the core.

She made herself smile at him then, cool and impersonal. "I'll be fine, Carson," she said, even though the place, mostly deserted in the storm, made her nervous. "Don't give it a moment's thought." She jumped out and was reaching for her bag when he came around and pulled it out for her.

Now that it was really goodbye, Lily's courage failed. She couldn't look at him, couldn't stop the tears that welled up in her eyes.

"Listen," he said gruffly. "I can take you back to the ranch. Give you time to think things through and figure out your next step, at least."

"No." She didn't dare return to the ranch. Didn't dare see the girls again. "Thanks for everything," she whispered, knowing her voice was barely audible over the lonely wind. "Tell...the twins... I love them."

It was all she could say. She couldn't look at his face. Instead, she grabbed her bag, gave his arm a quick squeeze and ran into the station.

As it turned out, she would have a long wait for the next bus south, but there was one going north in just three hours. She looked at the map given to her by a sleepy clerk and traced the routes with her finger, tears blurring her vision.

She'd thought to go back to Phoenix, because school and her apartment were there. But the idea of returning to the empty apartment was unbearable. If she went back, she'd have several weeks before the semester started, and she'd have nothing to do but sit and mope. And sink into despair.

On an impulse, she asked prices and distances to Kansas City, and discovered the trip was manageable. She could put the ticket on her credit card and use public transportation or a ride-sharing service when she got there.

It wasn't in the budget, but it felt like the right thing to do. Or at least, *a* thing to do. One more effort at atonement.

Four hours later she was on a bus north, riding through the night to Kansas City and a piece of her past.

As had happened before, Carson's twins were the saving of him.

Distraught as he was about what he'd learned about Pam, and about the vast secret Lily had kept from him, he still had to get up the next morning. Had to put on his game face and pack up their things and drive back to town.

Had to answer his girls' questions about why Miss Lily wasn't coming back.

"But she didn't say bye to us," Sunny protested when Carson said she'd had to go home.

"Is she mad?" Skye asked.

He shook his head. "No. She told me to tell you she loved spending Christmas with you," he said. It was a little modification of what she'd said—she'd said she loved them, plain and simple—but he felt funny saying that to the girls, when they'd probably never see her again.

He probably wouldn't, either.

Almost involuntarily, he brushed his fingertips with his thumb, remembering the feel of Lily's hair. He'd touched it only a couple of times, but it had been so soft and wispy.

He'd held her only the once, but the feeling was imprinted in his arms. Her delicacy, her slender strength.

He wouldn't feel those things again.

Wouldn't be as open to a woman, either. Not when it hurt this much to lose her. He'd always thought he'd eventually remarry, once he processed Pam's death and healed from it.

But the healing would be more difficult than he'd expected because of what he'd learned.

He doubted he'd remarry now. So this was how it would be: him ushering the girls out of the car—alone. Carrying their things inside their house—alone.

He could do single parenthood. He'd been doing it, and he could continue.

His reassurances had satisfied Sunny, but Skye was more sensitive. Spending the night at Long John's, and then coming home to an absent Miss Lily and a haggard, silent daddy, had upset her.

As they carried the last of their things back into their own house, he caught her wiping tears.

Carson dropped his load of suitcases and grocery bags right inside the front door and knelt to give her a hug. "What's wrong, muffin?" he asked.

"I wanted a mommy," she said into his shoulder, sniffling.

Carson's heart twisted, hard, and he tightened his arms around her. "I know you did. I'm sorry it didn't work out with Miss Lily."

Sunny shrugged. "Maybe someday, we'll meet someone else who can be the mommy of our family."

"But I liked *her*." The corners of Skye's mouth turned down.

Carson wrapped her in a big hug. "Me, too, baby. Me, too."

Fortunately, being kids, Sunny and Skye were quickly swept back into their town life of playmates and kindergarten and church activities.

Carson had a harder time of it. The days dragged by, even though he was immediately busy with the church. When he wasn't working, he looked at old pictures of Pam and wondered whether, even through her smiles, she'd been contemplating taking her own life. He tried to understand what might have led her to that pass. Wondered how much of it was his fault.

As it happened, he spent a fair amount of time counseling Gavin's family members. To be effective at it, he forced himself to read up on the subject of suicide, to understand the reasons for it. Despair, mental illness, hopelessness... Yeah. Pam had all of that.

If any good could come out of this awful situation, it was making him a better pastor. He could speak to Gavin's mom with real sympathy and understanding now, and she was doing better.

She felt terrible remorse for her actions. She agreed immediately with one of the catchphrases he'd shared with her: that taking one's own life was a permanent solution to a temporary problem.

Maybe Pam would have changed her mind, too, if she'd had time to think.

After a couple of weeks of ruminating about Pam, trying

to process what she'd done, thoughts of Lily began to creep back into his mind. He attempted to push them away, tried to maintain his anger, threw himself into his work.

On an unseasonably warm and sunny Sunday toward the end of January, Jack and Finn suggested they take advantage of the weather by doing some outdoor projects at the church after services. Since the twins had gone home with some friends for a playdate, Carson decided to join the other two men.

Better than going home alone.

They talked football championships for a while, and then somehow, they moved into more emotional ground. "I didn't think Lily would leave," Jack said, his voice casual, conversational. "She seemed like the type who'd stay. She fit in real well here."

"I thought so, too," Carson said. "But she kept a few secrets."

"What do you mean?"

As they worked on a fence around the church's new playground, Carson told his friend some of what Lily had revealed about Pam.

Jack shook his head. "That's rough," he said when Carson had finished the sorry tale. "I know how it goes. You're asking yourself why, what you could have done differently. That news just dumped a whole lot of guilt on you, but you can't let it. Suicide's complicated. And who's to say she was thinking when she did it? She could've been trying to get out of serving and come home."

Finn, who was listening from the other side of the yard, gave Jack a look.

Jack glared right back. "I know you're a war hero, but not everyone's like that. Some people get themselves injured on purpose so they can come home. Maybe that was Pam."

"Humph." Finn went over to a different side of the fence to work.

"*Could* it have been an accident?" Jack asked.

"Nope," Carson said. "There was a note. Lily had it." He paused. "She had it all along, but she didn't see fit to tell me until I forced the issue."

"Whoa."

They worked in silence for a while longer. Then Jack spoke. "Lily didn't keep that information from you for a bad reason. She knew it would hurt you, right? She was trying to spare you pain."

"I guess."

"So maybe you should talk to her." Then Jack lifted his hands like stop signs. "Although, don't listen to me. I know nothing about love. Never going there again."

"Never?" Carson was genuinely curious. He didn't know much about Jack's past, aside from the fact that he'd unexpectedly lost his wife at a young age, right after they'd adopted a baby.

"Never." Jack shook his head. "Me and women don't get along."

Finn carried a load of planks over their way. "If you like Lily, go after her. Don't get caught up in stubborn pride, like I did. I almost lost Kayla and Leo because of it."

Carson remembered those days, when Finn had spiraled into darkness caused by his past tragedy, and Kayla and Leo had packed up to leave the ranch. It had almost had a disastrous outcome, but with God's help, Finn and Kayla had overcome their hurdles and built a happy life together.

Funny how much easier it was to see that happen in others than to believe it could happen for him.

"Listen, Carson." Jack glanced over at Finn, who came to

stand beside him. "Even before what you said today, we…well, we were thinking you should talk to someone about Pam."

He leveled a glare at them. "Who's we? And talk to who?"

"Us," Finn said. "We think you should talk to a counselor."

"Because you're miserable," Jack said.

"And you pushed a good woman away," Finn added.

Jack pulled out his phone. "I called around. There are a couple counselors in the area who might be able to help."

"I can find my own therapist!" Carson narrowed his eyes at the pair. "How long have you been planning this conversation?"

They glanced at each other and shrugged at the same moment.

"I'm sending you names," Jack said. "Call somebody, man. Talk to someone."

"Do it." Finn, the taciturn giant, took a step closer and glared at Carson.

"Fine, I'll call," he groused as Jack's information pinged into his phone. But even through his annoyance at their interference, Carson felt grateful for friends who cared enough to do it.

Chapter Fourteen

After paying the Uber driver, Lily stood in the lightly falling snow and stared at her old home in Kansas City. Once a nice neighborhood, the area had gone downhill in recent years, with more people leaving their lawns uncared for and bars on many windows. For all that, a lump came into her throat.

This had been home to her. She'd ridden her bike up and down the street, had climbed the apple tree that still remained in the front yard. She'd sat on those porch steps, banished to them while her father and mother had it out inside. She'd brought stacks of library books home and read them, getting lost in another world.

This had also been her base of operations when she'd gone so wild as a teenager. She'd been the kid whose parents didn't check into things too closely, which gave her house appeal as a party spot.

But there had been good times with her parents, if her dad was home and sober and her mom was over whatever hurt or anger he'd last inflicted on her. She remembered building a snowman with both of them when she was barely as tall as the porch railing, how her father had lifted her up to put in the snowman's carrot nose.

Just as she'd done with Carson's twins.

The thought of the girls made her throat tighten. And the thought of Carson brought downright misery.

She'd handled everything wrong. She should have told him the truth right away. Yes, she'd been trying to prevent his being hurt, but it had all backfired so badly.

In the end, she'd been to blame for Pam's death. There was no way to get around that.

And there was no way Pam's husband and daughters could love someone who'd done something so awful.

Despair threatened to crush her down, down, down onto the snowy, broken sidewalk, so she did as her army therapist had always told her to do: she concentrated on now. She walked the neighborhood, knocking on doors of homes whose occupants she remembered, asking questions. If she could find her father, maybe she could help him. Do for him what she hadn't been able to do for Pam.

An hour later, she hadn't gotten a single lead, and she stood staring at her old house again. Down the street, children played. A car door slammed. Lily bit her lip and pondered what to do next. Had this trip been a mistake?

"Is it what you remembered?"

Lily spun to the familiar voice. "Aunt Penny! What are you doing here?"

Penny put an arm around her and smiled. "When you called to see if I had an address for your dad, I figured you'd come here searching for him. I had a day before I had to get back to the ranch, and some frequent flyer miles, so…it was easy to come."

"That was so kind of you!" Tears welled in Lily's eyes.

She'd never have expected her aunt to go so far out of her way for her.

"Just making up for what I wish I'd done years ago," Penny said matter-of-factly, looking around. "Your father doesn't still live here?"

"No. It's listed under a different owner." Lily gave Penny a quick hug, then turned to face the house. "I was just thinking about all the times we had here, good and bad. I remember when you came to visit, too."

Aunt Penny shook her head. "I should have come more. Your mom wasn't strong enough to give you what you needed. I wish I'd stepped in, even taken you to live with me."

"She wouldn't have allowed it," Lily said automatically, and realized that it was true. For all her mother's complaints and criticisms, she would never have let Lily be raised by anyone but her.

And that meant that her mother had loved her, even if she'd been too troubled to show it all the time.

"Any clues about your dad's whereabouts?" Penny asked.

"Not yet. The neighbors I remember don't live here any-more."

"What about him?" Penny pointed at a burly, white-haired African American man who'd just come around the side of the house next door, pushing a snowblower. His was one of the few cleaned-off driveways on the street.

"I don't think I know him, but—"

"But he might know something about your dad."

"Let's go ask."

The man shut down his snowblower and greeted them with a friendly smile, and after they'd all introduced themselves, Lily explained who they were looking for.

"I sure do remember him," the man, Mr. Ross, said, smiling more broadly as he shook his head a little. "Quite a character."

"So you know him!" Hope rose in Lily's heart.

"Any idea where he's living now?" Penny asked.

"Not sure," the man admitted. "But he was attending a program at the Church of the Redeemer, downtown. They might know more."

"He goes to church?" Lily couldn't restrain her surprise. While she and her mother had occasionally attended church during Lily's childhood, her father had adamantly refused to go along.

A smile curved up the man's face. "I wouldn't say he was attending steady, but he seemed to be moving in that direction. We had a few talks, he and I. He was lonely after losing his wife, looking for comfort in a bottle. We talked about how maybe there was a better way, and I pointed him toward their drug and alcohol program."

"Thank you." Lily reached out and grasped both of the man's hands. "I'm his daughter, and I so appreciate your reaching out."

"It's what we're called to do, isn't that right?" He smiled at her, then bent to start his snowblower again. "God bless you," he said over the sound of the motor.

"And you as well." If she found her father, then maybe some good would come out of this heartbreaking Christmas.

At the entrance to the downtown church, Lily froze.

Down the hall was a hunched figure, hair standing out crazily from his head, draped in a blanket that had maybe once been white. He stood at what looked like an intake desk, talking intently with the worker who sat there. The worker spoke back and finally appeared to be convinced; he stood, walked around the table and embraced the hunched man. Then they walked farther down the hall together.

The man's familiar gait convinced her of what she'd suspected, and her throat tightened. "That's him," she choked out in a whisper.

She gripped Penny's arm until the two men were out of sight. Then she turned to her aunt. "He's a street person. My father's on the streets."

Compassion crinkled Penny's eyes. "What do you want to do?"

Lily walked over to a chair in the church's entryway and sank down. "I want to help him. But how, when he's fallen this low?"

Penny sat beside her. "That man caused you and your mother a world of pain."

Lily nodded, releasing her breath in a shuddering sigh. "But he's my dad. And I can't believe he's here, in a shelter, looking like *that*..." She gestured in the direction her father had gone. "I feel terrible that I let it get to this point."

Penny shook her head impatiently. "No. This isn't your fault, and I'm not going to let you sit here and take responsibility."

"But he's my father. I could have tried harder to get him to come live with me." She'd invited him twice, once right after Mom had died and once a couple of months ago, but he'd refused both times.

And *she'd* refused to send him money instead, as he'd requested. She'd figured it would just go to alcohol, but maybe she'd been wrong.

"Your mother spent thirty years trying to fix that man. It's not something a human being can do. Only one way to heal that hurt, and we're in the place it can happen." Penny gestured around at the church. "Your dad probably hit bottom after your mom died, and maybe that's what he needed to do. That can be a step on the road. It's in God's hands."

The worker who'd disappeared with her father now came

back, skirting the desk and coming toward them. "My name's Fred Jenson. Can I help you ladies?"

Lily glanced over at Penny, who was looking back at her, one eyebrow raised. Penny was leaving it up to her, and Lily was grateful. "We'd like to see Donny Watkins, if that's possible," she said. "I'm his daughter."

"Of course! He seems to be back on the upswing again. You could join us for a meal if you'd like." Fred gestured toward the back of the church. "We're serving lunch in our Fellowship Hall, and it's open to everyone."

"Maybe just a chat with Donny?" Penny looked over at Lily.

"Yes," Lily decided. "And we'll make a donation."

Fred smiled. "That's always appreciated. This way."

He led them into a room that held many people milling around, some dressed in the ragged layers of the homeless, a few families and some individuals bustling around with serving dishes, apparently workers or volunteers.

Fred seated them at the end of a long table. "I'll get Donny," he said, and disappeared.

Lily's stomach started dancing. She shot up a quick prayer for strength and the right words.

Minutes later, her father walked into the room. When he saw Lily, his whole face lit up.

He's glad to see me? Lily stood, barely knowing what she was doing.

They walked toward each other and both paused for a few seconds at arm's length. Lily took in his greasy shoulder-length hair, his stained shirt, his bloodshot eyes.

He looked like everything Lily's mother had spent her life trying to prevent, making him shower and dress in freshly ironed shirts, covering for him by calling him in sick to employers, working two jobs herself, at times, to pay the mortgage on their property.

She'd worked and stressed herself to death, and yet in the end, the outcome for her father was the same. He'd slid down the slippery slope on which he'd spent his whole life.

"Dad," she said, her voice catching, and held out her arms.

He took two long steps and pulled her into a tight hug. She almost choked on his body odor, but at least she didn't smell booze.

Then he stepped back, his hands on her shoulders. "Look at you," he said, smiling. "You've grown up to be everything your mother and I always hoped you'd be."

Lily's brow wrinkled and she shook her head. "You guys talked about my future?"

"We sure did. She always thought you'd be a writer, and I thought an artist."

"I'm a photographer, finishing up school," she said through a tight throat. The idea that her parents had talked about her, had dreams for her, touched her beyond measure.

"And you did real well in the military, too. I sure am proud of you." He took her hand and drew her to a sofa in the parlor. "You were what held us together, you know."

She sat down beside him and gestured Penny to an adjacent armchair, and they spent a half hour catching up. It turned out her father had been in this Christian rehab program for a month, except for falling off the wagon a few days ago. He'd gotten himself sober and come back.

"They allow one relapse, and that was mine," he explained. "I can't mess up again. Seeing you makes me motivated to keep my nose clean."

Penny mostly listened, but Lily was the one to probe about his plans, asking about the length of the program and what might come of it.

"We're one day at a time," Dad said, "but after six weeks,

I need to start looking for a job and a place to stay. Move on, to make room for the next guy."

"Do they have aftercare, job counseling, stuff like that?"

"Yes, or if you want to move to another part of the country, they help you connect with a program there." He glanced speculatively at Lily.

"I'm sorry I didn't help you more," Lily said, fighting back tears. "I want you to get better. I wish there had been something I could do—"

Her father held up a hand. "Whoa. You're not responsible for me. You made efforts and offers and I turned you down." He shook his head. "I wasn't ready to live like a decent person then. Not sure I'm ready now, but maybe someday…"

Lily squeezed his hand, too moved to speak, too confused. Was this how they'd leave it, then? Would he make it or relapse again?

It was Penny who spoke up. "There might be a spot for a maintenance worker at the ranch I'm running," she said. "You're a veteran, right, Donny?"

"Navy man," he said proudly. "That's what drew your mother to me," he added to Lily. "She saw me in my dress whites and that was that."

Lily smiled through her weepiness, remembering the oft-told story.

"There's no alcohol at the ranch," Penny warned, "but there's a bunkhouse we're working on that could be a place for you to stay awhile. When you're ready." She put an arm around Lily. "This one has dreams to dream and a life to live, but I'm hoping she'll settle in Colorado. It would be nice if you were in the same area, at least."

Penny's protectiveness made Lily swallow hard.

"I always wanted to see the West," her father said. "Maybe

it'll happen." He turned to Lily. "I sure would like to make amends for the kind of father I was."

She shook her head. "No amends needed," she said, meaning it. But his words made her think.

She'd always blamed herself for the difficulties her mother and father had faced, and the fact was, her mom had sometimes blamed her, too. It was what had pushed Lily into acting out as a younger woman, living the wild, partying lifestyle she now regretted.

But maybe it hadn't been entirely her fault after all.

"Sorry to interrupt," came a voice at the door. "It's almost time for lunch, and you're on serving duty, Donny."

He stood immediately. "I need to get myself cleaned up."

Lily stood, too, and held out her arms. "I'm so glad you're finding your way," she said to him. "And I hope you do come to Colorado and work at the ranch. It's an amazing place."

All of a sudden she heard what she'd said. *Come* to Colorado. As if she'd be there herself. But she'd left, run away, broken off the relationships she had there. Hadn't she?

After an emotional goodbye, Lily spent a few minutes composing herself in the ladies' room and then met Penny in the parking lot.

"Where's next?" Penny asked. "I could take you to lunch before my plane leaves. In fact, those frequent flyer miles are burning a hole in my pocket, so if you'd like to fly back to Colorado with me...it's a lot faster than the bus."

Again, Penny's motherliness made Lily's throat tight.

"Seriously," Penny urged. "Come back with me, at least for a visit. If not permanently."

"I... I'd like that," Lily said. "Thank you. And I'm sorry, I'm not usually so weepy."

"Makes sense, on an emotional day." Penny put an arm around her. "Heard you left the ranch. Was it a good visit?"

"The best," Lily said fervently.

"Any chance you'll stay on in the area? I'd be glad to have you. And sounds like maybe your dad will be there, too, at some point."

"I love it there," she said. "But—" She broke off. Where to start?

Penny gestured Lily into the car and went around to the driver's side. "Get in. We'll talk."

Once they were heading toward the airport, Penny glanced over at her. "I spoke with Carson."

"Oh…" Lily said the word on a sigh. "How is he? How are the girls?"

"Everyone's managing. Missing you."

Lily frowned. "Did he say that?"

"Not in so many words, but I know him. I read between the lines."

Lily tried to process the tsunami of emotions inside her. Sadness, happiness, longing. And love. For her father. For Penny. And maybe, for Carson and his girls.

At the airport, Penny pulled into a parking space and turned off the car. "I'd be tickled to have you come live on the ranch, or in Esperanza Springs," she said. "I'd like to get to know you better as an adult. Seems to me you've grown into a very special person."

That warmed Lily's heart. "I do love it there," she said, propping her elbows on her knees, looking out the icy window. "But I don't want to make Carson's life difficult. His girls…they were getting attached to me, and I to them. It wouldn't be right."

"Those girls need a whole lot of mother figures. I'm one of them. What's wrong with you playing that role, too?"

"You don't understand. I… I really hurt Carson. I knew

his wife, see. And there were things I didn't tell him about her death."

"Huh."

A plane was taking off, lifting into the air with the elegance of a giant silver bird. Behind them, a family pulled luggage from a car's trunk, then headed toward the terminal, each pulling a suitcase.

"Is there any chance," Penny asked, "that you're carrying baggage that's not yours to carry?"

Lily tilted her head to one side, considering.

"Blame you're taking on for something that isn't your fault? Like you did with your parents?"

Was she doing that?

What if she weren't to blame for Pam's death, despite what Pam had said? Lily had done the best she could, given that the investigators had asked her direct questions. And she hadn't just been tattling; Pam's drug use while on duty had put a lot of people at risk.

Maybe she'd been right to say the truth. Even if what Pam had done with the results was purely horrible.

Lily had been wrong to keep information from Carson. A mistake, for sure, maybe even a self-protective sin. It wasn't likely that he'd forgive her.

But was it possible? As they walked into the airport, she thought about Carson, the girls and the town of Esperanza Springs. The ranch and Long John.

She did want it, all of it, if she were honest with herself. She wanted the closeness that she'd started to feel with Carson. She wanted to be near him and help him and care for him, and be cared for in return. Wanted to make a family with him and his girls.

It wasn't likely to work out, no—but it wasn't impossible. Maybe at some point in the future, they could reconnect.

Did she have the emotional strength to go back there again, to talk with him, apologize for the secrets, talk through what had happened to Pam? To try again, knowing she might fail, was actually likely to fail?

But something about today, the reconciliation with her father, the help Penny had offered so freely, had strengthened her. Or maybe just reminded her of the strength she already had. She turned to her aunt. "I have to tie up some loose ends at school and in Phoenix," she said. "But if you have space on the ranch, in a month or so, I'd like to come stay for a little while," she said. "I'll work to earn my keep."

Chapter Fifteen

Carson did *not* want to go back up to Redemption Ranch. His whole heart rebelled against it.

But he had to break the ice, jump in the water, get back on the horse. Whatever cliché you wanted to use, he had to do it. Somehow. It had been almost six weeks since Lily had left. His life and the girls' lives were back to normal. And for him, normal included serving as chaplain at the ranch.

Finn had let him know they were expecting more veterans soon, so Carson had to get used to going up there. He had to harden himself to being in the place where he'd fallen in love and lost his dream.

Those six weeks had been busy for him, because he had realized all the things he needed to work out. On the practical side, he had talked to army officials about Pam's discharge status and gotten a fuller picture of what had happened on the last day of her life, as well as the weeks leading up to it.

The information he'd received had been distressing, but in a way, not a surprise. He had known about most of Pam's issues. They had just gotten worse during her last weeks, when she'd stopped taking her medication and everything had gone wrong.

Carson had his own guilt to deal with. He knew why she'd gone off her meds: because she was pregnant. He wished he had considered that and talked to her about it, but he had been caught up in the joy of expecting another baby and the concern about her serving in the military while pregnant, and he hadn't stopped to think about the mental health issues involved.

Stupid, stupid, stupid.

Fortunately, he had good friends in Finn and Jack. And he had taken their advice and consulted someone who could help: not a therapist, but an older pastor who had lots of experience with similar issues. According to all of these men, his mistake was a mistake, not a sign that he was hopelessly and fatally flawed. According to them, the responsibility for taking the meds, or talking to a physician about how to go off them, ultimately rested on Pam.

Still, he'd struggled to understand, had wrestled with the issue in prayer. But the verse that kept coming to him was about seeing through a glass darkly now. Clarity might never come until he himself joined his Father in heaven, saw Him face-to-face and also saw the whole truth of life.

"Daddy, Daddy, we're almost there!"

"Do you think our doggy will be like Rockette or like Shoney?" Shoney, the cocker spaniel Finn had adopted right along with Leo, when he'd married Kayla, had plenty of challenges. But they did nothing to dampen her spirit, and everyone in Esperanza Springs loved her.

"Long John said we would like her," Carson reminded the girls. "What she's like will be a surprise. I'm excited, too."

And he was, as hard as that was to believe. In the midst of

all his other self-realizations, he'd come to understand that the reason he didn't want a dog had more to do with his parents and the way he was raised than with any actual dislike of having a pet. Once he'd figured that out, he had been glad for Jack and Long John to get the girls a dog.

"Remember," he said as he pulled the truck into the gravel space in front of Long John's cabin. "We're just meeting this pooch. If she isn't right for us, there will be another dog who is."

"I hope it's her," Skye said, her forehead wrinkling. "If we meet her and don't like her, she'll feel very sad."

"Come on, come on!" Sunny was already unbuckling her seat belt, and as soon as Carson turned off the truck, she opened the door and rushed outside. Skye wasn't far behind her.

As they tromped up Long John's steps, Carson's eyes strayed toward the cabin where Lily had stayed, and immediately his mind was filled with thoughts and images of her. How they had spent Christmas Eve right here, at Long John's. How they'd built a snowman with the girls, watched them go sledding, just over the hill.

But his girls needed him to be present now rather than reminiscing about the past, and so he shoved those thoughts aside and climbed the steps after them. Before they could even pound on the door, Long John opened it, and then the girls were inside with a fuzzball of energy like he had never seen before.

He tilted his head to the side and watched as the girls shrieked and rolled on the floor with the light brown fuzzball.

Fuzzballs.

He glanced over at Long John. "There are two of them."

"You have two girls."

"Yeah, but…"

Long John laughed. "You have to admit, it's a good surprise. For them and for you."

"For them, anyway." Carson blew out a sigh. How much more work could two dogs be than one? "What kind of dogs are they, anyway? I've never seen anything like them."

"Jack called 'em sporgis, or some such fool thing," Long John said. "A boy and a girl, some crazy mix of spaniel and corgi."

The dogs were, indeed, fluffy like some breeds of spaniels he'd seen. But their bodies were long and low-slung, corgi-like.

"Aren't they pretty, Daddy?" Skye looked up at him, her eyes glowing.

Carson was saved from having to answer by Sunny's giggles as her dog, an exact replica of her brother, barreled into her lap and started to lick her face.

"You'd better not have any other surprises up your sleeve," Carson warned Long John.

Long John didn't answer. Instead, he pushed his walker to the window and looked out. "Jack DeMoise was planning to come up so he could show you some things about taking care of them," he said. "Wonder where he is."

Carson came over to join him at the window. He looked out at the snowy landscape, then down toward the cabins where he, the girls and Lily had spent Christmas.

Again, memories assailed him. They'd had such a good time together. That warmth and caring between them had been real.

He'd been a real jerk to get angry with Lily for what Pam had done. He knew that now.

When a figure came into view, at first, he couldn't believe his eyes. Petite, royal blue jacket, wheat-blond hair fluffed out around a face he'd feared he'd never see again… Had he conjured Lily up out of his own imagination?

He turned to look at Long John. "Is that…" He trailed off.

The older man chuckled. "Surprise," he said.

Lily pushed the cabin door open. She didn't like to make Long John get up if he didn't need to.

She had been back at the ranch just a couple of days, but aside from the pain she felt every time she looked at the cabin where Carson and the girls had stayed, the place felt wonderful, like home. She had spent time with Penny, hammering out a job description that would let her help with the dogs, do PR for the ranch and still give her time to work on her exciting new project.

What her dad had said, how he and Mom had always thought she would end up in a creative profession, had impacted her. She had finished and turned in her thesis, and the feedback she had received had been so positive that she had decided to try to turn it into a book.

She was checking messages on her phone, so she barely looked up as she walked into Long John's cabin. "Hey, are you ready for me to take those dogs down to the kennel?"

"Not quite." There was laughter in the old man's voice.

"Miss Lily!" No sooner had she heard the words, the voices she'd missed so terribly, than the twins were flinging themselves on her. She sank down to her knees to properly hug the girls, inhaling their sweaty, soapy scent, listening to their excited greetings, her eyes closed.

She hardly dared look up, because if the twins were here, then… She took a deep breath and opened her eyes.

There was Carson.

The sight of him rocked her like an earthquake.

What was he doing here? Why were the girls here? And

most important, did he want to see her, or was this as surprising and even upsetting to him as it was to her?

She looked away, overcome with feeling, and then made herself look back up at him to discover that he was staring at her. Looking serious.

There was another knock on the door. "Come on in," Long John called, and the door opened to Jack DeMoise.

"Everyone ready to go down to the kennel and collect the paperwork and supplies for these two pups?" Jack looked around the room and smiled. "I'm assuming our plan was a success?"

"That remains to be seen." Long John made his way across the room toward Jack. "Come on, girls," he said. "Let's take the dogs down and start gathering up their things. That way, we can give your daddy and Miss Lily a few minutes alone."

Only then did the girls let go of Lily. Sunny ran to the door, ready to go anywhere as long as her new dog went with her. But Skye stood still, looking from Lily to her father. "Are you guys going to fight?"

"No, I don't think so," Lily said softly. "But we do have a few things to talk about."

She wanted to tell Carson how sorry she was. Wanted to hear what he was thinking, although from the serious expression still on his face, she didn't have much hope that he was feeling positive toward her.

There was a moment of flurry and chaos as Long John, Jack, the twins and the two strange-looking dogs headed out the door. And then it closed, and there was silence.

Feeling awkward, Lily got to her feet and walked over to the kitchen area, leaning her back against the counter. She didn't look directly at Carson. If she did, he would see her feelings in her eyes, and she didn't want the humiliation of that. Not when he didn't feel the same.

Besides, she needed to lean on something, because the very sight of him made her weak in the legs, like she might fall over. She still felt everything she had felt for him before. In fact, when you added in the realizations she'd had and the thinking she'd done in the past month, she felt even more.

"Lily." Carson cleared his throat. "I wasn't expecting to see you here today, but I *was* hoping to see you. I have a lot to say and an apology to make."

"About what?" She tried, unsuccessfully, to sound casual.

"I was judgmental before. I didn't understand anything."

Lily sucked in a breath.

He came to stand across from her, just an arm's length away, and his closeness squeezed at her heart. She'd been getting stronger, she knew that, but being in the same room with Carson was undoing her.

"I've been doing a lot of thinking about Pam," he said. "And a lot of talking to other people about her."

"You have?" Her voice came out husky, and she cleared her throat.

"I talked to her parents."

She cocked her head to one side. "You *did*? Don't they live overseas?" And if she recalled correctly, they hadn't been good to Pam.

He nodded. "I was able to track them down in the South of France. I found out something that shifted what I'd been thinking. It might shift your view, too."

"Okay." She squeezed her hands into fists.

"There's no easy way to say this." He sighed, then met Lily's eyes. "She'd attempted to take her own life twice before, once as a teenager and once in her early twenties."

"What?" Lily stared at him.

He nodded. "I didn't know. She'd never mentioned it, and neither did they, the couple of times I saw them." He tilted his head, watching her. "It wasn't about anything you did, Lily, no matter what she said, what the note said. I realize now that she lied a lot, and I think she lied about what was motivating her."

Lily let out her breath, her shoulders sagging.

"There were mental health issues all along, and imbalances that were at least partly chemical. Her medications were crucial," he went on, "but she had that rebellious streak. Her parents said they'd thrown up their hands about getting her to take her meds. And she concealed her need for them from her CO and her military doctors."

"Wow." Instinctively, she responded to the pain in Carson's voice. "That must be so hard to deal with."

"I didn't know how bad things could get inside her head. She was good at covering up, but I wish she hadn't felt she had to."

"I think...it wasn't under her control. Not entirely, anyway." Lily thought of her beautiful, wild friend. "If only I could have brought her closer to the Lord, maybe..."

He nodded. "I have the exact same regret. But, Lily, she *was* saved. She believed."

"And she's free now, free and happy." Lily's eyes filled with tears. "I wish she could have lived. For the girls to know."

"I'll make sure to keep talking about her as they grow," he said firmly. "All the good things about her, and there were a lot of them."

"There were." Lily's voice caught, and she grabbed a paper towel to blot her eyes. "There were."

They were both silent for a long moment. Lily was thinking of her friend, of her laughter and her beauty and her charm. What a terrible loss.

From the way Carson blinked and swallowed, she could tell he was having similar thoughts.

Finally, he walked over to the cupboard, pulled out two glasses and filled them with water. He handed one to her, and they both drank deeply.

"I'll always feel some guilt," he said. "But one thing her death has made me realize is that life is short. Too short to waste it on petty misunderstandings." He drained his glass and put it in the sink. "I'm sorry to have blamed you for what she did. It wasn't your fault, and I'm sorry I acted as though it was."

She walked toward him then. Reached out and grasped his hands. "I hope that means you can forgive me. And that we can be...friends, maybe."

"Lily." He drew in a breath, audibly. "I hope we can be more than friends."

"More?" The word came out in a squeak.

He didn't smile, didn't laugh at her. Instead, he squeezed her hands just a little, and Lily felt it, the warmth of it, wash through her whole body. "I know we haven't had much time together, but I also know how I feel. You are the woman for me, Lily. I know that without a doubt. And I would very much like to explore a relationship with you. I'll wait, and we can take it slowly, because I know you're not there yet, but—"

Lily extracted one hand from his and held it up, her head spinning. "Wait. Rewind. Did you just say you want a relationship with me?"

"I did. I do."

"Because of the girls?"

He shook his head back and forth slowly, a gentle smile coming over his face. "I'm thrilled that the girls love you so much, but that's not the reason. You're kind, and beautiful, and you fascinate me. I want to get to know you, and keep getting to know you, for the rest of my life." He held up a hand. "I know I'm getting way ahead of myself. I know we're just starting to reconnect. But I can't help telling you that for me, this is it and this is real."

Lily's eyes filled with tears, and she took deep breaths, just trying to stay calm and absorb what he was saying.

He took a step closer. "I'm not even the jealous type, but I get jealous whenever I think of other men looking at you. Because I want you. I want you because of your smile and the way you treat other people and that strength you've shown to get through the hard times in your life." He tilted his head to one side and his eyes clouded. "Do I have a chance, Lily? Do you think that, with time, you might be able to come to care for me? Even to, maybe, become part of my family, with me and the girls?"

She couldn't restrain the tears now, not completely, and she felt one leak out down her cheek as she looked up at him. Neither could she restrain the smile that broke out across her face. "I care for you. A lot."

His expression brightened, sunshine after clouds. "That night when we kissed," he said, "you felt so right in my arms." He took a step toward her, and his hands cupped her face, a thumb brushing aside her tears. Gently, he lowered his face to hers and brushed her lips with his. "I know it's early and I know we have a lot to talk about, but...can we try?"

Her throat was too tight to speak, so she just nodded. And smiled. And wrapped her arms around his neck to pull him down and kiss him again.

Epilogue

Carson straightened his tie and checked his cuff links, then glanced once more at the clock.

"We're ready, Daddy!" Sunny and Skye came running into the kitchen of the parsonage, dressed in identical green Easter dresses. They'd worn them to church this morning and hadn't wanted to take them off, which had fit in just fine with Carson's plans.

Trouble was, he was now questioning those plans.

Lily was fifteen minutes late to the home-cooked Easter dinner, which wasn't like her.

"Look, Basie and Boomer are ready, too!" Skye squatted and clapped her hands, and Sunny released the two dogs into the kitchen, both sporting green ribbons around their thick necks.

The dogs were still a bit odd-looking, and the frilly bows didn't change that. But they'd made the girls ecstatically happy, and Carson found himself enjoying their antics, too, and not minding the extra work they created.

He felt calmer and more peaceful generally. He'd laid memories from the past to rest. More than that, he and the girls had been spending a lot of time with Lily, working toward a future together.

Tonight, he would cement that. If she ever showed up.

"There she is!" Sunny spotted something out the window and ran to open the door for Lily, who was weighed down with a big armload of packages.

"It's like Christmas again!" Sunny crowed, and Skye clasped her hands together, her eyes excited.

Lily gave them a big smile and then dumped her bag of presents out onto the couch. "Okay, girls, you need to figure out which ones are for you and which are for the dogs."

She'd written names on the labels, and Sunny and Skye immediately discovered their own names and, after a nod from Carson, tore in. "Summer pajamas!" Skye said, holding up a pretty cotton pair.

"Look at mine!" Sunny's were brighter and louder, just like the child herself.

"And there's a book, too!"

"In mine, too!"

Of course, she'd bought them books, too. She was such a good influence, encouraging them to learn and grow.

But mostly, she was a loving influence. The girls were becoming more confident in her affection, in the fact that she'd be a part of their future.

The trouble was, Carson still wasn't sure she'd be willing to make it permanent. But he didn't want to wait, and Easter seemed like the right time for new beginnings.

"What are these packages?" Skye asked, indicating two more large packages on the couch.

"Read the labels to find out," Lily said, and they studied

the labels until they were able to read the dogs' names. "Open them," Lily urged, and the girls ripped in.

"Dog coats!" they cried and rushed to fit them on the dogs. Which had to be almost impossible, since the dogs were long like dachshunds, but bigger around.

"I made them," Lily confided, glancing up at Carson with a smile. "Because these dogs can't exactly do ready-to-wear."

"There's one more package, Daddy," Skye said, bringing over a flat package to Carson.

He lifted an eyebrow. "Should I open it?"

"Of course."

When he did, he couldn't believe his eyes. It was a framed photo of him, the girls and Lily on the sledding hill, that first Christmas they'd spent together. "Where did you get this?"

"Who knew that Long John was snapping photos with his camera?" She smiled at him. "I was so happy to see it. I thought you and the girls might like a copy, too."

It was the perfect segue into what he wanted to do. He pulled her toward the couch in front of the fire he'd built. "Sit down," he urged her, "so I can give you my Easter present."

"Oh, you didn't have to get me anything. I know you've been busy."

"Close your eyes!" the girls shouted.

"Well…okay." She did, and he and the twins got into position.

Carson's hands were sweating as he pulled the small box out of his pocket, and he shot up a quick prayer: *Not my will, but Thine.*

And please, make our two wills go together this time.

He held the red velvet cushion they'd found at a thrift store and nodded to the girls. "Open your eyes," he said.

She did and stared at the red cushion with the little box in the center.

"Lily," he said formally, "we would like to ask you to be part of our family."

He nudged Sunny.

"You could be part of it just by being our friend," she said, as coached.

"Like an aunt," Skye said.

"But we hope you'll be our mom!" Sunny blurted the words out and then clapped her hand over her mouth. They weren't supposed to put pressure on her.

"Now you know what to do," he told the twins.

"Do we have to, Daddy?" Sunny asked.

"We have to!" Skye grabbed her twin's hand and tugged.

"You *might* find some Easter candy up in your room," Carson said.

That was motivation enough, and they ran upstairs.

Leaving him alone with Lily. And very insecure about what she might be thinking. He looked at her, still on his knees, trying to read her face. "I love you so much, Lily," he said. "You've shown me the way to a new life with more happiness than I ever dreamed I could have."

She pressed her hand to her mouth, looking at him, eyes shining with what looked like tears.

"I hope you'll be their mom, too," he said. "They love you so much. But most of all, I hope you'll be my wife."

She reached down to put her hands on his shoulders, then leaned forward to press her lips to his.

A moment later, his head spinning, he let go of her enough to pick up the ring box that had fallen to the floor. "You... Wow." He shot her a smile. "You didn't even see the ring yet. I hope you like it. I... Was that a yes?"

She laughed, a joyous sound, and then there was a clatter of footsteps on the stairs that told him their time alone was over.

He had to know. "Lily?"

"It's a yes," she said. "Oh, Carson, it's my dream come true."

And as his girls threw themselves on both of them, all giggling happiness, he looked over the two blond heads and met Lily's eyes. "It's my dream come true, too."

★ ★ ★ ★ ★

SPECIAL EXCERPT FROM

LOVE INSPIRED
INSPIRATIONAL ROMANCE

*What happens when a beautiful foster mom claims an
Oklahoma rancher as her fake fiancé?*

Read on for a sneak preview of
The Rancher's Holiday Arrangement
by Brenda Minton.

"I am so sorry," Daisy told Joe as they walked down the sidewalk together.

The sun had come out and it was warm. The kind of day that made her long for spring.

"I don't know that I need an apology," Joe told her. "But an explanation would be a good start."

She shook her head. "I saw you sitting with your family, and I knew how I'd feel. Ambushed."

"I could have handled it. Now I'm engaged." He tossed her a dimpled grin. "What am I supposed to tell them when I don't have a wedding?"

"I got tired of your smug attitude and left you at the altar?" she asked, half teasing. "Where are we walking to?"

"I'm not sure. I guess the park."

"The park it is," she told him.

Daisy smiled down at the stroller. Myra and Miriam belonged with their mother, Lindsey. Daisy got to love them for a short time and hoped that she'd made a difference.

"It'll be hard to let them go," Joe said.

"It will be," Daisy admitted. "I think they'll go home after New Year's."

"That's pretty soon."

"It is. We have a court date next week."

"I'm sorry," Joe said, reaching for her hand and giving it a light squeeze.

"None of that has anything to do with what I've done to your life. I've complicated things. I'm sorry. You can tell your parents I lost my mind for a few minutes. Tell them I have a horrible sense of humor and that we aren't even friends. Tell them I wanted to make your life difficult."

"Which one is true?" he asked.

"Maybe a combination," she answered. "I *do* have a horrible sense of humor. I *did* want to mess with you."

"And the part about us not being friends?"

"Honestly, I don't know what we are."

"I'll take friendship," he told her. "Don't worry, Daisy, I'm not holding you to this proposal."

She laughed and so did he.

"Good thing. The last thing I want is a real fiancé."

"I know I'm not the most handsome guy, but I'm a decent catch," he said.

She ignored the comment about his looks. The last thing she wanted to admit was that when he smiled, she forgot herself just a little.

Don't miss
The Rancher's Holiday Arrangement *by Brenda Minton,*
available November 2020 wherever
Love Inspired books and ebooks are sold.

LoveInspired.com

LIEXP1120TRADE

LOVE INSPIRED
INSPIRATIONAL ROMANCE

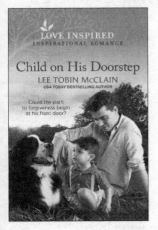

LOVE INSPIRED
INSPIRATIONAL ROMANCE

Child on His Doorstep

LEE TOBIN McCLAIN
USA TODAY BESTSELLING AUTHOR

Could the path
to forgiveness begin
at his front door?

Save $1.00
on the purchase of ANY Love Inspired or Love Inspired Suspense book.

Available wherever books are sold,
including most bookstores, supermarkets,
drugstores and discount stores.

Save **$1.00**
on the purchase of any Love Inspired or Love Inspired Suspense book.

Coupon valid until August 31, 2021.
Redeemable at participating outlets in the U.S. and Canada only.
Limit one coupon per customer.

52616916

5 65373 00076 2 (8100)0 12478

LOVE INSPIRED

INSPIRATIONAL ROMANCE

UPLIFTING STORIES OF FAITH, FORGIVENESS AND HOPE.

Join our social communities to connect with other readers who share your love!

Sign up for the Love Inspired newsletter at **LoveInspired.com** to be the first to find out about upcoming titles, special promotions and exclusive content.

CONNECT WITH US AT:

Facebook.com/LoveInspiredBooks

Twitter.com/LoveInspiredBks

Facebook.com/groups/HarlequinConnection

LISOCIAL2020TRADE